Dawood Ali McCallum

since the early 1980 ... been leading
justice and human ... across Africa
for the past 20 years. He ha worked in police ...
tions, prisons, prosecutor's offices and c ... rooms
in Botswana, E...pia, ...Niger... Somalia
and Zimbabwe ...e is ... of r... previous
novels, *The Lords of Anjan, Taz* and *The Peacock
in the Chicken Run*. He lives in the UK with his wife
and two children.

www.dawoodalimccallum.com

Also by Dawood Ali McCallum

The Peacock in the Chicken Run
Taz
The Lords of Alijah

THE FINAL CHARGE

Dawood Ali McCallum

SANDSTONEPRESS
HIGHLAND | SCOTLAND

First published in Great Britain
and the USA in 2015
Sandstone Press Ltd
Dochcarty Road
Dingwall
Ross-shire
IV15 9UG
Scotland.

www.sandstonepress.com

The publisher acknowledges subsidy from Creative Scotland
towards publication of this volume.

ISBN: 978-1-908737-92-2
ISBNe: 978-1-908737-93-9

Cover design by Mark Swan
Typesetting by Iolaire Typesetting, Newtonmore
Printed and bound by Totem, Poland

Dedicated to the memory of my Father,
'Archie' James McCallum

Transcript of Trial

Republic of Kenya vs Thomas James Miles
Day 8 (Extract)

Presented in Evidence by Prosecution: Twelve (12) copies of one
(1) black and white photograph.

Mr Muya, prosecuting: Dr Miles, can you describe what is
happening in this picture?

Ms Zain, defending: May it please the court, I must object most
strongly to the introduction of new evidence in this way.
Cross examination cannot be a licence to dispense with the
rules of disclosure. The prosecution has rested its case. I
urge that the court rule that this photograph is inadmissible.

Mr Muya, prosecuting: My Lord, I do sincerely apologise that
this document was not the subject of previous disclosure,
but it has only just become available. With the Court's
permission, we propose to enter it now among our exhibits.

Chief Justice, presiding: Proceed. Dr Miles?

Accused: The photograph . . . it shows the body of an African, the
head is propped up . . .

Ms Zain, defending: Objection . . .

Mr Muya, prosecuting: My Lord, I should perhaps have said
that this is an authenticated copy of a photograph which
is among the Colonial Office papers held by the United

Kingdom National Archives. Its authenticity has been certified however we will be happy to call the Director of the Kenya National Archives and Documentation Service to attest to its provenance. Please continue with your description, Dr Miles.

Accused: Beside the body kneels a British Officer. He has a Stirling sub-machine gun across his lap.

Mr Muya: As a doctor, can you describe the injuries of the dead man as they appear in the photograph?

Accused: From the photograph, I can say that the deceased has suffered severe head and facial injuries. The wounding is consistent with a gun shot. The stomach is considerably distended. This is consistent with internal bleeding, again, possibly as a result of gunshot injuries.

Mr Muya: From the photograph, can you identify the corpse?

Accused: No.

Mr Muya: Why not?

Accused: Because the head injuries are too severe.

My Muya: But you know whose body it is, don't you Dr Miles?

Accused: It is the body of Wilson Mumbu Muya. General Jembe.

Mr Muya: And the British officer kneeling beside the corpse. Who is he, Dr Miles?

Accused: He is me.

Mr Muya: Can you see the hands of the deceased in the picture before you, Dr Miles?

Accused: No.

Mr Muya: Where are my father's hands, Dr Miles? What happened to them?

Accused: They were removed. It was . . .

Mr Muya: What do you mean, 'they were removed'? How were they removed?

Accused: They were cut off. It was standard . . .

Mr Muya: Where are my father's hands at the time this photograph was taken, Dr Miles?

Accused: In the cardboard box on the ground beside me.

Mr Muya: Who cut my father's hands off, Dr Miles?

Accused: I did.

GLOSSARY

Ki-Swahili	English
askari	police constable
boma	village
debe	tin / can
dukas	shops
habariako!	Greeting. Lit: What news?
hiaya	come on
jembe	hoe
karibu	welcome
kipande	identity card
kodi	poll tax card
kwaheri	goodbye
matatus	taxi buses
mazungu/wazungu	white man/white people
muhindi/wahindi	Indian person/Indian people
mtoto	child
nyama choma	roast meat
panga	machete
shamba	farm
siafu	stinging ant
TKK	Acronym for Toa kitu kidogo. Lit: Give me something small. Request for a bribe or tip.
upesi	hurry up
wananchi	citizens

PART I

CHAPTER ONE

Five minutes earlier his biggest dilemma had been whether to attempt the crocodile steak.

It was the last evening of a fine holiday. Dinner at The Carnivore, feasting on exotic meats, prior to heading out to Jomo Kenyatta International and the charter flight back to Stansted was part of the package. They were on their second round of Tusker beer, when a rich preacher's voice, Oxford diction in Swahili rhythm, slowly intoned:

"Under the Provisions of Section 34 of the Kenya Criminal Procedure Code, I arrest you, Thomas Miles, for murder, contrary to Section 204 of the Penal Code, in that you did, on the 30th day of April 1955, at South Kinangop, location unlawfully kill Wilson Mumbu Muya, alias General Jembe."

The Nairobi restaurant exploded with flash photography and bellowed questions.

Tom Miles half rose, his mind and vision both out of focus. His face was reddened from two weeks fishing on the coast, his sparse white hair awry. The names echoed with the churning familiarity of an ancient nightmare: Jembe, South Kinangop. His eyes widened in horror and he froze. Guilty. The cameras caught it all. He couldn't have been more different from the erect, heroic figure who now placed a manicured hand on his shoulder.

Stony faced men in dark suits dragged Tom Miles out of the restaurant, shouldering their way through the cross-tide of reporters like fishing dhows in a brisk wind. Out to the car park, where a pair of gleaming E Class Mercedes saloons awaited, their engines running. They drove slowly down the Langata Road with six carloads of newsmen in their wake. Past Wilson Airfield into the city, heading for the Central Police Station. They took their time, easing over in response to flashing headlights to allow camera crews to speed past them so they could be in position to capture their arrival.

Tom Miles' confused and frightened fellow diners left behind at The Carnivore were relentlessly interviewed by the few journalists who had elected not to pursue the story back down to the city. They confirmed, over the debris of what had been a fine meal, what a decent sort Tom Miles seemed – how he loved Kenya. How, just that very evening, he had reminisced about the days – a half century before – when he had escorted the lorry loads of detainees to the screening centres. How he had described the camp that had been thrown up virtually overnight right there – within a stone's throw of what was now the most sophisticated watering hole in Nairobi.

Should one eat a crocodile, they recalled him asking, when a crocodile could eat you?

The Charge was in its thirty-first year. Leo 'Coke' Kane loved it, because it was a test not of strength, stamina and fair play, macho attributes he had always despised, but of intelligence, enterprise and sheer devious cunning. A fiercely fought competition with no rules.

The fact that it raised money for a good cause was for Leo Kane completely incidental.

Leo Kane was tall yet looked, as he had ever since a bout of childhood pneumonia had nearly killed him, somewhat gaunt and undernourished. Thin rather than slender; weedy more than wiry; weather-beaten, not tanned. Women, even those many years his junior, felt a need to mother him, to cook him meals and worry about how much he drank. From this, he did nothing to discourage them.

Leo and his two sons had driven in the last six Charges.

4

They had never won, or ever even been among the first four who qualified for trophies and car badges. Only twice had they completed the course, having on all other occasions ended up hopelessly lost. But they had loved every minute of it, as did all the other lawyers and their kin who took part. For men who made their living poring over volumes of rules, deducing principles, distilling precedents and delighting in interminable debates about definitions, interpretations, due process and pre-trial protocols, the Charge was a joyous, anarchic release. They said there were no rules, but there was one, pithily summarised by Nick Friedlander when accused of tampering with a fellow charger's ignition system three years earlier: You can cheat. You just can't bleat.

This year, Leo had assured his boys, victory would be theirs. He had told them that in every previous year too, but this year he really believed it. Why? Because he had a secret weapon up his sleeve – although he would never admit it to anyone, he had been practising. Every weekend. To win the Charge was suddenly very important to him. It was one of his resolutions.

Three years earlier, on his fortieth birthday, Leo had made a whole raft of such resolutions: all could be summarised under one heading – to hit middle-age head-on. He had traded in his sensible family car, the sole material possession the bruising divorce settlement had left to him, for a glitzy little 4x4. He had surrendered the lease on his apartment, forsaken his office in Nairobi, and moved back to the coast. He had even begun smoking again – something he had kicked in his late twenties.

He had decided to win the Charge – the final Charge.

For there was no doubt about it: this was going to be the final Charge. The authorities had made that abundantly clear. It smacked too much of a rich, white boys' game. It was also dangerous: not so much to the competitors as to those across whose path their bouncing vehicles careered.

Over the years, there had been numerous claims for crops damaged and cattle stampeded into barbed wire fences. All had been more or less amicably settled out of court.

Then, two years earlier, four youths had been flung from the back of a pick-up which had swerved to avoid the lead car.

Not that it was the competitor's fault; the pick-up had no headlights, and its driver was as high as a kite on miraa. But the competitor, an old hand sensing victory for the first time, and slightly nervous of mob vengeance, had kept going, relying on the softer consciences of those behind him to deal with any injuries.

Unfortunately, the pick-up was full of PNU Youth Wingers – the ruling party's young bloods – returning from a rally. The government had wanted to put a stop to the Charge there and then. For good and forever. The organisers pointed out that they had a contract with the Department of Wildlife which allowed them to race across National Park land and which still had two years to run. Even a government as authoritarian as the Kenyan regime was wary of breaching a contract with forty-two lawyers.

So, for its last two years, the Charge was restricted to National Park land, and notice was given that the agreement would not be renewed. A decades-old tradition was coming to an end, and Leo was determined that, in their dotage, his boys would be able to recall, if not a victory, at least a place in the first four, in this, the final Charge.

Leo glanced at his watch: Paul should have been here by now. He sat, waiting for his long-time friend and first-time navigator, with a dozen other men in the coffee shop of the plush Serena Hotel. Six months earlier, Paul Muya had agreed to make up the fourth for Leo's team in the Charge, but in the last few weeks they had seen little of one another. Paul was plenty busy, God knew: his parliamentary responsibilities and preaching took up enough time, let alone his legal practice, which seemed to consist these days solely of high profile court appearances. But that's why they called him the Total Man.

The nickname had first attached itself to Paul Muya several years earlier. It fitted and it stuck. An eloquent attorney. A Member of Parliament, a star of New Wave Kenya, a significant faction of a fragmented opposition. A lay preacher. An eloquent orator. A family man, heir of a martyred hero. A man of God. A man of the people. A man for his time.

The Total Man.

The absent Total Man, reflected Leo. It was not like Paul to let anyone down when he'd said he'd be there. Where the hell could he be?

The coffee shop was almost deserted. A couple of tables away, a European, an old man with thick grey hair, sat with a small girl. His grandchild, Leo guessed. Both devoured ice cream in distant silence. Out beyond the air conditioning, their voices muffled and indistinct, a party of young Asians chattered boisterously over Cokes at two tables pushed together amid the floodlit bougainvillaea beside the still pool.

At Leo's table, Nick Friedlander was, not for the first time, explaining how he could have, and bloody well should have, won last year. His protestations were greeted with a groan.

Leo's party were all European but for three Asians and two Africans. Not surprising, really. The whole mad idea of the Charge was typically White Kenyan – a hark back to the days of the White Highlands, Happy Valley and the settler mentality. The sort of bloody-minded, dangerous game that would appeal to a community renowned for its cross-grained, cantankerous individualism and gloriously self-obsessed pursuit of personal liberty. And for all that he decried it, Leo Kane was a child of that tradition.

If Paul didn't turn up soon, Leo realised, he would have to strike his name and enter a vacancy as fourth team member.

"I suggest we get started," he said, with a final glance at his watch. "If Paul joins us, that's fine. If not. . . ."

Nick Friedlander, a third generation white Kenyan, winked at one of the Asians before asking, "Don't you know where he is, Cokey? You surprise me. He told me he was hunting game tonight."

"Going after a big one, so he said," added Harvinder Singh, loyally. Leo could never understand the structure of their

7

relationship; what made Harvinder so willing to play Fried-lander's fag? Everyone knew Friedlander owed him a lot of favours and was reputed to be into him for a surprising amount of money too.

Leo sighed. "There's nothing I enjoy so much as a double act. Do you write all your own material?"

Friedlander chuckled, and nodded to the waiter, drawing a circle in the air with his index finger to call for another round of drinks. "He said we should catch habari – the news on KTN – if we want to see what he bags."

Leo checked his watch again. "It's ten to now. Can we get a TV in here?"

Tom Miles' arrest made the headlines. There were good quality images, although the sound was poor. There was Leo's friend Paul Muya, looking noble, confident and assured. And the ageing Englishman, confused, dishevelled and scared.

As a piece of pure theatre, Leo had to admit it was good.

Leo's party had taken over the resident's lounge, where they watched the unfolding drama in near silence. Heads shook slowly in wonder or confusion. An occasional gasped blasphemy punctuated the highlights.

The mobile phone in Leo's jacket pocket emitted its gurgling chirp, and they glared round at him, frowning.

He grinned apologetically, rose and walked out of the lounge towards the pool.

"Are you watching me on TV, Coke?" asked Paul Muya. Signal strength was poor but even through the distortion the satisfaction was clear in his voice.

"Paul? What the . . .?"

Paul Muya laughed "I look pretty cool, don't I? Get down to Central, and do yourself some good. You're listed as the Muzungu's attorney."

Leo frowned. "Me? Why?"

"Your Chambers handle British High Commission case work, don't they? Plus, I've just had your name put on the paperwork. It's an inside track to the big time, Leo. It's got

8

everything – media profile, political significance. Even a couple of fine points of law. Come on in and share my limelight."

Leo Kane felt for his cigarettes. Suddenly everything was happening too fast. "I'm not sure I want any part of this, Paul – I just want us to win the Charge . . ."

"Are you crazy? Who ever defends this one will be made for life – the Marshall Hall of East Africa."

"If he doesn't get his head blown off first," said Leo, unconvinced.

"What's your problem? Scared?" snapped Paul, then his voice changed, became pleading. "Come on, Coke, this isn't like you. Man up."

Leo had a suspicion that things might have made more sense if he hadn't drunk so much. "Why are you doing this?" he asked, weakening. He could hear the relief in Paul's voice.

"To say sorry for disappointing you and the boys about the Charge. I'm afraid I've known for some time I couldn't be your navigator, but I couldn't let you in on it before. Maybe this will make it up a bit . . ."

"You know that's not what I mean, Paul. This arrest. Why . . .?"

"Read tomorrow's papers. I've got to go. I'm about to give a press conference. Kwaheri, Coke. Get on down to Central."

Shaking his head, Leo switched off the mobile and checked his watch. Eleven ten, on a Saturday night. A press conference at such an hour needed advance planning. And pull. And plenty of both. What on earth was going on?

And where the hell was he going to find a fourth for the Charge now?

By the time Leo reached the Central Police Station it was near midnight. There was no sign of Paul Muya and the media horde had all decamped to wherever he was holding forth to the world's press.

Leo knew his way around Nairobi Central pretty well. He knew many of the Askaris by name, and all of the desk officers. His relationship with them used to be cordial, and efficient.

Small amounts of money changed hands easily to ensure that paperwork was completed properly and reached the appropriate file. In the past, he had always been greeted cheerfully on his arrival, no matter what the hour.

But not anymore. Not since he had successfully defended a Sikh youth charged with knifing an armed police officer. The cop had demanded money when he came upon the lad and his fianceé in a car late one night in Uhuru Park. The threats had included rape.

Leo told everyone that he hoped that the Judge's rather surprising decision in his favour, and the officer's subsequent dismissal, would make an important contribution to an enhancement of standards in the police service – because it had certainly cost him dear in terms of his working relationship with the guardians of the peace.

"Where's the big game?" he asked the desk sergeant, a man he had known for many years.

"You want something, Kane?" the desk sergeant answered, not looking up from the two-day-old copy of the Daily Nation he was perusing.

The ancient Bakelite telephone on the counter between them rang asthmatically. The sergeant recoiled as though vaguely offended. He glanced across at a slack-jawed Askari dozing on a bench and nodded at the phone. With a prodigious sigh, the Askari dragged himself up, slouched across and lifted the receiver. "Uh," he grunted as he reached for the Incident Book. "How much taken? What? You want us there? Got transport? OK, come in and get us. We'll come. But we'll need tea money."

Leo watched, unmoved. He'd seen it all a hundred times before. "Come on, Henry," he urged the bored sergeant. "The Muzungu: Paul Muya's white man. What cell is he in?"

"Sign the register," grunted the Sergeant, absently tapping a dog-eared book.

"Who else is on tonight's shift?" Leo asked conversationally as he filled in the ten columns of information required. The

Askari flopped back on to his bench, apparently exhausted by taking the call.

The Sergeant listed his other colleagues on duty. Leo nodded. "Has the British High Commission been informed of my client's arrest?"

"You here to interview the white man or me, Kane? Cell 4. You know the way . . ."

The cell was airless, and stiflingly hot. The door was a slab of metal, on which grey paint bubbled and flaked. There was a light bulb, burning continuously, and a reeking bucket in the corner in which the prisoner could relieve himself.

The cell had been painted with pale green emulsion since Leo had last visited a client in it, but the new paint was already marked with tiny blood splats of squashed mosquitoes, and other dried remains of human fluids.

"I don't suppose you've ever been inside a place like this before," offered Leo, sympathetically, after introducing himself.

"I have," replied Tom. "Many times. I used to be on a Police Surgeon rota back home. The cells I used to see people in weren't so very different. A bit cleaner, perhaps, but a cell is a cell. Plus I'm a Magistrate."

"Do you want to tell me what this is all about?" asked Leo. As he was here, he thought he may as well play the part. "I've seen the Charge Sheet. Murder."

"I don't think I should talk to anybody. Not until someone from the High Commission arrives."

"Fine by me," said Leo, turning to leave.

"I was out here as a soldier back in the fifties – during the Emergency," said Tom quickly, desperate not to be left alone. "You know, Mau Mau. But I swear to you I never killed any of them. Anybody. Ever."

"Did you know this General Jembe? This chap you're accused of killing?"

"Of him, yes. Who didn't? He was a cross between Che Guevara and Robin Hood."

11

"But you didn't kill him."

Tom shook his head emphatically. "No. I didn't kill him."

"Do you know how he died?"

"I – sort of – do."

"'Sort of do'; what does that mean?"

"He was killed by the unit I was with. C.A.T.12 it was called. The chap that got him bought it as well. A fellow called Foss. They both died in a little farm up on the Escarpment. I know that. But my recollection of the precise events is a bit hazy."

"But you were there when it happened?"

"Yes. No. I got cut off."

"Cut off?"

"Yes, you know, temporarily separated from my unit. Cut off. Lost."

"Lost?"

"Yes, lost."

"Smoke?" Leo asked, offering Tom Miles his packet of cigarettes. "No? I suppose not, you being a doctor," he concluded, lighting up and inhaling deeply. "OK, the first thing I'll do is challenge the legality of the arrest. I'll go and argue the toss with the Duty Inspector now. I'll bet he's as confused as everyone else over this. If that fails, I'll at least try to get the charges reduced to something bailable and get you out of here. First thing Monday morning. Then it's up to you and the UK Government what happens next . . ."

"Monday?" cried Tom, horrified. "This is crazy! I'm meant to be on a flight back to London in a few hours. I can't stay here till Monday! Look, I'm an innocent man. I didn't do it. I wasn't there, OK? It must be, what? A military operation more than half a century ago. No jury in its right mind would convict . . ."

"Dr Miles," Leo said, firmly, "let's get a couple of things clear. You're not going back home in a few hours. Or tomorrow. And this is Kenya. There are no juries here. If this case ever comes to trial it will be heard by a judge sitting with three assessors to advise him. If you are found guilty, the sentence of death is mandatory. So let's take it seriously, shall we? Very seriously. At least until we get you out of here."

Tom rose, and ran his fingers through his thin hair. "This is ridiculous, absolutely bloody ridiculous! I did my National Service here, like thousands of others. I've been coming back here for holidays for the past ten years, again like thousands of others, and no one's ever taken the slightest interest in me. What is this? Some cheap and shoddy political stunt?"

"A political stunt it may be," said Leo, "but not cheap and shoddy. The man who arrested you is no fool. He's making sure right now that by tomorrow this case will make headlines throughout the world. And in doing so, he's pissing off his own government, as well as yours. You can be sure he hasn't taken this step without a pretty clear idea of the next half a dozen moves."

Tom paused. "You know him?"

"Paul Muya? Yes. I know him."

"Do you know why he's doing this to me?"

Leo banged his fist on the cell door to summon the lock-up Askari. "I expect the fact that the man he says you killed – the famous General Jembe – was his father, might have something to do with it."

"Oh God," groaned Tom, then, as he heard the key turn in the cell door, "you will come back, won't you?" He continued, desperation forming his words into something like a sob. "Please?"

At the British High Commission, and half a dozen international news agencies, telephones began to ring on empty desks in darkened offices. New mail indicators flickered on e-mail screens before dozing duty officers. Social media stirred. Bloggers awoke. Something significant was happening in Nairobi.

Just when every diplomat and journalist in East Africa capable of handling a crisis of any significance was effectively the prisoner of the Acting President, hours away up country, cold in Eldoret.

"If you can give me any grounds to release him," the Duty Inspector assured Leo for the third time, "he's yours. And welcome. I don't need this any more than you do."

The Duty Inspector was in his early thirties, a graduate. He knew his law, and, whilst clearly uncertain about the events unfolding around him, was sufficiently unfazed to leave little opening for Leo's further pleas, or attempts at intimidation.

"Statute of Limitations?" offered Leo, grasping at straws.

The Duty Inspector guffawed. "Bullshit, and you know it. Next?"

"Unlawful arrest?"

The Duty Inspector picked up the chipped teacup from which he sipped at a steaming brew of tea and condensed milk. "I told you," he said, delicately blowing the skin formed on the top of his tea into fine, dark ridges on the far side of the cup, "I can find nothing wrong with the paperwork or the procedures followed. This is a private prosecution, and Mr Muya has done everything by the book. The offence is non-bailable. I say again: give me a reason, and your man walks. But so far, all you're giving me is a headache."

Leo wondered if the Duty Inspector's words amounted to a request for TKK, a financial inducement, but he doubted it. Not that he was all that convinced of the Inspector's honesty. Rather, it was Paul Muya's judgement that he was sure of: if there were any grounds for releasing Tom Miles before the courts opened for business on Monday morning, the Total Man would not have left the station so devoid of his presence. There would have been a couple of Muya minders hanging around, to guard the rear. No, Leo had to admit, he couldn't think of any reason to justify his client's immediate release either.

"Can he be moved to somewhere more . . . appropriate?" he ventured.

The Inspector smiled. Leo noticed how confident he looked, and how young. He was suddenly sure the Inspector had fallen under Paul Muya's spell. No bribes, no threats and only the vaguest of promises won Paul many such adherents. "Appropriate? What does that mean? We are the appropriate receiving station. He is safe here. This is where the people at his High Commission have been told he is. Short of a written instruction from my superiors I can think of no reason why I would agree to his movement."

"And where are your superiors?"

The Duty Inspector yawned. "At home. In their beds. And I don't intend to disturb them."

The phone rang on the Inspector's desk. He picked up the receiver, grunted once or twice, and then replaced it, a smile widening. "Is your car an Isuzu 4x4? I thought it might be. You have five minutes to remove it before it's impounded. Good night, Mr Kane, or should I say, Good morning?"

Leo got to his car just as the immobilisers were unloading a rusting wheel clamp from a battered van with which they had effectively boxed him in. After a brief but energetic exchange, and the handing over of a disproportionate amount of tea money, the immobilisers moved their van and Leo headed off in search of a parking place, and some kind of strategy.

He drove aimlessly around the collapsing infrastructure of the city, the car's A/C belching out chill waves of damp air and its radio, permanently tuned to Metro FM, crackling with late night blues. He drove along streets unlit, save for the glow of the heaps of smouldering garbage at every corner, swerving to avoid the worst of the potholes. Slowing, but never stopping, at the traffic lights set permanently flashing at amber, his car windows up, his doors locked. He glared out at the fractured pavements and the clogged drains. The dukas were all closed now, their windows covered by sheet metal, their doors caged, bolted and padlocked, with metal housings welded above the padlocks to box them in against bolt cutters. Nairobi, or Nairobbery as it was not very affectionately known these days, was a city he had never liked. It was, he thought, a place of bars, bolts, chains and blades, for not just the night-watchmen hunched over on stools and cocooned in thin blankets were tooled up. Even the beggars and cripples he saw huddled in doorways would be armed: the poorest would carry somewhere about them a panga, a long-bladed agricultural tool routinely

15

put to less pastoral uses in the city. The more sophisticated bore one of the innumerable flick knives that he had seen street traders thrust before passers-by, hopefully rattling a handful of change as they enthusiastically demonstrated the efficiency of the weapon's movement.

Only the lepers slept easy on these streets, safe in the protection of their grim deformities.

He was getting maudlin, he realised. Coffee, he decided, would help. The Casino at the Intercontinental stayed open till three to cater for the last gamblers who stood, round-shouldered, feeding coins into slot machines with a sad, mechanical avarice. He took a right onto Standard Street then a left and headed for the secure car park guarded by uniformed men with hippo hide whips and stout truncheons.

He parked the car, leant back, yawned and reached for the phone.

"Paul? It's Leo."

"Yes Leo, what can I do for you?"

Paul Muya had on his Sunday voice. It was not a good sign.

"I need to talk to you about this prosecution . . ."

"Not on the Sabbath," Paul Muya said, piously. "I can see you at, what, 10 o'clock Monday?"

"Oh, come on! By Monday this whole situation will have gone global. By then it will be too late to sort things out."

The silence was far more eloquent than anything even the urbane Paul Muya could have said.

"So what do I do, Paul?" pleaded Leo. "The Attorney General isn't available. The courts are closed. You won't talk to me. What am I meant to do till Monday?"

"Where are you now, Leo?" asked Paul.

"Outside the Casino at the Intercontinental."

"You won't find any answers in that den of iniquity," said Paul.

"So where do you propose I go?"

"You might try the house of the Lord, Leo."

"To seek divine inspiration?"

"Yes," said Paul, gravely, "and to hear what I have to say to my people. Get there early. We expect quite a crowd. God be with you, Leo."

"And screw you too," said Leo Kane, but only when he was quite sure Paul Muya's phone was disengaged.

CHAPTER TWO

"Rather you than me, Mr Miles," the corporal says to me, over the low growl of the Land Rover's engine as he grinds back down into first gear, low ratio. He's a Cockney. A regular. A real hard bastard, ten years older than me. An inch of burnt out roll-up dangles from his thin lips. His face is set in a permanent scowl of concentration, and the tattoos on his biceps writhe in permanent motion as he steers the bouncing vehicle away from the deepest ruts and craters. The headlamp beams throw up strange shadows ahead of us as they grope and probe into the dark like palsied fingers.

Four pasty-faced soldiers lurched and swung in the back of the Land Rover, their Patchett sub-machine guns on their knees.

Short-term shitehawks, south of Suez for the first time, I heard the corporal dismiss them as, when he ordered them to detach the magazines from their weapons. "Wouldn't want you blowing your balls off before you've found out what you've got them for, would we?" he cheerfully sneered. He's every inch the old sweat; been in Kenya for the best part of three years. Airlifted from the Canal Zone the day the Emergency was declared. Seen it all, so he says. He's equally contemptuous of me, a mere National Service Officer, I have little doubt. He can say 'Sir' in two dozen different ways – almost all sound like an insult.

He's a Lancashire. I ask him how a man so evidently from the East End had ended up in a county regiment.

"NFI," he grunts.

"What?" I ask.

18

"No *fuckin' idea,*" he replies, adding a reluctant "*sir*" suddenly wary that he has carried insubordination too far.

I lapse into an unsettled and unhappy silence, convinced that I should somehow impose my authority over the corporal but, knowing that's about as likely as me winning the Victoria Cross.

Men like the corporal have been the bane of my army life: brawny NCOs brim-full of swaggering arrogance, sure of their value and dismissive of anyone else's.

"Commissioned officers have pips on their shoulders," the adjutant had observed when welcoming me to the Mess, "NCOs have chips on theirs."

It was the only bit of military wisdom I found borne out in reality.

We had paused at Karatina an hour or so earlier for a brew and a smoke after the slow pull up from Nairobi. I'd offered round my packets of Wills filter-tips. The four squaddies stretching, stiff and cramped after two hours in the back of the Land Rover, had each muttered "*Sir*" in acknowledgement as they took one.

The corporal, in a stage whisper audible ten feet away, had dismissed filter-tips as nancy-boy fags, and proceeded to hand-roll the wire-thin cigarette, the corpse of which still hangs from his lips, its dead end black and its thin body veined brown with nicotine and saliva.

It's the first time I've ever travelled north of Nairobi. All new territory for me.

Apart from the initial journey up by train from Mombasa, where my troopship docked a lifetime ago, my only other excursions to date have been grim trips to the detention camps at Langata, McKinnon Road and Athi River. After Anvil, I had been one of those detailed to escort the convoys of Bedford lorries, their tarpaulin covers replaced by wire mesh cages, loaded with manacled detainees crammed in so tight they could only stand. I remember how they swayed in unison with the motion of the lorry, emitting a low, sullen moan as they contemplated a future in the pipeline of screening centres, detention camps and gallows.

19

I can't think of Operation Anvil – that massive sweep through Nairobi to apprehend every member of the Kikuyu, Meru and Embu tribes – without a return of the sick, distant uncertainty about what I did or didn't do, and what they said I should and shouldn't have done. Images of the mutilated, charred bodies of the two policemen in their burnt-out car haunt my dreams. They tell me it was my fault they're dead. Is it? How long had they taken to die? In their death throes, did they blame me?

"They eat women's tits and do it wiv goats, did you know that, Mr Miles?" the corporal bellows suddenly. "I saw what they did to a white woman and her kids near Naivasha. Fuckin' savages. Hacked them to pieces – and then there were the bits that were missing . . ."

The corporal hits the brake pedal. I am flung forward so violently I have to throw my hands up to stop my face hitting the windscreen.

I grope to free my service revolver, but pause, as the corporal nonchalantly reaches into his pocket for his petrol lighter, and carefully re-lights his cigarette, tilting his head to one side to avoid burning the tip of his nose.

"Over there," says the corporal, nodding and blowing out a thin stream of blue smoke in the direction he indicates as he snaps the lighter closed. "In that tree."

I follow the corporal's stare, my eyes slowly adjusting to the soft and short pre-dawn twilight after hours of following the harsh headlamps. I can just make out, suspended from the branch of a tree by a noose made of its own entrails, the eviscerated corpse of a domestic cat. "Bleedin' charmers, aren't they just?" the corporal grunts. "It's their way of keeping in touch with each other. They can pick up a scent for miles. They're like animals, see? They leave these little messages for each other. And to say hello to us, and let us know they're still here. Oi!" the corporal bellows out of the window at the four squaddies who, as the vehicle screeched to a halt, had thrown themselves out onto the roadside and deployed, in textbook fashion, in response to an ambush. "Boy Scouts! What the fuckin' hell do

20

you think you're doing? If this had been an ambush, you'd have been dead before you got out of the vehicle. Now get back in!" He shakes his head. "Wankers!" he mutters, under his breath.

Carefully, he pinches out the end of his cigarette before throwing it out of the window. "You know what someone once told me the smell is in this place?" he asks, with a grim smile. "It's the stench of God, rotting."

I can catch that smell now. All I have to do is close my eyes and inhale.

CHAPTER THREE

With no desire to sleep, no one to talk to and unable to think of anything better to do, Leo Kane returned to the Central Police Station and sat with a grateful Tom Miles until dawn.

He searched in his pockets for his cigarettes, but the pack was empty. He felt almost relieved: his throat was raw, his mouth tasted as though some lower primate had urinated in it, and his head throbbed. He cleared his throat. "Tell me about yourself," he asked, hoarsely.

Tom Miles glanced up, surprised. "About me, what's to tell?"

"All you've told me is that you were out here during Mau Mau, you're a JP, and that you're a doctor. We can talk about my various ailments if you'd prefer. No? OK. Are you married?"

Tom nodded.

"Is your wife out here with you? Do you want someone to contact her? Be with her?"

"No, it's OK. She's back at home. She, well, she finds trips like this a bit too much for her these days. Doesn't travel well. Apart from the occasional weekend, we take separate holidays."

"Kids? Grandchildren?"

"Yes . . . Look," said Tom, leaning forward, "I really need to tell my wife I'm OK. Can I call her from somewhere?"

Leo shook his head. "But I can. Once I get my phone back. It must be past midnight in Britain by now. Do you want to leave it until the morning? Where do you live?"

"Cromarty. On the Black Isle. Why hasn't anybody from the High Commission come here yet?"

Leo yawned. "I expect they're a bit thin on the ground. Just about everyone is up at this big jamboree in Eldoret with Ole Kisii."

"Who?"

"Ole Kisii . . . The President, or Acting President, to be precise. There's some big poverty alleviation thing being agreed. They're all tucked up in bed at least four hours' hard drive away."

There was an uncomfortable silence. Tom paced back and forth. Leo glanced surreptitiously at his watch: 3.15. A mere five hours earlier, he had been comfortably ensconced in the Serena with nothing more serious on his mind than the whereabouts of his navigator for the Charge.

Now here he was, spending the night in a stinking cell, babysitting a terrified seventy-year-old accused of a fifty-year-old murder in a war no one anywhere cared to remember.

Life, Leo Kane reflected bitterly, could be a bit of a pisser at times.

And he still had no idea who he could get to navigate for him in the Charge.

"Well?" yawned David Mowbray, Britain's High Commissioner to Kenya as he awoke in Eldoret.

"A British citizen has been arrested in Nairobi," explained his pyjama-ed Head of Chancery.

"Oh. Somebody significant, presumably?"

"No. Not particularly. Not according to our information. But . . ."

"But we are only hours away from signing the most significant aid package to Kenya, or anywhere else in Africa, for the last decade," completed Mowbray, waking up fully.

"And the charges relate to actions taken while this individual was a serving officer in the British Army," added the Head of Chancery.

"Right," said Mowbray, searching for his glasses. "Get me London."

23

While he waited for the call to be made, for he was one of the last of the generation of senior diplomats who eschewed, through arrogance or ignorance, typing their own documents and making their own calls, Mowbray wondered, not for the first time, what in hell Ole Kisii was up to: he'd known Kenya for many years, but he'd never known a time like this. Or a man like Ole Kisii.

Ole Kisii's political life had loyally dogged the mainstream: first in the Kenyan African National Union, KANU, which dominated Kenyan politics for four decades after Independence. Then came, if not democracy, at least multi party-ism, but the same old men changed colours and kept power and the elected President, Mzee as he was universally known, had become increasingly despotic and paranoid. Six months earlier, when the Vice President had been forced to resign in a massive scandal which brought down two major banks, an ancient Freedom Fighter, John Ole Kisii, was appointed in his place.

At the time, the few commentators who contemplated the matter imagined that the only reason anyone would pick John Ole Kisii was that he was the most uncontroversial person in the party. Intelligence assessments had dismissed him as a cog in the massive post-KANU voting machine. A cipher, an apparatchik, a spear carrier, a stolid plodder, an old man with few ambitions and no future whose appointment would please few but offend none.

Then, four months after Ole Kisii's appointment, Mzee had suffered a massive stroke and this arthritic non-entity suddenly found himself Acting President.

Within days of Ole Kisii assuming presidential powers the intelligence community and the media were clutching for other epithets: A dogged campaigner for an African Africa. A freedom fighter par excellence. A wily old bird. The black Castro. Another Mandela. A rabid Gandhi.

And, Mowbray had to admit, Ole Kisii was saying all the right things: Good Governance. Tackling radicalism. Promoting democracy, rebuilding accountability and re-establishing

24

the rule of law: he'd managed to get the African Development Bank, the Bretton Woods institutions, the European Union and the Chinese all lined up to pour in funds to support his ambitious reform and regeneration programme. In a few months, when the SEACOW Poverty Alleviation Partnership package came on line, Kenya would go from an international pariah to the number one aid recipient in Sub-Saharan Africa. All thanks to Ole Kisii.

The SEACOW signing was due to take place in less than seven hours time. The Chinese were enthusiastic, not least because the Acting President refused either to condone or condemn their record on human rights. The EU, the World Bank and the IMF were if anything even keener to move forward. The British, the first to start SEACOW rolling, were less gung-ho, but had stayed on board, determined that so many bigger players would not completely muscle them out of the game. SEACOW, Mowbray recalled explaining to a joint FCO/DFID briefing, was, like every other loan or gift, a pile of money with a raft of terms or, as the jargon had it, conditionalities, attached. What made SEACOW special, apart from its sheer scale and ambition, was that the biggest part of the money was coming from the Chinese, whilst the most taxing conditions were being imposed by the British. 21st Century diplomacy. Good governance assured, and all at someone else's expense.

By the time London was on the line, Mowbray was pretty sure he'd got the whole thing worked out.

"It's a last ditch attempt to get us to ease up on the SEACOW conditionalities," he explained patiently to the FCO Duty Officer, "and at the same time, Ole Kisii gets to portray himself as a hero in the struggle against imperialist oppression in general and British colonialism in particular . . . What? Yes, I do think you need to wake the Foreign Secretary. And give the International Development Secretary a ring too while you're at it. We're supposed to sign SEACOW in less than eight hours time. I'm out on a limb here . . . literally. We're completely out of touch with what's happening on the ground in Nairobi. Now listen, as I understand it, this is a private prosecution brought by Paul Muya – a man with no obvious links to Ole Kisii. So if it all goes tits up, the Acting President can wash his hands of the whole affair. It's been well thought out. Bloody well thought out."

Yes, he reflected. You had to hand it to him . . . But Mowbray had the measure of the man now. Or at least, he was pretty sure he had.

Many wondered why Mowbray had not risen further in the Diplomatic Service. Expressed surprise that, with his obvious intelligence and abilities, he had only ever held posts in Africa. But this was where he wanted to be. Where he would be more than content to see out his time. As a young fast-streamer three decades earlier, he could think of no higher accolade than to be described admiringly as an Old Africa Hand. And the FCO were willing to accommodate him because he was bloody good at what he did.

People said there was no other Brit who could think so like an African. But Mowbray knew they were wrong: his friend Nick Easton was every bit as good at getting inside an African's head. Better. That's how he'd made his fortune.

And Mowbray intended to run all this past Nick Easton the first chance he had.

Just to make sure.

CHAPTER FOUR

The Land Rover lurches drunkenly into the clearing where C.A.T.12 has set up camp. It seems like a vision from hell.

We are up high; I have no idea how high, but we have been climbing for hours. It's well past dawn now. We left the last track which could aspire to the name of a cleared roadway a good half an hour ago to follow tyre tracks through the bush.

The forest breathes and rustles around us. Branches groan against one another as though depressed at the thought of what the day will bring.

Earlier, there had been birds, singing their hearts out for the dawn. But as the day warms, there is little sound.

I'd expected the forest to be different; I'd anticipated a true, tropical jungle. Something much more foreign. Yet there is so much that seems familiar. Then I realise that I recognise many of the plants. I have seen them previously, in pots, in the conservatories of my parents' friends. But out here they grow wild, huge and vast.

Johnny Sandford told me later that, on Mt Kenya, the lobelia stands six feet high, and on the Moorlands of the Aberdares, heather grows so tall a herd of elephants can be lost from sight within it.

The Aberdare forest strikes me as like an English wood, viewed in a fever, with everything hot, pulsing and swollen out of proportion. The familiar, and the pretty, turned ugly, like the face of a loved one, bruised. I wonder if I am experiencing some kind of significant insight or, for I am already reading up in preparation for my first year as a medical student, whether

27

this is simply the first signs of dehydration. I make a note of my thoughts, in case it is the former, and I take a mouthful of water too, in case it is the latter. I am young, don't forget, and the young take themselves very seriously.

In the clearing before us there are three more Land Rovers and a Bedford truck, with its back wired in and caged like those I had escorted to Langata, packed with Anvil detainees. There are two dozen khaki tents pitched in four tidy rows and a radio mast around which a spaniel is sniffing, contemplating cocking its leg. Perhaps 30 or 40 Africans in an assortment of uniforms sit around, dozing, or simply squatting, in silence, in small groups. I recognise a clutch of King's African Rifles in bush uniforms, olive drab with high, laced boots: protection against snake bites and broken ankles. There are Police Askaris too, in dark blue sweaters with leather patches on their shoulders, in long socks and khaki shorts with brown shiny solar topis on their heads. They sit cross legged, cleaning their Lee Enfield rifles. Then there are older men, in greasy raincoats, their thin legs bare. They wear old trilby hats or knitted caps and sandals cut from car tyres. Their ear lobes are cut so that they hang down like loops of sagging cable. They carry spears and I learn later they are Kikuyu Home Guard. And furthest away, but not so far that I can fail to catch their rank odour, sit five men, in shorts and jackets roughly stitched from animal hides. Each wears a bag across his shoulder formed from skin. I recognise the long black and white hair of the Colobus monkey. They are bare-footed, and filthy, with long plaited hair. They seem barely human, yet one wears a wristwatch.

The Askaris stare indifferently at me. The soldiers slowly get to their feet when they see my pips.

"Welcome to the teddy bears' picnic, boy soldiers," the corporal bawls over his shoulder to my escort in the back of the Land Rover as he cuts the engine, and I climb stiffly down. "Twenty minutes, then we're out of the woods today before you get a big surprise."

A European in khaki trousers and a white vest, with shaving

cream still lathered beneath his chin and around his ears, ducks out of the largest tent. He waves cheerily, and then shouts to one of the Rifles, "Hiaya, upesi another debe of warm water!"

He strides towards me, one hand outstretched. The spaniel bounds over to him, tail wagging furiously, and tries to tangle itself around his legs.

"Major Sandford?" I ask, feeling suddenly self-conscious, tired and rather stupid.

For the first time, I see Johnny Sandford's full, wide smile. "Miles, yes? Welcome!" he cries. "Lob your gear over by my tent till we sort you out a billet." He looked hungrily towards the soldiers climbing out of the back of the Land Rover. "How many?"

"Six men. My escort," I tell him. "They're about to turn round and go back. They just sent me," I add, lamely.

His smile fades. "What?" he cries. "But I was promised 15 men and a wireless operator. Bloody hell! Have you got your orders?"

I shake my head. "Just to report to you, Sir. They said they'd be sent on later."

Johnny Sandford frowns. "But you are under my authority?"

I shrug. "I assume so, Sir."

"Well, don't. Look around you, Miles. I've got KAR, Police Reservists, Kikuyu Home Guard, and five de-oathed Mau Mau. Only half of them are under my direct command. All the police personnel are under Superintendent Foss, and presumably any British forces will be under you – except that, so far, you're the entire British contingent. Oh well, we'll get it sorted eventually, no doubt. But right now, it's all a bit of a bugger's muddle. You on your National Service?"

I tell him I've signed on for an extra year and that brings the smile back to his face.

"Good man! Want some coffee? Joseph!" he bellows, "kahawa for Bwana Miles. Seen any action?"

"Anvil," I say, hoping he wouldn't ask me to elaborate.

"Really? What did you do?"

29

I feel myself blushing. "Nothing, really. Held up the traffic while the search teams moved in."

Johnny Sandford shakes his head sadly. "No work for a soldier, is it? Still, now you've got your chance to do something really valuable. So what have you got to offer? What got you sent to us?"

"I got him sent to us," says a voice behind me that I know I should recognise.

I turn and I see him.

Ted Foss. I feel the old fear, afresh. I should have known.

CHAPTER FIVE

At dawn, the little interest the world had in Kenya was still firmly focused up country and on the imminent signing of the SEACOW agreement.

The Acting President's choice of Eldoret for the ceremony had been widely applauded. It was at the heart of the tribal homeland of the man who, nominally at least, still held the office of President (but who was now maintained in a vegetative state on life support simply, so cynics said, in order that Ole Kisii could consolidate his power base before bowing to the growing demand for an election). It was an area therefore that had been much favoured during the past twenty years, yet was still lacking in many of the basic amenities it had been consistently promised. It was a place from which millions of aid dollars had seeped away, as relentlessly as drinking water still did from the Municipality's cracked pipes although, three times, the city had been allocated the necessary funding for their complete overhaul. It was also a place in deep need of consolidation, rebirth and reengagement, having seen some viciously focused internecine slaughter following the disputed elections a few years earlier.

Therefore, for those who chose to see things that way, hosting the ceremony in Eldoret was the Acting President's method of simultaneously signalling the continuing influence of the smitten ruler and the healing that only heavy investment can bring. His way of demonstrating his deference to Mzee whilst at the same time emphasising to the old man's still powerful but suddenly insecure tribal interest that if it did come to an election, the Masai Ole Kisii represented continuity rather than change.

As ever more confused accounts of Tom Miles' arrest circulated, those who were inclined to attribute an almost Byzantine deviousness to Ole Kisii shook their heads in wonder and saw another dimension to the wisdom of the old man's choice – he had secured for those acting on his behalf in Nairobi a weekend during which the capital was effectively stripped of foreign reporters, senior diplomats and all accountable politicians, including himself. Through the early hours they could do little more than snatch at muddled stories of what was happening, stay awake and wonder what to do.

David Mowbray received his instructions at 4.02 am: until the situation in Nairobi was clarified there was to be no British signature to SEACOW. Mowbray knew the significance of this decision was more symbolic than real, for Britain was little more than a minor contributor. Nonetheless, the British position threw the meeting, which should have been little more than a pleasant ritual, into crisis as a succession of key players departed in fast convoys for Nairobi.

First to go was Mowbray himself, taking in his wake the delegation of development economists and London-based policy wonks who had flown out especially for the meeting. Next to leave were two Kenyan cabinet ministers and a clutch of senior civil servants from the Office of the President.

By 10 am, the Acting President summoned the remaining delegates together and announced, in a voice trembling with rage, that he proposed to defer the signing until what he described as 'this irrelevance in Nairobi' was resolved.

More than one pair of eyes narrowed at the Old Man's reaction; was he really as upset as he appeared? If so, maybe, as some were saying, he really had bitten off more than he could chew this time and things had backfired badly.

Within 15 minutes of his announcement, the Old Man was helped aboard the Presidential helicopter which had been hastily despatched from Eastleigh during the night, and was whisked back to the capital. The presidential motorcade, its outriders and escorts, set off shortly afterwards, following him south-east, horns blaring and lights flashing, forcing other vehicles to churn up the red dust at the roadside as it raced imperiously back to base, as though stung by its abandonment.

The sizeable press corps, for most networks still maintained Nairobi-based correspondents with a brief to cover the Horn and Eastern Africa, suddenly found itself similarly abandoned. They had trekked up to Eldoret for an event advertised as sig-nalling the dawn of a new era in the relationship between the rich world and the poor. Interesting but pretty routine stuff for hard-bitten newsmen who had cut their teeth on slaughters, wars, assassinations and famines. So, they had drifted up to Eldoret on Saturday afternoon, booked cars for their return journeys on Monday, and settled down to a pleasurable evening of lounge bar bonhomie and determined drinking in the Sirokwa Hotel. But as they rose on Sunday morning, hung-over but not unhappy, they had found to their horror that they were several hours away from the action, stranded in a profoundly Christian town in which, it seemed, just about everyone who had access to a vehicle for hire was chanting, clapping and swaying in one of Eldoret's many churches.

Like restrained hounds catching the distant scent of the chase, they barked and snapped and growled at one another, aching to be released from the confines of this suddenly deserted town, and to be off, in pursuit of their quarry. Men who had stood, beer for beer, arms around one another's shoulders swapping exaggerated stories the night before, nearly came to blows over the few matatus that could be found, as they offered ever more outrageous prices to persuade their drivers to abandon their local runs in favour of the four hour hard slog down to the capital.

Those lucky few who had driven up in their own 4x4s either sneaked off alone before their colleagues realised what was happening, or traded their empty seats against past kindnesses or assurances of future favours.

33

One way or another, most managed to find their way down to Nairobi by mid-afternoon, local time. Not that it was local time they were at all concerned about: it would be midday in Britain, early morning in Washington and New York. Ample time still to package up some quite respectable material for early evening and lunchtime news slots respectively and to draft some more considered pieces for Monday morning's newspapers.

Most had the text of their copy shaped in their heads or on notepads and laptops before they made the final descent from Limuru, indifferent to the breathtaking view across the Rift Valley. They polished their prose in sluggish traffic on Waiyaki Way. All they needed was a fact or two and they were home and dry.

None realised that their journey had taken them within a couple of miles of the site of the alleged murder. They sped past the rusting sign for South Kinangop without a second glance, for although it had been clearly stated at the arrest, and faithfully reported in the KTN broadcast, the quality of TV reception north of Nairobi was frightful – but then that had been among the matters the infrastructure stream of the now postponed SEACOW package had been destined to address.

CHAPTER SIX

Leo Kane, cold, hungry and wretched, drove out to what had once been his home in the expensive development on General Mathenge Road.

The irony had never struck him before: the road was named after a Mau Mau leader, a comrade of both the dead General Jembe, and the very much alive Acting President. A man who had fought for his country's independence commemorated in a wealthy enclave dominated by European professionals and Asian businessmen. Full of vast houses which were palaces and prisons both, mini mansions, clustered, like the huts of an up-country boma, fenced against marauding predators.

In these homes the encircling protection was not thorn bushes but high voltage electric fences and strands of razor wire atop a wall twelve feet high. Parked outside its permanently manned double gates were three minivans emblazoned 'Dieter Haas Security Services' packed with dozing, uniformed guards – privately contracted rapid response teams tooled up with pangas (machetes), iron bars and studded truncheons.

But Leo was white, and in a car. They didn't even bother asking who he was or where he was going, but swung the gates open, and, bored, waved him through.

At a personal level, Leo felt for Tom Miles; this was a shitty thing to happen to anyone, especially someone so old and after so long. At a professional level, he was already beginning to regret letting Paul talk him into taking the case and intended to avail himself of the first opportunity that presented itself to pass it on to someone else.

He had been planning to keep a low profile until the notoriety of his recent victories against the Attorney General and the police had died down. He had found himself gaining something of a reputation as a human rights advocate, a role in which he had no desire whatsoever to be cast. Such cases, he knew from bitter experience, represented precious little money and a belly full of hassle. All he wanted to do was to take on the odd high-value property squabble to pay the bills and win the Charge with the boys. Was that too much to ask?

He pulled up in front of what had once been his home, climbed out, stretching stiffly, and announced himself into the intercom.

Even electroplated with static, he could hear that his ex-wife's voice, and thoughts, were still thick with sleep.

"What time do you call this?" she grumbled.

"Early. Open the gate, Marianne."

"It's not your weekend for the boys," she said, and her words were followed with an abrupt double click which made Leo think she had left the intercom.

He pressed the buzzer twice more. "I haven't come for the boys."

"Good. Because they're not here."

"Fine. Just open the gate, will you?"

"Tell me what you want first."

"Jesus Christ! I want that blue suit you've got – you know, the one that didn't come back from the cleaners until after . . ."

". . . I kicked you out?" she offered.

"Debatable, but if that's how you want to remember it . . . Just open the gate, will you, and I'll be on my way."

"What do you want the blue suit for, at 7 o'clock on a Sunday morning?"

"Jesus Christ! Because I'm going to church, OK? Now open the fucking gate!"

"Where are the boys?" Leo asked, as he quickly changed into the blue suit. Freed after months in its protective sack of thin cellophane, it retained the bitter, chemical odour of the dry cleaners and there was a sharp horizontal crease across the trouser legs that looked like it would never iron out.

His ex-wife watched him, bemused. She leant against the wall, cradling a cup of coffee, which she'd made herself without offering him one, in both hands. She wore a bright dressing gown of some thin material. She'd always kept her hair cut short. She'd always looked so bloody neat, fresh and healthy first thing in the morning.

"They're staying over at Paul Muya's house."

Leo paused. "Since when has Paul taken such an interest in the boys?" he said, with a pang of something which felt disconcertingly like jealousy.

She shrugged. "Since, you know."

"Yeah. Have I got any ties here?"

"I shouldn't think so," she said. "You don't live here any-more, remember?"

"So how come Paul didn't mention they were there when I spoke to him last night?" He snapped back, looking round for a mirror.

She stared at him for a long, silent moment, weighing up whether to let this escalate into a full-scale row. "It was a last minute thing." she said, deciding against it. "Did you see him on TV last night?"

Leo nodded. "What do you think he's playing at?"

"God knows!" she said, pushing herself from the wall and taking a step towards the kitchen. She always took two cups of coffee in the morning.

"I'm sure He does," said Leo, suddenly irritated. "I thought you might too. Seeing as how you're such great pals."

This time she wasn't willing to let it pass. "What's that sup-posed to mean?"

"Nothing. Can I have a shave here?"

"No."

"Well, fuck you!"

"Fat chance," she sneered. "And on your way out, think

about the fact that just maybe the boys are at Paul Muya's because they need a father figure. One they can actually look up to."

It could have been a parish church in the Home Counties, except for the frangipani and bougainvillaea exploding in riots of colour in its grounds and the luxuriant, bright creeper which climbed the north-west face of its crenulated clock tower.

It was one of the few buildings in Nairobi to have survived from the pre-Independence period. The capital had grown out of a clutter of buildings cheaply constructed from local timber and corrugated tin around a railway depot. Quickly thrown up and as briskly torn down. Practically all colonial structures had been swept from the city centre in the heady days of the sixties and seventies to be replaced by twenty-storey glass blocks, wide roads and expensive hotels.

A crowd had already gathered outside the church. By the time Leo arrived, cars were cast up like beached boats on grass verges and pavements as far as the eye could see. Leo nonchalantly double parked, in a chorus of horn blasts, with the rear of his car jutting out into the traffic.

He wasn't quite sure why he had come, other than, as was this whole thing, it was something Paul had told him to do. He felt a sudden urge to back out. To just turn around, and head to the coast, but knew that things had already carried him along too far.

As he trod out a half-smoked cigarette at the church gates, he noticed two TV camera positions being set up.

Leo had seen himself on television. Giving interviews on the steps of the High Court Building on Kenyatta Avenue, mouthing easily digestible platitudes about the inalienable rights of the individual, the nature of justice and the importance of the rule of law.

But it wasn't what he'd said that stuck in his mind, it was how he'd looked – permanently in need of a shave. It was something that TV cameras seemed to do to him.

And that morning, sporting not just a 7 o'clock shadow but a full, slept-rough-in-a-police-cell stubble, he had no wish to be caught on camera entering Paul Muya's church.

Paul Muya, on the other hand, seemed to glow when the cameras were around; he was a good looking man, with prominent cheek bones and a well-formed mouth beneath a thin moustache. His eyes were bright, twinkling with mischief and his hair was cut fashionably short. He was slender and athletic. He moved with the lithe grace of a man who kept himself mentally and physically trim. He seemed to have a dynamo humming within him, generating energy dedicated to getting things done for the common good. He never approached a flight of stairs without sprinting up them two at a time. He was most at ease talking to a colleague with a hand on his shoulder, or at his elbow. He made people smile, want to be thought well of by him, and subsequently cherish the slightest acquaintance.

Leo caught a glimpse of Paul, shaking hands and embracing the faithful, as he slipped, carefully out of camera shot, into the dark, crowded church. He noticed that Paul was wearing his preaching suit: sombre and staid. A white shirt and a dark tie. His eyes were alive with God's own truth.

As was his wont when the media attended – and they quite often did these days – Paul Muya would preach in English, with a fellow preacher shadowing him, repeating his words, and mimicking his gestures and intonation, in Ki-Swahili. This led to a peculiar, dislocated sensation among those witnessing the phenomenon for the first time. Paul would speak, with passion trembling in his voice, and his body alive with the gravity and majesty of his mission, and then suddenly stop and stand stock still. His face expressionless, his eyes fixed on a point six inches in front of him on the floor, his hands, previously so animated, were still, clasped before him. Then his shadow preacher would repeat the chunk of wisdom verbatim, in Ki-Swahili.

Paul spoke briefly at first, simply to greet the faithful, and with a long, expressionless stare at Leo, one of the few white faces among the rapt congregation, to welcome strangers into their midst: lost souls come for guidance.

There were songs. Real Holy Roller stuff. Interminable, impassioned and repetitive. People stood, sang, gyrated and clapped. Next, a prayer with echoed choruses, praising the Lord and thanking him for His blessings. The temperature rose in pace with the fervour. There was a warm, rich smell of hot bodies, of honest sweat and clean clothes. A crying baby was passed from one pair of comforting arms to another along the pew in front of Leo. People cooed, clucked and made faces to calm the wailing child.

And then, Paul stepped forward with his shadow preacher at his right elbow, one pace behind him. He held up his Bible, worn and soft by much consultation, and shook it at the congregation like a weapon.

"Once, a young man came among a people. He was different from the others. His name and his appearance marked him out," Paul said, slowly. He looked down, as his shadow recited the same in Ki-Swahili. "He took up arms in a struggle not his own. He swore false witness, and with the Judas kiss, marked a good man down for death.

"What should the son of that good man do when, thanks to the Lord and the blessings of a free nation, he is grown to manhood and favoured with all his father fought and died for? Should he now stand idly by, and watch his father's killer enjoy the fruits of his father's land? Should he, silent, watch the evil-doer enjoy old age, dignity and honour when his father's bones lie cold, in an unknown grave? Or has that son a duty, to his father, to his law, his land and his God?

"This is not a story from The Book: this is no parable. This wrong was not perpetrated two millennia back, but a mere half century ago.

"And it is not Herod, the Pharisees and the Scribes who must come to judgement, but our own elders in our own courts!

"Last night, as some of you may know, with the help of God and the guidance of good men, I delivered a wrongdoer into the hands of those charged with delivering justice. Will they show themselves ready to confront the guilty, or will they show themselves unworthy now, and at that final judgement to which all men must come? I say to them, to you, to all of you, here and listening elsewhere, the words our Lord Jesus Christ spoke – by thy words thou shalt be justified, and by thy words thou shalt be condemned. Praise the Lord!"

At the end of the service, Leo eased himself into the queue waiting patiently to shake hands with Paul. There was an excited buzz of folk who felt they were where the action was. Cameramen and reporters seemed to be everywhere; people were calling to one another, laughing and shouting.

In the centre of it all, Paul stood. At peace in his skin, and with his God.

When Leo's turn came, he reached out his hand, and smiled, vaguely embarrassed. He had never seen this side of Paul close up before. Never attended his church or even watched any of his sermons on television. Now, as he studied his friend, he saw Paul's eyes were far away. Half closed. He looked to Leo as one might after good sex. Satiated, content, fulfilled.

"Looking good, Total Man," said Leo, uncomfortably.

Paul smiled. "And you look terrible, Coke. What's happened to you?"

"I spent the night at Central with the wrongdoer you're trying to visit the wrath of God upon."

"Not the wrath of God. Merely justice, long overdue. And this morning, you came to hear the word of the Lord. I'm impressed."

"Don't be. I came to hear you. To learn what this is all about."

"And did you?" asked Paul, suddenly very alert.

"No."

Paul smiled, relaxing. "Then you didn't hear properly."

"I listened."

"I'm sure you did. But you didn't hear."

"Fine," Leo sighed. "Whatever. Now you listen, Total Man. If you choose to cast the Mzungu as the villain in whatever

41

morality play it is you're staging, that's up to you. But I'm not going to play your stooge. And Tom Miles isn't going to be your villain as long as I'm representing him."

Paul Muya frowned slightly, as though struggling with how to make a complex issue comprehensible to a simpleton. "It's not up to Tom Miles. Or you. Or me. We are all in the hands of a higher force."

"I really get scared when you talk like that, Paul."

"And so do I, Coke. I quake before my Lord. But I'm afraid it's true."

And with that, Paul Muya half turned, grasped the extended hand of a hugely fat woman behind Leo and, laughing, kissed her on each cheek. Leo turned away – and found himself confronted with half a dozen cameras.

On the other side of the city the Acting President of the Republic of Kenya was, almost as reluctantly as Leo Kane, confronting the media.

One of the few traits he shared in full with his predecessor was an almost pathological loathing of the western press. As a result, he was even more brusque than usual when he appeared, no more than five minutes late, at the gathering of 30 invited correspondents who rose respectfully as he entered.

"I am an old man, with little time and a very great deal to do," he snapped, and the reporters smiled politely. "Questions?"

"Would you care to comment on the arrest of Dr Miles?" a tired American in a crumpled linen suit asked.

"Comment? No, I would not. I have nothing to say on the matter. It is a private prosecution properly brought according to our law. It is not a matter over which I have any influence, or in which I have a great deal of interest. I would much sooner discuss the SEACOW conditionalities."

"But the charges concern a struggle in which you were actively involved," prompted a middle-aged Zimbabwean – one of the few black faces.

Ole Kisii treated him to a wintry smile. "So I understand."

42

"Is Paul Muya acting on your behalf?" a sharp female voice asked, challengingly.

"To the best of my knowledge Mr Muya has not so far revealed himself to be a supporter of mine – what do you think?"

This response was greeted with a brief ripple of laughter.

"Did you know his father?" the woman at the back persisted.

"Jembe? Of course," said Ole Kisii quietly, as his aides took discreet steps to ensure the troublesome female would not ask the next question. "Jembe was . . . a martyr."

"So you are keen to see his killer brought to justice?" asked the man from a Frankfurt-based news agency.

Ole Kisii frowned. "I think Jembe would urge us to concentrate on the issues of the day and not waste our little time here righting ancient wrongs. Now, the SEACOW package . . ."

"This is the man defending British interests?" said Nick Easton, incredulously as he studied an image of Leo Kane downloaded and printed from the KBC website.

"I'm afraid so," High Commissioner David Mowbray confirmed.

Nick Easton shook his head, and looked at the picture again. There was Leo, emerging from Paul Muya's church. Unshaven, untidy and with dark shadows under his eyes.

"He looks more like something you might see selling 'The Big Issue' outside a London tube station. What does HMG intend?"

"To send someone out to take control, and try and get this sorry affair wrapped up quickly. And in the meantime, I've been told to try and talk Ole Kisii round."

"Do you think you have much chance?" asked Nick Easton, doubtfully.

"No, not really. But it can't do any harm, can it?"

"I suppose not," said Nick Easton, unconvinced.

Mowbray paused, and watched Easton reach into his pocket for a small cigar. There was a no smoking rule in the High Commission but Nick Easton didn't seem to feel it applied to him,

43

and no one, from the High Commissioner down, felt inclined to challenge his view.

Anyway, reasoned Mowbray, it's Sunday. Hardly anyone else was around, and he wanted Easton relaxed and expansive. After all, he'd given up his usually sacrosanct game of golf to come in and chat things over. Not letting him smoke would be a bit hard.

Nick Easton was an enigma. One of a kind. They broke the mould after him. But quite who 'they' were, or where the mould was, remained surrounded in mystery. A mystery, David Mowbray was convinced, that Nick Easton did everything in his power to maintain. He delighted in the slightly sinister and disreputable speculation about him that passed for news in the tabloid papers in Britain and in Kenya. He was at pains never to deny any of the fanciful tales, merely referring any enquiries to his entry in "Who's Who", which accurately described his many and varied business interests in Africa but was unusually vague about his origins and education. Indeed, anything before the early sixties, when he acquired at knock-down prices a raft of East African logging, mining and farming interests from settlers nervous of their prospects in the newly independent Kenya, was, to say the least, ambiguous.

Now in his late seventies, he had lost none of the energy and nerve that had made him a major player in the region. He was still a force to be reckoned with. Especially for the British High Commissioner.

Someone once said that British foreign policy in Kenya and Nick Easton's personal interests were one and the same, and whilst David Mowbray wouldn't, even in his own thoughts, go quite that far, it was certainly true that there was a considerable overlap between the two. Easton was by far the largest British investor in Kenya. He was in close contact with the ailing President's family, several of whom held directorships or consultancies with his companies, and had access to a lot of information simply not available to Mowbray and his kind.

44

A man who could thus pull a breathtaking range of useful strings.

Nick Easton was a mover and shaker. A well-connected, massively resourced maverick. He was also an enigma to the medical profession. A short man who must have been heavily set when young but was now simply, severely overweight, to the point that, had he ever retained a medical advisor willing to risk the generous fees he paid, he would have long since been diagnosed as clinically obese. He smoked, ate all the wrong things and generally lived a lifestyle that should have killed him decades earlier. But he kept going, his businesses, his influence and his belly ever expanding.

"But you do think our assessment is about right?" Mowbray asked, not for the first time. "SEACOW and self-glorification?"

"Yes, I think so," Nick Easton replied, yawning. He was getting bored.

"But what about Paul Muya? He's an opposition man. No friend of Ole Kisii. How does he fit in?"

"Oh come on, David," said Nick Easton. "You know as well as I do that Kenyan politics abound with just such behind-the-scenes deals and accommodations. I've no doubt Muya is lining himself up for a switch, and I'll bet Ole Kisii will offer him the Vice Presidency. The old warrior and the son of his fallen comrade, shoulder to shoulder into the future . . . I'd vote for them if I were a Kenyan!" Nick Easton chuckled dryly as he rose, in search of an ashtray. He paused and surveyed the Nairobi skyline from the High Commissioner's office.

"God, I love this country!" he sighed. "It's got such a future. Don't let's allow the past, and Ole Kisii, to fuck it up. Go and face him down, David," he added as he flicked ash onto the carpet. "Talk the old bugger round."

CHAPTER SEVEN

"So what have you got to offer? What got you sent to us?"
Johnny Sandford had asked.

"I got him sent to us," Ted Foss had replied.

I turn, and face him. "Inspector . . . Foss?"

"Superintendent Foss," he corrects me. I look from Sandford
to Foss, and back. It's clear that the two have little liking for
one another. Nothing in common, I guess. Sandford is tall and
long-limbed. He moves easily and his thin face, reddened by
exposure to sun and wind, is topped by fair hair, carelessly cut
and unruly. There is a lot of the wiry schoolboy still about him.

Foss, on the other hand, is square, squat and solid. His hair is
cut so short at the sides that it seems to be little more than a blue
stain on his white skin. A short, pointed nose thrust aggressively
from an otherwise puffy face. His lips are narrow, and his neck
is thick and florid.

He is heavier than the last time I saw him; the black leather
belt with its brass Kenya Police Reserve buckle bites into his
belly, which swells up over the top of his trousers.

"Miles was telling me all about his exploits in Anvil," Sanford says.

"All about?" smiles Foss mirthlessly. "I seriously doubt
that."

There is a silence, and then Johnny Sandford nods, slowly.
"He's the one you told me about." He says, realisation dawn-
ing. "The one who pointed Jembe out to you."

"That's right," says Foss, although his stare never leaves
my face. "He's the one. If Jembe's here, Miles can confirm the

46

sighting. He's the only one – the only one still alive – to have seen him close up. I'm taking my boys down to Nyere," he adds, bluntly. "We'll be back before sundown."

"Then I'll keep the gin slings on ice," says Sanford, with a sneer.

He seems to relax, as Foss strides off to round up his Askaris, and the smile returns. "Ever been in the Aberdares before, Miles? Fancy an outing now? Good man! Let's take a stroll over to the Salient. We had a Pembroke Skyshouter up yesterday announcing the ceasefire and we need to check our letter boxes. Who knows, you may even catch a glimpse of your illusive General Jembe: that would be one in the eye for Foss eh?" he chuckles.

Is this really more than 50 years ago? God, it seems like yesterday.

CHAPTER EIGHT

The Acting President of Kenya, the 78-year-old Masai John Ole Kisii, granted the British High Commissioner's request for an urgent interview more rapidly than expected. Mowbray had anticipated a display of measured petulance in response to the British prompted postponement of the signing upon which everyone said Ole Kisii had staked what brief political future he had. However, the messenger who had borne the High Commissioner's polite personal request had returned with its response – a fifteen minute audience at 8 that evening.

At 7.05 pm David Mowbray set off from the High Commission's purpose-built offices up beyond the Railway Golf Course. The High Commissioner's blue Range Rover, with its diplomatic plates and Union Jack flicking on its bonnet, was admitted with a crisp salute through the first ring of security around State House fifteen minutes later. Mowbray knew from tedious experience that the closer he got to Ole Kisii, the more time-consuming, inconsistent and illogical the security arrangements would become. Such were the political realities of Africa.

When he eventually reached the portico of the Presidential Palace, he still had a good six minutes in hand. He paused therefore to chat to the waiting aide, like the old man, a Masai. The aide checked his watch, Mowbray glanced at his. Their eyes met, they nodded to one another and Mowbray was ushered towards the presence. As they walked through State House itself to the garden, Mowbray heard the voices of children, singing. His escort caught his slight, questioning frown and beamed. "From an orphanage in Voi," he confided.

"Ah," Mowbray said, rearranging his face into a suitable expression of compassion and concern.

As they crossed the gardens, in darkness, towards the bright patch of neatly trimmed grass illuminated by powerful flood-lights, Mowbray saw first the choir: they looked so tiny, in their immaculate white shirts and shorts, conducted by a bespectacled teacher, singing their hearts out for the Old Man. Then he saw the Acting President, wrinkled as a burst balloon, a black sack of old bones in a safari suit, slumped in a wicker chair a dozen paces from the choir, one thin bony finger raised fractionally to wave stiffly in absent-minded appreciation of the thin, trilling voices.

He half turned to acknowledge the presence of the High Commissioner, and waved another chair forward.

"They sing like angels, no?" he said, his voice dry and friable. Then the single, bony finger paused, and the Acting President raised his hand, waving the choir away as though it was now an irritant.

"I hope you had a comfortable journey back from Eldoret, Your Excellency," offered Mowbray as the children bowed and were shepherded quickly away.

"Not really," sighed the President. "I took the helicopter. I don't like helicopters. The first time I saw one it was over Narok – dropping leaflets announcing the price on my head. Such things leave their mark. What do you want to speak to me about?"

The Old Man had exhausted his notoriously little patience for pleasantries.

"Your Excellency, we are most troubled about this situation with Dr Miles. I am sure you appreciate the potential repercussions . . ."

"Oh yes," agreed the President, grimly. "I am sure I do."

The High Commissioner shrugged. "Then perhaps if Your Excellency could see your way to exerting some influence to bring this matter to a speedy resolution . . ."

"Interfere with the due process of law?" the President cried in mock horror. "Really, Mr Mowbray, does your government know you are urging me to take such a course? Whatever may prevail these days in the UK, our constitution provides for an independent Judiciary."

It was clear that the old man intended to enjoy himself at the High Commissioner's expense, but Mowbray didn't intend to play.

"Her Majesty's Government would consider itself compelled to withdraw from the SEACOW package completely if this matter is not resolved satisfactorily," Mowbray said, evenly.

"Oh, it would, would it?" the Old Man snapped. His muddy eyes flashed, and his body twitched with a deep, repressed anger. "I will not be bought by pounds sterling, or bullied by public schoolboys, Mr Mowbray." He held up his hands against Mowbray's attempt to get the conversation back on course. "You think that by turning my signing ceremony into a fiasco you can flex your old colonial muscles and I will cringe? That I will bow to your whims out of a desperation for hard currency and foreign friends? You see this?" he demanded, hauling up the jacket of his safari suit to reveal a puckered scar an inch above his left hip bone. "A British bullet did this."

The High Commissioner watched, with a heavy sense of impending doom. He'd seen the scar before, and heard the story too. It was something of party piece for the Acting President. He resigned himself to a lengthy lecture on the Old Man's time in the forest, his capture, interrogation, screening and detention.

"I am not like the Africans of my generation you usually deal with! I was not taught the three Rs in a Christian mission school. I learnt to read in a detention camp. To write in internal exile, and to pray in the forest to a God you would think primitive. The only thing the British ever taught me was how to take a beating and survive a bullet.

"I know what young Muya is up to, far better than you do," Ole Kisii continued, trembling with rage. "But I watched your slaughters, bleeding from your bullets and bruised by your beatings. I say good luck to Paul Muya! Yes! Good luck to any son of Kenya who seeks vengeance on your type."

50

"But Your Excellency . . ."

"Silence!" the Old Man shouted, almost beside himself with fury. He leaned forward, shaking a fist beneath the High Commissioner's nose. For a moment Mowbray genuinely feared he was about to be struck. "Am I to spend my entire life listening to voices like yours?" exploded the President. "Who do you think you are, to come here, and threaten me?"

He paused, then continued, more measured, and with infinite menace. "What if this is only the first of many, eh? The French are still pursuing those who shipped their Jews off to concentration camps – why shouldn't we too demand that justice be visited on those who consigned thousands of our Kikuyu brothers and sisters to a similar hell? Yes. . . . Now get out! I will not bow to your whims, or dance to your tune!"

"Dan-ger-ous!" breathed the President's senior aide, the admiration clear in his voice as he joined his master to watch Mowbray's retreat.

The Old Man shook his head. "Danger has lesser dimensions at my age, but it still pleases me to make a Muzungu tremble."

"Is this really what you want to happen?" wondered the aide, helping the President up from his chair.

"Maybe," Ole Kisii said, stretching stiffly, "but if not, I could put a stop to this with a snap of my fingers – and never stray beyond my legal powers. You see, I have done my homework. They will make sense of it all, eventually. But first, they must do their homework, too. And in the meantime, let's watch the Muzungu sweat."

"But Paul Muya . . ." the aide began.

The President shook off the supporting hand. "Paul Muya is a small boy," he sneered. "They call him Total Man – I call him Mtoto – the child. He is not the man his father was – nowhere near! He thinks he's a leader, but he's just a Mtoto dancing in front of a crowd. A little drummer boy marching at the head of an army. He may think he is leading them, but he's just the first to fall when the bullets fly. Armies are led by generals, not little drummer boys. History is made by men, not Mtoto."

He paused, then continued, more gently. "Have the children gone?"

The aide confirmed that they had.

"Pity," said the Old Man, sadly. "Tell the Attorney General I want to see him first thing tomorrow morning."

CHAPTER NINE

"A land to fall in love with."

It is one of Johnny Sandford's favourite expressions. I lost count of the number of times I heard it during those weeks in the forest.

We sit, high up on the Salient, looking out towards the snow cap of Mt Kenya, and I first start to see it through his eyes. It is one of those mornings when the clouds cling to the trees like breath on a frosty morning, as though the forest itself sighs in glad anticipation of the day.

Until then, I'd seen precious little in Kenya to fall in love with.

Certainly not Nairobi. An ugly and vicious township built on hatred, greed and fear. With its rigorously enforced colour bar. Soldiers on the streets, police patrols, each man with his rifle chained to his belt, and white settlers armed to the teeth and considering themselves in mortal danger every minute. Then, outside the city, the Detention and Rehabilitation Camps; too hastily prepared, too cheaply built, too quickly filled.

It was in one of these stinking hell-holes, crammed with blanket-draped Kikuyu, I first heard the Mau Mau wail. It was like the keening of ten thousand souls lost in Perdition. It chilled me to the marrow.

But with Johnny Sandford, that morning, I first glimpsed a different Kenya.

"Travel up country from here, Miles, the first chance you get," he urged. "Up towards the Uganda border. Or into Tanganyika. The sky is higher there, and the horizons wider than *anywhere else in the world. Leakey reckons that's where Man first walked upright, and I wouldn't be at all surprised if he isn't right. It's the sheer bloody majesty of this place that hauled us up off all fours."*

I tease him about it. I say to him, "You love this country, yes?" And he says that he is proud to say that he does. And I say, "The Kikuyu love this country too, right?" And again he agrees. And then I say, "But what about all the others? The Indians? The Settlers? Foss?" And he frowns, and his normally open, cheerful face darkens.

"No," he says, brusquely, shaking his head. "No, they desire it. Want it for what it can offer. That's why they are not like me. Or the Kukes. If Foss and his kind are capable of love at all, then it is the love of an adulterer. A grubby, sullied hankering after the rightful object of another man's desire."

I will always remember the look on his face as he spoke. It was pinched and mean-looking. I'd never seen that expression before, and only once saw it after.

I never made light of his love of Kenya again.

CHAPTER TEN

Within 30 hours of Tom Miles' arrest Terry McKenzie, the East Africa Desk Officer in the Foreign and Commonwealth Office, was summoned back from his family holiday in a cottage in Totnes and despatched to Nairobi to take charge of what was fast becoming known as the Miles Affair.

A dour sort. Unshakeable, unflappable and clear-thinking; his was a reassuring presence. Within three hours of his arrival, dismissing suggestions that he allow himself a couple of hours downtime, he had established himself in the British High Commission and settled down to planning what to do next, liaising closely with the High Commission staff, smoothing ruffled feathers and resolving issues of protocol. By the end of his second day in Nairobi, he had been joined by a retained QC and two Ministry of Justice civil servants. Leo Kane found himself promptly sidelined and Tom Miles found himself treated with a distant, patient courtesy. McKenzie and his colleagues from the High Commission assured Tom they had everything under control, and made arrangements for him to speak to his family. They nodded intently whenever he spoke, and even took notes, but he could tell they weren't really listening. They assured him that they could resolve this matter to everyone's satisfaction the moment it got to court.

And they were as keen to dispense with Leo's services as Leo had been to be spared their brief, until they were reminded, much to the High Commissioner's chagrin, that Tom could only be represented by an attorney whose name appeared on the Kenya Role of Advocates. They had tentatively broached the subject of a change of local representation with Tom, only to be met by an absolute refusal. Not that Tom had a view one way or the other about Leo's relative competence. It was just that Leo had sat by him that first, grim night in Central, when he could have, probably should have, cleared off and abandoned him and that was not the kind of thing Tom forgot. So, making it clear that his role was to do precisely as he was told, they reluctantly asked Leo to remain. Not that their attitude troubled Leo overmuch: as the hours passed, and the media interest in the case became ever more strident, Leo was confirmed in his view that whilst a successful prosecution might well do Paul Muya's reputation a deal of good, win or lose, little glory would reflect upon Tom Miles' defender. So, he turned up to the interminable case conferences solely to assure himself of his fee and was content to daydream or doze while McKenzie and the pompous QC mapped out their path to triumph.

Except that they didn't. At least not in Leo's hearing.

Leo gazed out of the window, across the panorama of Nairobi centre. For the third time in half an hour, he rearranged his diary for the next few days – his ex-wife was due to be out of town representing a bankrupt haulier in Kisumu and his sons would be with him. He'd been thinking a lot about the boys, and who he could get to drive with them in the Charge now Paul had withdrawn . . .

They had a hell of a lot still to do. He had got small scale sponsorship from a friend who owned a tyre company, another who was a mushroom grower and a third who imported paint. Their names and logos needed to be displayed on the battered old Land Rover Defender they were preparing. Then there was the very generous funding offered by his scary neighbour on the coast, Dieter Haas, to again politely decline. A disinclination to drive a vehicle with Nazi-looking 'SS' flashes emblazoned on its sides wasn't Leo's only reason for saying no. The vehicle was currently painted yellow overall, but last year there'd been at least half a dozen other yellow Defenders. His meandering thoughts strayed to the hours he and the boys had spent reading

Thomas the Tank Engine stories. The recollection filled him with a mawkish nostalgia: he rather fancied he'd go for pale blue and red – Thomas' colours.

He'd taught the boys to read with those books: not the glossy, pathetic things that were everywhere now, but the original stories on hard card with hand-drawn illustrations of an ordered, tidy world, preserved from his own childhood. His ex-wife had conveniently managed to forget that, when she told everybody that the boys wouldn't miss their father because he'd never been there for them anyway.

Bitch.

A year earlier he would have thought hard about how the boys would react to the change of colour: would they feel they were being treated as babies? But thinking hard was another of those things he had given up. Bollocks to it, he decided. It's my Land Rover, and I'll be buying the paint.

"We do have a strategy, I presume?" Leo asked, suddenly deciding to take an interest, purely to rile the QC.

The QC and McKenzie glanced up from their papers, surprised.

"We?" asked the QC, rolling the word around his mouth like a fine claret. "Oh, you mean us? Yes. *We* have a strategy."

"And as Dr Miles' attorney, may I presume to enquire what it is?"

The QC treated him to a sad, professional smile, the type usually reserved for a deluded and confused simpleton. "Best not just yet. Suffice to say that we propose to see Mr Muya hoisted with his own petard."

"And you think *we* can do that, do you?"

"Oh, I think so."

"Don't make the mistake of underestimating him . . ." Leo began.

The QC made a show of glancing through the papers on the desk in front of him. "Ah yes," he murmured, almost to himself. "You're a chum of his, aren't you?"

Leo raised an eyebrow. "And?"

The QC paused, then glanced up and stared him straight in the eye. "And I'm wondering how you came to be involved in this case in the first place, Mr Kane. Your chum pulled a few strings, didn't he?"

Leo felt his temple throbbing, and a tiny muscle tugged at the corner of his mouth. He forced himself to smile, and chuckle, although the sound was hollow and empty. "If you're afraid that I would compromise the interests of my client . . ."

"Oh, I'm not afraid of anything you may or may not do," the QC assured him, blandly. "*We* shall make sure that Dr Miles' interests are amply safeguarded. From Mr Muya, and from his conveniently placed little chums."

As Leo left the briefing McKenzie ran to catch him up, just slipping into the lift as the door breathed shut.

McKenzie smiled, uncomfortably. Leo guessed he must be in his late thirties. Very neat, with sharp features, and a carefully trimmed moustache. "That was, er . . . out of order, what was said in there," McKenzie offered.

Leo shrugged, but said nothing.

"We've already worked out how we want you to handle the committal proceedings. You know that, don't you?" McKenzie continued.

Leo shrugged "I'd assumed as much. When am I going to be told?"

"In time. But only just." said McKenzie. "That's the official line. You're to be kept in the dark until the last possible moment."

The lift stopped at the ground floor. A messenger in a dark blue tunic, and brass lion and unicorn pinned on his breast pocket, eased in past them as they got out.

"I'm sorry but that's the way this has to be," said McKenzie. "Instructions from on high. Very high."

"I suspect I can work out most of it anyway," said Leo as they emerged onto the courtyard. "It's hardly rocket science. On Thursday we go for an adjournment in order to give us time

58

to gather the facts. Ask for an early date for the full hearing and seek bail for Dr Miles, yes?"

McKenzie frowned, as though debating how much to reveal. "No," he said suddenly, his mind made up. "We go for a full and complete dismissal from the outset. Get the whole business over and get Dr Miles home for the weekend. That's what everybody wants."

"And you think that's possible?"

"Yes, we do. We've got people working round the clock on this back in London. And we've got a trump card. Now that's the limit of my indiscretion, OK? We'll prove that Tom Miles was just what he claims to be: an innocent survivor of an ugly war."

"Tom Miles was a Commissioned Officer in a Combined Action Team," said Leo, slowly. "Those guys were no boy scouts. They were picked men, at the sharp end of a vicious and brutal counter-insurgency campaign."

"So what are you saying?" asked McKenzie. "That you think he's guilty?"

"I've no view on the matter either way," said Leo. "Just that I've read too many accounts of their methods over the past few days to be sure anyone can convince a Kenyan Court that such men are mere innocent survivors."

CHAPTER ELEVEN

Johnny Sandford strides briskly through the forest, a stick in his hand, with the confident, proprietorial air of a landowner walking through a wood his great-great-grandfather had planted. His spaniel is forever bounding off into the undergrowth, snuffling contentedly at mounds of elephant and rhino droppings. His de-oathed Mau Mau in their outlandish garb are out on his flanks, like beaters in some surreal grouse shoot. We move on, up through the deciduous forest to the edge of the bamboo belt.

Sandford is passionately proud of his small clutch of de-oathed Mau Mau, or pseudo terrorists, as he prefers to have them called. Proud, and a trifle wary too. He treats them as one might treat a pet leopard: glorying in its grace and the beauty of its movements, whilst never forgetting its capacity to kill and recognising that it can never truly be tamed. That it can at any moment turn; that it is still capable of devouring its erstwhile master.

The route we follow has been chosen not by Sandford, but by them.

"These chaps took the Mau Mau warrior's oath, and went into the forest, little more than village boys," Sandford tells me. "They may have left the forest, we may have de-oathed them, but the forest can never leave them. They've become the best bloody jungle fighters in the world. To hide their tracks, they can run for miles, barefoot, on the edges of their feet, or backwards. Re-kindled in them are senses I would have thought lost to mankind if I hadn't witnessed them in action. It's hard

to believe that men who stink like they do can pick up a scent over huge distances. But I tell you, they have to be seen to be believed. And the wonder of it is, it's all learnt! Oh, Foss and his kind say they've simply reverted to type. Become the savages they really are, but that's absolute rot. The Kukes were never forest dwellers: they're agriculturists. No, they've taken all we taught them during the war and developed it beyond anything we ever thought possible – then simply turned it back on us."

As though on a whim, Johnny Sandford suddenly pauses, and mutters a few words in Kikuyu. The men halt, and squat on their haunches.

"Come," he says, turning to me, "but don't touch anything."

We walk forward, in silence, emerging after a few minutes into a clearing. I feel the warmth of the sun for the first time, as it rises over the shoulder of Mt Kenya. The forest smells rich, with the sweet pungency of decaying vegetation. A slight breeze stirs the higher branches, and the trees come alive with sound.

Johnny Sandford holds up his hand, and I stop. At his signal, I slowly advance, until I am standing at his side. He points into the centre of the clearing, and I see a bamboo cane thrust into the ground, with a bottle upturned on it, a scrap of paper inside. In a circle of about 20 feet in diameter around the bottle on a stick, the ground has been cleared, and stamped flat.

"It's our way of communicating with them," Sandford explains. "We put that note there over a week ago now. It's to tell them that whoever tells us where we can find Jembe will receive a free pardon, and a reward.

"They always suspect booby traps, so we clear the ground all around to try and reassure them. Come on."

We skirt round the clearing to where the ground falls away. A hundred paces away, we pause again.

A light aircraft, a Piper Pacer, lays on its side, its wings broken and folded back upon themselves, like a crushed butterfly. It has clearly been there for some time. The gashes on the bark of the trees around it have begun to dry and scar over, and the forest has re-established itself around and through the wreckage.

"This is what they come here for. They strip out the wires. They make the best snares."

Two hours, and three other untouched letter boxes later, we enter the bamboo belt.

"Filthy stuff, bamboo," Johnny Sandford calls back over his shoulder. "It sheds these frightful hairs which itch like the very devil. Hell to move through. Still, you may as well get a taste of it before we have to go in there for real."

We move into the bamboo, stepping carefully over fallen stems.

Suddenly, to my left, I hear a loud report. I spin, dragging up my Patchett. Two more bangs, and I fire off a text book four-second burst as I throw myself to the ground. The three ex-Forest Fighters and Johnny Sandford drop like stones, and lie perfectly still.

After the staccato bark of the Patchett, there is an absolute silence for a long moment before an explosion of startled bird calls and monkey howls echoes above and around us.

One of the Kikuyu begins to chuckle, and raises his head from the ground. The others join in, a sibilant, insistent laughter. Johnny Sandford rolls over, and props himself up on his elbows, smiling broadly. "Congratulations, Lieutenant Miles! We shall have to mention you in despatches. You've single-handedly incapacitated an enemy stand of bamboo."

There is another muffled crack, further away, over to the right. I glance towards the sound, then back to Johnny Sandford. The confusion must be clear in my face.

Sandford laughs aloud as he gets to his feet, brushing leaf mould from his tunic. "I'm sorry, Miles, I should have warned you. That's the other thing the blessed stuff does. Gasses build up in the cane and, as the day warms up, they expand, and explode. Come on, boys!" He calls to his pseudo terrorists. "Lets . . ."

He pauses, picking up the warning in their crouched, still posture: they have smelt, or heard, something that we would never catch. Now they, the true jungle warriors, are in charge.

62

The five of us stand stock still. The three Kikuyu glance at one another, then up at the trees, selecting the quickest to climb.

"*Kifaru!*" breathes one of them. Rhino.

Suddenly, they are moving, incredibly fast. "Keep with them!" cries Sandford, haring off in pursuit. "Move!"

It comes at us from behind, and slightly to the right. A great, grey slab of muscle and bone. We grab at the thickest stems of the bamboo, and it is past us, throwing its massive horn from side to side and then stopping, and turning with the precise, almost delicate movements of a dancer. I try to hold my breath but can't. The blood is pumping too fast. The rhino picks up the sound. The three Kikuyu, high up, begin to call, whistle and hiss from different angles to distract it.

It turns, confused, and I see the grotesque scarring down its flank. The wound is livid and moist, alive with maggots. As the brute stands, crazed and pained, three tiny, brightly coloured birds land on its flank, and peck delicately at the oozing wound, using their beaks as a surgeon would use fine forceps to pick out minute shards of glass. The rhino, its side twitching and trembling, turns again, and moves away. After a few minutes, the Kikuyu climb down, and Johnny Sandford and I follow, scratching at our necks and forearms.

"Bombing," Sandford says, sadly. "Most of the elephant, buffalo and rhino in the forest have been wounded or driven mad. That one would never have troubled us but for the bombing. It's a terrible, ugly thing, Miles. Pointless, too. Just bloody awful."

Sandford's spaniel emerges from the undergrowth, keeping low, crawling to his master's feet, tail wagging in appeasement.

Sandford laughs. "Well done, Hero! I noticed you were well clear of the excitement, as usual." He turns to his pseudo terrorists. "Well done, chaps! Back to camp for tea and buns? I think we've given Bwana Miles a good introduction to the dubious joys of jungle warfare."

63

CHAPTER TWELVE

The Magistrates' Court was packed out with well-dressed, serious people on the morning of the committal proceedings in the case of the Republic vs. Miles. In addition to a shorthand writer Leo had hired to take a verbatim transcription of the event, and a mass of Paul Muya's supporters, there were several representatives of the world's media, numerous politicians, and a cluster of Embassy, High Commission and UN representatives.

The whole place seemed to buzz with nervous energy. It tensed up the public, the officials and the lawyers. But most of all it worked on the presiding Magistrate, who glanced nervously around like a trapped animal.

He was a public figure and a man of God, a political activist and a pillar of his community with an interest in a range of businesses. He was, people said, big in mangrove poles, the narrow, straight trunks of which were cut along the coast and transported throughout Kenya to serve as rafters, beams and scaffolding. He also had an interest in an ex-Lonrho wattle plantation and a couple of cut flower nurseries. In many ways he was a typical New Kenya man, successfully combining public office, political activity and private enterprise with few evident conflicts.

Until now.

It wasn't, he had moaned to a coven of sympathetic cronies the previous night, that he feared a difficult or unpleasant duty. It was just that, so far, no one had made it clear to him what that duty was. He didn't need anyone to tell him that the Tom Miles case was by far the most significant that had ever come before him, even if his involvement would only be at this committal stage. But in the old days, someone from State House would have explained what was expected of him. Now he found, to his distress, that his features dominated the front page of both the Nation and the Standard, uncomfortably sandwiched between those of Paul Muya and this man, Miles. As though trapped between the two. How apt, he concluded, checking his Rolex watch. Well, the case would begin within a matter of minutes and still no order, instruction, advice or guidance from above. Sometimes, he reflected miserably, the duties placed upon those willing to accept the burden of public office seemed almost too heavy to bear.

The court had a number of other cases to hear in its own right. Three charges of possessing African spirituous liquor, one of staying in Kenya unlawfully, one of being a rogue and a vagabond and one of possessing a game trophy unlawfully.

All were adjourned, pending further investigation. As the sad gallery of accused and their poorly prepared defenders came and went, the court grew restive. Deadlines approached, and this excursion into African jurisprudence would not cut it on the front pages of the Friday tabloids, half a dozen of which were paying serious money to have their best men on the spot.

At ten to eleven, Tom Miles was brought up, and the committal bundle – actually one thin file – was laid before the Court.

With immaculate timing the Attorney General arrived just as the case was announced. A sharply dressed man with a politician's smile whose bald head shone above his bespectacled face.

The Magistrate half rose, relief clear in his small eyes. The Attorney General frowned very slightly and shook his head, and the Magistrate hastily slumped back into his chair. The Attorney General nodded, and remained standing.

The Magistrate raised his hand to hush the Clerk who was still reading through the detail of the charge. With elaborate politeness, he welcomed the Attorney General, and invited him to act as *amicus curiae* – a friend of the Court.

Leo turned to McKenzie. "This could be a help," he assured him. "Look at Paul Muya: does he look happy?"

It was evident the Attorney General's arrival had discomfited the Prosecution. Paul Muya frowned, and fidgeted with his papers. He was clearly angry, and that anger swirled around him, finding no release. He looked like a man wrong-footed and furious about it. Not for the first time, Leo thought he glimpsed a hint of the hard edge to Paul's nature. The part, Leo guessed, which made Paul the successful politician. It was not so much how Paul looked or acted, but in the way his supporting counsel stared at the floor, hardly daring to move, like guilty schoolboys anxious to avoid the headmaster's wrath.

Leo scrawled a quick note on his pad, tore off the sheet of paper, folded it twice and, nodding towards Paul Muya, handed it to the policeman standing near Tom. The policeman crossed the room and placed it on the table in front of Paul who opened it, read it quickly, and glared across at the Defence. Leo rose and stood beneath the box in which Tom Miles sat, still and patient. Grinning broadly, he held up a brief, tied neatly with pink tape.

"What was that all about?" Tom asked.

Leo smiled up at him. "I just told him that when the beak kicks the case out we're going to sue his ass for wrongful arrest."

"Are we?" Tom asked vaguely.

Leo sighed. "That'll be up to you, Dr Miles. But right now, the more we make the good Mr Muya uncertain, the better. In many ways it's like sumo wrestling: the contest is decided as much in the posturing before battle commences, as it is in the rough and tumble of the brawl."

With that, Leo turned to the Attorney General, smiled broadly and with an exaggerated bow, hissed in a stage whisper that could be heard throughout the room, "So glad you could join us, Sir. Thank you *so* much."

The Attorney General treated Leo to a stony glare and sat dead still, looking attentively at nothing in particular, while waiting for a bevy of aides to bring him his briefing notes.

Once Paul Muya rose to outline the prosecution case it seemed as though Leo's theatrics had achieved little: his performance was assured and measured. A masterclass in clarity and restraint. Briefly, he outlined the basis of the charges, referring to the various depositions of the witnesses he proposed to call which formed the bulk of the neat file on the Magistrate's bench. He assured the Court that the evidence already deposited was more than enough to justify the proceedings and, in his view, sufficient to assure a conviction. He hinted at further, damning evidence still being pursued, but insisted that the Prosecution was ready to proceed whether or not these further proofs were obtained.

The Defence had been given access to the Prosecution bundle. There were two key documents: the situation report signed by Major Sandford, the commanding officer of Tom Miles' unit, which clearly described Tom as playing a critical role in the operation which ended with the death of Jembe, and a government circular issued several weeks earlier announcing a ceasefire. Paul's case was simple: there was a ceasefire. His father was invited to attend surrender talks where he was murdered, plain and simple. A pre-meditated, cold-blooded murder.

In some ways, Leo was relieved he'd been given such a precise brief to counter the charge. If he'd had to rely on his numerous discussions with Tom they would have been unhelpful, to say the least. The old man's account of the night in question remained muddled and inconsistent. He said the official report was inaccurate, but did he seem able or willing to say where it differed from his own recollection of events. He just kept insisting that he hadn't been the one who had killed Paul's father. Over and over again.

Paul Muya sat down. The Magistrate, with a quick glance in the Attorney General's direction for some approval or guidance, turned to Leo.

Leo studiously avoided any hint of a slur on Paul Muya's father but, as he had been instructed, focused entirely on the documents offered. He argued that the supposed ceasefire was without legal status. He pointed out that Paul had presented no evidence to support his contention that General Jembe was attending peace talks.

As he warmed to his theme, Leo became expansive about the high standards to which the Kenyan judiciary aspired. He waxed lyrical about the common legal heritage Kenya and Britain shared, and became almost tearful as he explored the deep humanity and high moral fibre of the man he had the honour to defend.

Then, with withering sarcasm, he set about Paul Muya's motives in bringing this private prosecution. As his hatchet job on Paul Muya drew to a close, so McKenzie bent forward and drew a slender file from his brief case. A file Leo had been shown for the first time earlier that morning.

The hairs on the back of Leo's neck tingled: he felt, with the crunching certainty of a sudden impact, that he was about to be made part of a classic blunder. He paused, and leaned towards McKenzie. "We don't need to do this," he hissed.

McKenzie glanced up, surprised, then smiled. "Yes we do. Take the papers."

A pulse in his left temple pounding, Leo opened the file. To the single sheet of paper he had been allowed to read just moments before court convened, marked Secret and dated early in 1954, had been added a further half page of text: his scripted statement.

"Mr Kane?" prompted the Magistrate.

"A moment, Sir," begged Leo. "Are you sure this will take him by surprise?" he whispered, leaning close to McKenzie.

"Oh yes," McKenzie assured him patiently, glancing back at the QC sitting in the public gallery making 'get on with it' gestures. "I told you, the file is subject to extended closure under the Public Records Act. No one's got access to this but us. It's going to take everyone by surprise. Even Dr Miles."

"You haven't discussed this with him?" asked Leo, horror-struck. "I was told he'd agreed to this."

"Look," said McKenzie. "We don't have time to debate that

now. You've got your instructions. I've got mine. The best legal minds in Britain have laboured long and hard over this stuff. All you have to do is read it into the record. Do your job, Kane. Now."

Leo turned, swallowed, and read aloud. "The elimination of General Jembe was in fact authorised by the document I now hold – Secret Circular number 10 issued in March 1954 – from which I quote: '*Whilst the apprehension of the terrorist popularly known as General Jembe remains a priority, and the neutralisation of his influence highly desirable, his prosecution in open court, or indeed any process of law which will permit him to make statements likely to be prejudicial to the early resolution of the State of Emergency, is not deemed to be in the public interest.*'"

The Magistrate halted Leo and turned to Paul Muya. "Mr Muya, do you wish to challenge this document?"

Paul rose: "Not at this point, thank you, Sir. I would however request that the entire document be read into the record and made available to the Prosecution."

The Attorney General was on his feet, counselling caution. "There is no duty on the Defence to disclose all the material it has. The Defence should be free to present such aspects of its evidence to the Counsel as it feels directly impinge upon the matter before this court."

Nodding, his brow slightly furrowed, as though complimenting this unlikely ally on the wisdom of his words, Leo continued his carefully scripted speech with slightly less trepidation.

"This document clearly shows that whichever member of the security forces actually killed General Jembe, and in whatever circumstances, they were acting on instructions from the highest authority. Properly framed instructions. Legally binding. However we might see the matter today, the killing of General Jembe was regarded by the lawful government then as a military necessity.

"Our case therefore is this: Dr Miles' role in the death of Wilson Mumbo Muya alias General Jembe – whatever that role may or may not have been – was that of a soldier engaged in a legitimate military action. I therefore respectfully suggest this Court has no alternative but to dismiss this unfounded and unnecessary charge and allow Dr Miles to return home to his family, and the relationship between the United Kingdom and Republic of Kenya to return to its former, mutually beneficial state. If I can be of further assistance . . ."

The Magistrate, clearly several fathoms out of his depth, looked, bewildered, towards the Attorney General as Leo sat down. The Attorney General did not disappoint him. With a shrug, and an easy smile, he said. "I'm afraid it is not that simple. In view of the content of the document now presented, I have no alternative but to intervene in the matter. By the powers vested in me by the Republic," he intoned solemnly, "I shall apply to the High Court to take over this case."

McKenzie and the QC shared a self-satisfied smile. Things were panning out exactly as predicted. Next the Attorney General would, having taken over the prosecution, announce his intention to discontinue it, just as London had assured them would happen.

All smiles froze however as the Attorney General continued, "I also give notice of the commencement of further proceedings against Dr Thomas Miles on charges of committing a War Crime and a Crime against Humanity. Henceforth this case will be handled by my officials and I require the Private Prosecutor, and the Court, to hand over all documents relating to this matter to my office by 10 am tomorrow morning. Thank you."

"Brilliant. Just fucking brilliant," Leo muttered as he glanced across at Paul, but then he paused, for he saw not the triumph he had anticipated, but cold fury in his friend's eyes. There were urgent, muttered consultations around him, but Paul sat dead still and distant, a sullen rock amid a churning sea, deeply, profoundly angry.

Leo shook his head and turned to the crestfallen McKenzie. "So much for the best legal minds in Britain. I suggest you get after the AG and see if you can find out what the hell he's up to."

"What about you?" asked McKenzie.

"Me?" asked Leo, bitterly. "I think I owe it to Dr Miles to be by his side right now. Don't you?"

Tom Miles was led to the cells below the Courtroom where, with Leo Kane's hand at his elbow to support him, he was formally charged with War Crimes and Crimes against Humanity.

Within ten minutes of the Attorney General's announcement, Ole Kisii himself appeared before the world's media, at a press conference in the Safari Club at which his Minister for Wildlife and Tourism was launching yet another anti-poaching initiative, and held up a piece of paper.

"This man Miles," he said, solemnly "is but the first. Indictments are being prepared in respect of twenty-three others named on this list. We will shortly be applying to the British Government for their extradition. Now, if you have any questions, ask them. As I may have told you before, I am an old man, with little time, and a very great deal to do."

"What?" cried David Mowbray, aghast. "War crimes? Impossible! The Kenyans aren't even signatories to the UN Declarations on war crimes, everybody knows that!"

"Well, I'm afraid they are now," said Nick Easton. "Since 8.15 this morning to be precise. I told you Paul Muya and Ole Kisii were hand in glove . . ."

"This was meant to have appeased them," the High Commissioner grumbled as he rushed for the nearest telephone. "Got Miles off the hook and showed that we could take responsibility for our colonial past. It was all agreed. What a . . ."

"Balls-up?" offered Nick Easton, amused.

CHAPTER THIRTEEN

I am with C.A.T.12 for four days before Foss speaks to me again. It's a joke, really, calling it a Combined Action Team: Sandford, his soldiers and de-oathed Mau Mau check their dead letter boxes and penetrate ever further into the forest, ranging through the bamboo belt and up onto the boggy moorlands at the top of the Aberdares, and I go with them.

Foss and his police Askaris scour the shambas and the settlements lower down. They both act completely independently. Without any desire or attempt to co-ordinate their efforts.

Neither is able to find a trace of Jembe, or indeed of any other Mau Mau. It all seems more like an exercise, but for the bomb craters, and the sight of slender, head-scarfed daughters of white settlers with red hands, and schoolgirl knees and revolvers strapped to their tiny waists, who come up with their machine-gun-toting fathers to bring us eggs and milk and exaggerated tales of renewed oathing ceremonies and hamstrung cattle.

Sandford doesn't have much time for them; most are fairly recent arrivals who have come out from Europe, or up from South Africa, on the promise of abundant, fertile land and cheap, acquiescent labour.

Foss, on the other hand, is very much one with them. He takes them all very seriously and spends hours following up their wild tales.

Nobody seems to be quite sure what to do with the Kikuyu home guard, except keep them well away from the de-oathed terrorists, for it's obvious that both groups would happily tear each other apart given the slightest opportunity.

All in all, there is very little combined action, and it certainly isn't my idea of a team.

Then, Johnny Sandford suddenly decides to go down to Nairobi to try and get his radio operator. It is typical of the way things are. They've given us some excellent equipment, and even sent a PWD team up to erect the mast, and not one of us has the first idea of how to operate it.

If he'd succeeded, then that night, with Jembe, would have been so different.

Or maybe it wouldn't. Foss is determined to go after him alone. Maybe he'd still have found a way to do so, who knows?

Foss is in charge, when Sandford is away. It has been raining hard, all of the previous night. During the day though, the sun shines and most of our efforts are devoted to drying out clothing and equipment. The clearing in which we camp looks like a makeshift laundry, with clothes, tents and tarpaulin sheeting all spread out to dry.

There's no fresh game, because no one has been out into the forest. We're eating out of tins. There is a bad atmosphere; Foss and I have already had to break up a voluble argument between the sergeant of the KAR contingent and the leader of the Home Guard Unit about who had killed the most terrorists. They had nearly come to blows, and there's still a risk that, even with the two of them confined to different ends of our small camp, their men might, in the sullen boredom of the evening, decide to continue the dispute with fists and weapons.

It's created a small bond between Foss and I. We need to stay alert. Need to keep an eye on things. So we talk, if only to keep one another awake.

He tells me about his life. I don't know why, but I'd always assumed he'd lost someone dear to him in a Mau Mau raid. He hasn't. Well, at least, not directly. His wife left him, taking their three children with her, and set up with another white settler while Foss was away on police business. She told him she couldn't stand the loneliness anymore.

73

Surprisingly, he speaks about it without the bitterness I usually ascribe to him. It's almost as if he understands, and sympathises with her.

It wasn't her fault, he seems to be saying, but theirs – the blacks.

He feels hugely betrayed by the Kikuyu. Like it was personal. He'd come to Kenya as a young man immediately after the war. He got a piece of land and, he'd thought, a good crowd of loyal blacks. He'd married, and his farm had prospered. He was, he insisted, a good boss. Hard but fair, he says. A decent man to work for and I suspect, by his own standards, he was. He's one of those who believes you have to treat Africans like dogs. Loyalty and devotion would be rewarded with trust and the occasional indulgence, but ill temper and indiscipline had to be thrashed out of them.

They need, he says, to know who is master. Always.

We start to drink. Not large amounts, just a tot of rum in our coffee to keep out the cold, for the nights can be surprisingly chilly up here.

I shiver. Foss looks at me, and then goes off to his tent, and fetches me one of his sweaters which, without a word, he tosses to me. He knows my kit has all been soaked and has still not dried.

I am surprised by the gesture. By how thoughtful it is.

But, as the alcohol warms us, the bile within him resurfaces. After a long silence, he turns on me, suddenly.

"You know why you're here, don't you, Miles? I asked for you because you know Jembe. I'm going to get him, and you're going to help me. I'm going to neutralise him, once and for all. I am. Listen to what I say carefully. Not us. Not we. Me."

He looks around, glaring at the camp, its inhabitants dozing, now and then out at the forest, black and impenetrable, beyond.

"I hate this place. Loathe it. It isn't up here we're going to bring this State of Emergency to an end. Poncing around like country gents chasing poachers. This isn't a war, Miles, and we're not facing a highly skilled enemy, no matter what

74

Sandford tells you. They're just a bunch of simple savages, out of control. It's not even their fault. It's a medically proven fact: we civilised the kukes too quickly and this sort of collective insanity is the result. We've got to cure them. Bring them back into line, that's all. Then bring them on more slowly. But we're not going to do that by chasing them through the forest like boy scouts at a weekend camp. We're going to do it by taking out the rabble-rousers who're feeding their psychosis."

He pauses, and lights another cigarette from the stub of its predecessor. "Nobody here knows about the cock-up you made in Anvil," he says, spitting a small piece of tobacco from his bottom lip. "Nobody except me, that is. I knew them, you know, those two. The two you got killed. I served with them. Good blokes. Decent, family men. I'm giving you a chance to wipe the slate clean, which is more than you deserve. A chance to put things right. Not for you, oh no. But out of respect for their memory. Just you and me," he concludes, as he gets up to take a leak. "I'm gonna bag Jembe, and you're here to help me do it, got that?"

CHAPTER FOURTEEN

Leo Kane glanced at his watch. How typical, he reflected, that the moment Tom Miles finally seemed to be getting ready to open up should coincide so precisely with his one day in over a fortnight with his sons. They were meant to be fixing the sticky accelerator pedal on the still yellow Land Rover, but instead, here he was in an Interview Room at the Central Police Station sharing a bag of croissants with Tom while his sons sat, watched over by a resentful Nick Friedlander, eating an unhealthy and overpriced breakfast in a nearby hotel.

"I know I should be focusing all my attention on these ridiculous charges," said Tom, wiping crumbs from the side of his mouth, "but every time I think about it I am ever more convinced that all of this has absolutely nothing to do with me. It is all such nonsense: I may not have covered myself with glory during the Emergency, but then, who did?"

Leo nodded, pushing the bag of croissants toward Tom and urging him to take another. "From all I've read it was a struggle without real heroes on either side. On Independence, Kenyatta as first President dismissed Mau Mau as a disease never to be remembered and its supporters as hooligans."

"So who does Paul Muya think he's kidding?" wondered Tom. "Speaking about his father as though he'd been a martyred saint? I'm not saying he deserved what happened to him. But let's at least be honest. The man was a leading terrorist in a movement which not only murdered dozens of white settlers but thousands of his own people. Mau Mau were responsible for the most ghastly atrocities; maybe you should get hold of the Horror Book and present that in evidence – let the court see the photographs of ritually slaughtered women and children that we were all shown on our first arrival in East Africa. That would make even Paul Muya sit up and think a bit."

"Or perhaps give him the chance to dismiss it as a bit of crude British propaganda?"

Tom smiled ruefully, and ran his fingers through his hair. Leo made a mental note to recommend a haircut before his next court appearance. "Probably. But still I wonder, why now? And why me? It is not beyond the realms of possibility that I could be hanged, yet this all feels like it's part of some process that really has nothing whatsoever to do with me."

"Because it isn't really about you, or Jembe," said Leo, wiping his fingers on his trouser legs. "It's about politics. Present day politics. Views differ only on whether it's internal positioning in preparation for the next election or international wrangling about some aid package, but that's what it's all about."

"And what do you think?"

"I think from where you sit right now it doesn't really matter. What does is that you get your day in court with the best representation money and influence can get for you. There's time for the British to get a dozen silks enrolled by the Kenya Bar Association. The AG has already promised he'll personally nominate anyone the High Commission proposes. And your people are now 100% committed to getting you off. Not only because it's the right thing to do but because they're terrified of Ole Kisii's list of others to be charged. They're going to throw everything at getting this particular genie back in the bottle."

"And what about you?"

"Me? This is now way out of my league. You are playing with the big boys now."

Tom said nothing for a long moment. Then he asked suddenly, "Are you married?"

"Divorced."

77

"Kids?"

"Two. Boys, 14 and 16," Leo told him, wondering quite where this was going.

"See them often?"

"Not as often as I'd like."

"And what do you do with them when they are with you?"

Leo frowned, bemused. Usually only other divorced Dads asked that. "Various things. We have a Land Rover we prepare and race once a year. That takes up plenty of time. We're meant to be working on it today. They're actually just across the road waiting for me."

"Oh, God, I'm sorry! Being in a place like this makes you forget other people still have lives to get on with. You should go."

"Why do you ask?"

"Well, it helps me to make a decision I've been mulling over," said Tom. "I have a son and a daughter. Much older than your two of course. And a grandson." He paused, as though unsure whether to continue, then offered Leo his hand as he asked quietly, "Who would your sons want standing next to their Dad if you were in my position? Wouldn't it be someone just like you?"

Leo shook the proffered hand. "Sadly, I expect they'd want Paul Muya. And even more depressingly, I think they'd be right."

'Morning Prayers', as the British High Commissioner's breakfast briefing was universally known, was usually a fairly amiable canter through the business of the day with his First Secretaries for Chancery, Aid and Trade. On the morning after Tom Miles' Committal Hearing it was more like a crisis cabinet of a government under siege.

The usual attendees were joined by McKenzie, the FCO desk officer for London, flushed from a difficult conversation with his wife, having just told her he'd been instructed to remain in Kenya until this matter was resolved.

"You've seen the papers, I suppose?" snapped the High Commissioner, waving a hand at the half dozen journals spread across the table beside which he sat, as soon as they were ushered in.

No one replied, although all had. The national dailies were full of gloating speculation about the list: two had even hired historians from Kenyatta University to postulate; as far as the laws on libel would allow, precisely which names it might contain. Things, as David Mowbray had observed to an unsympathetic Nick Easton the previous evening, were going decidedly pear-shaped.

Mowbray fussed about, gathering up the newspapers. "Sit down, gentlemen," he sighed. "What do we know about Ole Kisii's list?"

"There are, as he told the media, twenty three names on it, High Commissioner," the Head of Chancery began. "All were involved in events some have described as atrocities. The Hola Camp Massacre, for example . . ."

"The what?" asked the recently appointed First Secretary (Trade).

"The beating to death of eleven detainees under the orders, and before the eyes, of the British Camp Commandant," McKenzie explained.

"A lot of it makes Guantanamo seem positively restrained," admitted the Head of Chancery. "Dr Miles' case seems the weakest by far. It supports your initial contention, High Commissioner," he could not resist adding, "that the reason he was arrested was because he was unlucky enough to be in the wrong place at the wrong time."

"We also need be bear in mind the wider perspective." added McKenzie. "Let's not forget our peace-keeping responsibilities in Cyprus, Malaya, Palestine and a dozen other places. All within living memory. Then there's our European Community partners to consider, some of whom are rightly sensitive about their imperialist pasts. Think of the Belgians in the Congo, or the French in Algeria . . ."

"And it gives Paul Muya the opportunity to see his father's memory glorified," Mowbray added. "Well, they've got Miles, and they're clearly intent on trying him, unless we can persuade them otherwise. Perhaps we should let them. By all accounts there seems to be very little chance of them succeeding. And if they fail, it seriously reduces the likelihood of charges being pressed against anyone else."

Mowbray turned to McKenzie and raised an eyebrow, inviting him to speak.

"Based on an assessment of the official record in the public domain, they have nothing to go on, nothing at all. Of course there are some files still closed . . ."

"But unless we continue to give them such material on a plate," interrupted the Head of Chancery bluntly, "that's not going to be an issue, is it?"

"The choice of Dr Miles' defence strategy was not mine," bristled McKenzie.

"Well, it certainly wasn't ours," snapped back the Head of Chancery.

"What's done is done," said Mowbray. "How's the good doctor taking all this?"

"He's scared," said McKenzie. "And angry. Very scared, and very angry."

"Angry?" said Mowbray, frowning. "Yes, I suppose he would be. But not with us, surely?"

"I'm afraid so," said McKenzie "He feels badly let down by the way the committal proceedings were handled: 'betrayed' is the word he used to me. He's furious that we decided to accept responsibility without even consulting him about it first."

"Well, we don't want him angry with us," said the Head of Chancery, "otherwise there's no telling what he might say, or do. What might mollify him?"

McKenzie shrugged. "Leo Kane, his Kenyan brief, in charge."

Mowbray shook his head sadly. "You've met him. What do you think?"

"He seemed competent enough," said McKenzie. "I don't

think he's out to make a big reputation, and he knows the system, and the personalities. Particularly Paul Muya. I think we could do a lot worse."

"Very well," said Mowbray. "Let's keep talking to the Kenyans and let Dr Miles know he's got Kane, and anything else within reason he wants."

When Leo got to the hotel he found Nick Friedlander alone at a table well marked with jam and egg yolk and strewn with crumpled paper napkins, reading a newspaper.

"And the boys?" asked Leo with a sinking feeling in the pit of his stomach.

Bored, Nick Friedlander folded his paper and nodded at the mobile phone Leo had left with him on the table. "Their mother called. When she found out where they were, or more to the point, who they were with, she said she'd have them picked up. She's never really taken to me, you know. I've often wondered why. You just missed them."

"Fuck it! And you couldn't have lied, or played for time?"

"Of course I could. Had I been adequately briefed. Now I've got an appointment with Harvinder and the vehicle that's going to win the Charge this year, especially as you're about to be disqualified for failing to name a full team, so if you'll excuse me? The bill is just there." He concluded amiably, nodding to the leather-sheathed account.

"Did she say where she was taking them?"

"Did I say it was La Belle Dame Sans Merci herself? I don't think so. They were collected by one of the Total Man's ever growing army of suck-ups. Oh, and there was another call. Deepak Kapadia wants to see you."

Leo Kane was still, on paper at least, a member of Sena Chambers. An aggressive, expensive collective of attorneys who between them tackled everything from highly lucrative commercial law and intellectual property rights to the criminal cases at Leo's grubbier end of the spectrum.

Leo's name accordingly remained – fourth from the bottom, carefully painted in copperplate – on the old-fashioned board in the Chambers' otherwise ultra-modern reception, hissing with brisk air conditioning and the double-clicking of the receptionist's mouse.

The signboard was meant to recall the traditions and values of the Inns of Court in London to which no one in Chambers belonged. Perhaps not surprisingly the name board was a bone of general contention: several of Leo's younger colleagues considered it pretentious. One had even gone so far as to describe it as obsequiously neo-colonial – an observation which had deeply hurt the usually unflappable Kapadia, the Head of Chambers. Kapadia had indeed first joined Sena as a messenger back in colonial times. His subsequent progression to attorney had been made possible through the support and sponsorship of the then Head of Chambers, a brooding and solitary Welshman who had stayed on, only to drink himself to death within two years of Independence.

Deepak Kapadia remained profoundly, almost religiously, grateful to his mentor and benefactor. A portrait of the Welshman, the likeness copied posthumously from an old black and white photograph, also hung in the reception area. It was executed in garish colours and showed the Welshman with the full sensual lips and doe-like eyes of some lesser god from Hindu mythology, by the illustration of which, Leo was convinced, the artist had more usually earned his crust.

The portrait, however, did serve to counter-balance the board and give the reception a slightly less western appearance, particularly as Kapadia insisted on draping a garland of marigolds over it on the anniversary of the Welshman's death (and ruled that they remain there for several months thereafter, until they were withered down to a dusty string of crumpled, dry flower heads, fragile as burnt paper).

It had been the Welshman who had first introduced the board, and Kapadia decreed that his name should remain at its head, annotated (Dcd).

That was another thing that pissed Leo off about the board – its laboriously maintained inaccuracies. Not only the concept but the content was consistently out of date: for example, it still recorded him as occupying Room 7, when, months earlier, he had surrendered the narrow cell to a grateful junior who had anticipated hot-desking for several years more.

But what really, really pissed Leo off about it was that his wife's name was still there, two places higher than his, when it was well over a year since she had taken herself, her extensive collection of law reports and her lucrative client-base, half a mile across town to join Paul Muya's practice.

Sena Chambers occupied half of the 7th floor of International House on Kenyatta Avenue. Unfortunately not on the side which overlooked the High Court, but still a pretty prestigious address nonetheless, and although he no longer occupied office space there, remaining nominally in Chambers still cost Leo a hefty fund transfer each quarter – a payment which he knew was in arrears. He had assumed that was why Kapadia had asked to see him.

Kapadia, overweight, breathless and prey to a dozen ailments, real and imagined, called Leo in cheerily enough. His office was, as always, awash with paper. At various places on his wide desk (inherited from the Welshman), on top of bookcases and in the middle of his conference table, these papers coagulated into piles of files which bore witness to forlorn attempts to bring them into some sort of order. On top of the piles lay scraps of paper on which were written "Basement", "Bring forward in six months" and "Destroy". But these scraps were little more than failed prayers, for the paper never left Kapadia's office – at the last minute he just couldn't bring himself to part with a single scrap.

Elsewhere, the Chambers were a model of efficient information handling, thanks mainly to Jimee, the outrageously camp but breathtakingly efficient Chief Clerk.

But not in Kapadia's room. There the papers remained. The normally parsimonious Kapadia had even forked out for a tiny vacuum cleaner, designed to decontaminate old documents, with which he insisted the papers were, every six months, cleaned, for he was convinced that the patches of dry skin that erupted on the backs of his hands were an allergic reaction to dust.

Kapadia held up the most recent addition to this mass of paper. "Instructions, instructions, instructions!" he cried, cheerfully. "They want you to defend Dr Miles when he comes to trial."

Leo felt slightly nauseous. "Well, I don't want to defend Dr Miles, thank you very much. Not after the last fiasco. Tell them I'm not taking on anything at the moment. I've got to get ready for the Charge."

Kapadia sniffed dismissively at the mention of the Charge. "Come into money, have we? Afford to turn down cases and chase around in a 4x4 like a college boy now, can we? A rich Aunty died perhaps?"

Leo winced. "If you're thinking about my chamber fees . . ."

"I was thinking about the rest of your life, Leo," countered Kapadia, paternally. "This case is big. The biggest. Whoever defends Tom Miles . . ."

"Deepak," interrupted Leo, "I know, OK? This case is the road to fame, fortune and fanny . . . Sorry," he added, hastily, for Kapadia maintained strict standards of probity. "But just remember what the committal hearing was like," Leo continued, hurriedly. "They wouldn't even tell me what they were planning until the very last minute. Not again."

"People might conclude you are scared to go against the Attorney General," Kapadia ventured.

"Nonsense!" Leo cried, reacting exactly as Kapadia had anticipated. "I'll take on the AG anywhere. At anything. It's just that I've got other priorities, right now. My boys; the Charge . . ."

"And the fact that your ex-wife has joined Muya's chambers could make things difficult, no doubt," observed Kapadia, reasonably.

Leo's face split into a grin. "You're trying to wind me up! Jesus, Deepak, do you really think I'm that easy to manipulate? I don't give a flying fu . . . damn what my ex-wife does, or who she does it with, OK?"

"But you've got to admit it's going to look strange . . ."

"No, it isn't. Turn it down. I can assure you, Deepak, the only glamour and glory in this case will be heading Paul Muya's way."

Kapadia frowned. "But it's not Paul Muya's case anymore. And we can't turn it down or we'll be in breach of our contract with the British High Commission and that's worth . . ."

"OK, OK," said Leo, keen to steer Kapadia away from talk of money. "Then give it to somebody else."

"But they insist on you, Leo. Dr Miles has great faith in you."

"Heart-warming," said Leo, unmoved. He paused, and his eyes narrowed. "The High Commission picks up the bill?"

"Yes. And they say you can have whatever assistance you need."

"Do they really? Well, thanks to their efforts to date, the poor old sod is facing charges for war crimes now, instead of good old-fashioned conspiracy and murder. Tell them that I need support on the war crimes stuff. And I don't want some white twat who's going to tell me what to do and fuck everything up again . . . Sorry. Tell them . . . Yes. Tell them I want an African expert on war crimes."

Kapadia nodded, and smiled, encouragingly. "Anything else?"

"Yes. Tell them I'll do it if they can provide the expert. But I am to lead and be in sole charge of the defence strategy. Oh, and I want stenographers, too. At least three. They can be employed locally, but they have to be up to international standards."

Kapadia frowned. "And what if they won't wear it?"

"Too bad. I will not negotiate on this matter. This touches on justice and my professional integrity, both of which, as you well know, are dear to my heart. Now, if you'll excuse me, Deepak, I have a vehicle that requires my full attention, and a navigator to find . . . I don't suppose you'd . . . no? Oh well, never mind. An African expert on War Crimes legislation, OK?"

That evening one of his guards approached Tom Miles for medical advice. A large-bellied man with a mean streak, he did so diffidently, almost sullenly. Without a word he extracted a small brown envelope from his breast pocket and held it out for Tom's inspection. Tom stepped beneath the 40 watt light bulb in his cell and squinted at the pharmacist's scribbled description of the envelope's contents. "What's it supposed to be for?" he asked.

The guard looked sheepish. "My chest," he said, adding, almost as an afterthought, a plaintive cough.

Tom shook his head. "Complete waste of time. And money. Let me hear your cough again."

Two of his colleagues came in an hour later. An asthmatic and a hernia. These informal consultations, the first of many, gave Tom a role and activity to fill the long, dead hours. He found himself responding to their enquiries with an almost desperate enthusiasm, and they repaid him with whatever small kindnesses they could: old newspapers, extended exercise periods and home-cooked food. Offers to smuggle out letters or bring him in an illicit mobile phone, which Tom politely but firmly declined.

And a notebook, in which to record his thoughts and recollections as they came to him, which he accepted with thanks.

CHAPTER FIFTEEN

"*I've lost everything,*" *says Foss.* "*My wife, my kids. Even my farm is falling apart now my Kukes have all gone.*"

We are on a tour of the outlying shambas north of Nyeri which are still holding out. Every farmhouse has been turned into a small blockhouse with slits cut in window shutters to allow the inhabitants to fire out at any attackers, sandbags stacked against walls and rows of buckets filled with water and stirrup pumps to douse fires. Their gun racks – small armouries bristling with everything from Sten guns to Verey pistols – are padlocked but every weapon is kept loaded and is checked daily. Every farmer, and each member of his family over the age of fourteen, wears side arms as naturally as they do their boots and shorts. They would no more think of appearing before their African workers without a pistol at their hip than they would without trousers. In the evenings, they lock every internal door, and only admit the most long-serving and trusted houseboy, and even then at gunpoint.

"*They can turn,*" *they tell us, over and again with morbid satisfaction,* "*just like that.*"

They expect a lot from us, these farmers; far more than we can deliver. They demand our gratitude and admiration, too, for they are convinced they are doing us a favour. They are, in their own minds, the new frontiersmen. Heroes, holding out against the odds for God and the Queen. For civilisation, free enterprise, empire and race and all that's good and decent.

Yet Johnny Sandford says this whole thing actually has very little to do with them: it's a civil war, he says, between the

Kukes who believe British rule is the best way forward for the foreseeable future, and the Kukes who want Uhuru – freedom – now. And of course, the vast majority, like ordinary folk the world over, simply want to be left alone to get on with their lives, to grow their crops, educate their children and care for their old folk without us, or Mau Mau, or anyone else telling them what to do, where to live and what to think.

And of course they are the ones who are doing most of the dying.

When I challenge this view, Johnny quotes statistics at me: his favourite is the number of whites killed by Mau Mau across the whole of Kenya since the Emergency began compared to the number killed in car crashes in Nairobi alone over the same period.

The latter is the higher.

Of course the farmers, and Ted Foss, will have none of it. Today, we're inspecting the signal rockets each farm has been issued with, to alert the police and their neighbours in case of attack – a few days earlier one, on a tea plantation a few miles further south, self ignited. There was the inevitable panic; lorryloads of Askaris and a dozen farmers on horseback came charging in from all directions, armed to the teeth and fired up to slaughter all and sundry. Fortunately, the tea planter kept his head, got his workers rounded up and out of harm's way, but it could have been an absolute disaster. So, off we go, Foss and I, and a truckload of Askaris, from farm to farm, checking the rockets for signs of deterioration, listening to the hard done by, unappreciated, self-proclaimed heroes whinging on.

Even Foss is finding it wearing. "They don't know when they're well off," he says, removing his forage cap and wiping the perspiration from his forehead back over his closely cut hair as we set off from the third farm we've visited that day.

"They're lucky. I've lost everything. But I'll get it all back. And more."

He eases his belt a notch, folds his arms and slumps back in his seat. "Once this is over, once I've got Jembe. Then I'll pack this lark in and start again. But this time, it won't be just a farm. I'll take my gratuity, and what little I've managed to build up over the years, and start to buy out some of these buggers. It'll be years before things pick up again out here, and by then, I'll be the one who's laughing. Sandford and his sort have had their day, lording it like gentry. Acting like they own the bloody place. If the Emergency does nothing else it will have ended their time. Everything will be up for grabs then and I'm going to take my share."

He yawns, pulls his forage cap forward over his eyes, folds his arms and gets settled to doze. It's a good hour and a half to the next farm. It's early afternoon and he's taken a beer at each of the places we checked.

"You may not think so, Miles," he says, his soft body moving easily with the motion of the truck, "but I love this country. It's got such a future. Once we've liberated it from Jembe and all his kind and Sandford and all his."

CHAPTER SIXTEEN

Leo Kane lay beneath his Land Rover, an open manual and his mobile phone in a plastic bag beside him. He kept the Land Rover in a garage he hired out in a recently built industrial complex towards the airport. The garage was part of a compound owned by a friend of Leo's who imported paint.

The case in which his wife was due to appear in Kisumu had been adjourned – a witness had been ill – so he had not after all had his two sons returned to him after their day with Paul Muya. He was disappointed, of course, but he knew he had little grounds for complaint having so spectacularly fulfilled his wife's stereotype of him the last time they'd been in his care. Anyway, it had allowed him time to finish off his involvement in the Tom Miles case, for he was convinced his preconditions for any future involvement would never be met. Could never be met. Whatever African experts on War Crimes existed were all on massive retainers at the UN International Criminal Tribunal in Arusha or in The Hague. Accordingly, he had spent the weekend painting the vehicle and getting the names of their sponsors stencilled on.

In the end, he'd decided against blue and red and gone for a remarkable deep purple. He wasn't sure if he'd made the right decision, but it was too late to worry now.

He'd selected that shade because the paint importer from whom he rented the garage had a special offer on the colour. He had bought several thousand gallons of it cheap, which he was busily re-labelling 'Zambrau', the Ki-Swahili name for the fruit of the same hue. If the source of the paint was prominently displayed on the Land Rover, he had promised he would meet the cost of a subsequent re-spray. He'd even thrown in four pairs of overalls he had got run up in the same colour for Leo and the boys, and the as yet still unknown navigator, to wear.

So Zambrau it was.

Leo was attempting to refit the accelerator linkage without his sons. The manual from which he worked defined the complexity of tasks by the number of shaded-in spanners, ranging from one to five. Leo was currently working on two-spanner tasks, although even these he routinely had checked afterwards by a qualified mechanic.

Two spanners was described as beginner level. Well, maybe. The exploded diagram and the accompanying list of parts assured him that there were 63 separate components in the accelerator pedal and linkage mechanism although he would have sworn there were at least twice that number scattered on the garage floor. Leo worked with a growing suspicion that fitting them all back together might well prove beyond him.

It wouldn't be the first time: three weeks earlier he had attempted to remove and refit the water pump – another two-spanner task. He had failed. Dismally and absolutely.

Uncertain quite what the implications of this were, he had coughed up a couple of thousand shillings to fetch a grinning mechanic out from a garage in town to put the whole thing back together for him.

The money was nothing. The indignity, crippling.

To make matters worse, he was in a hurry. He was due to collect the boys – overdue – but he wanted to pick them up in the Land Rover.

It was odd, he thought idly as he worked, but in a society that delighted in giving nicknames to people, places and things, he and the boys had never named the Land Rover. He wondered why.

Leo used to get everything done on the Land Rover by someone else, either as a favour, or for a fee. But these days – another of his resolutions – he tried to do as many of the jobs himself, or with the boys as he could. Not that he enjoyed it; far from it. He detested the grimy, oily feel of the components, loathed lying on his back under the vehicle and cursed loudly every time he barked his knuckles – which was often. Most of all, he hated having to get the compound Askari to help him to release a rusted nut, or fit a heavy component because he hadn't the strength – especially as the Askari invariably managed the task without the slightest exertion.

Still, it was worth it, if only for the common bond it sealed with his younger son, Josh.

Josh, unlike his father, had a flair for things mechanical, an enthusiasm for tinkering with motors, and a haughty disinclination to take his school work seriously.

Leo's eldest boy, Zeke (named, at his ex-wife's insistence, after her father, Ezekiel) had always done well at school and looked set to follow his parents into the legal profession. But Josh – between his increasingly frustrating school reports (he had it in him, they insisted, but just didn't seem able to apply himself) and his near obsessive dismantling of every piece of equipment in the home from the can opener to the old CD player – was a constant cause for concern. A worry for his future was one of the few things Leo and his ex-wife still shared.

Four years earlier, Leo had had his brainwave. Without discussing it with his wife, he had gone out and bought a battered old Land Rover, and before long the then ten-year-old Josh, who a few weeks earlier had been resentfully struggling with Ladybird books for five-year-olds, was poring over the dog-eared manuals that came with the vehicle.

As a strategy to get their son to read, it had received even his wife's tacit approval – or so he assumed. Even in those days, she would sooner have torn her tongue out at the roots than say he'd done well, but she remained uncharacteristically quiet about the Land Rover, and their efforts in the Charge, whereas every other activity in which he indulged was routinely drenched in waves of effortless criticism.

The mobile chirped. With an oath, Leo wiped his hands on his monogrammed handkerchief, cursed again when he saw the oily smudges on the crisp linen and eased himself out from under the vehicle.

"Yes?" he snapped, as he sat up.

It was his ex-wife.

"What time are you coming for the boys?"

"Soon."

"Have you collected the DVD?"

He closed his eyes, and took a deep breath. The DVD player had been the latest victim of Josh's enthusiastic attention. Leo had taken the disembowelled machine to a guy he knew who promised him it would be ready for collection at the weekend. It had simply slipped his mind.

"You've forgotten, haven't you?" his wife said, resigned.

"No. Yes. Look, I've been very busy . . ."

"No you haven't. You've been playing with the Land Rover. You promised . . ."

"It's a DVD, not a fucking life support machine. I'll swing by there on my way, all right? Anyway you let them watch far too much crap."

He slid back under the vehicle, and continued to tinker. He smiled, as he thought of how, when he picked up the boys, he would tell them about what he'd done, and Josh would point out precisely how he should have done it, and Leo would act stupid, and feel good, then Zeke would be drawn into it, and they'd both patronise him terribly.

The phone rang again "Jesus Christ!" he shouted as he snatched it up. "What now?" he bellowed into it.

"Kane?" an affronted male voice asked.

Leo frowned. "Yes."

"Leo Kane, of Sena Chambers?"

"That's right. Who is this?"

"My name is Mwangi. The Attorney General has instructed me to inform you that he has decided to withdraw the charges against your client. Dr Miles will be released from Central at 7 pm."

Leo glanced at his watch: less than an hour.

"Have you told the British High Commission?"

"The Attorney General told me to tell Dr Miles' representative. That is you, isn't it, Kane?"

The line went dead. Leo punched out the British High Commission's out-of-hours number and got through to the duty officer.

"Tom Miles will be out in less than an hour's time," Leo said, simply.

"What?" the Duty Officer cried. "Blimey. I'll need to get hold of the High Commissioner. We'll have to make a statement . . ."

"Can you just get a vehicle to Central to pick him up?" said Leo.

He could hear the Duty Officer sucking his teeth. "Not that quickly. They really should have given us more warning; all the vehicles are in the compound. I suppose I could go round there in a taxi, but it would be better if they held on to him for a bit longer till we're ready . . ."

Leo rang off in disgust. He checked in his Organiser for McKenzie's hotel number, leaving oily fingerprints all over it.

"It's Kane," he said when McKenzie answered. "They're releasing Tom Miles."

"I know," said the unflappable McKenzie. "A deal's been done. We're going to sign the SEACOW agreement and they're going to drop the charges against Miles. And any others. It's supposed to be all set for tomorrow . . ."

"Well, it isn't. It's tonight. Tom Miles is going to be on the streets in about 45 minutes, and the High Commission needs to get round there and pick him up. Can you put a firecracker under them?"

"Sure. I'll get on to it right now, but if I were you, I think I might drive round there myself. Just to be on the safe side."

Next, Leo rang his wife. "I'll be a bit late," he said, simply "and I probably won't get the DVD today. I'll be there as soon as I can."

He heard her intake of breath as she prepared for a diatribe.

"Save it," he said. "Even you would think this was worth being late for."

"I doubt it."

"Really? What if I told you I was about to go and collect Miles from prison? Suppose I told you someone, somewhere, has buggered Paul Muya's grand plan, eh?"

There was a long silence, then she said, quietly, "Is this true?"

"Have I ever lied to you?" he said, airily, and switched off the mobile before she could reply.

It was some time after sunset when Tom Miles emerged from the Central Police Station. The streets looked bleak, unfriendly and severe.

He smiled, relieved, as he saw Leo Kane, in purple overalls, leaning against an ancient Land Rover of the same, tasteless shade, and began to laugh.

Leo laughed too, and extended his hand. "I won't pretend I know why you're out, but we can worry about that another day. Let's go."

They climbed into the Land Rover, and headed fast across the city to the British High Commission, but as Leo drove past the golf course, he braked, and pulled over to the curb, the engine still running.

He chewed his bottom lip in concentration. Tom followed his stare, and a lump formed in his stomach as he saw the gaggle of demonstrators outside the entrance to the High Commission. Tom didn't have his glasses on, but he could make out his own name, and that of Jembe scrawled on hastily prepared placards.

A dark blue bus with mesh over its windows was parked further down the street. The policemen inside stared out at the demonstrators, but showed no sign of being about to get involved.

"Have you got your passport?" Leo asked, drumming his fingers on the steering wheel.

Tom nodded.

"Right," said Leo, making up his mind. He released the hand

brake, and swung the Land Rover in a tight turn, heading back down toward the Uhuru Highway, the main, broad artery leading away from the city's heart. "We go straight to the airport. There's a British Airways flight sometime near midnight."

"I flew out with KLM . . ." Tom said, inconsequentially.

"When we get to the airport," said Leo, ignoring him as his mind raced. "We'll buy you a first class ticket. That will get you into the VIP lounge. Once you're through immigration and customs, you're out of Kenya. You're going to have to sit there for a few hours, but it's going to be a hell of a lot more comfortable than where you've been sitting for the past week."

He reached into his pocket, pulled out his mobile, and tossed it onto Tom's lap. "Do you want to call your family? Tell them you're on your way home?"

"I'll have plenty of time to call from the airport," said Tom. "Can you come into the lounge with me . . .?" He realised Leo wasn't listening, all his attention fixed on his rear-view mirror. "What is it?"

"There's a Merc behind us. It's been with us since we left the High Commission. I think it might be one of Paul's."

Tom looked round desperately. "Can you get away from him?"

"In this? Only across rough ground . . ."

Matching the action to the thought, Leo swerved suddenly, off the dual carriageway, and into the anonymous suburbs of the Mariakani Estate. The roads were straight, laid out on a grid, but brutally pock marked with vicious potholes. He engaged four-wheel drive, and hit them hard. Tom's head hit the roof. He reached around for a seat belt, but there wasn't one.

The Mercedes lost ground. Leo took a sharp left onto Mukenia Road, then a sudden right, fast into Mkoba, but not quite quickly enough to avoid being seen. Suburban houses behind high walls and steel-plated gates lined the road, with big reconditioned cars parked in compounds illuminated by neon strips suspended from the branches of stunted trees. On the pavement, occasional booths, secured now, boasted their wares – vegetables, soft drinks, cigarettes sold singly and soap in long bars sold by the inch. But here, the surface of the road improved and the Mercedes gained on them. There was a slough of carelessly parked vehicles ahead; Leo headed for them, negotiated them like a chicane, and raced on.

The Mercedes sounded its horn furiously and braked to a crawl to ease its way through.

Leo chuckled. He guessed that they must be running parallel to the main Mombasa Road and maybe a mile north of it. He was sure there was a lane around here somewhere that would lead them out through Plains View and back on to the dual carriageway just opposite the derelict Belle Vue drive-in, but even if he missed it there were plenty of dirt tracks where his vehicle would be at a considerable advantage.

He took a right and accelerated.

Then realised, too late, he had turned into a dead end.

He tried to reverse, but the Mercedes eased gently across the road, blocking his exit. Leo stopped, and hit the steering wheel with his fist. "Fuck! Stay here," he said to Tom, and leapt out.

There, emerging from the Mercedes, was Paul Muya, and three heavies in ill-cut suits.

Leo put his hands on his hips, and fixed his face into a sneer. His heart was beating rapidly and he felt sick, and scared, but he was damned if he was going to let Paul Muya know that.

And although he tried to look cool, and in control, Paul was breathless, and he had a wild, desperate look in his eyes.

"You'll have to do better than that in the Charge, Coke," he panted.

"What is it with you, Total Man?" said Leo. "Don't you know when you're beaten? Or maybe your bosses haven't bothered telling their boy yet: a deal's been done. The Attorney General's dropped the charges. It's all over, and you lost. Want to get back on the team now, Paul? Looks like you'll have plenty of time on your hands."

Paul Muya smiled. "I'm not interested in what the Attorney

97

General's done. Only in the man you're trying to smuggle out of the country. He's mine, Coke. Give him to me."

"You've got no right . . ."

"You think not? Two of my friends here are police inspectors, and they wouldn't agree with you," Paul said, triumphantly. "Remember the decision in Kimani and Kahara? '*The Constitution safeguards a private individual's right to pursue a prosecution against the capricious, corrupt or biased failure of the prosecuting authorities to proceed.*' I thought the Attorney General might choose to withdraw the charges, so I applied to the High Court for a declamatory judgment to confirm my constitutional right to retake the prosecution in such circumstances, which it did. Now stand aside please, Leo."

With a nod, Paul called the plain-clothed policemen forward. Leo glanced desperately back towards the vehicle, then reached out, and placed a restraining hand on Paul's chest. Paul looked at him, surprised.

The policemen were on Leo before he knew what was happening. One pulled him back and the other drove his fist into his stomach, doubling him up, and knocking the breath out of him. Leo, with a moan, crumpled to the ground.

He was vaguely aware of Tom's sobbed protests through the pounding in his ears as the policemen dragged him struggling and kicking out of the Land Rover.

Paul knelt down in front of Leo, eased him over onto his back, and massaged his solar plexus. "You shouldn't have touched me, Coke," he said, gently. "They don't like it, you see. They worry for my safety."

"You of all people should understand, Coke," he continued, as he eased Leo up to a sitting position, brushing dirt from his clothes and tutting like a mother. "This is just like the Charge: there are no rules, but the need to win. You must forgive me, and you must try to understand. I have prayed to the Lord, and the Lord has told me to seek justice. And I cannot allow Ole Kisii, or the British, or even you, my friend, to stand in my way."

Yes, thought Leo, as he let Paul Muya help him, breathless, to his feet, it was like the Charge. It's for real, and there's no appeal.

And, just as in the Charge, Leo was suddenly resolved to win.

"Re-arrested!" cried the High Commissioner, incredulously, "but you told me we had an agreement!"

The Head of Chancery shrugged. "We did. Or so I thought. They seem to be playing some kind of cat and mouse game. We met all their demands on SEACOW, but they just reneged on the deal. Thank God we agreed to keep quiet about the release until Miles was out of the country . . ."

There was a knock at the door, and Nick Easton's head appeared round the side. "May I?" he said, easing himself into the room.

"Not just now, Nick," said the High Commissioner testily. "I'll call you."

Nick Easton withdrew, confused. He wasn't used to being dismissed by the likes of Mowbray.

He turned, hoping no one was witness to his embarrassment, and saw McKenzie approaching. "Looks like we're back where we started," said McKenzie by way of a greeting.

Nick Easton tilted his head to one side, and smiled, pleased to be given the opportunity to show his breadth of vision. "Not at all. We're actually quite a long way forward. Paul Muya can continue his private prosecution against Dr Miles only because he has *locus standii* – a personal involvement in the case. But as far as the authorities are concerned, the case is closed, just as the Kenyans promised. And they won't pursue any others. They've kept to their side of the bargain, and the major threat has been averted. On second thoughts, maybe you're right. Maybe we are back where we started. But even that's a hell of a lot better than we were 48 hours ago. All we have to do now is to secure a not guilty verdict for Dr Miles and we are home and dry."

"I still have an African war crimes expert to find," said McKenzie.

"Search no further," said Nick Easton, tapping a slender file he held under his left arm. "That's what I popped in to tell David."

He held the file close to him for a moment, as though considering and then, with the grin of a bully magnanimously returning a smaller boy's ball, offered it to McKenzie. "It's a scanned copy, of course. The originals are on their way to you in tonight's diplomatic bag."

McKenzie raised a doubtful eyebrow, and took the file. "So how do you come to have this?"

Easton looked deeply offended. "My view on her credibility was sought."

"It's the first I've heard of it."

Easton smiled. "It's a personal thing. Above your pay grade. Political."

"And what is your view?"

"I said I thought she'd do fine."

McKenzie glanced through the resumé and CV, then flipped back through the papers, quickly absorbing the key factors.

"She hardly sounds like an expert . . ."

Nick Easton waved away the objection. "Expertise is a relative concept. The DPP says she's bright and competent."

"But an African? With a name like Aliya Zain surely she's Asian."

"Only ethnically," said Easton with a complacent smile. "She was born in Kenya. Like Paul Muya. Like Leo Kane. That makes her an African in my book. Look, I can't hang around here all day, why don't you give David the good news, eh? It would look better coming from within the FCO, don't you think?"

PART II

CHAPTER SEVENTEEN

Aliya Zain sorted through the papers that had dominated her every waking hour for the past fifteen months for one last time before despatching all the files to the Registry. They were already in perfect order, but she just couldn't seem to let them go without one more last glance. She knew she was making a meal of it, but she justified herself on the basis that this was a necessary part of the grieving process. For she was in mourning. Not for the withered old fascist whose cruel heart had finally given up, but for his prosecution, and her ambitions.

There were a number of things about Aliya Zain that set her apart from her colleagues. While she was not the only Asian in the CPS, nor the only woman, she was the only member of the War Crimes Branch who wasn't white, male, or over 45.

She didn't drink. That made her colleagues uncomfortable too. It wasn't a religious thing, she assured them. She just didn't like the taste. But more than one was secretly convinced that she was disguising some strain of Islamic fundamentalism and they all remained excessively cautious about what they said in her presence or joked about in her hearing. Not that she was a prude, oh no, though behind her back she had been described as something of a language fascist. In the office, her verbal exchanges were peppered with swear words. However she could be icily prim when others spoke in ways she thought inappropriate.

She was not known to have had any relationships: that was odd too. Though not classically beautiful by either western or Asian stereotypes, she wasn't unattractive. Many found her quite appealing, albeit in a fiery, intelligent, vaguely intimidating sort of way. Yet when she'd been invited to a christening the previous spring, and last summer, when one of the Admin staff had got married, the invitations had included a partner, spouse or friend, but on both occasions Aliya had turned up alone.

Finally, she rode a Yamaha WR125X to work. The hatstand in the room she shared with four others looked more appropriate for a dispatch rider than a lawyer, groaning under her helmet and leathers, and she was engaged in a long-running feud with Facilities Management about where precisely she could chain up her City Scrambler.

In short, Aliya Zain was different. In an interesting way, most of her colleagues were agreed, for she was universally liked, but perhaps too in a distant and slightly threatening way. And now, in her mid-thirties, these various facets of her personality were bedding down: quirkiness maturing into eccentricity.

Her Team Leader Harry Fitzsimmonds, in an unguarded moment, once told her she should lighten up, advice she had more than once received in the past. She joked that she must be the only first generation Asian in Britain whose parents urged them to try less hard. She behaved, Fitzsimmonds had said, as though she were still on probation. She knew that was true because, deep down, she suspected she always would be. She was good at her job. She knew that. But she also knew that as a latecomer to the Law, having first studied accountancy, she was still years away from the really important work, and that her eventual ascent to the great cases would depend on the good will of the Fitzsimmondses of this world as much as on her steadily amassing a raft of lesser successes. She knew too that her advancement, perhaps more than that of her colleagues, would be forever jeopardised by one careless slip in court or in the office. For that would prove the unspoken supposition – she didn't fit in. She was out of her depth. She wasn't up to the job.

The screen on her desk flashed with an incoming message: Could she spare Mr Fitzsimmonds a moment?

She crossed the corridor to the Team Leader's room.

The Crown Prosecution Service was her second position. Her first had been with a small town practice in North Wales known as Christie, Manson and Sutcliffe.

It had been one of over 80 to which she had applied at the time her articles were coming to an end. One she thought least likely to be interested in her. She'd only written to them because the idea of a practice bearing the name of three serial killers had struck her as amusing. Whilst there she'd been drafted in to devil for one of the seniors on a libel action. A local newspaper had dredged up some old stories about a Polish pensioner being implicated in war crimes in what had once, in a different world, been Yugoslavia.

It had come to nothing. All fizzled out to an apology after an initial flurry of publicity, but she had found the law she had researched fascinating. From then on she was hooked. She read everything on the subject she could lay her hands on, and even penned a paper which was published in a law journal and had been quite well received.

That was what had led a friend in the CPS to encourage her to apply to join their moribund War Crimes Branch.

"Come," bawled Fitzsimmonds as she tapped on his door. "Ah, come in, Aliya," he said, not looking up from the file before him. "Bloody shame about your Ukrainian," he commiserated, as he waved her to a chair. "Still, he's answering for his sins before a higher tribunal now, eh? Have you sorted the papers?"

"I'll be finished by this afternoon. Tomorrow morning at the latest. If there's anything you'd like me to get started on . . ."

"As a matter of fact, there is. Presumably you've been following the Miles case in Kenya?"

"Of course."

"Would we prosecute it?"

Aliya shook her head. "Absolutely not. Nor should they. The first prosecution against an agent of an erstwhile colonising

105

power? From what I've read, this hardly seems the one to make a test case."

"How do you think the defence will handle it?"

"First, acknowledge that any society which wants to live at peace with itself has a moral imperative to prosecute war crimes and crimes against humanity. Then with the utmost respect question every detail; challenge every fact; cast doubt on every memory. Then, conclude by arguing the arbitrariness of any such prosecution."

"The FCO wants to know if the fact that Kenya didn't even exist as an independent nation when the alleged crime was committed is a basis for challenging jurisdiction." He said, handing her the file.

She snorted as she read it. "Pathetic! Such prosecutions almost always involve a *post facto* claiming of jurisdiction. Look at Nuremberg. A court comprised of Russians, Americans, Britons and Frenchmen claimed the right to try Germans for their actions in Poland. Israel tried Eichmann for crimes committed in Europe before the State of Israel even existed. Then there's . . . Fitz, why are we talking about this?"

"Because the FCO's looking for someone to help out on this case, and the D thinks you'd fit the bill."

"Me?" said Aliya. "I don't think so."

"Why ever not?" asked Fitz, genuinely surprised. "International experience always looks good on a CV. I'd jump at the chance if it were me. A high profile case. A few weeks in the sun, all expenses paid . . ."

Aliya shook her head. "I don't want to be stuck in Kenya defending some ageing colonial hit man just when the next tranche of International Criminal Court jobs come up. So Dr Miles off-ed some terrorist? News flash: they're giving out medals for that from Washington to Ouagadougou." Seeing that made little impact, she changed her tone, her voice pleading. "Oh, come on, Fitz! I want to be prosecuting genocide, not defending heavy-handed policing. Give it to Davidson and give his casework to me."

106

"That's hardly fair, Aliya. Even if he were as well placed to handle this case. His wife is expecting their second child in the next few weeks."

"Hawks?" Aliya said, with increasing desperation.

Harry Fitz shook his head.

"Levin? Crombie?"

"No, Aliya," said Fitz, reaching over the desk and taking the file from her hand. "You."

Aliya's eyes narrowed. "But I know nothing about Kenya, the Emergency, or Mau Mau."

"Until you started investigating them," Fitz replied, "you didn't know much about Nazi atrocities in the Ukraine either. You pick things up very quickly. One of your many strengths. Now trot off and immerse yourself in the background. And learn to recognise a golden opportunity when one comes along."

"Can I appeal against your decision?"

"Of course you can," Fitz said, "but I wouldn't advise it. The D specifically asked for you."

Aliya's eyes narrowed. "Did he? Why?"

Fitz puffed out his cheeks, and shrugged. "Who knows how the D's mind works? Because he knows how good you are, perhaps? Or maybe because of your ... background. As a Kenyan Asian ..."

"Whoa! A Kenyan Asian?" said Aliya. "I don't think so. I'm a British Citizen. So are my parents, so were theirs. I'm a black Briton. Asian British, if you prefer. I am *not* a Kenyan Asian."

"What does it say on your Passport under Place of Birth, Ms Zain?" asked Fitz, suddenly very much the prosecutor.

"On my *British* passport? Mombasa, Kenya" replied Aliya, unintimidated. "A place my parents left when I was less than two years old. To come here. If this has anything to do with the decision to send me, you do know I could claim racial dis-crimination?"

"If you were stupid, which you aren't. Whatever the reason-ing behind it, this is a great opportunity for you, which we are going to accept on your behalf. An announcement to that effect will be made tomorrow. Now, I suggest you get in touch with Dr Miles' attorney."

When his eldest son Zeke told him that the call was from London, Leo broke one of his cardinal rules and took it although they were only three quarters of the way through lunch. Josh gazed longingly at the iPhone he had been forbidden, on pain of a thousand torments, to touch, and his fingers itched.

"Mr Kane?" a distorted female voice asked, sounding like it was wrapped up in tin foil. "Good morning. My name is Aliya Zain. I believe we're to work together on the Miles case."

"It's afternoon here," Leo mumbled through a mouthful of nyama choma he'd had fetched in from the restaurant in town. "You must be the stenographer I asked for."

The eloquent pause crackled with static. "No, Mr Kane," said Aliya, evenly, "I'm with the UK Crown Prosecution Service. I'm your support on war crimes legislation."

Leo held the phone away as he half choked, coughing on a mis-directed chunk of lamb. "I asked for an African," he wheezed.

"Oh really? That explains a great deal. Well, I can hear this isn't a good time. Good bye."

"Wait a minute," said Leo, blinking his watering eyes, and clearing his throat. "Uh, Zain, you said. Right? I guess you must be, what, Muslim Asian?"

"British," said Aliya, icily, "actually."

"But you were born out here, right?"

The silence confirmed his supposition. "So how do you think I should handle this?" Leo asked. "He was just obeying orders?"

"Let's not play games with one another, Mr Kane. That's never been a defence, and you know it. The British Military Legal Manual has emphasised every soldier's personal responsibility for his acts since 1944. The fact that his superiors may have given an illegal order is little more than a mitigating factor."

108

"Hold on, hold on," said Leo. "Who says it was an illegal order? And what about Erich Priebke? I thought his lawyers got him off at his first trial on that basis?"

"Actually, he was found guilty, but ineligible for sentencing. There was a whole range of other issues involved, including statute of limitations and the role of military tribunals. None of which translate to this case. You are going to have to do a great deal better than that."

"Jurisdiction? Dr Miles is being tried by a state whose very existence post-dates the event to which the charges refer."

"Never heard of the Vienna Convention on State Succession? Anyway, there's universal jurisdiction on war crimes."

"Is this a war crime?"

Aliya put the phone on Speaker, leaned back, put her hands behind her head, and quoted from memory: "War crimes: namely, violations of the law and customs of war. Such violations shall include, but not be limited to, murder, ill-treatment or deportation etc, etc not justified by military necessity."

"So I'll argue that this was justified by military necessity."

"I guess you're going to have to, but you'll have to prove it, and that might be difficult, given that there was a ceasefire in effect at the time. They may simply argue that it's a crime against humanity, namely, murder, extermination, enslavement, deportation and any other inhumane acts committed against any civilian population . . ."

"OK, OK. I'm impressed."

"And you are going to have to decide whether you argue that Mau Mau was a military force or not: as far as I can see it was never accorded that status at the time, nor has it been so designated subsequently. As far as the authorities were concerned, they were terrorists and the killing of terrorists is much more legally acceptable these days. Was it a war? Is a State of Emergency the same as a war?"

"How many of these cases have you defended?" he asked, feeling the need to reassert his authority.

"None."

"No, of course not, sorry. You said you were in the CPS. How many have you prosecuted?"

"None beyond a committal hearing."

"But you're content to be offered up as an expert?" he asked, feeling somewhat better.

"No, Mr Kane, I'm not. So please feel free to say you don't want me and we can both get on with the rest of our lives."

"Bear with me a moment or two longer," said Leo. "Can you drive?"

"Yes. So what?"

"And read a map . . ."

"I was a Ranger Guide. What do you think?"

"I think you might be just what we've been waiting for, Miss Zain," said Leo, chuckling. "Email me your CV and Practising Certificate and I'll sort things out this end."

"There really is no way I can persuade you to look elsewhere?" asked Aliya.

"Not in a million years," Leo assured her.

She sighed, resigned. "Very well. Is there anything I should be doing as prep?"

"Yes. Practice double declutching."

"What?"

"Never mind," he said. "Just get here as soon as you can."

CHAPTER EIGHTEEN

It is my eighth day in the forest when we stumble across the headless corpse.

Johnny Sandford's dog Hero has sniffed it out, although its stench is so strong that we would have picked it up too before much longer.

Johnny says that six months earlier, his pseudo-terrorists would have picked up the scent before Hero, but they are losing their edge. Getting soft.

The corpse must have been there for some days. He'd been bound, hand and foot with moundwi, the long, tough grass that can double as short lengths of rope. He'd struggled, before he'd died, and his bindings had bitten into his flesh.

Tree rats have gnawed away great gouts of flesh. Some larger creature has fed on him, too.

But his head has been severed with a blade.

"I feel sorry for them, sometimes," says Johnny Sandford, his voice muffled by a handkerchief over his mouth and nose as he gingerly turns the stinking corpse over with his foot. I express my surprise.

"I really do," he insists. "It's not just us, and the RAF bombing and all the other police and army and Kikuyu home guard units out after them, but every big game hunter with a reputation to enhance or a final thrill to feel is up here taking a pot shot at them, too. I suspect that's who got this chap. Just think about it: a chance to bag the biggest prey of all – and quite legally too. We stopped a white hunter up near here a couple of months ago who boasted that he'd already bagged seventy-three, can

you believe that? He said he'll score a century before this is over, and I expect he will. He had two heads in a sack when we stopped him. Personally, I doubt if they were Mau Mau at all: they looked far more like Wandorobo than Kukes to me and it was in their traditional range for gathering honey. Still, it's a prohibited area now and he claims he challenged them first so the law's on his side. We had to let him go. Makes you think though, doesn't it, Miles? Makes you wonder what this is all about. I mean, the Mau Mau remaining out here have lived in the forest now for years, through every weather, constantly on their guard, constantly alert. Do you know the first thing they do when they wake up each morning? They sit dead still, utterly silent, for up to half an hour. Just listening. Listening to the forest. They can hear, and smell and see things we aren't even aware of. What a quarry, eh? Man at his most savage perhaps, but also man at his finest!

"We closed down their schools, took their land and herded them into reservations to make farms for men like Foss. And now, we hunt them for their heads.

"Who's the savage, young Miles? You tell me."

CHAPTER NINETEEN

"Welcome to Swahili Land, Miss Zain," said Leo Kane.

It was late on a Saturday night, and it was hot. A slight breeze moved the damp air around, but was unequal to the task of cooling the night. It eased its way sluggishly through the fronds of the palm trees that edged the airfield, and tugged at the limp and dejected wind sock.

Mombasa Airport struck Aliya as stark, and squalid. Constructed from slabs of concrete, it looked like a vast, floodlit processing plant designed to herd and channel beasts through and be swilled down with bleach each morning.

They stood just outside the arrivals hall. The baggage carousels had clearly not worked for some time: the arriving suitcases, knapsacks and backpacks were being off-loaded from a tractor-drawn trailer.

Aliya watched, with a mixture of relief and concern, as her two suitcases hit the ground hard, bounced once and flopped on their sides.

She turned back to Leo, smiled, and shook the hand he extended towards her.

"It was kind of you to meet me," she said. "I hope I'm not causing you any inconvenience."

"Inconvenience, she says," said Leo, casting his eyes skywards. "This is my weekend to have my boys, so my clerk has had to write to my ex-wife's clerk to reschedule, and if you knew my ex-wife, or my ex-wife's clerk for that matter, you'd know what inconvenience was. Still, never mind. I have a feeling that your presence will make up for it."

"I was quite happy to fly into Nairobi on Monday," Aliya said.

"Nairobi's full of TV crews, reporters and other assorted lowlife. We're taking our responsibility for your personal safety very seriously. Hence the change. We can secure things better, down here."

He glanced back over his shoulder, and with a jerk of his head called forward a young man who reached, with a welcoming 'Jambo', for Aliya's shoulder bag. She pulled it away, gently but firmly. "I can manage, thanks. The rest of my luggage is over there, if you wouldn't mind . . ."

She looked around, as the youth loped off for the bags, and squinted slightly into the halogen lights. "So this is Kenya?" she said, lamely. "Africa."

"No, Ms Zain. This is Swahili Land, the Coast. The only place our type of Kenyan can claim any right to be."

"I'm not any type of Kenyan, remember?"

"Sure, sure," he said, soothingly. "Whatever. You're still welcome in Swahili Land. Because this is the land where everybody fits in. You know why? 'Cos there's no such thing as a pure Swahili. Wonderful, isn't it? All the rest of the world is obsessed with race and ethnicity, yet here there's a healthy, happy, functioning and perfectly well adjusted community whose entire culture is based on mixed blood."

"I've never really thought about it . . ."

"No, I don't suppose you have. But I have," he continued as he led her to his car. "Welcome to Swahili Land: what, if the world were a better place, the future would look like."

They drove from the airport, headlights on full beam picking out small stalls illuminated with guttering flames of oil lamps, and the bright eyes of people walking the roadside. They turned on to the main road where what had once been a drive-in cinema now doubled as a container park. Here, there was more traffic. Huge lorries, dragging equally vast trailers, belched out clouds of thick smoke. Minibuses, sounding their horns, raced along, then braked furiously to disgorge or pick up further passengers. Crammed with people, with a tout hanging from

114

the doorway, shouting their destination and waving a fistful of folded notes. Private cars, air conditioners misting the insides of their windscreens, and long distance buses, their passengers dozing already, settled for the night, to sleep away the interminable climb up to Nairobi, Kisumu, and on.

Aliya was tired and a heavy depression seemed to descend on her which the dismal streets through which they drove did little to alleviate. Where was the colour, the buzz and the thrill? All she saw was the locked up and closed down face of Mombasa. Sheet-metal shutters over every window and every door so that no glimmer of light or even any sound spilt out from either houses or shops. There were people around, but for every passer-by, there seemed to be a uniformed guard, a pickaxe handle across his lap, dozing on a stool.

And the few public places, the bars and street eateries, seemed dimly lit and dismal, half full of figures slumped over Formica tables, or leaning against tiled walls, sipping soft drinks. Occasionally, she caught sight of brighter, more enticing places to gather: paan houses, neon-lit, tinsel-bright with posters of Bollywood stars she barely recognised, cut from the centre pages of Cineblitz and Stardust. And ice cream parlours, where expensively dressed youngsters, primarily Arab and Asian, hung out. Their cars parked carelessly, their bright shirts, and labelled sunglasses declaring their parents' wealth.

It all seemed too easy to reconcile with her parents' grim recollections. She sighed, and looked forward to going home.

"Your folks are from Mombasa?" Leo asked.

"That's right," said Aliya warily. "How did you know?"

"I was told. I asked around. No one remembers a Zain who left in the '70s."

"We were called Zainuddinbhai then," Aliya said reluctantly.

"As in Zainuddinbhai Mithaiwalla- the sweet shop on Kilindini Road?"

"Don't tell me it's still there."

"Sure is! Still trading under the same name too. Still got folks here?"

115

"Distant cousins in Nairobi. I'll try to catch up with them if there's time."

"There'll be time. You know how these cases are. Lots of hanging about waiting for things to happen."

"I hope there aren't going to be too many delays and continuances. I have a life to get on with."

"So does our client," said Leo, coolly.

"I realise that," countered Aliya, unfazed. "How is he?"

"As well as can be expected, poor devil. Safe and comfortable at least, now he's been moved out of a cell in Central Police Station. I thought Paul would object, but he was actually very decent about it."

"Tell me about Paul Muya," Aliya asked.

"The Total Man? He's a Bintu."

"Ah," said Aliya, nodding seriously. "That's his, er . . . ethnic group, is it?"

Leo laughed. "In a way. Been to London, been to Paris, been to Washington. That's what they call well travelled Africans here; Bintus. Actually, he's a Kikuyu. He's going to be a big man, one day. That's why everyone calls him the Total Man."

"And what do they call you?" asked Aliya idly, not really expecting a reply.

"Coke."

"Really? Why?"

Leo shrugged. "An unfortunate misunderstanding involving a prohibited substance which necessitated a rapid and somewhat undignified departure from the Land of the Free."

"What?"

"I was expelled from the United States in my 20s for being in possession of a minuscule quantity of cannabis resin."

"Not cocaine?"

"No. But with my surname I suppose it was inevitable. If it had been Brown, I would probably be called Hash."

Aliya smiled. "Let me guess: you were looking after it for a friend."

"As a matter of fact, I was. Still, what the hell? It's given me an unwarranted reputation as something of a Jack the Lad, and earned me an almost embarrassing amount of money defending possession and trafficking cases."

"Hence, Coke Kane."

"You've got it. Pretty much everyone has a nickname out here. What should we call you, I wonder?"

"A cab back to the airport?"

"Pathetic. No, I think something that reflects your role in guiding us through the complexities of War Crimes legislation. The Navigator, perhaps . . ."

Suddenly, they were in complete darkness. The buildings, the trees, everything simply disappeared on both sides of the road, and it took Aliya a moment to realise that they were crossing a bridge. Far away, she could make out the intermittent glimmer of some kind of an industrial complex: docks maybe, or a factory. The tiny pinheads of light came and went, as invisible vegetation blocked her line of vision.

On the other side of the bridge were the remains of toll booths, broken down now to little more than concrete stumps, like smashed teeth. A few yards further on, they took a sharp right, and entered an area of expensive housing, clustered together behind high walls and electric fences, dominated by huge satellite dishes, like some frontier settlement on a distant planet.

"Nyali," said Leo. "This is where I live. Not much further now."

"Do you want to see where it all happened?" he asked after a long moment, as though the thought had just crossed his mind.

"What? Half a century later? Do you think that's really necessary?"

"Oh, absolutely. It hasn't changed much. We'll drive up there next week. As it happens I need to be in that area anyway. You see, there's this event called the Charge . . ."

Aliya slept poorly. Tension, the time difference and a general sense of disorientation kept her tossing and turning every bit as much as her inability to get the atmosphere of the room right.

With the air conditioner on, the room was chilly, damp and draughty. With it off: cloying, stifling and airless. The mosquito net tenting her bed was dusty, and made her sneeze. With the dawn, watery-eyed and ill tempered, she was glad of an excuse to get up and explore.

She looked out of the window, down into the compound of which, in the darkness of the previous night, she had only been vaguely aware. Then it had seemed stark and dismal. In the morning light, its beauty left her breathless. Bushes covered in bloom billowed up: oleander, frangipani and bougainvillaea frothing with bright colour. There was a swimming pool, the pump already running, the water circulating, sparkling in the sun and gurgling, chorusing the cool contentment of the morning.

A thin man in khaki shorts and a faded Hard Rock Café t-shirt lifted a confetti of fallen blossom from the surface of the water in long, slow sweeps with an implement that looked like a giant tea strainer on the end of a 15 foot pole.

Aliya slipped into the kimono she customarily wore as a dressing gown on the few occasions she had visitors, and wandered down stairs.

Leo Kane was already up, sitting beside the pool, leafing through the Guardian and Independent she had been reading on the flight and had discarded.

He looked up, as she approached, and smiled. "How do you like it?" he asked.

"It's . . . beautiful," she admitted, almost reluctantly. "When can I meet Tom Miles?" she asked.

"We'll fly up to Nairobi on Monday. Or maybe we should take the train. It's a beautiful journey. You'd enjoy it."

"I'm not on holiday, Mr Kane," she said, primly.

Leo smiled. "Of course not, Miss Zain, and even the Fundi – handyman – calls me Leo. Or Coke. So can we drop the formal stuff?"

She nodded, tilted her head back, and ran her fingers through her hair. "Sorry. But we've only got a couple of weeks before the trial and I want to . . ."

"See where it all happened?" Leo said, quickly. "Yes, you said so last night. Well, it just so happens that my boys and I are driving in a sort of cross country event around there, and if you liked, you could come along as our navigator. We could start to prepare this coming weekend."

Her eyes narrowed. "What sort of an event?"

"Oh, we take out a bunch of old vehicles and we have to get from the start to a certain point on the map travelling the least possible distance. It doesn't matter how long you take, it's whoever manages to clock up the fewest miles that wins. It's really good fun . . ."

"Doesn't sound too difficult. Why can't you just go in a straight line?"

"Because of the terrain. The start and end points are deliberately chosen so that the ground in between has got all sorts of obstacles. Last year, there was a river, a ravine, an army firing range, and a forest to get through. It was a hoot. Nick Friedlander nearly got himself arrested . . ."

"And how did you get on?" she asked, feeling herself being drawn in, and not resenting it too much.

"Well, we didn't actually complete the course. Nor the year before. Or the year before that. But this year, we've got great hopes. And it's for a good cause. Do you like rhinos?"

"I don't know. I suppose so."

"Well there you are then; it raises money for rhino conservation. And it will give you an excellent opportunity to see the sort of environment all this happened in. Do you want me to put your name down for our team?"

Aliya smiled, and nodded. "As long as it doesn't interfere with what we're here to do. Or delays my return home, why not?"

Leo laughed. "Well done! Want some breakfast, teammate?"

He reached behind his chair, and offered her a plate of small, plump bananas. She took one but recoiled in disgust as, revealed

119

beneath the fruit she had pulled free of the bunch, the bananas at the centre were black and rotten, and a mass of tiny ants fled from the pulp across the plate. She dropped the banana, the corners of her mouth turned down, and she brushed her hands on her kimono.

"The reason why everything you see here is so beautiful, and so perfect is because it's all on the edge of decomposition, decay and death," said Leo, patiently. "The most beautiful blooms fall within moments of your joy in them. The sweetest fruit is a rotting pulp a few hours later. It goes with the glory, I'm afraid. For Europeans, and I'll categorise you as that for the moment, the implication of that fact either enthrals or disgusts."

"It disgusts. Believe me, it disgusts," said Aliya. "I just want to get my involvement in this case over, and get out of here. Now if you'll excuse me, I'm going to shower."

The day slid by amiably enough as they picked over the issues and explored tentative defences.

Over flasks of Ethiopian coffee, Leo outlined the second committal hearing – a brief, five minute affair, little more than a formality, for all the salient facts had been disclosed at the initial hearing. The only real achievement was Tom's relocation. Leo had applied for bail, arguing that continuing to hold Tom in a police cell was an abuse of his human rights whilst his transfer on remand to a Kenyan Prison was likely to threaten his wellbeing and physical safety. Paul had agreed that it was in no one's interest for Tom to be in danger, but pointed out that his temporary release on bail was not risk free either. The compromise solution was that Tom should be housed in the Police Staff Club, free to move about the club house and grounds but restricted to the compound.

The prosecution said it was ready, and keen, to proceed as soon as convenient to the Court. Leo had asked for two weeks to prepare and a trial date had been set, with the Chief Justice himself presiding. Paul had already emailed Leo a list of the witnesses he intended to call and had couriered to him copies of the key documents he intended to present.

And that's what puzzled both Leo and Aliya. The prosecution witnesses named were a couple of historians, six ex-Mau Mau, one of whom had since become a successful writer, and a yet to be identified international authority on war crimes. The documents were exactly the same as in the initial bundle, plus certified copies of the secret circular so disastrously presented at the committal.

"Not much of a case, really, is it?" Leo said.

"No, it isn't," Aliya agreed. "The DPP would never allow us to proceed with such a prosecution if this is all we had. Paul Muya's holding something back. Got to be."

"And what do we need?" asked Leo.

"Witnesses. Evidence. An alibi and another possible perpetrator."

Leo smiled. "Right now I'd just be grateful for a client who can give a clear account of the night in question. But Tom Miles claims he can't remember what happened. It's all so vague. We can talk to his commanding officer, Sandford. Think seeing the scene of the crime might help?"

"Can't do any harm. We've got precious little else. Think we can?"

"Oh, I'm sure that can be arranged," beamed Leo.

They worked on into the evening.

"I propose we admit everything Paul offers on Mau Mau and the Emergency except Tom's part in the death of Jembe, or in any other act that they claim to be a war crime. That way, it can be read into the record unchallenged, and Tom Miles doesn't end up standing trial for the failings of the entire British Colonial system," Leo said.

Aliya paused, frowning slightly. "Fine. As long as we don't let in anything which Paul Muya can subsequently use against our man."

"Like?"

"Like his part in Operation Anvil. As I understand it, the whole thing was designed to apprehend every member of three particular tribes in Nairobi and ship them off to detention

121

camps where many of them were held for years without trial. Camps in which – and this is well documented – some were tortured, and others were beaten to death. Doesn't that sound like a crime against humanity to you?"

"But Tom Miles can't be held responsible for that."

"No?" wondered Aliya. "He didn't refuse to take part in it, did he? Then there's the unsavoury record of many of these Combined Action Teams: can we produce any evidence to show that Tom Miles resisted his posting to C.A.T.12?"

"Surely on that we can argue he was just obeying orders? To have disobeyed would have been unreasonable and unjustified."

"You know, bright German lawyers spent millions searching for a record of anyone who refused to take part in the extermination of the Jews and was punished as a result. That, after all, was the classic defence: *I was just obeying orders. They sent me to that place and once I was there, if I hadn't done it, I would have been killed.* Do you know what they found, after years and years of searching? A small town policeman, who had been transferred to a concentration camp as a guard. He saw what was going on, and refused to be a part of it. Do you know what happened to him? He was simply transferred back to his small town. And, unfortunately for us, the prosecution will be able to produce dozens of examples of National Service conscripts who wrote to their Member of Parliament, or back home to the newspapers, blowing the whistle on all manner of things they found unacceptable. Good luck arguing that Tom Miles was an unwilling participant in these events."

"He was young, naive. Not a professional soldier."

"He was older, more senior and better educated than many of the conscript whistle blowers. Also, he signed on for an extra year. He could have been back home when all this happened. He actually went out of his way to remain. Not a conscript any more, a volunteer. In order to take part in a campaign in which you now propose to argue he didn't believe. I agree we should try and distance Dr Miles from the general behaviour of the

122

security forces in the Emergency, but I don't think it's going to be that easy."

"You sound like you'd be more comfortable supporting the prosecution?"

"Of course I would. That's what I've been trained to do. But I'm a professional. I'll give this my best shot. And take it from one who knows, it's a lot easier to defend these cases than it is to prosecute them."

"So what have we got going for us?"

"A, or one: the apparent lack of any eye witness. B, or two: the fact that the official record compiled at the time, or shortly after, is riddled with inconsistencies and contains conflicting accounts of what happened that night . . ."

"C, or three," Leo interrupted her, "this Special Circular No 10 which apparently authorised Jembe's termination."

"Wrong. It may have been useful in defending our man against murder, but it actually helps in the prosecution of a war crime. Don't forget, for a war crime it's not necessary to prove intent. He simply has to have taken part in an action – obeyed orders, if you like – when he should, as a decent human being, have refused to be involved."

"Can we build an argument out of the fact that no other government, or even an individual, has ever brought a prosecution against the British in such circumstances?"

Aliya smiled. "The Dresden fiction."

"The Dresden fiction?"

"Yes. The Dresden fiction. It goes something like this: take the blanket bombing of Dresden. The deliberate, premeditated slaughter of thousands of German civilians. For no military objective. Solely to create terror among civilian populations. Is it a war crime? No. Why not? One reason. Because the British are incapable of committing a war crime. That, in a nutshell, is the Dresden fiction."

"Good one. Where does that come from?"

"Me, actually. Do you want to try that argument in a Kenyan court?"

"But surely that doesn't apply these days: what about that British soldier in Iraq who pleaded guilty to committing a war crime in 2006? And even in this case, where atrocities on the part of the security services were proven, those guilty were punished for their actions. Black. White. Asian. Your Dresden fiction may apply to the British, but we are talking about Kenyans."

Aliya's eyes narrowed. "Part of the legislation which introduced the Emergency conferred the death penalty on those found guilty of a range of crimes including consorting with people illegally armed, aiding insurgent groups, and administering unlawful oaths. People could be, and were, hanged simply for drinking beer with a man who unbeknown to them had a bullet, not a gun mind you, but just a bullet, in his pocket."

She flicked through her notes: "Between 20 October 1952 and 12 November 1954, 756 Kenyans were executed, including 294 for the unlawful possession of arms and ammunition, and 45 for administering unlawful oaths. Every one of them black. Now, let's examine your contention that wrongdoers in the security forces were punished irrespective of race, creed or colour."

She searched for a moment among the books she had brought with her, and found the page she wanted. "Captain P M Carthew – a Kenyan, white – charged with the murder of one or two Africans. Acquitted because the prosecution was unable to prove the identity of the murdered men. Harry Snelgrove – another white Kenyan – ordered paraffin to be poured on a suspect – fined £25. Assistant District Commandant Hatton – is a pattern starting to emerge at all? Participated in burning a prisoner – fined £20. Reserve Police Officer Kallenbach – white, Kenyan – inflicted illegal and heavy floggings – fined £50. Reserve Police Officer Mason – set a fierce dog on a prisoner – fined. Sergeant Joyner and Police Officer Meacham – convicted of beating an African to death – fined. Need I go on?"

Leo sat quiet for a moment, studying Aliya contemplatively. "Is there a racial aspect to this?" he asked, gently.

Aliya's eyes flashed. "Are you high? Of course there's a

racial aspect to this! If you're black and simply happen to be a member of the wrong tribe, you get strung up, beat up or locked away for years in abominable circumstances, no matter how loyal you are. If you're white, and you torture, burn and murder a black man, you get a small fine and a slap across the wrist. I would have thought the racial aspect was crystal clear to the meanest intelligence."

"No, I meant for you, as a non-white."

"A non-white?" she exploded. "What sort of fucking stupid expression is that? Why don't you call me a non-Martian? What's your ethnicity, non-Chinese?"

"OK, OK. Calm down. I apologise. Jesus! What I am trying, and clearly failing, to ask is if the racial aspects of this case present you with a personal dilemma?"

She shook her head vigorously. "Not in the least. I spent the last 18 months putting together a case against a Ukrainian who allegedly killed Jews and gypsies 60 years ago. This case is no different. Both are distant and foreign. You should be asking yourself that question. You're the one who specified the race of your war crimes expert, remember? My only interest is in doing the best job I can because I'm a professional. I want us to win this case, because it will be good for my career, and then I want to be out of here."

"Fair enough," said Leo, pushing himself up out of the chair. "Look, we're both tired; there's nothing more we can do, just now. Why don't we call it a day, get in a pizza, crack open a bottle and download a film?"

Aliya, still frowning, shook her head, and continued reading the transcript of the committal hearings.

Leo ran his fingers through his hair. "It doesn't have to be Hollywood," he said. "They do really good Indian films, too. Everybody says so."

"Hmmm," said Aliya, only half listening "I don't expect they'd have the kind of films I like."

"Well that's just where you're wrong, Miss Smug and Superior," Leo said, brightening. "They have the latest. They've probably got more up-to-date films than you can get in London."

Aliya put aside the papers and stared up at him. "I loathe modern Bollywood," she said, yawning. "Anything made after 1962 is crap, with a couple of notable exceptions."

"Well then, what sort of films do you like?"

"Anything by Guru Dutt. Most early Raj Kapoor. Do you think they can oblige?"

"How about going out for something to eat?"

Aliya sneered. "What did you have in mind? I've seen the tourist brochures. The mock Italian pizzeria or the mock German beer garden? I don't think so."

"I was actually going to suggest we go to Ali Asgar's B and B. It's a cheap little guest house down by the bridge. But the cook's a Dawoodi Bohra, which I assume you are, and she does a fine Biryani. Blimey, what is it with you?" Leo sighed. "The time of the month or something? I thought you might appreciate something approximating to home cooking . . ."

Aliya frowned. "Please don't be crass, Mr Kane. What sort of Biryani?"

"How the fuck do I know!" cried Leo, exasperated. "Do you want to go or not?"

CHAPTER TWENTY

Tom Miles found that his move to the Police Club improved the quality of his life whilst simultaneously complicating it. The regime he had previously been held under was austere and uncomfortable, but it had at least been straightforward and simple. The cell he had occupied had been below ground, horribly airless and stiflingly hot. The sergeant in charge of the holding area, one of the ever growing number to whom Tom was giving medical advice, had arranged for three other prisoners to scrub it out and repaint its walls. Though much cleaner, the cell then reeked of distemper, which made Tom feel nauseous and gave him an almost constant headache whilst failing to mask the all-pervasive odour of stale sweat, vomit and urine.

The sergeant had broken a fibula a year earlier which had been poorly set, resulting in chronic pain and a limp. Tom had quickly learnt not to ask how such injuries had been incurred but to focus solely on their remedy, or at least the easement of their more severe symptoms. Difficult, without patient records, books or instruments, but his custodians were happy to check things on Google for him on the Station's one PC with internet access. They were genuinely sorry to see him go, and pressed on him further small presents to show their appreciation. Only later realising the vaguely surreal nature of his farewell, Tom assured them they were more than welcome to visit and consult him at the Police Club whenever they liked.

His new place of confinement, on the north-west outskirts of the city, was larger, lighter and almost unimaginably luxurious by comparison with his previous surroundings. His room was on the first floor of a neo-colonial clubhouse. Furnishings were Spartan and somewhat the worse for wear, but compared to what had gone before, seemed little short of palatial. Bare floor-boards and a narrow bed with a lumpy mattress on a sagging wire frame that creaked every time he moved. A single pillow, two blankets and thin but gloriously clean, starched sheets. A shelf, on which he placed the two books, one religious pamphlet and the small carved giraffe his previous hosts had given him, and a wardrobe, with warped doors, one of which was stuck fast. Next to the bed was a small, chipped table with a lamp and a Bible.

Most glorious of all, he had daylight and a view over a regularly watered and carefully tended cricket pitch to tall trees and a high, wide sky over the city skyline beyond. And a door that wasn't locked.

On arrival, he had been met by the Club President, a retired Deputy Inspector General, who, with profound gravity, asked Tom to give his sacred oath not to attempt to abscond. Having done so, Tom was promptly asked his preferences for breakfast cereal. It was clear that whilst possible attempts to flee might be a concern, self-harm was not, for he was allowed to keep his belt and shoe-laces and even permitted a pitcher of water and a glass. Within hours, McKenzie arrived, and he and Tom walked the well-kept gardens, hands behind their backs, for all the world like two English squires inspecting the estate.

"Your clothes will be here shortly," McKenzie promised. "We collected your stuff from the hotel and have been storing your bags at the High Commission. And we've had a whip-round for books for you. I hope you like American detective fiction."

Tom smiled, "That's very kind. Anything will be fine, really. I never realised before what a blessing being able to lie in bed and read is. I'm really looking forward to it."

"Plus your wife and son are here. They arrived last night. I think we can arrange for them to visit most days. We just need to agree a schedule. Everyone seems very keen to be accommodating so . . ."

Tom had stopped, and McKenzie, who had walked on a few paces, turned. "Is there a problem?"

"I didn't know they were coming."

"No. Your son asked us not to tell you. Didn't want you building your hopes up, just in case there was some hitch. Do you want to sit down?" McKenzie asked, concerned.

Tom looked likely to fall. He swayed back and forth, his face horribly pale and his forehead damp with sweat. He took out a handkerchief to mop his brow and McKenzie noticed with concern how much his hand was shaking.

"Let's get you into shade," he said, placing his hand on Tom's arm as he glanced around for the policeman pacing a discreet distance behind them for possible help. "We shouldn't have spent so long in the sun on your first day out."

Tom jerked his arm away. "Take your hands off me! Who the hell do you think you are? Didn't it even occur to you people to ask me if I wanted my family here?"

"We just thought . . ."

"No, you didn't. You didn't think at all. Or you would have stopped to ask yourself if just maybe I might not want them to see me like this. To read what the newspapers here are saying. To hear what's going to be said in court. About me. About what we did. All this was over long before I ever met my wife. I've never even spoken to my children about my time out here. You think I want them to learn about it like this? I am charged with War Crimes, for God's sake!"

"It wasn't up to us. Your family want to stand by you. We didn't ask them to come. This is where they want to be. By your side."

"The only people who should be standing by me is the Country in whose service these things were done. And I see precious little evidence of that right now," continued Tom, in disgust. "They say even the War Crimes expert you provided Leo Kane

129

with is little more than a joke. Some Indian girl barely out of Law School."

"That's hardly fair, Dr Miles," replied McKenzie. "Kane is happy with her. We are doing everything we can to help."

"Like bringing my family out here behind my back? Have you met them?"

"Just before I came here. Your son asked me to give you this." McKenzie took a small package from his pocket, but the policeman following them, who had moved in closer as voices were raised, cleared his throat noisily. McKenzie looked over, and offered the tissue wrapped package to him. The police-man carefully unwrapped it. A small silver cross lay among the crumpled tissue. He offered it to Tom, who took it and held it in the palm of his left hand, his thumb, trembling still, caressed it.

"My mother's," he murmured, and then, after a moment. "How did my wife seem?"

"OK," said McKenzie, non-committally.

"She has Huntington's disease," said Tom quietly. "She shouldn't be here. The journey itself ... Let alone ... She just shouldn't be here. This is going to do far more harm to her than any good her presence can possibly do for me. I don't need to see her to know she cares. We've been married for more than 40 years, for Christ's sake. This is just wrong. Stupid."

"Your son felt ..."

"My son," sighed Tom, exasperated, "is a man of the cloth. He has what many, including me, think is a naive belief in the benefit of prayer and the virtue of suffering. In that, and in many other things, he has far more in common with Paul Muya than he does with me. Much as I love them both, I really don't want either of them here right now."

"Well ..."

"Yes," said Tom, testily. "I know. I have no option but to see them now. Another example of a duty foisted on me by my government against my will. You people need to understand that if you push me too far you'll be sorry for what happens. Now understand this: I will do everything I can to get them to return to the UK as quickly as possible, and I expect you, no, I *need* you, to help me. Agreed?"

"Agreed," sighed McKenzie, who suddenly missed his own wife and children very much indeed.

Paul Muya listened, nodding and smiling affectionately, as Josh Kane described Leo's newly repainted Land Rover over a late Sunday lunch. Paul had always had the ability to seem to focus wholeheartedly on the person with whom he was engaged at any given moment. He could make that person feel they were the only one he had ever, would ever, truly care about. That every word they spoke was an insight, an inspiration, of massive importance to him. Even if he couldn't make the blind see, Paul Muya could perform the more politically useful miracle of making the stumbling feel clever and the superficial, profound.

Not that giving them his full attention was any hardship when it came to Zeke and Josh Kane. He couldn't have loved them more if they had been his own. He took real pride in Zeke's intelligence and felt genuine affection for Josh's unfocused enthusiasms. He liked in them the things he liked in their father, and admired in them the aspects of their personalities he recognised as their mother's. Whilst Mrs Muya might resent the increasing amount of time her husband seemed to find it necessary to spend with the boys and their mother, Paul was uncharacteristically untroubled about it. He glanced up at Marianne Kane, caught her eye and winked. The darker side within him, or the realist, told him he could probably take Marianne Kane as a lover without too much difficulty. She had certainly given out the signs. Was right now. But Paul Muya was not an adulterer. Nor was he looking for a second wife or a surrogate family.

Driven, as always, by duty, he felt quite simply his friend's sons needed a rather more . . . *substantial* father figure, an African father figure. And it was a privilege to fulfil that need.

"You have never seen anything like it!" enthused Josh, and

his elder brother, though wired into his iPod, nodded in agreement. "It is, well, bangin'!"

Paul frowned slightly, unsure if this was swearing, and Zeke picked up the brief chill in the atmosphere.

"It would be great if you were coming with us though, Uncle Paul. Josh wants you to. So do I. So does Dad."

Paul shook his head. "I wish I could, but it's just not possible. And the more I think about it, the less sure I am you and your Dad should be going either. These are tense times."

"Oh, I think they'll be fine," said Marianne Kane, putting a hand on Zeke's shoulder. "It's the last chance they'll have and it means a lot to them. And you can say what you like about Leo, but he'd never let any harm come to his boys."

Paul looked at her for a long moment. "Neither would I," he said, quietly. "Ever."

There was an uncomfortable silence. "You see the Miles family have turned up at last?" asked Marianne, hoping to break the suddenly sombre mood. "The papers are full of it. The son is a vicar."

Paul continued to stare at her. Then he smiled and returned his attention to the boys. "Has your Dad got that accelerator fixed yet? Don't tell me he managed to do it himself?"

CHAPTER TWENTY-ONE

After I'd been in the forest a couple of weeks, our chaps picked up the trail of a lone terrorist, wandering, apparently aimlessly, across the salient. Poor devil was half starved, and chronically dehydrated.

Johnny Sandford was always dead keen to turn more Mau Mau, get them de-oathed and working on his side, so we set an ambush, and bagged him. He was overjoyed to be taken alive. Apparently he'd been marked down as a traitor, and he'd been wandering for days, avoiding both them and us, fearing every shadow, and never daring to stop to sleep.

He turned out to be one hell of a tracker, and a valuable addition to our little force, but we didn't know that then.

What struck me most about him was the crude, home-made musket he carried. It had a rusty wire spring for a firing pin, and a piece of old pipe for a barrel, all lashed onto a roughly carved stock.

How could these people ever think they had a chance of taking us on with such primitive weapons?

When I mentioned it to Johnny Sandford, he shrugged. "They all started with things like this," he said.

"How has it taken us so long to beat them?" I wondered.

Johnny frowned. "You know, before we could have many British troops out here to help us, we had to establish NAAFIs, allocate BFPO numbers, set up Quartermaster's stores. The whole kit and caboodle. That's the difference between us and them. We think we need to have everything organised, ship shape and tickety-boo before we can move a muscle. They decided to make war, came up to the forest, and simply set about it. This weapon just about sums up the difference. You see it as crude copy of a gun, hardly more than a joke. But that's because you're looking at in comparison to your own Patchett. Your machine gun is just that: a machine. Designed for robust efficiency and longevity. It should outlast you, and be passed on to your successor, and to his. This, on the other hand," he said, holding up the home-made musket, "is only designed to fire once. It's designed to kill or incapacitate one of our chaps so that they can take his more sophisticated weapon. Why do you think policemen and prison guards in Nairobi walk around with their rifles chained to their belts? Why do you think it's a criminal offence here for a civilian to have a gun stolen from them? Get the idea? When we're presented with a problem, we pride ourselves on our ability to think through all the implications and ramifications, before we make a move. They think one step a time."

"But what if that one shot misses?" I asked. "What then?"

Johnny shrugged. "Either the firer gets taken, or he makes himself another weapon. But what if you lose your Patchett, young Miles? Could you manufacture another? No. We'd have to send you down to Nairobi to indent at the Central Stores, and fill out page after page of paperwork to account for the loss of Her Majesty's property. That, my young friend, is why they think they have a chance."

CHAPTER TWENTY-TWO

General Sir Malcolm Harris MC, DSO (retired), cast his newspaper, with its front page dominated by a picture of Tom Miles' wife and son arriving in Nairobi, aside in disgust, then chewed the knuckle of the index finger of his left hand.

It was a gesture those who had served under him would have recognised as indicating not confusion or uncertainty, but a build-up of energy, like static electricity in the air before a thunder storm. And they would have done their utmost to merge with the background, for that energy invariably exploded into action. 'Hack 'em' Harris was contemplating another of the notoriously impetuous decisions which characterised his rather roller-coaster military career.

"Someone's got to make a stand . . ." he muttered, causing the young executive across the corridor tapping away at his laptop to glance up, his fingers poised above the compact keyboard.

The General glared across at him, and the younger man looked away.

The irascible old man into which the General had almost enthusiastically metamorphosed on retirement had already composed three different letters to British Rail – or whatever the blighters were calling themselves this week – demanding that they ban electronic gadgetry from first class compartments. The tough commando still within him ached to grab the infuriating machine and attempt to insert it into one of its owner's narrower orifices.

The General, on his way to a meeting of the Board of Governors for a service charity which, in a moment of weakness, he had agreed to chair, was making one of his increasingly infrequent visits to London. He'd become something of a recluse, devoting himself to his farm and, although he didn't like it to be generally known, collecting 18th century china.

His military career was characterised as successful rather than distinguished. This was through no fault of his own; he had the heart of a hero, won the affection of his men, and planned and executed some of the most audacious actions of his time. It was just his misfortune to have been born that little bit too late to play a major role in the Second World War, and to have spent the bulk of his active service in a series of unfashionable postings: Malaya, Kenya, Suez, Palestine. His memories were not of celebrated triumphs but of a weary, thankless series of peacekeeping and anti-insurgent campaigns in a suddenly unfashionable Empire being dismantled with ungainly haste around them.

He'd landed a couple of interesting advisor posts in the 60s though, and was held then to be something of an expert in helping to weld together ex-colonial regiments and the guerrillas they had once fought into unified forces capable of defending newly independent nations.

He'd been in Kenya during the Emergency for example, and then gone back there in '64 and again in '67, to conduct reviews of the Kenyan army and make recommendations. Recommendations which, by and large, had been well received and fairly effectively implemented.

It was around that time that he'd realised he was never to be a man of destiny. Ever after, he was suspicious of situations which suggested to him that he had a unique role to play. But despite this he was convinced, as he glowered once more at his discarded newspaper, that somebody needed to stand up and be counted beside this poor bugger the Kenyans had the gall to charge with war crimes, and he felt in his old hero's heart that it had to be him.

A trill ping, and an irritating twitter of electronic music, snapped his attention back to the young man working at his laptop.

For no logical reason, this made up the General's mind.

"You," he said, gruffly. "Either you switch that damned machine off now, or you shift yourself to another part of the train."

The young man blushed furiously. "You don't own this compartment . . ." he began.

"True," the General acknowledged, his voice crisp with the supreme self confidence that had once halted an angry mob on the edge of riot. He felt that same reassuring increase in his heartbeat now, and the tightening in his loose sinews. Steadily, he rose, with a glint in his eye, and raised his hand to the emergency alarm. "But I do have more time than I know what to do with," he said, with a hard, 'try-me' smile revealing his false teeth. "And more than enough money to pay the fine. Now shift yourself, Sonny Jim, or prepare to sit here for some time to come!"

Never much given to procrastination – or, his detractors might have said, mature reflection – General Harris rang the number he found at the foot of the back page of his newspaper the moment he arrived at Paddington station.

His Knighthood got him through to the editor's office. The headline value of his proposal got him an interview that afternoon.

The editor, who looked to the General as though he should still be in school, called in two equally youthful sub-editors and a feature writer, and asked the General to run through his idea again.

Over polystyrene cups of vending machine cappuccino, the eye contact sparked and locked. It could be, they said silently to one another, it just could be . . .

The editor asked the General if he would like to take a look around the place while he made a couple of phone calls. The feature writer delegated to escort him made a crack about inspecting the troops which prompted a baleful glare from his boss. The General didn't notice: he was enjoying himself too much.

The editor rang the proprietor.

The proprietor agreed the plan and approved the budget.

And 'Hack 'em' Harris found himself on the front page the next morning, and he had to admit they'd done a pretty decent job. There he was, dignified, and proud. A veteran of too many campaigns to recall, an old soldier with a straight back and still a hint of the old 'damn you, Dago' glint in his eye.

They'd dug up some old photos of him in Africa. Inspecting a GSU platoon in Nakuru, if his memory served.

And they'd agreed to fund his trip, and contacted the lawyer representing this poor devil Miles to tell him that he was on his way.

And they quoted his words. "I was out there then, too. I can remember what we were fighting against. And what we were fighting for. I won't see another old soldier abandoned. There is such a thing as comradeship and solidarity. There is such a thing, still, as standing shoulder to shoulder against a common foe."

John Ole Kisii, one time Mau Mau Freedom Fighter, KANU time server, and now Kenya's Acting President, sat alone in the dark and entertained unwelcome thoughts about the future.

He had, in his own, quiet way, taken them all by surprise. First his party, then his country, and now, quite literally, the world. They had written him off, all of them. Years ago. Seen him as little more than a rote voter who would do as he was told, and keep his nose clean, and remember his place.

Not one of them had felt the heat of the flame that still burnt within him, every bit as intensely as it had in his youth.

Even then, they hadn't taken him seriously – dismissed him as an outsider, this man of a different tribe – a Masai in a Kikuyu war. Oh, they used to treat him well enough! Even in the forest, there'd been a political correctness of sorts. But he'd never been one of the chosen few. No, the Kikuyu had made sure they kept the key places to themselves. Always had done. Always would.

He'd taken to reading biographies of late. Gorbachev and

de Klerk. They, perhaps surprisingly for a black African patriot, were his inspiration, rather than the Nkrumahs and Mandelas of this world. He knew it had fallen to his lot to be the one who made the transition from the out-moded and out-dated, to the more near-to-the-real. And he knew, from all that he had seen over the past decades, that that was an unfashionable, unpopular and ultimately unpleasant role in which to be cast. But that was his lot, and that's all there was to it.

He would not, he knew, reap the harvest of the changes, so long overdue, that he had already begun to introduce. Indeed, given his advanced years, it was unlikely he would even live to see them fully implemented, but he knew that it was for him to plant the seeds. Deeply. So that no matter what or who followed him, they could not be dug up, and cast away, before they'd had a chance to put down roots and sprout.

Although he'd never met them he imagined Gorbachev and de Klerk were, like him, pragmatists. Like bareback riders, they hung on grimly to the bucking, kicking beast beneath them, hoping for the best. Determined not to be unseated, until the crazed thing calmed, and they could begin, once more, to exert control.

As he was sure they had, it was his turn now to feel the weight of the world's interest in him. He knew that, whilst there were many silent watchers who wanted him to succeed, there were far, far more who would rejoice in his failure.

The pressure for an election was mounting, day by day. How much longer, people asked, should the Republic struggle on under these interim arrangements, with a stand-in at the helm, whilst its elected President lay cocooned in tubes and wires, in a permanent vegetative state?

He had secured the SEACOW package; that had eased the pressure. Soon – but would it be soon enough? – the benefits would start to become evident. Already, they were clearing a site for a teaching hospital out towards Langata: the first of two dozen massive infrastructure construction programmes. And that was only the visible tip of a vast iceberg of capital investment.

But first, before all other considerations, there was this trial. The ghost of Jembe to lay, once and for all.

He remembered the hours he had spent with Paul Muya's father. The laughter, the teasing. The arrogant certainty of young men with a purpose shared, a war to fight and a country to win. The mutual respect, the occasional rivalry. Like young lions, playfully cuffing one another, roaring loud, but with claws retracted.

He was a good man, Wilson Muya. Jembe – the hoe. A martyr to the cause, like ten thousand others – but one whose spectre seemed determined to return and haunt him until he was avenged.

Yes, Jembe's was the ghost, howling in the wind. The spirit, moving with the leaves. He was out there, in the dust devils on the floor of the Rift Valley, and in the creaking branches of the high forest. He was there, in the night clouds. He was there, in the empty dawn.

He was there, in the bright eyes of his son.

Kenya's Acting President had read that it was the penalty of great men to sleep badly. He wandered, in the dark, from room to room in State House. The various security men and retainers found it eerie, his capacity to move about silently and with no light. He would laugh, if anyone commented on it. How do you think I lived for all those years, with the British after me? He would ask. Once you learn to see in the dark, it never leaves you.

Once the elections have come, and gone, maybe then I shall sleep, he promised himself, without really believing it. Or maybe when the Jembe business is finally resolved.

His intelligence advisers had told him about the announcement of this General Harris coming out to help the Defence. Kenya's High Commissioner in London thought the General must be a publicity seeker, but the Acting President knew differently. Something the General had said had struck home. About standing shoulder to shoulder against a common enemy. The Acting President understood the General, and respected him, as he had respected many of the British officers he had fought. The way the General talked about Miles was the way the Acting President thought about Jembe. They were both old warriors, who knew where their duty lay, and if the fulfilment of that duty was going to be painful, for themselves or for others, well, they were sorry, but that's how things had to be.

The Acting President wondered briefly whether he should invite the General to a reception at State House, but as quickly dismissed the idea. It would be just one more confused message in an already muddled situation. Better to let the battle lines be drawn, and the traditional stances taken. There would be time later, if things turned out right, for grand gestures. For now, as back in those days, when they had been young, the fight, and the final victory, were all that really mattered.

PART III

CHAPTER TWENTY-THREE

Leo and Aliya took the Monday morning flight up to Nairobi. On arrival, they were met by a uniformed police inspector and two armed Askaris.

There had been death threats, the Inspector explained. The State had a responsibility to the British Government to ensure Aliya's well-being. It also had a duty which, the Inspector made clear, it accepted with much less enthusiasm, to safeguard Leo Kane. Henceforth, the two Askaris would escort them everywhere.

They went first to visit Tom.

"This is our expert?" Tom said, frowning slightly, and glancing doubtfully at Aliya as Leo Kane made the introductions.

Aliya smiled, and held on to the hand that he had extended after the handshake was complete. It was as dry as old parchment.

"I am indeed, Dr Miles," she said. "However, as I have already advised leading counsel, you are entirely free to dispense with my services. You will find I will not object in the least. Is that what you would like to do?"

"Are they treating you OK?" Leo cut in hastily. The last thing he wanted was to lose his potential navigator for the Charge. He was also worried about Tom. He'd seemed to have aged by a good ten years since they had last met a mere four days earlier.

"What?" said Tom, vaguely. "Oh yes. Not too bad."

"Have you been seen by a doctor?"

"No. Why?"

"I just wondered."

"You're very young," said Tom, returning his attention to Aliya.

"I'm ten years older than you were when you completed your military service in Kenya. Dr Miles, would you like me to go, or would you like to tell me about General Jembe?"

"It's all in the briefing notes . . ." said Leo.

"I've read the briefing notes," said Aliya, her stare not shifting from Tom's face. "If Dr Miles wishes to retain me I want to hear it from him. Tell me about the first time you saw Jembe."

Tom shrugged. "It was at a rally we were policing. A loyalist gathering in one of the Nairobi suburbs to demonstrate the strength of pro-British feeling. I don't remember exactly where. There were newsreel cameras and photographers there. It was during one of the phases when it looked like surrender talks might begin in earnest. The price on Jembe's head had been lifted, but we'd been told that if we saw him, or any of the other leaders, we were to search and detain them but on no account to prompt a firefight. He just appeared, briefly, in the middle of a part of the crowd which was jeering the loyalist speeches, and chanting the Mau Mau version of the national anthem.

They had this trick, you see. It took us ages to work it out. Ridiculous, really, when you look back. They'd all been taught Christian hymns at school, but translated into Kikuyu by missionaries. A language which none of us understood. So they would chant these hymns, but simply replace the name of Jesus with the name of Kenyatta, and any reference to the devil with the British. At this rally there were perhaps fifty men that kept forming up at different points in the crowd, chanting out their songs. Then if the security forces made any move towards them, they simply dispersed and then gathered again somewhere else in the crowd.

When I thought I saw Jembe, I sent one of my men off to

get a Special Branch officer – there were half a dozen of them, sitting in cars in the side road, ready to move in if necessary. This fellow came, and I pointed out the man I thought was Jembe. Just as I pointed, Jembe turned, and saw me pointing at him. He smiled, and waved, like we were old friends, and then simply disappeared."

"And that officer was Edward Foss?" asked Aliya.

"That's right."

I am standing on the bonnet of the Land Rover, legs apart, binoculars to my eyes, scanning the crowd. I am not looking for anything in particular. Guns, or trouble, I suppose I would say if anyone had asked me. But actually, I am just killing time.

There's another ceasefire. Nothing's happening. It's several months after Anvil. Weeks before my posting to C.A.T.12. I, like everyone else, am just waiting. Waiting. Waiting.

That's the thing about being a soldier that no one ever tells you. The sheer bloody boredom. Hours and hours, and then more hours of sitting around, half hoping that you're not going to be needed, but half hoping that you will, simply to interrupt the tedium.

That's how it was at that moment. I probably cut a pretty sharp figure, up here, I think. After all, I am young, tall, and in good health. My uniform is freshly pressed, my leathers highly polished.

The sun warms me; I feel good. I have just decided to sign on for an extra year. Although I am staring through binoculars into the crowd, my thoughts are all about the future. Miles away.

Three days before, I got a letter telling me that I'd applied too late for a place at medical school but as I am on National Service, I'll be given priority for the start of the next academic year.

That's why I've decided to sign on again. What's the alternative? How can I just go home? Just sit around at my parents' house, watching the grass grow, after what's happened? I think maybe if I hang on a while I might be able to put right what went wrong in Anvil.

Although I'm still not clear about the right, and wrong, of it.

I am daydreaming. Feeling warm, and good. No one expects any trouble. I've even sent my lads off, in twos, for a smoke.

Then I see him. General Jembe.

He is staring straight at me. It's as though he was waiting for my gaze to fall on him. They are all wearing hats. Trilbies are particularly popular among the Africans, and they all seem to wear them, pulled down low over their eyes.

He takes his hat off, half in greeting, and half in challenge. It's the scar down the side of his face that makes me positive it's him.

They've got this kind of routine when they're trying to evade our efforts to track one of them down. They swap hats, as they move through a crowd, so it's virtually impossible to keep track of them. They're smart, but I am determined not to lose sight of him. Not that he's trying to avoid my stare very hard at all.

Without lowering my glasses, I shout for my NCO and send him to fetch a Special Branch Man.

I keep watching him, not even looking away when Foss arrives.

"Where is he?" Foss hisses.

I point him out, but it takes Foss a while to spot the man I mean. There are several of them aware of what's going on by then. It's become a kind of game: they know we could never get to them before they could get away. Three or four of them start to taunt us, waving their hats, jeering and whistling, then Foss says, "I've got him."

We both continue to keep him in our sights.

"Grin, you fucker," Foss mutters. "Yes, that's right. Laugh, nigger. I'll see you spill your guts before this is over."

Then Jembe simply disappears. Folds back into the crowd. Foss and I drop our glasses, and Foss looks at me.

"You're the one, aren't you?" he says.

148

Suddenly I'm not scared anymore. "That's right," I say, meeting the challenge. "I'm the one."

"Do you know this man?" asked Leo Kane, showing Tom the front page of the daily sponsoring 'Hack 'em' Harris' visit.

Tom squinted at the image of the general. "I don't think so."

"You never knew him? Never served under a man named Harris?"

"Not that I recall."

"Well it looks like he's on his way to stand by you, whether we like it or not."

"I seem to be spoilt with people I didn't invite wanting to stand by me. Do you intend to have him give evidence?"

Leo shrugged. "It depends how well he comes over. He looks like a bit of a maverick; he's not an establishment figure, and that could be a help. He was out here during the Emergency, and that's useful too, as long as there's nothing very embarrassing in his background.

"The fact that he came out again after Independence, and it says here received the personal thanks of Kenyatta for his contribution, could be very valuable. He might be useful for drawing Paul Muya's fire; taking some of the heat away from you. I'll talk to him. Then we'll decide."

There was a pause, then Tom turned to Aliya. "I'm sorry," he said. "We started badly. I'm just . . ."

"It's OK," Aliya assured him. "I understand."

"Thank you," said Tom. "I'm just . . ." he said again but he left the sentence unfinished. "My family were here. It was . . ."

"We're going to see Sandford," said Leo, uncomfortably, recalling Tom's thoughts from far away. "Tomorrow."

"He's still out here?" said Tom, surprised.

"Where else would he be?" asked Leo. "He's a Kenyan."

"I thought . . ."

"Yes?"

"Oh, I don't know. Where is he?"

"In some kind of a home in Naivasha."

149

"Is there anything in particular we should ask him?" Aliya asked "Apparently he's a bit, you know, muddled."

Tom thought for a moment. "You could ask him about his dog, Hero. Or the day I shot the bamboo. Or what he told me about the two types of killing competitions. Yes, ask him about that."

CHAPTER TWENTY-FOUR

I'd forgotten all about the killing competitions . . . I remember it so clearly, now. Yet I'll bet if someone had asked me about it yesterday, I'd have denied any recollection of what Johnny Sandford said that day. Odd, really, how memory works.

"Let me tell you something," says Johnny. We are heading back to camp. We are up high, and it's cold. Soon it will be dark. "You watch the wildlife, and you'll see that there are only two types of killing competition. The first is the fight between the hunter and the hunted. If the hunter doesn't make a kill, he starves to death. If he does, then the hunted dies. It's deadly serious, but it's not personal. Do you understand? The hunter will exert only so much energy in the pursuit of his targeted victim. He works out a complex equation – a calculation which sets the energy expended and the risks incurred in the hunt against the calorific value of the prey. If the victim is too fit, fast or strong, he gives up, and they both walk away. The hunter isn't obsessed with the death of his prospective victim or determined to achieve a kill at all costs and at any risk. He doesn't hate his prey. He just does what he's there to do. Quickly, cleanly and efficiently. That's us. You and me."

"And the second kind?" I ask.

"That's a fight for territory: for a place to breed, and make a home. And that's personal. Passionately personal. You'll see two male bush-bucks gore each other to death, rather than give ground. You'll see rival packs of hyena rip each other to shreds, until neither pack is viable."

"And that's Mau Mau?"

"Yep, that's Mau Mau. It's the settlers too. Men like Ted Foss. That's what makes his sort different from you and me. For them, this is personal. Always remember, we're the professionals. We may be professional killers sometimes, but it is never, ever, personal. All our professional skills are engaged in the pursuit, but not our emotions or our passions. This is what we have been trained to do. When it becomes personal, we become vulnerable. We lose the right to keep the peace. And we become a liability to those around us. Always remember that, and you'll get through."

CHAPTER TWENTY-FIVE

Leo and Aliya separated for a couple of hours, each with a police officer at their side, to attend to a few personal matters.

Leo and his shadow, whose name, he learnt, was Tyson, headed out to the compound where the purple Land Rover was garaged.

"You know much about these vehicles?" Leo asked his protector as he pulled back the tarpaulin sheet that covered it.

Tyson grinned. "Nice colour."

Leo gave him a hard stare; was he taking the piss?

He wasn't. Tyson walked round the vehicle, touching the paintwork here and there, admiring the finish. He was, Leo guessed, in his late twenties. His hair was cut fashionably short, shaved at the back. His skin was the colour of the earth, up on the Escarpment, a rich, deep black. His eyes shone with life and enthusiasm, and he had a habit, with thinking, of slowly licking his upper lip.

He looked hungrily at the Land Rover.

Leo smiled. "Do you drive?"

Tyson nodded.

"What about your mate? What's his name?"

"Joseph. Joseph drives too."

"Fancy an outing?"

They drove back into town. They had agreed to meet Aliya and Joseph at a pizzeria on Kimathi Avenue.

When they arrived Aliya and Joseph were already seated. Aliya was staring disconsolately into a half glass of coke.

Leo sat down.

"You look glum," he said.

"I went to visit my relatives. To drop off some gifts from my folks."

153

"Oh yeah. The distant cousins. How did it go?"

"It was . . . uncomfortable. They didn't seem that glad to see me."

"I don't blame them. I wouldn't have been either if I were them. Have you ordered yet?"

He beckoned Joseph to join them and ordered a round of beers.

"When I was a teenager," he continued when the drinks arrived. "The Air Force attempted a coup. It failed. It was all over in a matter of hours. But the mob came out. Raped, burned and looted their way through the suburbs where the Asians lived. It was weird for quite a while after. Dusk to dawn curfew. Troops on the streets. When you drove through a shopping precinct, you'd see every African-owned shop untouched. Even the plate glass windows intact. Whilst every Asian duka was looted and gutted. I don't blame your relatives for feeling threatened by your presence. You add to their profile at an uncertain time. Anyway," he said, looking at the menu, "put it all behind you. Pack yourself full of pizza, cos we're off on an adventure."

Aliya eyed him warily. "What sort of an adventure?"

"One totally legit and all chargeable to the British taxpayer. We need to talk to Sandford, right?"

"Right."

"And you said you wanted to have a look at where it all happened, didn't you? No? Oh. I could have sworn you said you did. Oh well, too late now. After lunch, we're going to take the Land Rover and head off up to Nyeri, overnight there then next morning cross the Aberdares to South Kinangop, just as Tom and this man Foss did, and try and find the shamba where Jembe got whacked. We've got the map reference, so it shouldn't be too hard. Then down to Naivasha, see Sandford and back into Nairobi by Wednesday lunch time latest. OK?"

Leo smiled with exaggerated innocence, and Joseph was grinning and nodding as Tyson whispered to him in Ki-Swahili. Aliya was sure they were up to something, but couldn't work out what. Leo waved over a waiter, and ordered.

154

"We're taking your Land Rover?" Aliya asked.

"Of course! We'll need a four by four to tackle those roads. It'll be cheaper than hiring a vehicle. Think of it as an economy measure. No pepperoni, right?"

"This wouldn't have anything to do with the Charge, would it?"

Leo spread his hands and let his jaw hang loose in a gesture of exaggerated innocence. "We'll be going through the area we *may* be driving across in the Charge, yes. But that's just coincidence. The guys here are on duty, and so are we. So we can charge the mileage, as well as our time. What's the problem?"

She relaxed, and sank back in her seat. "I'm not promising to do any of the driving . . ."

"No problem! The guys and I will take turns."

The first of the pizzas arrived. Leo rubbed his hands together. "Let's get stuck in. The sooner we get started, the better. By the way, how did Tom Miles strike you?"

"Pretty vague," Aliya said, through a mouthful of margherita.

Leo nodded. "He was, wasn't he? He seems to have a genius for half-truths and vague memories. But he wasn't as bad as this before. He was perfectly clear about what was going on, and seemed very much more in control of what he said and what he didn't."

"The visit from his family clearly upset him. And, he's of an age where dementia could be an issue. This can't have been easy for him."

"Yeah. I think we need to have him checked over. Who knows? We may even be able to argue he's not fit to stand trial on medical grounds. I'll get someone at my Chambers to arrange it. Also, I want to send someone round to ask him to recall everything he can about Foss, and anyone else who was at or near the shamba that night."

Aliya frowned. "You think there might be something that we've missed?"

"Not really," Leo admitted, "but did you notice how his concentration clicked back in when we started talking about

155

Sandford? It might help to keep his wandering thoughts grounded a bit. I'll pop into Sena and get that organised while you and Joseph go and get us some maps. OK?"

He slipped his mobile phone from his pocket. "I'll just let my ex-wife know where I'll be for the next few days. Just in case . . ."

Leo had intended to be no more than five minutes in his Chambers, however, as invariably happened, he got drawn into the day's current crises, and when Aliya and Joseph, with an armful of maps, came for him, Kapadia greeted her like a long lost daughter. After 20 minutes of attempts to identify common acquaintances in fast Gujarati, and assurances that she would come home for dinner when they returned to Nairobi, and meet his wife and children, they finally set off.

The encounter made her feel a lot better. Welcome, briefly, for the first time since her arrival.

Kapadia walked her to the reception, told Leo to make sure he looked after her properly, and then treated their bodyguards to a three minute harangue in Ki-Swahili about their responsibility for Aliya's well-being and the dire fate he would ensure awaited them if he heard of the slightest dereliction of duty. He sniffed their breaths, caught the hint of beer, and listed the senior officers with whom he was on first-name terms to back up everything he'd said.

In all, they were well over an hour behind schedule by the time they eventually set off.

They got to Nyeri shortly after sunset. The White Rhino where Leo had planned to stay was closed for redecoration so they booked instead into the more luxurious, and expensive, Outspan Hotel. There was an embarrassing five minutes during which a debate ensued about whether Tyson and Joseph could sleep in the drivers' quarters, but both were quite clear about their instructions to remain close to Leo and Aliya, and were keen to enjoy the facilities of the hotel which in normal circumstances was light years beyond their meagre salaries.

"What the hell?" Leo concluded finally. "It's all chargeable.

156

Give us four rooms together. And first thing tomorrow, it's into the Aberdares."

The Aberdares and Mount Kenya – the prohibited areas in which we are authorised to shoot to kill without warning – must be among the most remarkable places in the world. For centuries, accounts of snow-capped peaks on the equator were dismissed as fanciful tales, told by charlatans to entertain the gullible. Such places, the savants confidently assured themselves, simply could not exist.

There is still something unbelievable about the place. A primeval forest where the palm and the pine grow side by side. Twelve hours tropical day; twelve hours arctic night. A scorching summer and a bitter winter every 24 hours. Every day since forever, for forever.

The Kikuyu believe their god, Ngai, lives on, or is, Mount Kenya. They pray towards it. Having seen it, at dawn, when the light seems to seep into the mountain and bleach the darkness out of it until it glows, I can understand why. This is a formidable place of bleak faith and acid beauty. Sometimes dark, forbidding and terrible, sometimes gorgeous, lush and generous – a vision of Eden. It is easy here to believe one is in the close proximity of an awesome deity.

I am out on patrol, with Johnny Sandford. As usual. There is a stark, absolute quiet. That's usual too. It is cold. Bloody cold. Again, nothing new. When you are lower down, especially at the coast, it is impossible to imagine how bitterly cold it can be in the Aberdares. When you are up here, you have to keep reminding yourself you are in Africa.

It is a normal day for us. Entirely normal. Routine.

We stop for a breather. We have chocolate. I break up a couple of bars and pass it around. We are silent, as we check. My attention is absorbed by a rotten branch on the ground beside me: its bark is still perfect, but the wood within is little more than white powder. Delicate filaments, weightless as a spider's web, dust-dry and fragile as spun sugar. I think, not for the first time, that for all the misery around me and the heavy, repetitive condemnation of the memory of Anvil, I am physically at my peak. I have never been, and I am pretty sure never again will be, so fit, strong and in tune with my body. I move easily, and can keep going for longer than I would ever have believed possible. I feel a deep, inner tranquillity that comes with well honed, tested muscles. It is a moment of consummate ease. Peace.

Then I catch a flash of black and white above me and I see the first Colobus monkey, wild eyed, come hurtling down from the high branches from which they normally regard us with a wary detachment. Then a second, and a third, carrying its young. They practically throw themselves down, and scuttle along the ground to where we lay, amazed. They look vaguely ludicrous, close to, with their long black and white fur alive with ticks and nits. Like a comic wig come to life, or the result of a horrific experiment. A bonding of a long-haired cat, and a man. Their teeth chatter and they shiver with an abject terror.

They cringe at our sides and we are mystified by the stark absurdity of their behaviour. The African Rifles have seen nothing like it, although they have been in the forest for many months. They are, frankly, scared. Their eyes widen. One giggles nervously. Another swears, half rising. A third looks to Johnny for some explanation, but he has nothing to offer. I am struck by how perfectly formed are the tiny hands of the creature nearest to me as it clasps desperately at nothing.

Only the de-oathed Mau Mau, our pseudo terrorists, fellow creatures of these forests, understand. One touches a finger to his lips, and then cups his hand to his ear. Silently, obediently, we listen.

Then we catch a distant drone. A throb in the air which grows until it reverberates off the hills and trembles through the trees and the whole forest resonates with it so that we too begin to cringe and cover our ears. Amidst this din, a myriad of creatures screech and wail. Then the bombers – vast, cumbersome Lincolns – sweep directly overhead.

The sound declines, and gives way a few minutes later to the

*dull whump of distant bombing. Johnny Sandford shakes his
head sadly at the destructive futility of it all. The African Rifles
laugh, tension easing, and make a joke in Swahili that's too fast
for me to catch, as the pseudo terrorists, who prize the Colobus
pelts highly, methodically club the petrified monkeys to death.*

*Strangest of all, not one of the monkeys flees. Still paralysed,
they submit. As though they prefer a brutal death at the hands
of a man to the incomprehensible horrors of the bomb.*

The next morning, Leo, Aliya and their bodyguards set off
at dawn, entered the Park through the Ruhuruini Gate, and
climbed steadily, up through the bamboo belt, and onto the
central moorland.

It reminded Aliya of Dartmoor. Tussocks of tough grass.
Bleak, boggy marshes. High, empty skies.

The Park authorities insisted they took a Ranger with them
for protection, much to the chagrin of Tyson and Joseph, who
seemed to feel that their manhood had been called into question.
The three Africans sat in hostile silence in the rear of the vehicle.
The two policemen cradling automatic weapons, and the Ranger
his ancient rifle. As they drove, they saw no other vehicle, and
little sign of life, other than brilliantly coloured birds that darted
low over the rough ground. More than once, Aliya held her
breath as a scarlet-tufted malachite sunbird, its long, slender tail,
and its feathers emerald green, flashed across their path.

She had never seen Leo Kane so focused, so intent. This, she
surmised, must be the part of the job on which he thrived. The
investigation of the facts on the ground. Although even that
scarcely seemed to justify his avid note taking. He bombarded
the bemused Park Ranger with questions about watercourses,
game tracks, drainage and terrain. Every half mile or so he
called a halt and jumped down, to study the ground or examine
a distant mound through powerful binoculars.

When she too stepped down to stretch her legs she found the
ground beneath her feet marshy, soft. It was a harsh, forbidding,
empty place. For Leo, she assumed, anywhere this far up from

the coast was to be regarded with a jaundiced eye, and Tyson and Joseph, committed city boys both, also seemed to find the vast openness oppressive. Ironically, only Aliya felt at ease and Leo fell silent as she chatted with the Park Ranger about good treks, common hazards and the joys of a night under canvas. They paused at the Chania Falls to consume the packed lunch the hotel had supplied them with and drove down the serpentine road that took them round the side of the Kinangop to the scene of the alleged crime.

There Aliya, to her quiet satisfaction, impressed even the Park Ranger with her map reading skills by taking them, with barely a hesitation, to the shamba.

It had been abandoned many years before. The land around it had been absorbed into the periphery of neighbouring holdings. The remains of the burnt out building could just be made out, and the small pile of stones that had been stacked up as some kind of memorial.

There was nothing for them there. They headed on to Naivasha, and checked in at the lodge shortly before sunset.

They agreed it was too late by then to visit Johnny Sandford. They rang the hospital to make arrangements to call round the next morning, only to be told that, sadly, he had passed away, just the previous night.

As Leo and Aliya had lingered over coffee on the veranda of the Outspan the night before, and their guardians had drunk one too many Tusker beers, Johnny Sandford had lain in his bed in a retirement home on the other side of the Aberdares, propped up by three pillows to ease his laboured breathing. There was a plastic sheet beneath him and wadding was packed around his withered loins. The room smelt of old age, stale urine, cheap disinfectant and the talcum powder his sole relative – a niece in Canada – sent every Christmas. His eyes were half closed, their corners caked with white matter. His left hand skipped and trembled in constant erratic motion above the single sheet which covered him.

160

It was late. Into the early hours, but a bedside light was on for he was troubled by the dark. A Tommy Tippee child's cup with a sipping lid filled with mango juice and water was placed beneath the bedside light next to a plastic bowl. Every two hours, a nurse would enter, ease him forward and thump his back to loosen the phlegm which he dutifully coughed up into the bowl. Then he would be given a sip of juice. For months, his cough had been the only indication of his awareness of a world around him.

He still had a fine head of hair, which one of the nurses took great pride in combing every evening before going off duty. They used to leave a radio playing in his room, but when the batteries had faded six months earlier he hadn't seemed to notice so no one had bothered to replace them.

He had no medication now, and had not eaten solids for several weeks.

At 1.13 am, the night sister checked on him, tried unsuccessfully to get him to sip some juice, and continued on her rounds.

At 1.55 am, a man in a white coat entered. Carefully closing the door behind him, he waited for a moment, seemingly getting his bearings, before moving to Johnny Sandford's side. He reached out, to ease Sandford forward and the old man coughed. The man in the white coat recoiled in surprise. Regaining his composure as Sandford showed no further awareness of his presence, he placed one hand in the middle of Sandford's back to prop him up, and then removed one of the pillows. He gently eased the old man back and placed a pillow over his face.

When the night sister returned at 2.42 am, Sandford lay as she had left him. Everything in the room was just as she had seen it before, but she was immediately struck by the silence and the stillness. His palsied left hand lay motionless on the sheet.

Major John Wynn Sandford, King's African Rifles (retired) was declared dead by a yawning Sikh doctor at 3.35 am.

A blessed release, everyone agreed.

CHAPTER TWENTY-SIX

You were wrong, Johnny, when you told me there were only two types of killing competition. I realise that now. You told me to watch the game, out on the Savannah, and I did. But I also watched the game in the Aberdares. Like you, I saw the elephant, the buffalo and rhino, wild-eyed, and driven mad by the bombing so that ever afterward they would charge a tree, or a rock, and beat their own brains out at the first clap of thunder.

I think I started to realise it then, but it has only really come home to me now. Now that you're gone, too.

There's a third killing competition: one which defies your analysis. It's the killing of those creatures crazed by the violence. Their behaviour is not defined by the laws of nature, because what's happened to them is not natural. They are an abomination. An aberration. Because of what's happened to them, their understanding of the world has gone all awry. I'd seen it, and so had you, but we didn't realise what we were watching. Not then.

Did you recall in later years, that day, when the monkeys climbed down out of the trees, and laid, shivering, beside us. At the first sound of an aircraft, so distant that we couldn't even hear it? Crazy, unnatural things. We should have known it, you and I, because we'd seen it. The lion should lay down with the lamb, not when the Kingdom of God is at hand, but when the Lincolns had bombed the simple reason out of the natural world.

That was the madness of the rhino that first day. The madness of the monkeys.

It was also the madness of Ted Foss. You didn't know that, because I never told you. But I did, and I think you might have sensed it, too.

Did you?

PART IV

CHAPTER TWENTY-SEVEN

The High Court building in Nairobi, like the law practised within it, pre-dated independent Kenya. The dark, panelled courtrooms, the judge's chambers. The split wooden direction signs with their faded gold lettering. The robing rooms. The overgrown courtyards. The notice boards honeycombed with pinholes on which the daily Cause Lists were posted and the broken benches labelled *For Advocates Only*. All proclaimed the dignity of age amidst the shabby melancholy of indifferent care.

A sea of complainants, witnesses, respondents and victims daily surged and churned through its corridors, leaving a grubby tide mark at shoulder height on the flaking green emulsion paint. Gowned and bewigged figures clutching ribbon-bound briefs thrust imperiously through them. Bent old men in the traditional garb of their various tribes, sporting heavy, significant jewellery, doggedly searched for their hearings – their withered old legs bare, their sandaled feet dusty. Outside, traffic roared, horns blared and touts shouted.

Built from red sandstone with broad stairways and Doric columned entrances, the High Court sat four-square and solid beneath its tiled roofs, the very heart and uneasy conscience of Nairobi, overlooking a dusty park of scorched grass, enlivened only by bright litter tumbling lightly across it in the easy breeze. The building seemed to stare out, world-weary and baleful, at the sheer cliff faces of steel and mirrored glass that towered around it, as though despising them, with the confident superiority of its colonial builders. But it was with a broken-winded and rheumy-eyed arrogance, for its own glory had faded over the decades. The authorities had proven themselves as indifferent to maintaining the fabric of the building as they had to preserving the principles for which it stood. Its courtrooms were still cleaned and the benches regularly polished but, behind the facade, the floors of its registries were awash with un-filed judgments and lost dockets. Its exhibit rooms were a dusty clutter of unlabelled pangas, simis, iron bars and flick knives and the awesome reek of its public toilets could be caught 50 yards away.

The case of the Republic vs Miles (for, even though this was a private prosecution, form dictated it be pursued in the name of the Republic) was posted for Court 3 – one of the smallest in the building yet the scene of many a previous cause célèbre. Superficially the reason was simple: it was nearest to the side entrance. It was thus preferred for the more dramatic cases for it ensured that the cameras, crowds of sightseers and the heightened security arrangements such cases always attracted need not penetrate deeper into the building and intrude upon other, more sedately paced proceedings.

As with most aspects of public life in Kenya, there was a more subtle reasoning at work beneath the surface: the size of the court justified a tight restriction being placed on the number of spectators – a fact that the State had found particularly useful in the past. As a result, there was fierce competition for access to the trial of Tom Miles.

The atmosphere in the corridors around Court 3 was one of tense and almost inappropriately cheerful anticipation among the reporters, diplomats and legal observers who, by a myriad means, had secured entry. In the Robing Room, Paul and Leo said little to one another. Neither was much in the mood to talk, particularly as – by convention – conversations in the Robing Room were always conducted with the false heartiness of an English public school.

Kenya's lawyers, judges and court officials had not only adopted, with few subsequent adaptations, English law, but they had also taken to themselves many of the traditions, conventions and conceits of the English Bar. One of these was that a tattered gown and bedraggled wig, like the nicks and chips on a samurai's armour, proclaimed an advocate's hard won experience and years of successful combat. Paul Muya's gown was faded, at odds with his otherwise fastidious appearance, but well cared for. His horse hair wig was discoloured with the passage of time, but appeared near pristine compared to Leo's, which had a good decade of further wear and tear distressed out of it. The difference was surprising, given that Paul had qualified years before Leo. Paul was not alone in suspecting that the dramatic ageing Leo's wig underwent in his first few years at the Bar proclaimed more eloquently the effects of overnight soaking in cold tea than extensive adversarial experience.

Elsewhere in the Robing Room attorneys were sharing a joke, smoking a final cigarette, or chatting amiably about golf, tennis, the cost of phone rental. Good drivers. Dogs and blood lines.

Leo looked around with something like love for these people and this place.

There was Charlie Monkton and Billy Kimoni, horsing around, as usual. Monkton was grumbling about his losses in the casino. And over in the corner of the room, Nick Fried-lander and Harvinder Singh were locked in a conspiratorial huddle, close as lovers, talking tactics for the Charge, which was now less than a week away.

Leo felt a sudden, overwhelming kinship swell within him: a love for these, his learned friends and fellow Chargers. These men, of different races and widely varied backgrounds with whom he had shared the past twenty years or more. He had a strong sense too that this, just like the Charge, was all coming to an end. That what was about to happen in Court 3 would sound the swansong of something which until now he had taken entirely for granted and never really valued. Yet the sudden contemplation of its loss struck him with an intensity that took him completely by surprise.

It welled inside his chest with the bitter magnificence of the end of a glorious affair. He felt as he had on his last day at university, or when he finally realised his marriage was over.

169

Light-headed and cast adrift, scared yet excited. Free, yet with a large part of him aching for a safety that until then he had dismissed merely as confinement. He wanted to slap backs, shake hands and wish everyone well, but then realised that though they occupied the same time and space, they may as well have been in another dimension. For them, this was just another day.

"Friedlander, you bastard," he roared across the room to force this oppressive sense of foreboding from him. "Five hundred says you don't make it to the end."

"A thousand says you don't, Cokey," Friedlander called back, cheerily.

"You're on. This is gonna be our Charge this year."

"The Charge?" said Friedlander, aping innocence. "Oh sorry, old mate. I was talking about your trial."

Leo and Paul strode to Court 3, side by side, in silence, indifferent to the baying reporters around them.

Aliya was already there, gowned and wigged, waiting.

Leo smiled, when he saw her. "Why, Miss Zain!" he cried. "You look quite fetching!"

"You look different too," Aliya said, after she had been introduced to Paul Muya.

Leo shrugged, modestly. "More dignified? Dashing? Statesmanlike?"

"Fatter."

Paul laughed, and everyone around smiled, as they invariably did, when the Total Man was amused.

Leo glared at both of them. "I think we have rather more important matters to engage us than personal appearance, don't you?" he said, glancing at his watch.

As they prepared to make their way into Court, Paul paused and held out his hand. "Good luck, Coke," he said, softly.

"Break a leg, Paul," said Leo, shaking his hand.

Five minutes later, Tom Miles was brought up.

The Chief Justice sat erect, beneath the coat of arms of Kenya.

The Bible, the Koran and the Oxford English Dictionary lay side by side on the bench before him. His face, already glistening with sweat under his bench wig, was impassive, his eyes expressionless behind dark-framed glasses. His mouth, with its corners permanently turned down might have been registering disapproval, or impatience, or then again might merely have been set in such glum reflection by the lies, ugliness, and simple vicious pettiness he had heard recounted in his two decades on the bench.

The Chief Justice leaned forward, his left hand resting on his notebook, whilst the right was in constant motion, recording verbatim all that was said in a cramped scrawl that was the bane of the High Court typist's life. Every so often he would clear his throat softly and the clerk would halt in mid-sentence to allow him to catch up.

A brief nod would indicate that he might continue.

After the charge was read and the 'not guilty' plea entered, there was a palpable sense of anti-climax as the court settled to a range of necessary but unglamorous preliminaries. Paul Muya introduced his team: four other attorneys from his Chambers, including Marianne Kane. Leo introduced Aliya and offered the Bench her certificate of membership of the Kenya Bar.

The Chief Justice was fulsome in his welcome to Aliya, assuring her of his determination to make her feel completely at home. Paul was quickly on his feet to add the Prosecution's welcome: it was all so polite, courteous and refined.

The rest of the morning was given over to the selection of Assessors.

Prior to Independence, Africans were arraigned before a white Magistrate with three native Assessors to judge fact and advise on local custom whilst Europeans would have been tried before twelve good men and true – and white. The most significant change in procedure following Independence was the removal of that privilege. Thereafter, all major trials, whatever the race of the accused, were conducted by a judge sitting with Assessors.

171

Six potential Assessors had been summoned to attend court, drawn from a list compiled in consultation with the Provincial Administration. People whom the nominating authorities – government ministries and the like – were satisfied met the basic qualification: an adult aged between twenty-one and sixty, leading an ordinary life. The first two, both men, were middle-aged, solidly built, serious individuals who seemed determined not to be overawed by the events in which chance had caught them up. The first was sharply dressed, in an expensive lime green suit, white shirt and bright tie. His hair was salt and pepper grey, and he wore gold-framed spectacles, an expensive watch and heavy rings on three fingers of his left hand. His name identified him, to Leo and Paul, as a Luo. The second was less well dressed. His jacket was ill-fitting and shiny at the elbow and the shoulder. The collar of his shirt was frayed, and he wore no tie. His head was shaved, and his face round. A coast Muslim.

Of each, the Chief Justice asked the ritual questions: Did they know the accused? Did they know anything about the circumstances of the offence? Both acknowledged having read newspaper accounts of Tom Miles' arrest and of having heard of Paul Muya and General Jembe, but nothing more.

Leo and Paul accepted them both.

Third up was a Hindu. Nervous, and seeming desperate to please. Leo objected to his inclusion, and he was, to his evident relief, discharged.

Next on the list was a woman: older than the two men, thin and striking. Her skin had the deep, rich tone of the highlander. She wore little jewellery, and no make-up. Her near-white hair was brushed back and tied in a no-nonsense little bun. Her long neck and sharply defined features gave her a fragile look. A large pair of spectacles perched on the tip of her nose. She was delicate, bird-like in her movements. She answered the Chief Justice confidently, and Leo immediately took a shine to her. "She'll do nicely," he whispered to Aliya, as he rose to accept her.

The Chief Justice explained the Assessor's role to them, and asked them if they understood. They confirmed that they did.

172

The Judge turned to Paul Muya and nodded. "The Republic may open its case."

Paul Muya's warmth, charm and innate decency were deployed in full measure as soon as he began his opening address. He spoke in a deep, rich voice that was a pleasure to listen to. His words, well formed, and impeccably chosen, were of a rhythm and intonation that marked him clearly as a Kenyan. I may have been educated abroad, his accent seemed to say, but I'm a Wananchi – a citizen – one hundred percent.

"My Lord, on the last day of April, 1955," he began, "a man died in a shamba in South Kinangop. That man was Wilson Mumbu Muya. He was known, to comrades and enemies alike, as General Jembe. It was a violent time. Many thousands of our people died. What was so special about this man?

"Well, for me, he was special because he was my father. Had he lived, historians of all political persuasions agree he would have taken a leading role in an independent Kenya. I was robbed of that father. He was robbed of that future. Our nation was robbed of that man.

"We will show that this death was an extra-judicial execution carried out with profound brutality. We will demonstrate how the accused, Miles, with his compatriots, hunted down and slaughtered this man who was no longer a threat to them but whom they killed simply to rob this country of a future leader.

"So how did it come about that Wilson Mumbu Muya's life bled away on a distant hillside on the last hours of that last day of a far past April? Taken unarmed, shot in cold blood and allowed to perish slowly and in great pain without even the basic humanity of a quick death? We will show you the so-called Secret Circular No 10 that was my father's death warrant. We will demonstrate the full, calculated evil of this determined and premeditated slaughter."

Paul Muya's eyes shone, and his voice rose, trembling slightly with a preacher's passion. He thrust an accusing finger toward the Dock. "I charge this man Miles with war crimes and crimes against humanity. Some may say that it is inappropriate to base such grave charges on the unlawful killing of a single individual. They may say that those tried at Nuremberg, in Arusha and The Hague slaughtered hundreds, thousands, millions. But those who pose this argument fail to appreciate that such a crime is not defined quantitatively: there is no numerical threshold which the perpetrator must cross in order for his deeds to merit description as a crime against humanity. When John F Kennedy fell to an assassin's bullet, the entire world held its breath. The killing of such a one – the slaying of a Malcolm X, of a Martin Luther King, of a Mahatma Gandhi – is an event of such profound magnitude that it touches us all. We will demonstrate that the killing of my father was just such an event: a crime of war, against humanity. For with his death, a part of all our futures died. We will also show, beyond any shadow of a doubt, that this man Miles played a full, knowing, crucial part in that cruel and unnecessary act.

"The accused, Miles, stands alone today to face these charges. There are others, still alive, cowering in the shadows who should be in the dock with him. Their day of judgement, I give them notice now, approaches! But their absence today does not detract one iota from Miles' responsibility for my father's murder."

Leo, arms folded and chin tucked into his chest, leaned ever so slightly towards Aliya and whispered, "Do you notice how Paul studiously avoids calling Tom 'Dr Miles'? This is a country in which medics are held in high regard."

He rose, and with a little half gasp, a frown and a confused shake of his head, he began, "My Lord, I hesitate to interrupt my friend's opening oration, but my client has not as yet been found guilty of any crime. Surely he can be accorded the simple courtesy of being addressed by his name *and* the title of the profession that he has pursued, nobly and honourably, for the past forty years."

"I'm inclined to agree with you, Mr Kane," said the Chief Justice. "I would also be obliged, Mr Muya, if you could refer to the alleged victim by his name rather than by his relationship to you."

Paul bowed to the bench. "So be it, My Lord." Paul turned

174

to Tom. "The accused, Doctor Miles . . ." he said, as though trying it out for size.

Leo looked down, to hide a smile. There were times when his respect for the Total Man knew no bounds. Paul had placed heavy emphasis on the 'c' of doctor and dragged out the last syllable, – 'dock-tour' – making the word heavy with menace. Pronounced the way Paul had, it conjured up not decent, wholesome images of a country GP, in tweeds and stout shoes, toting his bag around the farms and villages of some picturesque landscape, but a white-coated demon in a death camp perpetrating ghastly experiments on helpless victims.

Yes, Leo mused, he could see how Paul Muya got to where he is today. If ever there was a man who could enslave language to serve his needs . . .

"I was but a few months old when Wilson Muya's life bled away into the rich soil of our beloved nation. Killed by this man, Doctor Miles. This country was robbed of a great and noble son. By this man, Doctor Miles. This, beyond a shadow of a doubt, the Prosecution will prove. We will present to you evidence from experts, who will explore for you the motives and motivation of this man, Doctor Miles."

Paul Muya, his chin trembling with emotion, turned once more from the bench to stare straight at Tom. "Look at this man!" he roared. "This old man, this kindly looking man. This gentle man. His hair is white, and his shoulders round. Age dignifies him. But we will show you a different Thomas Miles, before he was a doctor. Thomas Miles as he was, at that shamba in South Kinangop on that cold April night in 1955. We will peel back the intervening years! We will reconstruct for you those times and that place! And there, at last, you will see, revealed in the incandescence of this transformation, the vicious, complacent face of white colonialism!"

I sit here, and I watch my fate unfold around me. I watch this man, Muya, thrust his finger toward me, stabbing at me, accusing me of killing his father, and I think: he's a very fine speaker.

How can that be? Why am I not afraid of him? Why am I not angry?

I suppose it's because I've come to accept now that all this really is happening to me. When they first snatched me, and during that first terrible night in the police cell, I thought I was going mad. That my head would burst with the impossibility of understanding what was happening.

But now, after so many more such nights, it's become normal.

It's the rest of my life I can no longer conceive: not comprehend.

It's like the intervening years have never happened. Val. The kids. All the things we enjoyed together and all the things we fell out about. All the daily pressures and questions in the surgery. All the friends. The holidays, the joys and triumphs and tragedies of a normal life. Weddings and christenings. Bereavements. Val's decline. All boxed up and carted away, so that there's a clear, obvious and, it seems now, inevitable continuity between 1955 and today. As though nothing of any significance took place between that night in the shamba in South Kinangop and that night – was it only a few weeks ago – when they took me from that restaurant in Nairobi.

I watch the son, accusing me, but I see the father. In his eyes, and in his movements.

Jembe was a good looking man too, just like his son. He had the same bearing.

Both, through no wish of mine, are my enemies. They say I killed the father and now the son wants me destroyed.

How can you have enemies – literally, deadly enemies, and not hate them?

I suppose Paul Muya feels about me as we felt about his father. It was time for him to die. And there's an end to it.

"There's something I have to ask you," said Aliya, as they took lunch.

"Let me guess," said Leo, resigned. "Why did I discharge the Asian Assessor, right?"

She nodded.

"Simple. He was as much on trial as Tom Miles. If he spoke up on our behalf, everyone would simply dismiss that as some kind of Asian solidarity, or ethnic conspiracy. If he spoke up for the Prosecution, then he would simply be currying favour, no pun intended. Let's face it, poor old Tom's case is hardly aided by his skin colour, or yours, or mine. There are enough complex racial agendas at play in this matter already. The last thing we need is to add one more."

"It doesn't occur to you that he could simply have done his duty, like the others?"

Leo frowned as he checked through the plastic-wrapped sandwiches. "I doubt it, in the circumstances. Anyway, he hardly looked disappointed I turned him down, did he? Couldn't get out of the place fast enough. Look, we talked about this before, right? Indians here are living on borrowed time. Their every action, or inaction, is viewed with profound suspicion. Now what sandwich do you fancy? Chicken or egg and cress?"

"You're quite a racist, really, aren't you, Mr Kane?"

To her surprise, Leo laughed. "Not at all! Merely an observer and reflector of society around me. I would also have objected to a white or a Kikuyu Assessor for exactly the same reasons."

"Bullshit! You've made it perfectly clear you despise Asians. You said it yourself."

"Right, I'm having the chicken. And if you're ever going to amount to anything in this profession, you really must learn to listen to what people are saying before you launch into these ill-directed offensives! We talking about what Kenyan Asians are. That's quite different. On Asians as a whole, I have no view. Or if I do, it's a positive, rather affectionate one. I spent my honeymoon in Kashmir. I love Indian food. I think the Taj Mahal is magnificent. But if you really want to know, then yes, I think Asians in Kenya are a drain on the economy, a threat to our political stability and a danger to themselves. And in saying that, I do not discriminate in any way between Hindus, Muslims, Sikhs or Christians. As far as I'm concerned, the whole lot of them should take a long, hard look at themselves, and focus on what they want to be, who they think they are and where they think they're going."

"And being a white man, of course," snapped Aliya, "you have the advantage of being able to offer this view as a fully paid up member of a community whose behaviour has always demonstrated the highest standards. The kind of things we're going to be talking about in court: the extra-judicial executions. Hola Camp. The torture, the slaughter. They were all acts of some other, foreign entity I suppose?"

"Yes, that's absolutely right," agreed Leo, "and it's you that is being a racist, not me. Simply because I am white, you feel that gives you the right to group me with Sandford and Foss and the British Colonial administration? I am a Kenyan. I was born a Kenyan, and I will die a Kenyan. If I'm unlucky enough to die abroad, I'll have my body flown home. That's the difference. We white Kenyans are members of a minority tribe. These days it's *our* land that's being taken from us and given to others without any compensation. *Our* businesses which are subject to controls and regulations that do not apply to our more fortunate, black fellow citizens. Yet we remain loyal Kenyans. We have made, or are currently making, the transition. We are no longer the shielded protégés of a colonial bureaucracy. We are just another minority, hanging on, doing our best to contribute, and hoping for better times. Unlike, I am sorry to have to say, your lot."

"My heart bleeds! You poor things! Discriminated against, victimised and put upon. Nobly holding on, serving the country you love. Unappreciated, unloved. What utter crap! I'd like to know what the per capita wealth of your minority tribe is, compared to the rest of the population, or even compared to the Asian community. Hard times for your type means only one aeroplane per household and having the same houseboy serve the soup and the sherry."

Leo exploded in great guffaws of laughter, which eventually died away into a choking cough. He shook his head, and with the heel of his palm, wiped a tear from the corner of his eye. "Oh, that was very good! Beautifully put. You really are an absolute joy to have around."

Aliya's eyes flared. "You're not taking any of this seriously, are you?"

Leo frowned, a caricature of bewilderment. "You've lost me again. Do you mean this conversation, or the trial?"

"Either. Both. None of this is really important to you, is it?"

"Oh, both are extremely important to me. But if by taking things seriously you mean to ask whether I'm convinced of the truth of every word of my defence of us poor, hard-done-by white Kenyans or what will be my equally eloquent defence of Dr Miles, then no, I'm not. I am however sure there is justice in both."

"Isn't the truth all that really matters? Isn't that what this is all about?"

"No. It isn't the truth that matters. It's justice."

"Aren't they the same?"

"Sometimes, but not always. In fact, the older I get, the less the two seem to have to do with each other."

"You're playing with words again."

"No, on that occasion, I wasn't. But I forgive you for being unable to see the difference. Now, are you going to eat that sandwich or not?"

After lunch, Paul requested the Court's indulgence to change the order in which he called his witnesses. This, he explained was simply due to the poor health of their first expert who, it was hoped, would be well enough to take the stand the following day.

Leo assured the Court that he had no objection. "We can afford to be magnanimous at this stage," he murmured to Aliya. "We may be glad for a favour or two in payback later on."

The first of the reordered list of prosecution witnesses appeared. A plump, brisk man in his sixties who nodded affably to the bench, the prosecution and defence teams while waiting to be sworn in.

He wore a charcoal grey safari suit, the left breast pocket of which bulged with a swollen Filofax. He licked his lips, his tongue wide and pink, before reading the oath. As he handed the card back to the Clerk of the Court, he closed his eyes tight, clenched his interlocked fingers into a fat knot pressed tight to his chest, and cried "Oh Lord Jesus, guide my words today! Help me speak with wisdom and truth! Let not pride blind my vision! Amen!"

The witness opened his eyes wide, and smiled cheerfully at the Judge, who raised an eloquent eyebrow at the outburst. Paul Muya rose, to receive an equally encouraging beam.

"Your name is Philip J Kimeto?"

"It is."

"Can you tell me how you are employed, Sir?"

"I have the honour to be Professor of Modern History and the Chairman of the School of History at Moi University."

"And you've held that post since . . . ?"

"1992."

"Could you describe for me your academic background?"

The professor looked down, and smiled, almost bashfully. "I received my first degree, with honours in 1973. This was a Bachelor of Arts Degree in History from Kenyatta University. I then had the fortune to be a Rhodes Visiting Fellow in the University of Oxford. This was followed by an M.Phil. at the School of Oriental and African Studies, in the University of London. I received a Doctorate in 1986 from Nairobi University."

"What was the subject of your Master of Philosophy degree?"

"The Social and Economic Factors Governing the Conflicts of Interest in the White Highlands of Kenya from 1900 to 1970."

"And your PhD?"

"It was entitled 'The Rise and Demise of the Land and Freedom Army: A Structural Reinterpretation.'"

"Is the Land and Freedom Army known by any other title?"

180

"It is. It is generally, erroneously I would say, referred to as Mau Mau."

Throughout the Prosecution's opening questions, Aliya had been scribbling notes furiously. Leo leaned across, and laid a restraining hand on her arm. "Don't look too keen," he advised. "Look bored."

"Would you say you are an authority on Mau Mau?" Paul Muya continued.

"Oh no!" exclaimed the professor.

"No?"

"No. The Bible warns us to guard against pride. It is not for a man to judge his own worth."

Paul Muya could not resist catching Leo's eye and holding his stare for a moment, his eyes expressionless. Leo winked.

"Do others describe you as an authority?" Paul Muya persisted without any hint of exasperation.

The Professor nodded. "Frequently."

"Have you studied the counter-insurgency campaign in the Aberdares?"

"Yes. Such has been my special study."

"Are you familiar with the activities of the Security Forces in the winter of 1954 and spring of 1955?"

"I am."

Aliya leant forward, her fists clenched beneath her chin. Leo, watching the tension in her arched back, studiously slouched lower in his chair and yawned. Tom Miles sat, as he had throughout the morning, still and quiet. He didn't fidget, speak, or make any notes. It was as though he were in church, listening to a sermon on a subject of precious little interest and even less relevance to him.

"Professor, are you familiar with the hunt for Wilson Mumbu Muya, popularly known as General Jembe?"

"I am. I have a particular interest in this operation."

"And why is that?"

The Professor beamed indulgently at Paul. "For many reasons, but for two in the main. Firstly, your father . . ." The

Chief Justice cleared his throat, threateningly. The Professor glanced up guiltily, and apologised. "*General Jembe* was a figure of great potential political significance."

Leo rose, "My Lord, rivetingly interesting though this is, I fail to see its relevance. 'The potential political significance . . .' what has that got to do with anything? What does it even mean? Surely under our law the only questions are whether the alleged victim was unlawfully killed, and if so, by whom, and then whether that action constitutes a war crime. Whether the victim was a rich man, a poor man, a beggarman or a thief surely has no impact on the matter."

Paul Muya, who had nodded patiently throughout Leo's interruption, began. "Your Honour, it goes to motive. We hope to demonstrate why the Wazungu were so keen to see General Jembe dead . . ."

Leo threw up his hands in mock horror. "Oh My Lord, I really must protest! This is the second time my learned friend has made a blatantly racist observation. The first, out of courtesy, I let pass. But I cannot in all conscience hear my learned friend describe the Security Forces of Kenya in 1955, the overwhelming majority of whom were black African citizens, as white men. It is as offensive as it is inaccurate."

The Chief Justice removed his spectacles, and rubbed his remarkably delicate hands over his eyes.

"If the potential significance of General Jembe, had he survived, touches on motive, I will allow it. But I agree with Mr Kane's second point. I warn all parties to this matter to avoid ethnic, racial or tribal generalisations. Kenya is a multi-racial democracy, and it is the responsibility of us all to be sensitive to such matters. Would Counsel please approach the Bench?"

As Paul and Leo stood at the Bench, looking up like guilty but unrepentant schoolboys, Aliya smiled. She looked across to Tom, and mouthed "OK?"

Tom smiled bleakly, and nodded.

Leo returned to the defence table and sat.

"The Chief Justice can be quite witty when he puts his mind to it," he admitted, grudgingly.

"Why, what did he say?" asked Aliya.

Leo shifted his wig. "His exact words were that he considered Paul's opening remarks unnecessarily histrionic and politically motivated and my objections trivial and designed primarily to pander to the western press. Then he said he found the sight of us parading our respective talents reminiscent of a couple of dock-side pansies touting for trade when the fleet comes in. Finally, there was some stuff about the high standards of our profession."

Aliya smiled broadly. "Offensively homophobic, unacceptably sexist, but otherwise I'd say he was right on the mark."

"Oh good," said Leo, with another yawn. "I must remember to tell him his comments met with your approval. I'm sure he'll be massively interested in your opinion. He also asked us to dinner tonight."

"That's kind of him," said Aliya.

Leo glanced at her and shook his head. "When I said we, I meant Paul and I. The three of us are members of the Muthaiga Club."

"Oh," said Aliya, feeling clumsy, stupid and angry.

"Professor Kimeto," Paul continued, "you said there were two main reasons why the pursuit of General Jembe warranted particular interest."

"I did. The second was that it was a unique example of the combined operations mounted by the Security Services. At the time there were British regiments, the Royal Air Force, the King's African Rifles and Kenya Regiment, the Police, the Kenya Police Reserve and the Kikuyu Home Guard in action. All with different command structures, many accountable to different parts of Government. Liaison was poor, and discipline in many units a disgrace. In an attempt to bring about some form of cohesion, a small number of joint units were formed, called Combined Action Teams or C.A.T. Units. In total, 23 such units were created, although many only existed on paper. Approximately seven were functioning military units, and of these, only two or three actually took part in any direct operations against the Land and Freedom Army. The remainder devoted their energies to . . ."

Leo was on his feet in a flash. "Your Honour, the activities of these other groups are surely of no interest to this court."

"Sustained," sighed the Judge. "Mr Muya, please help your witness to focus on issues directly relevant to this case. Professor, please try and confine your answers to matters which we are here to address."

With a nervous, giggled apology, the Professor continued: "The only C.A.T. unit to undertake large scale de-oathing and to engage the Forest Fighters at all was C.A.T.12, the unit which pursued and ultimately killed General Jembe."

"Professor Kimeto, can you describe the composition of C.A.T.12?"

The Professor reached for his Filofax, then turned to the bench, a question clear on his face.

The Judge nodded and briefly explained to the Assessors the dividing line between hearsay and expert testimony while the Professor flipped through the bloated volume, a frown making a sunburst of ridges spread from a point between his eyebrows, until he found what he was looking for.

"C.A.T.12 was under the overall command of Major John Sandford, a commissioned officer of the King's African Rifles. His second in command was Edward Foss, a Superintendent in the Kenya Police Reserve. The British Army Liaison Officer and effective third in command was the accused, 1st Lt. Thomas Miles. The non-commissioned officers and the rank and file, which comprised about 50 men, were largely seconded from the KAR, KPR and Kikuyu Home Guard. There was also a small number of what were called pseudo-terrorists – ex Forest Fighters who had changed sides and been de-oathed."

Paul led the Professor through a description of the oathing and de-oathing processes to the detail of the interrogation techniques used on suspected insurgents captured by C.A.T.12, regularly pausing as the Professor listed his documentary sources. Leo raised several more objections, all of which were overruled, and the prosecution focused on the events of 30 April 1955.

"It is my considered view," the Professor assured the Court, "from the evidence I have studied as part of my research, that C.A.T.12 set out that night to find and kill General Jembe. It would have been perfectly possible to have placed him under arrest . . ."

"Objection," Leo said quickly. "The witness can't possibly know that."

"Sustained." said the Judge, not looking up from the notes he was taking. "The witness may however, as an expert, indicate what his interpretation of the information in the written record would be. Mr Muya, perhaps you could help the Professor through this?"

Paul bowed to the Bench. "Professor Kimeto, on the basis of the evidence you have studied, do you think it would have been possible to have affected the arrest of General Jembe without bloodshed?"

"I do. He was, after all, unarmed."

"How then do you, as a historian, and an expert, account for his death?"

"I believe it was a deliberate extra-judicial execution. Part of a purge of men who would otherwise form a significant part of any future independent government."

"And have you encountered any evidence that this was justified by any military necessity?"

The Professor shook his head. "On the contrary, at the time, the campaign against the Land and Freedom Army in the forests was winding down. Only a few days after the death of General Jembe, control of operations was returned to the police. The British had moved from the terror, detainment and death policies which characterised the early part of the struggle to a 'hearts and minds' campaign in the settled areas and in Kikuyu reserve. As Wamweya observes, by this time, the Forest Fighter was out of favour with all sides – with the Colonialists and with the Wananchi."

The Professor paused. The Chief Justice smiled at Aliya. "That means the citizens."

Aliya rose. "I'm obliged, My Lord, but I am acquainted with the term."

"Is there any evidence whatsoever of a military strategy of targeting the leadership of the Mau Mau movement?" Paul continued.

"None."

"Can any such policy be deduced from the general behaviour of the Security forces at the time?"

"No," said the Professor, firmly. "Numerous military leaders were captured and put on trial. General China. Dedan Kimathi. The Secret Circular No 10 which authorised Jembe's killing refers specifically and exclusively to him."

"Then how do you account for this singling out for death?"

"Simple. In killing Jembe, C.A.T.12 was silencing one of our future political leaders."

"Were none of the others future political leaders?"

"I think not. Only Jembe."

"What about John Ole Kisii?"

"Have a care, Mr Muya," warned the Chief Justice.

"Although he is now our Acting President, in 1955 Mr Ole Kisii, or *Siafu* to give him his war-name, was not in a leadership position or in fact seen as particularly significant at all."

Paul opened his mouth to ask another question but before he could speak the Chief Justice cut him off. "I think we need not discuss Mr Ole Kisii any further at this point. Move on Mr Muya."

"I have nothing more for this witness, My Lord. Thank you, Professor Kimeto."

The Judge adjourned the Court for the day, and as they stood for his departure, Leo nodded to Paul. "Not bad."

Paul Muya smiled as he gathered his papers. "Let's see what you can do with him tomorrow, Coke."

CHAPTER TWENTY-EIGHT

I hear from my family every day. We have e-mail and Skype and Leo Kane has arranged for his chambers to receive everyone's messages and for them to be passed on to me. Val doesn't write of course: it's been a long time since she touched a keyboard or even held a pen. No, one of her carers, Claire, I think, talks to her and jots down notes and thoughts.

It's not a formal arrangement. I don't think the High Commission is even aware of it, but it's one of the numerous minor breaches of the rules in which both my old and new jailers happily conspire to thank me for what little advice I can give them on their medical problems, and those of their kith and kin.

There have been two telephone conversations as well since Val and David went back home. These were official, above board. Organised on my behalf by the High Commission.

They were terrible. There were so many people sitting around at each end, listening and watching, that both Val and I were completely tongue-tied. We mouthed platitudes about health, and even, believe it or not, the weather. But they were distressing. Horribly upsetting. Val became very agitated, and I simply couldn't hack it. David said something infuriating about praying I find my way which, as his pious platitudes always do, infuriated me. It all left me massively depressed. It was as though they were an opportunity that had been missed to say something profound. Something as grave and important as the events in which we now find ourselves entangled.

Val is, as anyone who knows her would expect, passionately loyal. She hasn't said a word about how all this is affecting her.

187

Not a complaint, not a grumble. Yet I know, from the sad, tiny messages that pass subliminally between a long married couple, that she is angry. With me.

Not so much, I suspect, because I now find myself in this situation, but because, back when it might have made a difference, I never confided to her that there had been anything in the least significant about my time in Kenya.

After all, it was long over before I even met her. Yet maybe it's here that I have done all my real living, and maybe Val has every right to be angry and hurt, because all we shared turns out to be but a shadow existence, a sedately paced, two-dimensional approximation of a life played out in sepia tones. Whilst out here, in fast bursts of livid Technicolor, I have fought, and faced death, and truly lived, and really killed.

How could I even think such nonsense? How can I deny those most important relationships, all that's really mattered, all that's really important? My wife, my home, my family.

My ex-colleagues in the practice have been good, too. Although it can't have been easy. I still cover for holidays and do a clinic every Thursday morning. Or did. So they are still meeting my part-time salary and having to find the cost of a locum. The last I heard from the Practice Manager, they were pressing for their insurance policy to cover their additional costs, and whether they would or not all comes down to whether there is some sort of legal agreement between Kenya and Britain which covers prosecutions. They tell me I shouldn't worry myself about them, and to be honest, I'm not. Oh, I know I should be. I owe it to them, but right now, it's very difficult not to be completely selfish. Self-centred. After all, who I am, what I am, and what I might once have been capable of seems to be a subject of all-consuming interest to a remarkable range of people right now. Why shouldn't it absorb all of my attention?

My colleagues on the Bench, my fellow Magistrates, have inevitably been somewhat more circumspect. They have no choice. They can't be seen to remain too chummy with one of their own who now faces criminal charges, let alone ones *of such gravity. I suppose I'd be the same, were the situation reversed, but I can't help feeling just a little let down. Some word or gesture would be nice.*

My room here at the police club is 10 feet by 12 feet. Spacious, by Kenyan standards. Luxurious, too. But it's odd what one misses from home. Often, and with an almost unimaginable intensity, things one never really cared that much for. Heinz Cream of Tomato Soup in my case. Can't remember when I last tasted the damned stuff back home. Years, probably decades ago. There was a can at the back of the pantry that remained there untouched since God knows when. Still there, I imagine. Now, it's not even a comfort, it's a craving. The food here is not at all bad. Institutionalised, bland, very British. Lots of boiled potatoes and roast chicken. Puddings I remember from my army days. Soup too. But not Heinz Cream of Tomato . . .

One of the guards on nights has a daughter of eight who has an extreme allergic reaction. Together, he and I are working through strategies to isolate whatever is triggering it. He keeps me supplied with my Tomato Soup. Francis, his name is. The kitchen staff are happy to warm it through for me.

I'm troubled by dreams, all of which are about the forest, and I awake, deeply scared and horribly alone at night, and my heart swells like it's going to burst each morning when I catch the strains of children singing in the near-by primary school. Yesterday, when their thin voices trilled, "Here we go round the mulberry bush," I started to cry. But at heart I am a survivor and have adjusted to my incarceration now. What I still find most difficult is the heat, and the lack of air. At home, even in the winter, we sleep with one window slightly open. Here, I find it difficult to breathe at night.

I discovered, early on, that the coolest place was the wall beside my bunk. I slept for two nights with my back pressed up against the plaster. As a result, I have some kidney infection which refuses to clear up. It is most embarrassing in court: I keep having to ask to be excused, and I am sure the judge, who is politeness itself, thinks I am incontinent.

189

I mentioned it to an official from the Prisons Department who are nominally responsible for me and who carry out a weekly inspection. "Physician, heal thyself" he said, unsympathetically, and then berated the guards for letting me have the newspapers and magazines I had foolishly failed to hide. Thereafter, things were unpleasant for a day or two, but they gradually went back to normal.

I should be writing to Val, now. There's no problem about getting word out; I can send whatever I want out with Jimee, from Leo's chambers. It's strange, I can scribble in this notebook all night, and still have more I want to put down, and yet I can't write a line to my wife.

Maybe it's as I've thought before, that in that life, back home, I am already dead. That Val, the kids, my partners in the practice and my colleagues on the Bench are, quite literally, those I have left behind. That I await judgement knowing that whatever lies ahead, there is no going back.

I wonder if Jembe had any inkling of that as he approached the shamba that night? I probably shouldn't look for any kind of kinship with him, after what happened, but I can't help but wonder. We killed him, and now they want to kill me. We are both victims. Do we share more? Are there other common trends, common players? Do we feel similar things, and are we fated somehow to be tied together forever? To live, and die, each for the political requirement of a government we don't serve, participate in or support? To satisfy some political requirement we don't comprehend? Executed, sacrificed for someone else's greater purpose? Am I responsible for his death, and is he responsible for mine, or are we both just two more irrelevant, unconnected victims in an inexorable, relentless process that just goes on for ever?

Last night I awoke massively aware of something I had never really thought about before: I am already nearly 20 years older than my father was when he died. The years I had up to the day Jembe died is the extra life I have been granted over him.

And with such thoughts churning in my mind I am once more

190

subject to the fear I last knew the night Jembe died. How do I write anything that is worth communicating to friends and family that seem more foreign to me now than any of the faces that tomorrow will stare at me once more, hoping for some sign, or semblance of recognition? Some indicator which will allow them to relate what they are hearing with to what they see when they look at me, once more, in court tomorrow?

Tomorrow? I have no more tomorrows. Only vacated yesterdays.

CHAPTER TWENTY-NINE

There was less of a buzz about the Court on the morning of the second day: already a routine was beginning to establish itself. Most observers made their way to the same places on the public benches they had occupied the day before. People who had been strangers nodded affably to one another, and a few exchanged business cards. It was as though the Court was bedding down. It's going to be a long and wearisome journey: let's shift ourselves up and hunker down so that we can travel it together as comfortably as we can.

Paul and Leo had dined with the Chief Justice the previous evening. There was nothing unusual about that. It was something of a ritual: the CJ entertaining leading counsel on the first evening of a major case. It was the old boy's way of doing business. Amicable, measured, pleasant. Civilised. It gave them the opportunity to talk through the way in which the three of them could best ensure the case proceeded as efficiently, equitably and uncontroversially as possible.

Of course, there were some young firebrands who declined these invitations: Harvinder Singh, for one, and Paul, too, when he was younger. But most people recognised the simple wisdom of working within the system. That, after all, was what they were all about.

It had been a good dinner. The Chief Justice was usually good company, and Paul and Leo invariably enjoyed being together. Ironically, considering that their professional lives were now so tightly entwined, they had seen less of one another over the past three months than they had at any time in the past twelve years.

There'd been an inevitable distancing when Leo's marriage failed. The family picnics, the outings and safaris inevitably became problematic, especially as Leo's wife had almost simultaneously joined Paul's Chambers. On the one occasion they had all got together, it was Paul and Marianne Kane who now shared the in-jokes and work-related asides, much to the irritation of Leo and Paul's increasingly withdrawn wife, Victoria. So when Paul and Leo did meet these days, it was without their families. And that made things difficult, too. For Paul had so many other calls on his time. What with Parliament, the church, and his practice, time with his family was at a premium, and it was an evident wrench for him to sacrifice a couple of hours even for the sake of his friendship with Leo.

Aliya had spent the evening reading over the transcripts of the first day, making notes while watching television in her room. She was staying at the Intercontinental. She was on the 8th floor, and she could see the High Court from her bedroom window. Her cousins had half-heartedly urged her to stay with them, and so, with greater conviction, had Kapadia. But she had been struck, more than she would ever admit, by what Leo had said to her in the pizzeria on that first day in Nairobi about the possible threat her presence represented to her family. The Intercontinental was the better option, even allowing for Joseph's insistence that he should sit outside her door, a small assault rifle across his lap.

Although she was ashamed to admit it even to herself, she was secretly enjoying moving around with a bodyguard. She didn't really believe it was necessary. She was certain it was all show, but there was something, well, almost thrilling about it, really. The way it made people get out of her way, turn their heads, and watch her.

She'd finally persuaded Joseph to take the night off by promising faithfully that she wouldn't leave the room until he returned the next morning. As a result, she arrived at Court bright-eyed and alert after nearly twelve hours of sleep. Leo, she suspected, was hung-over. He and Paul both looked like men who'd had a late night, and the Chief Justice, whom she studied as he removed his glasses and wiped his face with a large white handkerchief, looked puffy eyed, and somewhat the worse for wear.

He'd sent her a little note, to apologise for not including her in the invitation, explaining, in his cramped handwriting, that it was customary for him to dine only with leading counsel, and assuring her of his determination to meet with her socially as soon as this was all over.

As he put on his glasses, he saw that she was watching him, and he smiled, kindly. She rose a fraction and nodded her greetings.

The Assessors filed in, Court was declared in session, and Leo, slightly hoarse, took a sip of water, and began his cross-examination.

"So Professor, bit of an expert on Mau Mau, are we?" he asked.

The Professor shrugged. "Others say so."

"Oh yes. I recall your reply when Mr Muya asked you a similar question. But you wouldn't say so?"

"No," the Professor replied, glancing towards the Judge, then back to Leo, "No. I would not say so."

"Then who would you suggest we consult who is an expert?"

"I don't know," began the Professor.

"Oh, come now, Professor!" cried Leo. "Surely you must know who leads your own field? A field in which you have worked and studied for years?"

Paul Muya half rose, to protest Leo's style. "He's badgering the witness, My Lord. He knows the Professor is merely being modest."

"I know of no such thing!" Leo insisted. "My learned friend has presented the Professor as an expert witness. I have a responsibility to my client to test the measure of the fellow's expertise."

"I will give you some side, Mr Kane," murmured the Chief Justice, "but not very much. Proceed."

Leo continued for a further five minutes, referring to the list of works Aliya had devilled. Published and unpublished. Conference papers and proceedings of learned societies: had the Professor read these documents, attended those gatherings? In each case, yes. Aliya wondered what the point of all this was. All Leo seemed to be doing was further establishing the credibility of Paul's expert for him.

Leo paused, as he noticed the Chief Justice put his pen aside and absently massage his writing hand.

"My Lord," he said, softly, "I have professional stenographers taking a verbatim record of the proceedings. I'd be delighted to make these available to the Court."

The Chief Justice smiled. "Thank you, Mr Kane," he said. "The Chief Registrar told me of your kind offer. But it's old dogs and new tricks, I fear. I've recorded longhand every trial I've presided over for more than 20 years now. Give me a moment, and then we'll proceed."

"Have you consulted primary sources?" Leo asked the Professor when the Chief Justice indicated he was ready.

"I have. I have carried out extensive research on the original documents in the Rhodes House Library in Oxford, the UK National Archives and the Kenya National Archives. I have also interviewed numerous ex-squatters and ex-Freedom Fighters over a number of years. Records of all of these interviews I have deposited in the University Library for anyone to consult."

"Approximately how many interviews would you say you had carried out, Professor?"

"Over 200."

"Between what dates? Roughly will do."

"Between 1979 and 1984 for my thesis, and at whatever opportunities have arisen since."

Leo nodded, clearly impressed. "And you claim to have made a special study of the activities of the unit known as C.A.T.12? Did you interview its commanding officer, Major Sandford?"

The Professor smiled, patronisingly "Major Sandford was an

ill man. For many years he was unable to speak coherently or commit to paper any recollections."

"Yes, he was," said Leo, evenly. "But not when you were carrying out research for your M Phil or for your PhD, was he, Professor? In those days he lived, in rude good health, a mere two hour drive from your university, didn't he, Professor?"

The Professor glanced around, first to the Judge then to Paul Muya as though seeking reassurance and guidance. Leo tore into him, relentlessly.

"And how about my client, Professor? Did you ever attempt to interview Dr Miles during any of your many visits to the UK? No? Not even when you were beavering away so diligently in the Rhodes Library in Oxford, and Dr Miles was then working in Swindon, less than an hour's drive from you? I'd have thought it would have made a nice afternoon out. Have you ever interviewed anyone who actually served in C.A.T.12, Professor?"

"I have read extensively . . ." The Professor began, flustered and sweating.

"My Lord, will you please direct the witness to answer my question?" Leo cried. "I didn't ask him what he's read, but who he has interviewed. Professor, I ask you again: have you interviewed any members of C.A.T.12? Ever?"

"I have interviewed their victims," snapped back the Professor, "and where their victims did not survive, their next of kin . . ."

"Are you being deliberately obstructive, Professor, or am I somehow failing to get through to you?" shouted Leo. "Let me make it even simpler: Have you ever interviewed any members of the Security Forces? Anywhere? Ever? Even once?"

There was a silence. Leo counted to 20 before concluding, quietly. "Isn't it true that all of your research, without exception, has focused on the perceptions and recollections of the guerrillas who fought in the Mau Mau campaign, and the squatters who supported them and supplied them with information and food? Isn't that so, Professor?"

The Professor shook with anger, his eyes blazing. "I see nothing wrong with attempting to redress . . ."

"Oh, I see nothing wrong with what you have done, Professor. I'm sure your work will live on after you, a proud legacy. A major contribution to our cultural heritage, I don't doubt. But where is the objectivity, the impartiality the court has the right to expect in an expert? Not, I am sorry to have to say, in you."

Leo sat down and glanced, with a smug and triumphant grin, at Aliya. He had expected her to be more struck, and maybe even on the edge of hero worship. He was disappointed, but not by much.

Aliya puffed out her cheeks, and whistled silently. "You certainly roughed him over," she said, with grudging admiration. "Are you sure you weren't too hard on him?"

Leo snorted derisively. "Kane's first principle of cross-examination: everybody hates a smart-arse. Judges and Assessors both love to see an expert humbled, hurt and bleeding. It makes them feel good. Ergo, expert witnesses are always fair game. You can't be too hard on them."

Paul's next witness was another expert: Dr Jacob Ochino. A small, soft-spoken man who, with a nervous smile, explained that he was the author of several books on Mau Mau and the State of Emergency. Paul led him through a brief but telling description of Kenya in the 1950s: a place where Black Africans could not buy hard liquor or go out after dark without a kipande or kodi. Could not assemble publicly or privately to listen to their leaders. Could not buy land in the White Highlands. Could not vote, grow coffee or sisal, visit restaurants or cinemas, walk on beaches or use public toilets reserved for Europeans or Asians.

He explained how discontent had grown among the Kikuyu squatters, who had for generations farmed the land in what became known as the White Highlands. How, overnight, they had found themselves dispossessed and the land they had regarded as their own packaged up and leased out to newly arrived Europeans. He told of farmers forced to tend what they

197

regarded as their own land for a white master and a pittance wage, or face compulsory repatriation to a Kikuyu reserve far too small and impoverished to provide a livelihood for the thousands crowded there.

Unsensationally, he described the generation of young Africans who had fought with the British in the Second World War in South East Asia. How, having lived with British soldiers in the equality of danger and death, many returned to find their father's lands given away to new immigrants from the very countries they had been fighting.

They had a grievance; they had military training. They had also seen that the white soldier was no greater, no braver, no more impervious to shot and shell than were they.

Among the dispossessed squatters in the White Highlands, and the repatriated Kikuyu in the Reserve, the swearing of oaths of secrecy and loyalty began. Two Mau Mau armies formed, one in the Aberdares and the other on Mt Kenya. Both areas were declared 'Prohibited' – within which the army and police could use weapons freely and without preliminary challenge, on a straightforward war basis.

Ochino's style of presentation throughout was understated: he spoke almost diffidently, and his evidence was all the more telling because of its deadpan delivery. The Court was hushed and attentive. The female Assessor sat back for long periods, erect, eyes closed, absolutely still but clearly absorbing and weighing every word. She leaned forward slowly at one point, and scribbled a quick note which she passed to the Chief Justice, who raised his pen to signify a pause.

"Dr Ochino," he asked after reading the note, "was the shamba in South Kinangop where Wilson Muya died within a Prohibited area?"

"No sir, it was not."

The Chief Justice glanced across at the Assessor, who tilted her head to indicate she was satisfied.

"Proceed."

"She's the one we have to convince," murmured Leo to Aliya.

"Watch her every reaction. Gauge what has an effect. We need to get her on our side."

Dr Ochino continued to stack up his evidence. Over 50,000 Kikuyus arrested and screened in Operation Anvil. More than 1,000 individuals executed. The death of 10,000 supposed insurgents in the field. Thirty-two European civilians and over 2,000 Africans killed by the insurgents. Sixty-three European members of the police and security services killed. 132 prosecutions for brutality among police officers . . .

It was late in the afternoon when Leo rose to begin his cross-examination. The entire Courtroom seemed to hold its breath, anticipating a repetition of his savaging of the Prosecution's first expert. The Chief Justice asked him if he would prefer to adjourn early and begin the next morning. Leo, with thanks, declined, and there was an audible gasp as he announced that he had no questions for the witness. With that, he resumed his seat, hand thrust deep into his pocket.

No one was more surprised than Aliya. "You're not going to challenge any of that?"

"What's to challenge? We agreed we'd get it on the record and move on. There's no advantage to our client in getting embroiled in a defence of the indefensible. The behaviour of the colonial authorities isn't his responsibility. Defending it isn't ours."

Leo rose again to thank the witness for his illuminating evidence, congratulated him on the intelligent way it was delivered, and then paused.

"On second thoughts, if you'll forgive me, your Lordship, I do have just one question for this witness. Dr Ochino, I hope you are fully recovered from whatever indisposition was troubling you?"

Dr Ochino smiled, "Fully, thank you."

"And you'll be available to reappear if we need any further elucidation?"

The Court was in a relaxed, almost sleepy, end-of-day mood. Paul Muya rose to object. Leo had said he had only one question; surely he had just asked two? The Chief Justice smiled and nodded, Leo bowed in acknowledgement. There was a ripple of laughter. Even Tom was smiling. It was all so calm, so ordered, so civilised.

I suddenly remember what this whole thing reminds me of: I've been trying to recall it all day.

Medical school.

In part, it's the mix of races in the people gathered to watch the proceedings: Africans, Indians, Europeans. Even a couple of Orientals. And there's something too in the way they're looking at me. With this mix of forensic interest, fascination, professional detachment and mild revulsion. I'm not a person to them, any more than the cadavers we used to watch dissected had been people to us.

They watch, as Paul Muya explains his diagnosis, and then proceeds to open me up for their education, describing, organ by organ, the spread of the disease he perceives evidenced in me.

And like the cadaver, I'm at one and the same moment both the centre of everyone's attention and the least significant thing in the room. They stare, study and talk about me, then they go home at the end of the day to their loves and worries, homes and heartaches and I am simply returned to my cold slab. I'm just the inert thing it's all happening to. The being it's all about. Yet I don't matter a jot to any one of them.

It was on the second day of the trial that General Harris arrived in Nairobi to a flurry of media curiosity and, ever the showman, immediately held court in the bar of the Grand Regency, where, at the sponsoring newspaper's expense, he established his field HQ.

A little love affair immediately developed between the media and 'Hack 'em' Harris. A cosy intimacy which prompted those who had served with him many years before to recall his habit of cultivating war correspondents and cameramen. Long before it became MOD policy, decades before the concept of embedded

200

reportage was adopted, he would invite journalists to the Mess, and give them unrivalled access to the front line in his sector, thereby guaranteeing himself the lion's share of the headlines when things went well, and the opportunity to put his side of the case to a sympathetic audience when they didn't.

He was a natural at handling the media, seeming to know by instinct when to share confidences, and when to restrict himself to a knowing wink. He looked good on camera and spoke in clipped, unqualified sentences that were the delight of news editors.

As the Prosecution case settled itself down to lengthy descriptions of the grimness of the Emergency years, and the media tired of trying to find ways of casting the rather two-dimensional and lacklustre Tom Miles as either a hero or a villain, in clattered 'Hack 'em Harris', to the rescue. A real, larger-than-life eccentric with an opinion on everything, who could be relied on to fill several column inches of newsprint every day.

That evening, Leo and Aliya sat in Kapadia's office in Sena Chambers waiting for the final pages of the day's transcripts to be produced.

Kapadia was out of town, putting together a last minute appeal for commutation of an imminent death penalty. Given that Leo no longer had an office he could call his own, Kapadia had offered them his.

Amid the piles of papers, they went through the sheets of the transcript already prepared, circling errors, and re-examining the day as the bald, bland words captured it.

The transcript was as revealing as a series of sharply focused monochrome photographs. It showed a clear image, accurate within its own parameters; precise, but without the colour, heat and movement. Just occasionally, the words would capture the speed or feeling behind an interchange. Here and there the word 'laughter' in brackets sketched in a bit more background, but generally it made for tedious reading.

"Is it what you expected?" yawned Leo, as he completed his perusal of the sixteenth page, and passed it to Aliya.

201

She paused, a slight frown on her face.

"Well?" Leo prompted.

"Well, so far it's all just setting the scene. And it's all so . . ."

"Mannered?"

"I was going to say civilised, but realise that might sound patronising."

Leo nodded. "During recess, I was standing next to this guy in the john. Some big shot columnist from Britain. Said he's going home tomorrow. He's hired a local stringer to keep an eye on things for him. He said this was turning out to be about as thrilling as Sunday afternoon at a grammar school debating society. Said if the defence was going to be as dreary he'd only come back out for the decision."

"Why do you think Paul Muya's spending so long on the background?" asked Aliya.

"I think he's wary of launching into the case proper. Not surprising, really. He doesn't know any more than I do about war crimes legislation. And he hasn't got the funds or friends to hire in world class expertise. With you on our side," Leo added, with a smile. "We have him outgunned."

Aliya gave him a hard look, suspecting he was making fun of her and was then irritated with herself for feeling good because he wasn't. "So what do we do?"

Leo arched his back, yawned again and stretched. "Get a good night's sleep, and tomorrow, I intend to make that hotshot journalist regret heading back to London."

CHAPTER THIRTY

Leo's change of tactics was evident from the moment Court convened for the third day of the trial. Paul's next expert was an ex-Freedom Fighter who was the author of a book on the life and career of Wilson Muya. Leo had read it, and so had Aliya, more than once. As a literary work, both had to admit it was good: it was impossible not to feel a sense of outrage and loss when, in the final chapter, Jembe is put down like a rabid dog.

As soon as the author, George Githunguri, took the oath, Leo began. Eye rolling, head shaking, tutting, and little, ironic smiles.

Paul was untroubled by his performance: he'd seen it before. The Chief Justice was irritated, and treated Leo to several withering glares, which Leo studiously ignored.

But in the witness box, Githunguri found it deeply upsetting.

A master of the written word, the underground publisher of Mau Mau broadsheets before being hauled off to years of detention in Manda Island camp, Githunguri was a clumsy and uncertain speaker. He had a slight stutter, which grew progressively worse during the course of his examination-in-chief, not least because whenever his delivery faltered, Leo, with a huge sigh, would look at his watch, and shake his head, sadly.

Having established the writer's credentials, and given him ample opportunity to expand upon his own part in the Mau Mau campaign, Paul picked up a copy of his book, in which a series of pages were marked with Post-it stickers. Turning to the first, he asked the writer to describe the incident in which Jembe sneaked three terrorists out of the High Court building itself on the very day they were to be sentenced to death.

This prompted another massive sigh from Leo, who reached down to his briefcase and extracted a large paperback copy of a Wilbur Smith novel. Holding it up so that it was clearly visible, he made an exaggerated display of reading it.

"Mr Kane?" the Chief Justice asked. "May I ask what you think you're doing?"

Leo clambered slowly to his feet, his face a picture of astonishment. "Me, My Lord? Why, I'm doing exactly the same as my learned friend: browsing through a work of African fiction."

There was a general titter of amusement around the Court, which the Chief Justice cut dead with a glower around the room. "Put your props away, Mr Kane, and attend to the matter in hand. I have warned you before about playing to the gallery; I will not warn you again."

Like a schoolboy unfairly admonished, Leo shrugged eloquently, and put the book away.

Paul, momentarily thrown off his argument by the exchange, asked the author to reiterate the research he had carried out: Leo objected. "Surely we have heard all this before?" he argued.

The Chief Justice agreed, and asked Paul to move on.

But whatever question he asked, Leo objected. Almost always, to be overruled. Eventually, the Chief Justice could tolerate it no longer.

"What is your problem, Mr Kane?" he asked, exasperated.

"My problem," Leo said, innocently, "is that my learned friend is not presenting a prosecution but indulging in a lesson in family history for the benefit of his own ego."

The Chief Justice nodded and to Leo's horror seemed almost inclined to agree with him.

"And he is doing so with the active collaboration of this Court," Leo added quickly.

"That is a serious contempt, Mr Kane," snapped the Chief Justice, furiously. "Twenty thousand shillings, non-rechargeable."

Leo held the Judge's stare, "By all means, My Lord."

"This is more like it," he whispered to Aliya, as he reached

204

for his cheque book. "Worth every cent in tomorrow's newspapers."

"Mr Kane," said the Chief Justice, beckoning.

Leo approached the bench, holding his cheque. The Chief Justice leaned forward, and whispered. "Don't think I don't know what you're playing at, Mister. You will not provoke me into giving you grounds for a mistrial, so I advise you to reconsider your current strategy."

Leo stared him straight in the eye. "I have no idea what you mean, My Lord."

The Chief Justice sat back. "Very well, Mr Kane. We shall have to see whether your bank account or my patience gets exhausted first then, won't we?"

Leo returned to his seat, and was as good as gold for the rest of the author's examination-in-chief.

In response to Paul's prompting, the author outlined Wilson Muya's war service in Ethiopia, Madagascar, India and Burma with the Army Signal Corps, 22nd East African Brigade.

After the war, he had returned to Kenya, trained to be a teacher, and subsequently taught at a number of different institutions.

In December 1952, he took the Mau Mau oath. A month later he was appointed Commander to the First Reinforcement Division by the Nairobi War Council, charged with liaising between the Mt Kenya forces and the Nairobi activists supplying them with weapons, troops, and money.

He instigated a number of highly effective strategies: the use of women to transfer weapons to the fighting forces; the commitment to attempt to free any Forest Fighters brought to Nairobi for trail. The oathing of African servants employed by senior British government figures, including the Governor, the Chief Native Commissioner, and the Commissioner of Police. Also, he began the campaign of letter writing and speech making that eventually led to the authorities' determination to silence him. It was while publishing and distributing those writings that Githunguri came into contact with Jembe.

In May 1953, Githunguri explained, Wilson Mumbu Muya was promoted to full General by the Nairobi War Council, and took the war name Jembe – the hoe.

The author had actually discussed the symbolism of the choice of code name with Wilson Muya at the time. Muya had not wanted to be known as a weapon of war, Githunguri explained, preferring the imagery of an implement to root out the unwelcome weeds.

In October that year, General Jembe freed four Freedom Fighters on trial for possessing weapons and pistols – a trial which was bound to end in the death penalty.

He acquired a uniform, and arrangements were made for him to sweep the remand toilets in the High Court. Before 8 o'clock on the final morning of the trial Jembe, equipped with a broom and a pail of water, sneaked into the very building Tom's case was being heard in. As the prisoners on remand were brought into the cells below the court, so he followed them, as though going to clean the latrines.

Spotting the four he had come to rescue, he caught their eye, and nodded towards the toilets.

Quickly, he explained that he couldn't get them all out, but if he could walk out with the principal accused, then the trial of the others must inevitably collapse. Accordingly, he dressed the Freedom Fighter who had been caught in possession of the pistol and ammunition, in his sweeper's uniform, and gave him the bucket he had carried. Jembe slung the broom over his shoulder, and together they simply walked through the High Court, past the guards, and all the way to the cleaning department at City Hall.

As he had predicted, without the principal accused, the others could not be found guilty of complicity and they were duly acquitted.

Paul and Githunguri settled into a rhythm. The war stories were flowing easily. Leo watched the Assessors, trying to gauge how much impact these tales of dashing escapades were having. The female Assessor, as usual, was giving little away. She sat erect, intent, making occasional notes. The wealthier of the two male Assessors, today dressed in a pale blue safari suit, shifted uneasily. His cheeks ballooned out momentarily as he belched silently and his face set in a grimace against the taste of bile. His recurring dyspepsia, evidence of which Leo had detected before, in the traces of chalk at the corners of the man's mouth and the occasional peppermint, discreetly sucked, seemed to be absorbing his attention far more than Githunguri's evidence.

The final Assessor, Leo was pleased to note, was fighting a losing battle to stay awake. His eyelids drooped. He crossed his arms, then uncrossed them. He cleared his throat and shifted in his seat but all to no avail. His eyebrows rose, and fell, and his chin slowly sank onto his chest. Leo smiled to himself, and jotted down the time. It was a trivial point, but if it came to an appeal . . .

"Mr Githunguri," said Paul, "Can you describe Jembe's actions on 24 January 1954?"

"Twenty-three Freedom Fighters were held in Nairobi prison awaiting trial under the Emergency laws, all for offences which carried the death penalty. Using female Freedom Fighters, Jembe had the prison spied out, and a number of prison warders in his control.

"Jembe concluded that the best way to free the prisoners would be when they were being transported to court in a mabiga – a large, caged-in van in which prisoners on remand were transported to the court.

"Jembe arranged for one of the prison warders in his pay to close, but not snap shut, the padlock on the rear doors of the van. At the interception of Railway Loco Shed Road and Unga Road, the van drew up at the junction, slowing before turning left.

"Jembe himself was waiting there. He snatched off the pad-lock, and flung the doors open. Before the guards sitting in the front of the vehicle realised what was happening, the prisoners were out, and mingling with the many pedestrians along the street at that time, heading for work.

207

"As soon as the workers realised what was going on, hats and jackets were swapped to help the escapees disappear into the crowd.

"A few moments later, when the guards realised what had happened, a search was instigated. The prison authorities quickly formed up a squadron of prison and police vehicles, and swept through the city. Not one of the escapees was re-arrested."

"Could you name any of those escapees?" Paul asked.

The author, clearly well briefed for the moment, paused, and looked carefully round the room. "I can. I was one of the escapees. John Ole Kisii was another."

"The current Acting President of the Republic of Kenya?" Paul asked, unable to resist emphasising the word 'Acting'.

"The same," the author confirmed.

In the benches, people turned to one another, murmuring, and nodding as though an important piece of the jigsaw had suddenly fallen into place. The Chief Justice sighed.

"When was Jembe identified as Wilson Mumbu Muya by the authorities?" Paul asked, once the buzz had subsided.

"In March 1954."

"What happened to General Jembe then?"

"In a clash with the security forces during Operation Anvil the following month, he received several wounds. These put him out of action for some months. He was kept in a cellar we established as a Mau Mau hospital, cared for by a Kikuyu male nurse from the general hospital, and supplied with drugs stolen from the dispensaries around the town. I visited him there several times. I brought him fruit and newspapers," he added, with a sad smile.

"Operation Anvil broke the back of our force in Nairobi: most of our men were dragged off to detention camps, those few who remained were too scattered, and poorly organised, to maintain the struggle.

"When he was well enough, Jembe tried to rally our forces, but he saw that it was hopeless. While recovering from his injuries, he concentrated on his writing: in particular his vision of an independent Kenya which is a standard text in schools today. I last saw him in December 1954. Two days after I saw him, I was arrested and spent the next three and a half years in detention camps."

While the author had been talking, Leo had been thumbing idly through his papers, and he paused on the notice served on the defence informing them of the prosecution's intention to call Githunguri: he whispered to Aliya, who rose, bowed to the bench, and at a crouch, moved back to where their transcribers sat.

She rummaged through the notes, found what she was looking for, and returned.

"My Lord," Leo began. "I wish to object to this witness giving evidence, and ask that his statements to date be struck."

The Chief Justice put his pen down, wearily. "Somewhat late in the day for a stunt like this, isn't it, Mr Kane?"

"I'm sorry, My Lord, but it has only just come to my attention that the notice served by the prosecution in respect of this witness is inaccurately drafted and does not comply with Section 301 of the Criminal Procedure Code."

With obvious reluctance, the Chief Justice turned to the Assessors, and said "I am afraid I must ask you to withdraw. Mr Kane has questioned the admissibility of this witness's evidence. This requires us to hold what is known as a trial within a trial, in your absence. It is a matter of law and not fact, whether or not this witness's statements are admissible. It is practice that you leave us for this discussion, so that you are not prejudiced by it in considering the facts. I will recall you as soon as I have made a decision on the matter."

He glanced up at the clock. "Given the time, I think it highly unlikely this matter will be resolved before the end of the day. I therefore excuse you for the rest of the day but require you to attend from 10 am tomorrow morning."

Once the Assessors had filed out, Leo outlined his argument: the Criminal Procedure Code describes the formal requirements of the notice. That served in respect of Githunguri, Leo argued, was indeterminate and insufficient to meet those requirements.

The Chief Justice invited Paul to respond: Paul was furious at having his carefully staged day interrupted. The debate snapped back and forth for three quarters of an hour. A classic lawyers' issue, largely lost on the reporters, diplomats and spectators in the public gallery.

"I've heard enough," said the Chief Justice, eventually. "The objection is overruled. The witness's evidence is admissible. We will continue in the presence of the Assessors tomorrow morning."

Leo half rose from his seat. "If I could crave one further indulgence, My Lord, what code of law are we working to now? We clearly seem to have put that of the Republic to one side. If your Lordship would be kind enough to advise me I'll have the appropriate texts fetched in for the morning so we can attempt to keep up."

This time, even the Chief Justice couldn't hide a smile. "Very witty, Mr Kane. Most amusing. Fifty thousand shillings. Non-rechargeable."

"I shall write the cheque now," said Leo, unfazed. "If Your Lordship would be kind enough to instruct the Clerk to prepare a receipt."

"Consider it done, Mr Kane. But let me remind you: this does not appear on your bill."

Leo bowed "I fully understand, My Lord. The receipt is for tax purposes. I hope to persuade the Principal Collector of Income Tax to allow me to write these charges off as an unavoidable business expense."

"My, we are on form this afternoon, Mr Kane!" observed the Chief Justice, clearly relishing the exchange. "Add a further twenty thousand to that cheque."

Leo opened his mouth to reply but the Chief Justice held up his hand.

"And before you utter another word, Mr Kane," he added, picking up his pen. "Be advised that even my legendary patience has its limits and you have taken us to it. The next penalty will be custodial. Now, do you have anything to say?"

"Not a thing, My Lord," Leo assured him hurriedly.

"Splendid. Then once you have got your receipt, perhaps we can adjourn for the day?"

"And I look forward to greeting you tomorrow, Mr Kane", added the Chief Justice, with a twinkle in his eye. "A poorer but wiser man. I advise you to save your more flamboyant strategies for the Charge. Learn from this expensive lesson; in my court there *are* rules, and you will observe them."

The revelation that Ole Kisii, the Acting President, was one of those freed by Jembe re-awakened speculation that he was behind Tom Miles' prosecution. The fact that he had not previously volunteered this information was also thought to be significant. It hadn't been evident from Githunguri's book, although all those freed had been listed in an appendix, for Ole Kisii had been recorded under his war name, Siafu – the stinging ant.

Questioned on the subject as he emerged from an African Union meeting at the Kenyatta Conference Centre, he glared, as though caught out in a secret, but then grimaced his lined old face into a humourless smile. "Jembe was a loyal comrade, a good friend, and a great man. Yes, he probably saved my life that day. But I was no one special, and neither was he. We were merely two young men among thousands, fighting to free our country. The greatest tribute I can pay to him is to continue in my efforts to make this country worthy of his memory. Tonight, as a lesson to all that our children will be protected from evil, I will be confirming death sentences on four men found guilty of abducting and murdering a thirteen-year-old girl in Kakamega. Tomorrow, I will be officiating at the ground breaking of a water purification complex in Athi River and a new hospital here in Nairobi. It is for these things, rather than to have our names and deeds recorded in old books, that Wilson Mumbu Muya became Jembe, and I became Siafu."

But his statement did little to discourage the speculation. Many thought it had been specifically designed to fuel it further.

211

CHAPTER THIRTY-ONE

"Jesus Christ!" Aliya murmured, stopping dead six paces short of the defence table as they entered Court No 3 for the fourth day of the trial.

Leo cannoned into the back of her, and saw she was staring, transfixed, at the Prosecution.

"No, that's Paul Muya, actually. But it's an increasingly common mistake: especially when the light's behind him. I think it's called aura."

"Not him, dickhead. The Mazungu."

Leo followed her stare, so taken aback by her reaction he didn't even comment on her use of a Ki-Swahili word. Paul Muya sat, surrounded, his usual coterie of supporting attorneys, augmented by a European in a crisp suit and a wide tie.

"Now we know why Paul's been holding off the war crimes stuff," Aliya muttered. "And why he was so keen to wrap up Githunguri yesterday."

"You know him?"

"Oh, yeah."

The European glanced up, saw Aliya, and his face split into a huge grin. He excused himself, and strode across to her, his arms wide and his head cocked to one side in a gesture that was both appealing and predatory.

"Hey!" he cried. "Ally!"

He embraced her, and then turned to face Leo, his arm still draped around Aliya's shoulder.

"This is Michael Rosenberg," said Aliya. "Chief Prosecutor at the Sons of Zion Centre."

Rosenberg was leonine. A great mane of dark hair flecked with grey swept powerfully back from his broad forehead. His dark, deep-set eyes shone with intelligence and purpose. His skin was olive brown, with a designer tan, and he had a smile so perfect that Leo suspected sourly that it had probably paid for his orthodontist's holiday several years running. He wore a suit that Leo was inclined to suspect cost more than his entire wardrobe and he stood, with his arm around Aliya, relaxed and assured.

Rosenberg thrust his hand forward. "Heard a lot of good about you, Leo. How you doing?"

Leo took his hand, and was treated to a manly, no-nonsense grip, and a firm-jawed, eye to eye, nod. He promptly decided he didn't like Michael Rosenberg, and he wanted him, above all else, to take his hand off Aliya's shoulder.

"You've got a great girl on your team, Leo. She's gonna be one of the best."

Aliya eased herself gently from under his arm. "Michael and I worked together a year back," she said, turning so that she was at Leo's side, facing Rosenberg.

Rosenberg gave her a considered, momentarily disappointed look that made Leo suspect there had been more to their relationship than a professional engagement. His dislike congealed and matured into mild hatred.

Rosenberg's easy features set into a contemplative frown. "Ally, we're kinda hoping you can cut us some slack. It would sure help me out of a bind."

"What sort of slack?" Leo asked, before Aliya could reply.

Rosenberg's eyes flicked between the two of them, and then he shrugged, ever so slightly. "I've agreed to help Paul out on this one: pro bono, naturally. But I've only got a two day window – gotta be back in Tel Aviv Sunday. Paul thought you might be amenable to holding over your cross of this writer guy till Monday."

"Absolutely out of the question," Leo said, moving to walk past Rosenberg to his table.

213

Rosenberg placed a restraining hand on his shoulder. "Paul told me to tell you that he'd remember the favour," Rosenberg said.

Leo lifted Rosenberg's hand away, like it was a soiled rag. "A word of advice, painfully learnt. Never do that to Paul Muya. And I don't care what he told you to tell me. The answer's still no."

Rosenberg turned to Aliya. "Ally . . ." he began.

Aliya shook her head. "Forget it, Michael. You heard the boss."

"Who is that shit?" Leo muttered, as Rosenberg returned to the Prosecution table, spreading his hands in a 'What more could I do?' gesture.

"I told you; Chief Prosecutor at the Sons of Zion Centre. He's probably one of the half dozen or so leading authorities on war crimes."

"Knows his stuff, does he?"

"He wrote the book."

"Yeah, yeah."

"No, really. *Rosenberg on War Crimes* is the definitive work on the subject."

Leo smiled, and bent so that he and Aliya were eye to eye. "But you can take him, right?"

Aliya nodded "Oh, yes. By the time I've finished with him he's going the think he's been fucked fourteen ways this side of Friday."

"Just reassure me: That's a bad thing, yes?" asked Leo, trying not to look shocked by both the language and the vehemence behind it.

Aliya smiled grimly, but said nothing.

The Chief Justice welcomed the Assessors back, told them that Githunguri's evidence was admissible and that they would shortly move to hear the cross-examination. He then treated everyone present to a ten minute homily on the role and responsibilities of advocates.

"Overnight I consulted with the Chairman of the Law Society,

214

and the Attorney General in his role as Head of the Bar," he concluded. "Both concur with my view that any further histrionics by counsel – but let us be clear, I have you particularly in mind, Mr Kane – will only serve to lessen the regard in which the legal profession is held in this country, and overseas. I warn all parties here for the last time that I will tolerate no further attempts to entertain the world's media at the expense of the good name of the judiciary of this nation. Am I clear, ladies and gentlemen? Am I understood?"

All attorneys rose, and muttered their acquiescence.

"Very well," said the Chief Justice, mollified. "Now Mr Muya, I see a new face at your table. Perhaps you would care to introduce him?"

"We could go for a filibuster," Leo murmured, as Paul introduced Rosenberg. "I could drag out the cross for two days and then he'll be on his bike."

"No way!" hissed Aliya. "I told you, I can take him. I just need an hour of internet access."

"OK. I'll keep Githunguri on the stand until 11. Off you go."

"Do you wish the Court to recognise Mr Rosenberg?" The Chief Justice asked as Aliya rose, bowed and slipped out.

"No, I thank you, My Lord," Paul replied, "but it is our intention to call him as an expert witness."

Leo was on his feet. "Objection: Not notified."

The Chief Justice turned back to Paul, and raised an eyebrow.

"I would respectfully suggest that Mr Rosenberg is covered under the general notification of our intention to call an international authority in this field," said Paul. "We have given the defence ample indication of the areas we intend such a witness to explore. We were simply unable to provide a name because, although we have been in discussion with the Sons of Zion Centre we were unsure precisely who they would be able to furnish to assist us. Mr Rosenberg only became available last night due to the rescheduling of a matter in which he is currently involved elsewhere."

The Assessors, recognising the similarity with the previous

afternoon's debate on admissibility, began to rise, and prepared to leave.

"No, no," the Chief Justice said, waving them back to their seats. "You may remain. I intend to allow this witness to appear and for his evidence to be heard by you."

Leo shook his head. "I trust, My Lord, my objection has been noted?"

"You are so assured, Mr Kane."

Paul was still on his feet. "Given that Mr Rosenberg's time with us is so strictly limited, we would be very much obliged if my learned friend would agree to delay his cross-examination of Mr Githunguri in order to allow the court to hear Mr Rosenberg's testimony straight away."

"I regret, My Lord, I must disappoint my learned friend," Leo said.

"Mr Kane has refused," the Chief Justice noted. "And I support him. In the face of Mr Kane's arguments, the Prosecution urged the Court to hear your earlier witnesses, and you, Mr Muya, chose to spend a considerable part of yesterday having Mr Githunguri read into evidence large tracts from his book. I will not see the Defence put at any potential disadvantage simply because you failed to manage your time as effectively as you might."

"My Lord," Paul began again.

The Chief Justice treated him to a withering glare. "I have ruled on the matter, Mr Muya," he snapped. "I will hear no further argument. Now, let's have Mr Githunguri back on the stand. And Mr Kane, I shall be watching carefully for any deliberate prevarication on your part."

Leo stood, arms spread, shaking his head slowly from side to side as though shocked to the core by the very suggestion. "My Lord! As if . . ."

Leo's cross was the very image of probity and discipline. Circumspect, patient, and well constructed. He progressed steadily, probing the reliability of Githunguri's recollections of events, questioning the veracity of the other sources quoted and

216

challenging the conclusions drawn. Throughout, he attempted to cast doubt on the author's perception of Jembe's importance in the eyes of the security forces in the 1950s. Githunguri remained unshakeable in the face of Leo's patient questioning.

It was the presence of Rosenberg as much as anything that determined Leo to demonstrate his mastery of cross-examination. Something about the man's exaggerated enthusiasm, and the intense concentration with which he followed what was going on around him, reminded Leo of a parent playing with a bunch of five-year-olds: trying too hard to show how seriously he took it all. Letting the kiddies just get to the ball first. Earnestly pretending the little ones were in charge, capable and competent.

And there was something about the way he had embraced Aliya and called her 'Ally'. And about the way she had stiffened, and seemed to recoil.

"Call Michael Rosenberg!"

Rosenberg didn't hurry to the witness box, nor did he dawdle. He strode, purposeful and intent, yet relaxed and confident. Like an American presidential candidate, striding to the podium to receive his nomination. Leo was vaguely surprised that Rosenberg didn't stand, arms raised, making victory signs rather than taking the oath.

With uncharacteristic obsequiousness, Paul thanked Rosenberg profusely for finding the time to be present. He established his credentials: the papers presented, the cases prosecuted, the books written. He asked him what he was currently working on – the extradition of a 93-year-old Nazi from Uruguay accused of executing several hundred partisans outside Krakov – and asked him to explain how he had come to be available at such short notice, clearly determined to have Rosenberg's account read into the record to prevent Leo using it in a subsequent appeal.

Paul took Rosenberg through generally accepted definitions of war crimes, got him to spell out the universal nature of jurisdiction, and the main points of the UN Charter to which Kenya was the most recent signatory.

"Mr Rosenberg, is it possible for a war crime to be committed where there is no officially declared war?"

"Certainly, although it may then be more properly categorised a crime against humanity. Rwanda and the former Yugoslavia are two recent examples."

Paul picked up a document, labelled and stamped, in a clear plastic envelope. "My Lord, this is the Republic's first exhibit: an authenticated copy of the so called Secret Circular No 10."

Paul handed the document to an usher, who took it across to the witness stand, and held it up to Rosenberg. While he was reading, Paul read aloud from a copy of the wording.

I am standing to attention in front of a large desk covered in files and photographs. It is the day of Anvil. The window is thrown open. The room looks down across a wide compound, full, as is every other secure area in Nairobi, with row upon row of Kikuyu men, sitting, silent, waiting.

The corridor beyond the closed door echoes with booted feet, running up and down. Everybody is talking urgently and denying responsibility. The detainees are coming in too fast, they insist. They are running out of places to put them. Anvil is either a success beyond their wildest dreams or a total bloody shambles, and no one yet seems to know which it was turning out to be.

I am sweating. In part, because I am scared, but mainly because it is so bloody hot. The ceiling fan is out of action.

"Do you realise how much damage you've done, you bloody idiot?" the Chief Superintendent shouts at me.

He seems more exasperated than angry.

I don't reply. I just stare up at the autographed photograph of the young Queen above his head, and wait.

The two policemen by the window smirk.

The one in the jacket, his trilby hat tipped to the back of his head, mops at his sweating neck with a balled-up handkerchief, but keeps his hat and jacket on.

"I hope you can sleep at night, young man," the Chief Super-intendent adds.

"How do we handle the . . . paperwork, Sir?" prompts the other Special Branch Officer – the one in the short-sleeved shirt.

The Chief Superintendent frowns, and gives me a long hard look. "That depends on whether Lieutenant Miles understands the sensitivity of his current position: what happened this morning is covered by the Official Secrets Act."

He pauses, then orders the other two out.

He tells me to sit down, and his tone changes. Angry teacher to disappointed father.

He flicks through the papers on the file in front of him, finds what he is looking for, then turns the file for me to see. "Look at that," he says. "Read it."

It is Secret Circular No 10.

"Whilst the apprehension of the terrorist popularly known as General Jembe remains a priority, and the neutralisation of his influence highly desirable, his prosecution in open court, or indeed any process of law which will permit him to make statements likely to be prejudicial to the early resolution of the State of Emergency is not deemed to be in the public interest."

"Do you understand what that means?" asks the Chief Super-intendent when I look up from the document. "We have more than enough to hang him, but we don't want to have to try him. Because we don't want him making speeches before the world's press. So our orders – your orders – are that when we find him, we neutralise him. We want him dead, but we don't want him martyred. Now do you understand what you've done?"

"How would you categorise the document in front of you?" Paul asked.

"It appears to be a statement of policy that the man referred to should be killed if apprehended, rather than be the subject of due process."

"So in killing General Jembe, the men of C.A.T.12 were act-ing under orders?"

"Apparently so. But unless such an order is justified by military necessity, it is an illegal order."

"But surely responsibility for any illegality rests with those who drafted the order, not those who, maybe in good faith or out of a sense of duty, obeyed it?"

Rosenberg shook his head vigorously. "No sir. A soldier has a duty only to obey legal orders. He has a responsibility to refuse to follow orders which are illegal, or which he considers immoral, or improper. This is an absolute responsibility, placed on every individual. When a soldier puts on a uniform, he doesn't put his conscience, or his personal responsibility for his acts, into mothballs with his civilian clothes. Obeying orders may be a mitigating factor, but it is never, on its own, a defence."

"Can you summarise the case law on which you base that opinion?"

He could. And did. At length.

It was a strong performance. Rosenberg made a powerful impression. Unemotional, uninvolved in the specific case yet passionate and absolute in his conviction that certain deeds were war crimes, and that even if perpetrated long ago, war crimes should be, could be and must be prosecuted.

In spite of the disapproval of the Chief Justice, Leo's antics the previous day had generated a sense of levity in the Court. It was all a long time ago, seemed to be the general view. Wasn't it all rather academic now? Sure, it mattered to Paul Muya, but the alleged crime had not, until Rosenberg took the stand, been made a reality to the Court. Rosenberg's testimony, delivered with the clinical assurance of a pathologist, first gave the Court a sense of a body somewhere, the slaying of which needed to be accounted for, and a growing sense of wrong.

In the first three days of the trial, Tom had been treated almost like one of a working party trying to resolve an old mystery. Like the storeman, helping the visiting auditors with the annual stock take. Perhaps he knew a bit more about where things were than the others, and how they were organised, but he seemed, at the end of the day, merely another participant in the process. Yet as Rosenberg spoke, so people began to look anew at this nondescript old man in the dock, and then, not to look at him at all.

"In your expert opinion, were a member of the security forces to carry out the policy outlined in Secret Circular No 10, would that constitute a war crime?"

"Unless justified by military necessity, yes, I believe it would," said Rosenberg, with a nod and a wink to Aliya as she eased herself discreetly back into court.

"Previous expert witnesses have testified that by the time Jembe was killed, the Emergency was virtually over, and the military campaign almost at an end. Other Mau Mau leaders were captured rather than slaughtered. In such circumstances, do you conclude there is evidence of a military necessity?"

"Given the circumstances you describe, there would appear to be no evidence to justify the act."

"Then in your expert view . . ." prompted Paul.

"This killing was, is, a war crime, pure and simple," concluded Rosenberg, on cue.

As Rosenberg's examination-in-chief came to an end, there seemed to be a general sense of pressure released and, like riders on some roller coaster slowly coming to an end, everyone in the court seemed to breathe out, stretch, slump, and sigh.

Leo glanced at his watch, and was amazed to see that it wasn't even 12.30: Rosenberg seemed to have been on the stand for hours, yet it was barely 50 minutes.

"I suggest we break for lunch now," the Chief Justice said. "We will reconvene at 2.30. That will give you a little longer to prepare, Mr Kane, bearing in mind your earlier objection. I would be grateful if you would note that."

Aliya rose. "With Your Lordship's permission, I will be leading the cross-examination of this witness."

The Chief Justice smiled. "Then I shall look forward to our return even more," he said, courteously.

As they left the Court, and Joseph and Tyson fell into step

behind them, Leo gave Aliya an odd look. "What do we do now?" he asked.

Aliya was absorbed, and seemed irritated by his interruption.

"There's just a couple more things I need to check in his book. I have a copy back in my room. Then I just want to be alone, to think this through."

"Shouldn't we discuss how we're going to play this?"

She turned, her eyes burning, and emotion tugging her mouth in strange shapes as she spoke. "This is what I'm here to do, Leo. If I'd known they were going to call Michael, then I would have killed to get this case. I told you, I can take him. Now let me do what I'm going to do, OK?"

Leo smiled, "OK. But let me at least buy you a sandwich."

"I'm not hungry," she said, and she and Joseph headed off for the Intercontinental without a backward glance.

"How are war crimes tried, Mr Rosenberg?"

"Different countries have different systems, Miss Zain."

She felt good, she felt easy. She had dreamed of this: she knew what she was doing, and just at that moment, for one of the very few times in her life, she didn't want to be anywhere else in the world, or doing anything different.

She treated him to a sweet smile. "But jurisdiction is universal?"

"Correct."

"Could you describe the Kenyan system for handling war crimes?"

Rosenberg looked around, rather theatrically, Leo thought. There was a ripple of laughter as he replied, "Isn't this it?"

"Are you aware that this is a private prosecution?"

Rosenberg frowned, nodding seriously. "I am."

"Is that usual?"

"Not usual, no. But not unheard of, either."

"Are you also aware that the British authorities inquired into the circumstances surrounding the death of General Jembe at the time, and exonerated Dr Miles of any wrongdoing?"

"I am."

"Well, doesn't universal jurisdiction mean that such a conclusion is binding on all other tribunals in all other countries?"

"It does."

"Then surely it follows that Dr Miles has no case to answer before this Court?"

Rosenberg tilted his head forward, pursed his lips, and then looked at Aliya from below bushy eyebrows. "As I understand it, both the essence of the matter which that body enquired into, as well as the extent to which it could be regarded as an impartial judge, have been challenged."

They danced around that for a while longer, before Aliya suddenly changed tack.

"Has international law changed substantially over the past half century?"

"No. Not significantly."

"So what this all comes down to, at the end of the day, is whether or not the killing of General Jembe was justified by military necessity?"

"Correct. And in my experience, most tribunals would conclude that the extra-judicial execution of an unarmed insurgent already in the custody of the security services is unlikely to be justified by military necessity."

"But you accept that this is the essence of the matter here? The question of military necessity?"

"I accept it is a key issue."

"Is it *the* key issue?"

"Yes, I guess it is. The key issue."

Aliya paused, rocking back and forth on the balls of her feet. Should she continue, letting him get more comfortable, and expansive, before launching into a full frontal assault, or was now the time?

She decided to give him a bit longer.

"Mr Rosenberg, are you familiar with the policy pursued by the Israeli Government in the mid-1980s with regard to the targeting of senior figures in the PLO?"

"As a layman, but not an expert."

"Then let me illustrate it with an example," said Aliya, reaching for the sheet of text she had quickly put together on her laptop during the lunch recess. "On 16 April 1988 at 1.30 in the morning, in a suburb of Tunis, an Israeli assassination squad broke into the house of Khalil al-Wazir, better known as Abu Jihad. They killed Wazir's driver, and two guards, and then proceeded to pump more than 60 bullets into Wazir himself, while he stood on the stairs of his house, with his wife only a few paces away. One of the assassins then fired a number of bullets into the wall above the bed of Wazir's infant child?"

"I'm not sure I see the relevance . . ."

"Really? I put it to you that that action is an extra-judicial execution of a man of similar status in the PLO to Jembe's position in Mau Mau. The Israeli commandos had secured the house, and to all intents and purposes, Wazir was in their custody. Yet when writing about this event, you explored the legality of this action and concluded, on the basis of military necessity, that this extra-judicial execution was a justifiable act of war."

"I did. And that remains my view."

"But how is it any different from the circumstances we see in this case?" insisted Aliya. "The Israeli forces had their target in their custody prior to his execution, did they not?"

"The status of the two campaigns is quite different . . ."

"Really? How? Read again the words of Secret Circular No 10, Mr Rosenberg. Doesn't that precisely describe the Israeli policy? I quote: The neutralisation of his influence is highly desirable: His prosecution in open court is not in the public interest?"

"As I understand it, and I reiterate my assertion that I am not qualified to offer expert testimony on this issue, the Israeli authorities were concerned less with silencing Wazir than, yes, neutralising his influence, but in a way that would avoid reprisals against civilian populations, including the taking of hostages to attempt to force a subsequent release. In Jembe's case, it appears that the authorities were more concerned with stifling a dissident voice than in containing a military threat."

"And you can deduce that, from the wording of this Circular alone?" asked Aliya, incredulously.

"Such an interpretation would be consistent with the facts as so far presented to me," countered Rosenberg.

The verbal parrying continued. Neither gave ground. Each scored the occasional touch, but after a further hour honours were still pretty even. There was something in the competition. A kind of intimacy which made more than just Leo feel they were witnessing an interchange that was going on at several different levels simultaneously.

Rosenberg was clearly enjoying himself. He treated Aliya to ever longer bursts of amused eye contact before answering. He even started playing with her, quoting her own "Dresden fiction" to support an argument she was trying to destroy.

Aliya decided it was time.

"Mr Rosenberg, on what basis do you appear in this matter?" she asked, veering off the line of questioning she had doggedly maintained for the previous twenty minutes.

If Rosenberg was wrong-footed, his recovery was little short of miraculous. Half a breath, and he smiled, and looked down, modestly. "I make a certain proportion of my time available at no charge to assist in matters such as these."

"But the Prosecution is meeting your reasonable expenses? Airfare, accommodation?"

Rosenberg shrugged, and glanced momentarily at Paul, who picked up the message, and objected.

Patiently, the Chief Justice heard him, and posed his challenge to Aliya: what was the point of these questions?

Aliya spread her hands, in a gesture of innocence that would have done Leo Kane credit, and said, guilelessly, "My Lord, I am about to challenge the integrity of this witness."

For a moment the Chief Justice thought he had misheard. "Are you quite sure you have grounds, Miss Zain?"

"I believe so, My Lord," Aliya assured him.

"Very well," said the Chief Justice, reluctantly. "You may continue, but I warn you, I take a harsh view of unsubstantiated slurs on a witness's character." And with a deeply suspicious frown at Leo he added, "I hope you have not been unwisely instructed by your leading counsel."

She turned, with an easy smile, to the frowning Rosenberg. "Michael, do you have any financial interest in the outcome of this trial?" she asked.

Paul was on his feet again, but the Chief Justice waved away his objection with a cautionary. "Have a care, Miss Zain . . ."

"Mr Rosenberg?"

"I have already said my appearance in this matter is unremunerated."

"So you did. I was wondering whether you and the Prosecutor in this matter had come to any agreement about, for example, exclusive rights to material in the Prosecutor's possession with regard to future publication?"

Rosenberg stared hard at her, his mouth a tight, straight line. Beneath his tan, strange things were happening to the colour of his face.

"Mr Rosenberg?" prompted Aliya.

"I believe I would be within my rights to decline to answer that question."

"I'm not so sure you would be, but I'll let it pass. Let me give you a straight yes or no option instead: have you done a deal with Mr Muya to write the book about this case?"

"We have held some exploratory discussions about . . ." he began, then pulled himself up short. "I decline to answer that question."

"Mr Rosenberg, how would you estimate the market value of a book on a successful war crimes prosecution compared to the market value of a book about an unsuccessful one?"

"I do not believe I am in a position to give expert testimony on this matter."

Aliya suddenly felt wrung-out, as though she had swum far further than she had intended and with a mixture of fear and relief found an unanticipated shore. Beneath her gown, her blouse was drenched in sweat. She rested her hands on the table in front of her, and blinked hard. "On the contrary, Mr Rosenberg," she said, quietly, "I think the court will agree with me that you sound eminently qualified to hazard a view. My Lord, we contend that this witness has a direct financial interest in the outcome of this trial, and for that reason his evidence fails to meet the necessary tests for objectivity to allow it to be admitted as expert. I have no further questions."

She almost fell back onto the bench, and let out a long, trembling breath.

Beside her Leo shook his head in wonder. "And you thought I was hard on the Professor?" he said, admiringly.

"Zain's first principle of cross-examination. Fourteen ways this side of Friday. And now," she said, huskily, "you can bring me that sandwich. I'm starving."

"How did you know?" Leo asked again.

They were in a hotel bar, with Tyson and Joseph. Court had adjourned for the day barely 30 minutes earlier. Aliya ate ravenously. They ordered another round of sandwiches. Nick Friedlander, Billy Kimoni and Harvinder Singh dropped by to catch up on the day. Against her better judgement, Aliya had accepted the congratulatory glass of a sparkling South African wine Billy Kimoni bought for her, and it had gone straight to her head.

"Leopards and spots," she said, her cheeks stuffed with peanuts off the bar. "Just as you can't stop yourself making racist statements . . ."

"Ha, ha . . ."

"He can't help doing deals. He once told me how much he earns from the books he's written. Not just the great texts, but the far more sensationalist stuff he writes under a pen name. He even showed me one of his royalty cheques. I think he was trying to impress me."

"Well, that's a Jew for you . . . Look at old Friedlander

there . . ." He paused, waiting for the inevitable reaction. "What? Come on! You set that one up. It's a joke, OK?"

Aliya shook her head. "Dickhead."

"You must have known Rosenberg pretty well," ventured Leo.

"Pretty well," she agreed, and said no more.

One of Paul Muya's people entered the near-deserted bar, paused for a moment, and then headed straight for Leo and Aliya.

Tyson and Joseph, as one, eased themselves from their bar stools, and stood, a solid wall of hard flesh, in his path.

"Its OK, guys," Leo said. "Habari, Solomon." he added, holding out his hand.

Paul Muya's man shrugged, took an envelope from his pocket, but made no effort to hand it over. "It's for the lady," he said.

Aliya took the letter, tore it open and read it, a smile growing into a beam by the time she'd finished.

"How kind! Paul Muya's sent me a note congratulating me on how well I handled Michael. Oh, and he's offering us a deal."

Leo frowned. "Why?" he asked, reaching for the note.

"Don't you want to know what it is?" asked Aliya, playfully holding the letter out of his reach.

Leo sighed. "Of course I want to know what it is. But I'm even more curious about why he's offering us any deal at all. And why now?"

"Maybe he's running scared now he knows what a real international authority looks like."

Harvinder hooted his appreciation and offered her a high five, which, after a momentary pause, she accepted.

"One little triumph . . ." said Leo, sourly. "OK, I give in. What's on offer?"

"He says he'll withdraw all the charges if Tom will sign a sworn statement describing everything that happened that night to Paul's father, and naming everyone who was involved."

Leo shook his head, confused. "Why would he settle for that?"

228

"Maybe he really does just want to know the truth. Maybe that's all this has been about from the start."

"Pull the other one!" said Leo.

"Do we care? It will get Tom out."

"Yes, but not acquitted. This has a sickeningly familiar ring to it. Remember what happened last time? The state dropped the charges, and let him out, only to let Paul take up the running? Maybe this is yet another elaborate game. Now that everybody knows Ole Kisii owes his life to Jembe, maybe the State wants to take over the Prosecution again, and this is some gambit to side-step the earlier dismissal of their application. Maybe Paul needs more time to try and recover from the kicking we've given him . . ."

"Who's given him?"

"We've given him. What ever it is, this isn't the deal to accept."

"Isn't that up to Dr Miles?"

"Of course it is!" snapped Leo. "But it's up to me to advise him on what I perceive is his best interest. And right now I think that's hanging on in there a while longer. Clearly something's bothering Paul, otherwise he wouldn't want out now. Another day like today and we may get a deal we can accept, and if the trial goes right through to judgment, well, who knows? Between the two of us, it's not beyond the realms of possibility that we might win!"

They had another round of drinks, and ordered snacks. Aliya was still hungry.

They chatted amiably, Tyson and Joseph dropping into the conversation, which was bespattered with laughter, and light teasing. The mobile in Leo's pocket chirped. Leo grinned. "Guess who this is going to be," he said, as he took out the phone, and pressed the receive button.

"Mr Muya! What a surprise! Habariako! I guess my international authority pretty much kicked your international authority's ass. I won't tell you how she described what she did to him, but I think your man would agree that's how he feels right now." He added with a smile in Aliya's direction.

229

"All I want is a statement," said Paul, "I just need him to tell me what happened that night. I've got no further interest in him. Just get him to tell me the truth. Please."

"And what are you offering in return?" asked Leo. "Until you close, any freedom you offer Tom Miles is the freedom of a chicken in a snake pit. Sure, you can withdraw the charges, so he's out on the streets, but then what? Another of Ole Kisii's boys hauls him back into prison to face the same set of charges all over again? Total Man, I won't let you do it. You're tearing the poor old bugger apart. You saw him that time you took him on the way to the airport. It almost destroyed him. And you should have seen him that first night, in the cells. You're killing this guy by playing these games. As surely as . . ."

"As he killed my father?" said Paul, bitterly.

"If that's what you believe then let him have his day in court. We're ready. So is he. Listen," said Leo, more conciliatory. "We're not ruling out a deal, but it's got to be copper-bottomed. Solid. We're not playing games any more."

"You don't know what you're doing," pleaded Paul. "Don't force my hand, or we're all going to suffer. I mean it, Bwana."

Leo sighed, theatrically. "See you in court," he said, disconnecting the phone. He winked at Aliya. "That is one scared guy," he said, laughing. "Where's the action tonight? How about we find a party or some society bash to gatecrash? Go somewhere and have our photos taken with the beautiful people. Let's go and bask a while in the warm glow of the limelight!"

I learn so much from Johnny Sandford. He isn't that much older than me – maybe six or seven years. But he has taken me under his wing. Halfway between an older brother and a young uncle.

It's become a bit of a routine. He and I are up before dawn, even when there's no operations planned. With his pseudo terrorists, we set off, climbing to a high point, where we can watch the dawn.

The pseudo terrorists stand, silent, watching for Mount Kenya to appear out of the darkness, and they mutter prayers to Ngai, each with a handful of soil, their earth, in their hands.

And Johnny and I talk, in whispers.

They are good, these mornings. Cool draughts of peace in an otherwise grim fog of misery. The air up there, after dawn breaks, has the crystal brightness of a frosty October morning. Everything is so clear, and your senses seem heightened, as though you are on some mind-expanding narcotic.

I am young, of course. At that age, it doesn't take much to rekindle the natural optimism and zest for life all young men have. And by the time we head back down to camp, our fatigues drenched in the dew, and our blood pumping hot and fast in our veins, our stomachs gurgle with hunger, and the smell of fresh coffee hits you and, with luck, there will be some eggs frying. If Foss has been off round the farms, or into Nyeri, there might even be bacon. It's good to be alive, just then.

Then the realities take over. Foss and Johnny bicker and snipe at one another. And we hang around with nothing to do, or be off on another wild goose chase because one of Foss' army of informers has told him Jembe is going to be at such and such a place. It's always rubbish. Always nonsense. Until the last time.

CHAPTER THIRTY-TWO

"You may call your next witness, Mr Muya," said the Chief Justice.

Paul Muya rose, almost diffidently. He looked wrung-out. As though he hadn't slept the night before. If it had been anybody else, Leo would have thought he was hung-over, but with Paul, that was out of the question. More likely he had spent the night in prayer, seeking divine guidance.

Well, if he had found it, it seemed to sit far from easy with him. His fingers tugged at the border of his gown, and fussed with his papers.

"With the Court's permission, the Prosecution proposes to dispense with the evidence of the remaining witnesses listed, and wishes to call instead one further witness not previously identified."

The Chief Justice sighed, "I am listening, Mr Muya . . ."

His voice trembling, Paul hauled himself erect, threw back his head, and announced, "The Republic calls John Ole Kisii."

There was a gasp, and a murmur. Then silence. In the back of the Court, four men in suits, ignoring the Chief Justice's prohibition, surreptitiously reached for their mobiles and autodialed State Security.

"Mr Muya?" the Chief Justice asked carefully, his head tilted back, and his eyes narrowed.

"We call John Ole Kisii," Paul repeated. "The Acting President of the Republic of Kenya," he added, for the world's media, and simply to hear himself say it.

"Jesus!" Leo gasped. He turned to Aliya, opened his mouth, thought better of it and just shook his head in wonder.

The Chief Justice reached for his copy of the Constitution, to check the reference. "You know as well as I do, Mr Muya, that anyone exercising the functions of the office of President is protected from legal proceedings, either civil or criminal."

"We are not instigating proceedings against Mr Ole Kisii, My Lord," said Paul, drawing on some deep reserves of confidence. "We are merely asking him to appear to help to clarify a matter to which he was party. We would respectfully point out that Cabinet has not enacted Paragraph 12 (2) of the Constitution and invited you to appoint a tribunal to enquire into the question of whether the elected President is unable to exercise the functions of his office. In the circumstances Mr Ole Kisii cannot therefore be regarded as discharging the functions of the office, as it still rests with the elected postholder. He is not therefore entitled to the protection described in the paragraph to which you refer."

"Mr Kane?" said the Chief Justice, motivated by desperation, and in order to give himself time to think rather than by any real desire to avail himself of the benefit of Leo's perceptions of the matter.

"My Lord, this is about politics not justice. You rightly admonished me for implying this court was being complicit in Mr Muya's personal advancement. I fear now my learned friend is guilty of a far more grave and cynical contempt. With your usual incisiveness, Your Lordship has indicated why this desperate measure on the part of the Prosecution is unconstitutional, and I can do no more than commend Your Lordship's wisdom on the matter."

There was silence. The Chief Justice sat, tapping his pencil idly on his pad, staring intensely at Paul Muya. Paul returned his stare. The two glared at each other, like poker players, staring each other down over a table heavy with wealth, hoping to detect, in some flicker, or blink, that the other was bluffing.

After what seemed like an age, the Chief Justice raised his hands slightly and let them fall, with a heavy slap, on the bench. "Court is adjourned, until Tuesday morning at 10 o'clock. In the meantime, I shall take advice on the legality of Mr Muya's petition. I will receive written submissions from Counsel until midday, Monday. Mr Kane," the Judge concluded. "I recall you drive in the Charge this weekend. I am sure all of us here wish you well in your endeavours, and in recognition of your prior commitment I extend the deadline on submissions to 6 pm Monday. Usher?"

The Chief Justice rose. Paul and his team, like a delegation from some far off land who understood not a word, resumed their seats on his departure and sat in silence, still. They clearly felt the full magnitude of what they had done, and in their stillness, exuded a massive uncertainty about the outcome.

As Leo gathered up his papers, Paul reached out and offered him his hand.

"Good luck, Coke. Remember what I told you; you're going to have to drive faster than you did on the road to the airport."

Leo paused for a moment, then took the offered hand. "Thanks, Total Man. But this time, I'm the one with the policemen at my back."

Paul frowned, and shook his head, not understanding. Leo's face split into a grin. "Come on, Total Man! Don't tell me you haven't noticed. Our bodyguards: our shadows. We've got police protection. Don't say you didn't know. I'd assumed it was you who'd arranged it."

Paul shrugged, clearly still confused, and then, without a word, turned to one of his supporting attorneys and began the process of organising the drafting of their petition. Leo was left standing, shaking his head, wondering, not for the first time, whether Paul Muya was the smartest guy in Kenya, or just another sad chancer, fathoms out of his depth.

CHAPTER THIRTY-THREE

As tradition dictated, the start and end points of the Charge were posted on the notice board outside Court No 6 at 3 pm, on the Friday preceding the event.

The Ruhuruini Gate. More than 2,000 metres above sea level, on the southern side of the Treetops salient. Across the Aberdares to a spot two miles short of the Mutubio West Gate.

The very route Leo and Aliya had traversed barely two weeks earlier.

Aliya's eyes narrowed as she and Leo eased themselves into the wigged and robed huddle watching the High Court Registrar ceremoniously post the notice.

"How does the route get selected?" she asked suspiciously, amid the disappointed groans of the many who had been secretly rehearsing other routes, and the joyful cheers and clapping hands of the few who were in the know.

Leo shrugged. "There's a committee . . ." he said, letting the words trail away.

"Comprising who?"

"Various regular competitors. It rotates."

"And this year, it included you?"

"Yes, it did, as a matter of fact. I chaired it."

He looked at her, smiled slightly, and winked. "Remember, there are no rules."

She found herself laughing, and Leo roared too. He looked around, and felt again the sensation that had almost overwhelmed him on the first morning of the trial. He knew every face, and could tell good stories about each one of them. He'd seen more than a few age from smooth cheeked, bright-eyed young devils into sagging, bagged and balding senior counsel. He'd smoked dope with some, and played cards with others. Attended weddings, christenings, weathered family crises, boozed with them through their disappointments, chided them through their divorces and sat silent with them during their tragedies. He'd felt a sudden oppression, as of a gathering crisis, as though the air had become weighty, pressing down upon him. Leo felt himself at the eye of a storm. Round them, in every direction, the horizon was closing in. Dark, oppressive skies, bloated with menace, churned and swirled. Yet where they were, at its heart, all was still, tranquil, and normal. Unaware, at the epicentre of the hurricane.

He thought this must have been how those with the vision to see what the next few years would bring must have looked around the messes and clubs of the officer corps throughout Europe on the eve of the Great War. As they organised dances, small arms competitions and tea parties while the forces that would thrust them, indifferent, through the meat grinder were inexorably powering up.

He shook himself, and turned to grin, as Harvinder Singh called him a devious bastard, and he reached out, took Aliya's hand, bowing deeply, and waving his other hand, like some 18th century courtier escorting his lady onto the floor. "Come, madam," he said, with exaggerated chivalry, "Let me escort you to the field of tourney, and let these base ruffians have a first taste of our dust."

Aliya, still light-headed on the high praise her crushing cross-examination of Michael Rosenberg had attracted all morning, was happy to play along. She curtsied, and with a flick of her head, walked with him down the corridor.

CHAPTER THIRTY-FOUR

They've started to allow me letters here. As well as the ones that get smuggled in by Leo's clerk. But they're all opened, of course. And thoroughly checked through. They've left me my belt, ties and shoelaces but remove any staples and paper clips, although what harm they think I could do to myself with them escapes me. They even tell me when they've decided not to let me have something.

I get hate mail. Not much locally, perhaps surprisingly. Oh, a few now and again. All so poorly written and full of such over-blown threats that it is impossible to take seriously.

No, it's the stuff I get from home that really distresses me. The threats against my family. And against Aliya Zain. And me, of course.

Most is from cranks. Obvious sad cases who have neither the wit nor wherewithal to carry out even a tenth of what they threaten. Some of it is obscene. Most of it, just pathetic. Then there are the messages from the groups. Some are organisations far beyond the fringe of mainstream politics. Those are the ones that scare me most. Here at the Police Club, they've asked me if I want to continue seeing such letters. Offered to put them to one side for the High Commission, or Leo Kane to look through. To spare me the distress.

Sometimes I think the authorities here are the only people who care for me at all.

But I've said I want to carry on seeing them. If that is reality, then whether I am destined to leave it or rejoin it, I want to see it for what it is. In all its grim entirety.

And I mustn't get too maudlin about it. For every threat I receive, I must get ten, or even 20 letters wishing me well.

Some of these too are over-blown and sound a bit hollow. Pompous declarations from various ex-servicemen's associations who are far more concerned for the good name of the regiment, the service or the regime than they are about me. They offer me their support but really they see me as an embarrassment and a threat to their own reputation or their memory of what they hold to be true.

The vast majority of letters are from individuals. Some are poignant beyond belief. From ancient matrons who lost sons in other forgotten campaigns and who are reminded of their dead boys by my plight. Others who did their duty and see in me a re-awakening of the dilemmas they had themselves, unsatisfactorily, resolved.

And then there are the letters which scare me most of all. The strident bellow of approval, championing me as a hero of the white right – a man who knew how to put a black man in his place.

With one letter, from some neo-fascist bunch of young thugs, I received a contribution to my costs of £100.

Whilst the party for which I have voted, campaigned and championed for forty years talks uncertainly of me, finds me an uncomfortable embarrassment, and wishes that I would simply, quietly disappear.

I am despised by those I admire, and admired by those I despise.

And out here, Leo Kane and Aliya Zain are emerging as the heroes of the hour, too busy giving press conferences and having their photographs taken to care very much about what I have to say, or what I want, or think anymore.

And Paul Muya, it now seems, is no more than a pawn in the hands of John Ole Kisii, one of the Mau Mau thugs who these days have the sheer gall to call themselves heroes, revolutionaries, and freedom fighters.

So, the game plan emerges. The strategy is revealed. Ole Kisii will have his moment on the stand. Another moment of glory. Another boost to his political ambitions. And then they will either let me go, or they will kill me. I am reconciled now to the massive extremes of my fate. It's another part of the continuity from those days in the forest. I feel now, as I felt then: In twelve months time, this will all seem like a nightmare and I'll be back at home leading a normal life, or I'll be dead. I could live with that thought then, and I can live with that thought now. Somehow, it's almost comforting. Reassuringly simple. It allows a certain fatalistic recklessness which in its way is quite intoxicating.

It almost makes me feel young again. No shades of grey. No reconciliation, compromise and accommodation. Them and us. Him or me. Death or, well, not glory. No, never that.

CHAPTER THIRTY-FIVE

Yet another unwritten tradition of the Charge, albeit one exclusive to the Kane family, was that Leo and his navigator would drive the Land Rover to the rallying point the previous evening and his wife would bring the boys to join them at the starting line on the morning of the event. It was something they had done even when they were still married. The night before the Charge, again by tradition, was a boozy, boisterous affair. Aliya was not the only woman at the party, but the few others present were white, horsy, outdoor types who stood round for round with their male fellow competitors, held their own in the raucous banter and flirted outrageously, with an easy confidence which the silent Aliya found both offensive and impressive.

A handful of Asian men were competing, and from among them a couple of Sikhs, and a Hindu who was some vague relation of Kapadia's, took an avuncular, protective interest in her. Lording about her triumph in court, and keeping her well supplied with soft drinks and uncomplicated platonic company.

The party was even more riotous than usual: the fact that this was the final Charge fired them with a determination to make it an event to remember, a source of outrageous stories for years to come. Friedlander, for example, had painted his Land Rover the same outrageous purple as Leo's – and to the front bumper of Leo's vehicle he had tied a bunch of plastic flowers, and drenched the seats with cheap perfume. He'd protested, to the delight of his fellow Chargers, that he'd assumed making your vehicle look like a pansy wagon was a requirement this year. There was all the forced bonhomie of the last night of a festival,

240

the tear-bright glorying in the final game of the season as they celebrated, with a lump in their throats, the end of something special.

They drank at the Outspan, but staggered back to the White Rhino several hours after Aliya turned in, to grab a couple of hours of dizzy sleep before being up with the dawn to check their vehicles over in a sour, hung-over silence, and setting off, in convoy, to the starting point.

Aliya alone was alert and cheerful, breakfasting on mangoes, and thin slices of papaya. She marvelled at the trenchermen, Leo included who, despite their churning stomachs and pounding heads, piled into heaped plates of crisp bacon and pale fried eggs, washed down with pot after pot of strong coffee.

Leo, as Chairman of the Routing Committee – another tradition – led the convoy up from Nyeri to the Park Gate. There were 27 vehicles in all: the majority Land Rovers, with the occasional jeep or old Toyota, and one custom-built monstrosity, all wide tyres and bright chrome.

At the starting line, Leo handed her a pair of purple overalls. As she unfolded them, she saw that he had had her name stencilled across the shoulders. She shook her head, smiling, as she stepped into them. Sometimes she wondered why people bothered to make the distinction between boys and men.

He shook out his sons' overalls, marked out with their names and smiled, proudly. He glanced at his watch: thirty minutes to the start.

"They'll be here soon," he said, confidently.

Tyson and Joseph, their bodyguards, had travelled up with them. There was no question of them travelling in the Land Rover: each team was restricted to four. However, there were a few dozen assorted marshals, mechanics, camp followers and hangers-on who would make their way sedately along the longer but much faster metalled roads to the finishing line, and their protectors had, reluctantly, been persuaded to join this motley crew, to be re-united with Leo and Aliya at the end of the event.

They too had joined in on the periphery of the previous

night's revelry. They too were hung-over, and ill-disposed to conversation. All in all, it was a sombre, sullen gathering.

Aliya, for the third time, arranged her maps, with the route Leo had selected marked out with a pink highlighter pen. She checked her compass and ran through the list of supplies. A high-level jack, and a metal plate on which to set it. A spare wheel, and the four spades with which to bury it to form an anchor. Rope. Sacking to wrap round tree trunks when using the winch. Spare parts and a first aid kit.

Leo glanced at his watch again: where were the boys?

The Chief Marshall fired off a starting pistol: ten minutes to the start. Several competitors started to turn over their engines. The sun was rising, and the day warming. The excesses of the previous evening were loosening their grip. The banter began, and a few last minute bets were offered and accepted. A military helicopter swept overhead, so low several people ducked, and one or two cursed the downdraft of its rotors.

When the Marshall announced five minutes to the start, Leo's phone sounded. With a muttered curse, and a powerful sense of foreboding, he strode away from the roar of the engines, and the reek of diesel, and took the call. As he walked back, thrusting the phone into his pocket, Aliya didn't even need to ask: his expression told her all she needed to know.

"So what do we do?" she asked, gently.

Leo's eyes were bright with tears of anger and frustration. "Who the fuck does Paul Muya think he is?" he snapped. "She says Paul says it's too dangerous. Because we've got police bodyguards. They're my fucking children. Yet that bitch will trust Paul Muya's judgement . . ."

"Use me as an excuse," she offered, quietly. "Say it was me who insisted we withdraw."

"Withdraw?" cried Leo. "Are you crazy? Look, this is an event for the legal profession, right? Well, what are Joseph and Tyson if not members of the legal profession? They're policemen. They're just a different part of the legal system. Hiya!" he shouted, and beckoned the two policemen over.

242

He explained the situation to them in Ki-Swahili. They grinned, and nodded. Their submachine guns quickly joined the rest of the equipment in the back as they eyed the overalls. Joseph produced a small knife and began to cut the stitching where they had been taken in and turned up, to fit Leo's boys.

The three minute gun fired. Leo ran across to the Chief Marshall, and explained the situation, got into a brief, heated debate, and then loped back, smiling a forced, mirthless grin.

"Right. We go," he said, clambering into the driving seat, and tugging on a pair of light cotton gloves.

There were, inevitably, those among the Chargers who delighted in facts, statistics and trivia. Fastest times. Most commonly encountered problems. Best performances in the wet, on sand, or across rocky terrain. One piece of folk lore that every competitor knew was that, in all the years of the Charge, the first vehicle away at the start had never won, or even been placed. There was therefore a superstitious reticence to be first over the line. When the starting flag dropped, there was an agonised pause, while engines were gunned, and battle cries were roared – and everyone waited for some other bugger to set off first.

Leo, still furious, suddenly decided that it would be them. The purple Land Rover practically leapt across the starting line and roared off along the tarmac road for a quarter of a mile before heading on into the bush as the road bent away.

Aliya, bouncing at Leo's side, shouted out what could be deduced from the map about the terrain ahead. Leo grunted to acknowledge the information. Only one other vehicle followed them, the others having decided that the shortest route would be achieved by sticking to the road for a while longer.

The following vehicle was the purple Land Rover sponsored by Kenya's second largest dairy, part of Easton Investments, driven by Nick Friedlander and navigated by Harvinder Singh, with two giggling secretaries, with one of whom Friedlander was having a current fling-ette, in the back.

Leo's phone sounded again. Not taking his hands from the

243

wheel, or his eyes from the thickening bush ahead, he shouted to Aliya, "Take that thing out of my pocket and lose it!"

Aliya reached into the breast pocket of his overall, took out the phone, and tossed it into her bag. In the back, at a bellowed order from Leo, Tyson and Joseph searched out two long bladed pangas. They checked the blades and then sat poised, ready to leap out whenever the Land Rover ground to a halt and hack away at the thicket blocking its path.

Catching sight of Nick Friedlander in his mirror, Leo pulled up and got out. Raising the bonnet of the Land Rover, he stood, frowning, as Friedlander drew up beside them.

"Problem, Cokey?" Friedlander asked, innocently.

Leo shook his head. "Don't know what it is, Mate. Still I'm sure we can handle it. You carry on."

Friedlander laughed. "No way, Coke, you sly bugger! You've driven this territory before. We're sticking to you like shit to a blanket."

Leo sighed, and slammed down the bonnet. "Suit yourself, Nick."

"We will. You've sussed out the shortest route, you devious sod, and we're going to be with you all the way. At worst, we'll tie for first place. At best, we'll shave a few hundred yards off your distance. Say hello to your shadow."

They were doing well: keeping as near to a straight line as possible. Time didn't matter, but Friedlander could be a problem, so Leo was keen to try and tackle some of the roughest terrain. Maybe shake them off, or force them to bust something. Ever one to put his disappointments behind him, and look for the advantage in an unexpected turn of events, he quickly realised that having Tyson and Joseph on board instead of his sons meant that he had considerably more muscle, and could thus take even greater risks. Risks which Friedlander and Harvinder Singh, with just two giggly lightweights in high heels in the back, could not afford.

True to his promise, Friedlander stuck close, but made no effort to assist in clearing a pathway through the bush. Instead, he and his teammates lounged around with exaggerated indifference, trying to rile the lead crew. Harvinder Singh stretched luxuriously, yawned, and watched them, whistling tunelessly. Nick Friedlander leant on the bonnet of their vehicle, smoking a cigarette. The girls read magazines. When Aliya insisted on taking her turn at hacking a pathway through the bush there was a chorus of wolf whistles from Friedlander's vehicle. Joseph spun, his eyes flashing, and for a moment it looked as though he was seriously contemplating using the blade in his hand on the jeering men.

Aliya straightened up, one hand on the small of her back and caught the look in his eye, saw the loathing, and glanced over to see the sneering disdain in the two lawyers.

She placed a restraining hand on Joseph's arm.

"Leave it. They're not worth it," she said, then smiled to herself, reflecting that if ever there was an expression she could less have envisaged herself saying, in any circumstances, let alone halfway up a mountain in Africa . . .

They continued like this for over an hour. Driving a few hundred yards, stopping, cutting a path through, then continuing. All the time under the smirking scrutiny of Nick Friedlander and his crew.

And they were climbing, all the time. Up the bleak slopes of the Kinangop before they would drop down toward the scene of Jembe's death.

They had hit a clear patch of heath, and were moving well. Joseph and Tyson were drinking from the flask of water Aliya had handed back, and she was massaging the start of a blister on the palm of her right hand, when Leo stopped so suddenly that Tyson slopped water over himself and Nick Friedlander nearly drove into the back of them.

"What is it?" Aliya cried, "I can't see anything. What's wrong?"

Leo was staring ahead up into the clear sky, rapt. As though some heavenly visitation had appeared before them. Friedlander pulled past them, whistling and banging his hand on the side of door panel. "See you, losers!" he roared, as they raced on, leaving two neat tyre tracks across the grass. "We can take it from here!"

"Where were C.A.T.12 based?" murmured Leo, as though speaking from far away.

Aliya frowned. "A couple of miles from where we started. What is this, Leo? Are we going to follow Friedlander now? Let them clear the path for us for a while? Smart move."

Leo shook his head, impatiently. "How long did it take Tom Miles and Foss to get from their camp to the shamba in South Kinangop on that night?"

"Who cares?" said Aliya impatiently. "Three hours, I think the report said. Maybe more. It took us, what? Two and a half hours when we drove that route a couple of weeks ago? Assuming the roads were pretty much the same then, it must have taken them at least that. It was night. And raining. Probably longer. What is this?"

"And where was Jembe, after Anvil?"

Aliya sighed, "In the Aberdares of course. It was him C.A.T.12 was up here looking for."

Leo turned to her, shaking his head slowly. "Was he? Think about the route we took the other week: think about the route we've been driving now. Then tell me why in the name of all that's holy would Jembe have climbed up through the forest, and the bamboo, and half way up a bloody mountain, cross the moorland, and trek down the other side in order to meet men who were in the very place he started from. It doesn't make any sense."

Aliya leaned back, and stared up at the roof of the vehicle. "I don't know," she said. "Maybe he wanted to be sure he wouldn't run into a different army unit, or the Kikuyu Home Guard."

"Why? Why should he care, if he was just going to surrender anyway? And if that was his reasoning, then he put himself in far greater danger by crossing several different sectors, and open ground. It just doesn't make sense."

246

Aliya sighed. "Then what does?"

Leo switched off the engine and felt in his pockets for a cigarette. "I'll tell you what does. And I'll tell you why Paul Muya hasn't called any witnesses to give evidence about his father's activities in the forest, too. Because Jembe was never in the Aberdares, that's why. Not until the night he came up to South Kinangop to surrender."

"Then where was he?"

"I don't know. Maybe he never left Nairobi."

"But that makes even less sense! If he was in Nairobi all the time, then there were countless opportunities for him to surrender. All your earlier arguments apply with even greater force: why should he risk travelling all the way out to South Kinangop, to a farm in the middle of nowhere, when he could have given himself up in broad daylight with journalists watching? They couldn't have killed him then. You're raising questions, Leo, but you're not providing any answers."

Leo turned over the engine, looked back over his shoulder, and put the Land Rover into reverse. "Where are we going?" Aliya cried.

"Back to Nairobi. We're going to go through this all over again with Tom Miles. And again. And again, until it makes some sort of sense. He's holding something back, and we need to know what that is."

"But what about the Charge?" cried Aliya desperately, taken by surprise at how much she cared. "We could win. You told me so yourself."

"What does it matter?" said Leo, bitterly, "What does it matter if my boys aren't here?"

Forty-five minutes later, Nick Friedlander's purple vehicle dropped down into a hollow, reduced its speed to a crawl and came to halt as it was flagged down by four men in Park Ranger uniforms.

The Park Rangers explained that a large herd of elephant was browsing up ahead, and one had just calved. They advised them

247

to remain in their vehicle and assured them that they would not be delayed for long.

The Park Rangers retreated, promising that they would return shortly with permission for the vehicle to proceed. 45 seconds later, the Land Rover's petrol tank exploded. Harvinder Singh and the two girls in the back perished almost instantly. Nick Friedlander, his hands on the back of his head, which had been fractured with the neat precision of a split coconut, staggered blindly from the burning vehicle with his clothes ablaze, then collapsed, and died, six metres away.

The Park Rangers returned ten minutes later, and helped extinguish the blaze. The pall of black smoke had already attracted several horror-struck Chargers, come in vain, armed with inadequate fire extinguishers to see if they could offer any assistance. Overhead, the military helicopter circled.

The last Charge was officially abandoned at 11.23, Nairobi time.

"I don't know what to tell you," Tom Miles said, for the third time.

"Listen," said Leo, still shaken by what had happened to Friedlander and Singh, "There's something evil here. Something more than Paul Muya and Ole Kisii kicking around old memories of dead heroes to forward their respective careers. Too many people this comes close to are dying. Not 50 years ago, but today. Now. We set off to see Johnny Sandford and, would you believe it? He dies in his sleep hours before we get there. A vehicle in the Charge that looked exactly like ours and was precisely where we should have been disappears in a mass of flames. They were my friends, and I have an uneasy feeling it was meant to have been us. So don't tell me you can't remember, OK?"

They were at the Police Club. It was mid-afternoon. Leo had driven hard and fast down from the Aberdares. He and Aliya still wore the purple overalls they had donned just that morning. Tom sat on the edge of his narrow bed. Leo sat facing him on the single chair in the room. Aliya stood in a corner leaning against the wall, hugging herself, hunched over. She felt profoundly cold, deep inside. Had done ever since she'd heard what had happened to Friedlander and friends.

Tom looked away. "Of course I remember. It's not about remembering. God, I wish I could forget it all. It's about how much I should say."

"You need to be telling us a lot more than you've done so far. We can't defend you when we don't even know what Paul Muya's going to produce. Was Jembe ever in the forest? How did he get to the Shamba that night? How did Foss know he would be there? Well?"

Tom shook his head. "Not yet," he said, simply.

"Then find yourself a new lawyer."

"Leo, please . . ." pleaded Tom.

"You do know what happened?" Aliya interrupted.

"Yes."

"But you're not willing to tell us?"

An odd expression passed across Tom's face. Part wince, part smile. As though in contemplation of a thought which amused, as it hurt. "I don't know. I don't know what to do. For the best, you understand? There are . . . security implications. I signed the Official Secrets Act. What about that? Maybe Johnny Sandford died of natural causes? Are you really sure what happened to your friends was anything other than a tragic accident? When you're locked up like this, it's impossible to make sense of the outside world. Unreasonable for anyone to imagine that you're going to react reasonably, yet that's what I've got to try and do. To work out what's the right thing to do. I need time to think."

"Come on," said Leo to Aliya as he stood up, "we have to go. This is a waste of everybody's time."

Tom looked up at him, desperation and a hint of something darker in his eyes.

"Give us something, right now," said Leo, staring down at him. "Or find yourself new representation. This isn't a game."

"Alright," said Tom, running a hand through his hair. "Anvil. Operation Anvil. That's the key."

"What you did then? Did it involve Jembe?"

"Yes. Now let me ask you something first: suppose I was guilty of murder that night. I'm not saying I did kill Jembe," he added quickly. "But just suppose. Then . . ."

"Stop!" Aliya said quickly. "Don't say another word."

"Aliya's right," said Leo, sitting back down. "Stop right there and listen to me very, very carefully: Firstly, you don't get to say if you're guilty or innocent of anything, unless you change your plea. Secondly, you're not charged with murder. This is much more complex. Even if you did kill Jembe, and neither of us heard you say you did, right? It's for the court to decide your guilt on the war crime charge, not you. But understand this, neither of us, nor any other lawyer, can walk into that courtroom and defend you on a Not Guilty plea if you tell us you actually committed the crime. So think very carefully what you say next. Neither of us is going to ask you directly whether you killed Jembe or not. Not now. Not ever. But if you tell us you did, then as Officers of the court, we are duty bound to report the fact to the CJ."

"Let's all take a step back," said Aliya. "This is helping no one and we are all in danger of saying something we'll later regret."

Leo nodded. "We'll talk again on Monday. I'm going back to Mombasa on tonight's flight. Friedlander's wife and kids are down there, and I need to talk to them about arrangements."

"Arrangements? Oh, I see. Of course," Said Tom. He looked at Aliya, professionally logging the symptoms of shock. "What are you going to do?" he asked her, concerned.

Aliya hadn't given it much thought. Return to the Intercontinental, she assumed. She began to reply, but Leo cut across her. "She will be coming to Mombasa too," he said, decisively, "I need her with me. We have arguments to prepare for Monday, remember?"

It was late by the time they cleared the airport in Mombasa and reclaimed Joseph and Tyson's hardware. Most restaurants and hotels had long since stopped serving food, and the town was closing down, but for the rougher bars that stayed open 24 hours, and the nyama choma spots down by the dhow harbour.

Both Leo and Aliya felt the need for something familiar, something shared. They headed for Ali Asgar's where, after saffron mounds of Biryani and too much coffee consumed in an otherwise empty dining room in near total silence, they began to feel better. So much so that Leo suggested they walk to his house along the beach.

It wasn't recommended, he explained. After dark, the beach was the haunt of thieves, who preyed on any tourists foolhardy enough to venture out at night. But with a pair of tooled up bodyguards it was an ideal opportunity for a walk along a picture-postcard stretch of coast.

They strolled side by side along sands silver in the moon-light, using the line of seaweed and debris cast up by the last high tide as their guide. The sea hissed and whispered onto the beach, each wave breaking easily with a rumble and a sigh. The warm breeze sounded in the palm fronds above them, a constant rattle, like seeds in dry pods. Their exhausted protectors plodded along a discreet twenty paces behind, silent but for the occasional cough – Tyson was coming down with a cold. Recalling their training on the merits of converging arcs of fire, they paced wide apart, so they could provide maximum cover. Joseph paused and lit a cigarette, shielding the match from the wind in a cupped hand.

Leo slowed, and turned over a flattened polystyrene cup with his foot. "Sometimes," he said, "I imagine a young woman on another beach throwing away something like this on the other side of the ocean: Bombay, perhaps. Some place as full of colour, noise and excitement as this is silent and tranquil. Hers is a careless, indifferent act. And then, God knows how many months later, that discarded scrap washes up, here, on my beach. An ocean away. A world apart."

Aliya knelt to pick up a shell. "They call it Mumbai now."

"I knew that. Sadly, I also knew that was what you were going to say."

There was a silence between them as they listened to the sounds of night, wind and sea.

"Your boys must have been really disappointed about the Charge. Have you rung them?"

"Of course. They want to come down next weekend. Their mother's been very reasonable for once. Says they need to be with me, which must be a first. Paul Muya was right though, wasn't he? As usual," mused Leo. "About the danger I mean." He paused, then continued, more to himself than to her, "Do you know what my dream was? To walk with my sons along the beach, just like this, every night. To end each day talking with them about . . . things. Not to impart knowledge, or to press on them my view of the world. Just to share the darkness with them. To hear what they see in the driftwood. To know how they smell the sea, and feel the sand."

"But it didn't work out," said Aliya, softly.

"Hmm? Oh, no, it didn't work out. Other things intervened. No one's fault. No great act of betrayal. Life moved on and so did their mother and I. But at different speeds, and in different directions, that's all." His voice cracked, "You know, you have a kid, and you think you can't possibly love another as much. You think that one has claimed all of the love that's in you. And then his little brother comes along and you find out this peculiar thing about love – it has an infinite capacity to go on growing. It has no end. It can expand to infinity. If you just give it the opportunity." He wiped away a tear with the heel of his palm. "I don't know what I'd do if any harm ever came to either of those two."

Aliya felt desperately uncomfortable and was totally unsure how to react. Cautiously, she put out a hand, patted his arm clumsily. "It will be good for them to be with you next weekend."

"No," Leo said, sniffing. "I said no. Better they stay with their mother. Just until this is all over. There'll be time then,

252

please God. I am not sure I can ensure their safety, and that has to be the paramount concern."

"Do you really think what happened was deliberate? That it was meant to have been us?"

"I don't know. But until I do, I don't want the boys anywhere near me. I suspect I'm toxic right now. And if you're wise, you'll think seriously about quitting too. This would be a very good time to get out. Just say the word and I'll dispense with your services. You've done your part brilliantly. Covered yourself in glory. Neutralised their expert. Fourteen ways this side of Friday. We don't need you any more."

"Yes, you do. You know you do. And I have never heard a more pathetic attempt at nobility. Anyway, I want to find out what happened in Operation Anvil."

"Suit yourself," said Leo. "Our nursemaids must want their beds," he said, glancing behind them. "Let's get on."

That night, after Leo and Aliya have gone, one memory comes back, very strongly, of the road they will be following, the great road that links the busy port to the sprawling capital. It's a clear image, though I suspect it's an amalgam of many different times. I am escorting a convoy of trucks, packed full of manacled detainees. Before I joined C.A.T.12. It is in the days following Anvil, when the enormity of what happened, of what I may have done, heightens my senses to everything around me. I forget how many times I did that journey: back and forth, usually out to Athi River. And usually at night. If I close my eyes, I can see it, oh, so clearly.

The road shines in the moonlight, as though it has absorbed and refracted some luminescence from each of the tens of thousands of pairs of headlamps of the trucks which had ground their way, transporting load after load up from the coast. The road seems to have a life all its own. We are not its travellers, but its creatures. Never sleeping, never resting and never arriving. Merely moving, back and forth, things of the night, alive only when caught in the beam of another vehicle's lights.

And there's me, tired, tense and confused, like some latter-day slaver, plying a new, abbreviated route from the screening camps around Nairobi to the detention centres on beyond. Feeding a new, imperialist hunger for retribution and revenge.

The road ahead in the brief horizon to the furthest edges of the Bedford's headlights shines, as though wet. We catch up with the vehicle in front of us, and I notice that the rear lights are reflected in the road's surface. It's only the greasing of so many tyres, and so much spilt oil. The surface of the road is like an artery, slick with fat.

And me? What am I in this memory? I am merely the purveyor. I am no innocent. I am not guiltless. But I, in common with every other poor, feckless youth who dons identity tags, and allows himself to be re-defined into a rank and a number, am merely the pimp in the transaction. I am not proud of that, but I refuse to be ashamed, either. I have been that in the past and for far too long. In private. Pandering to my guilt like a grubby fetish. Only exposing it in the twilight, alone. Behind secure doors.

Now, against my will, I have been dragged before the world into the daylight. Hauled up and held to account – but for what?

For the deliberate sins of others.

I will take my share of the blame, but I will not be used to absolve all the others. White, or black.

No matter what happens, I have decided. I now know what I must do. What I owe Johnny Sandford, and in a strange sort of way, what I owe Jembe, too. A full account. I shall take the stand. I will speak. Whether it is in my own defence, or as part of my own prosecution, time alone will tell.

But first, there is something I must know.

CHAPTER THIRTY-SIX

Leo had another reason for wanting to return to Mombasa. One which he decided not to share with Aliya.

For he had concluded, as he contemplated Nick Friedlander's fate, that he was overdue a chat with his neighbour, Dieter Haas.

Dieter Haas was one of many losers, shiftless drifters and wastrel sons that had washed up on the shores of Kenya and unexpectedly fallen profoundly in love and accidentally found a role.

He had started with a property clearance outfit.

It was an idea that had come to him when, virtually penniless and doing odd jobs at the Bier Keller set up to meet the needs of his fellow German visitors, a despondent Khoja sipping a Tusker beer from a plastic stein told him about his problem. And Dieter's life changed forever.

The Khoja owned three blocks of flats, comprising a total of 60 apartments, all occupied by tenants who were paying rents so low that they fell within the rent protection scheme designed to protect small farmers up-country from rapacious landlords. As property values steadily rose, and the value of the shilling fell, so the rents had become increasingly unrealistic.

If he'd been an African, the Khoja moaned, then he could have had the tenants out years ago and whopped the rents up to something realistic. But as it was, he was stuck with three sizeable properties which were bringing in far less than the cost of their own maintenance. There was nothing he could do about it: there was no legitimate course of action open to him, and his attempts at reasoning with his tenants had, not surprisingly, fallen upon deaf ears. He couldn't even sell the properties at anything near their market value, because he couldn't give notice to his tenants on their protected pittance rents.

On the spur of the moment, Dieter offered to solve his problems for him at a premium of 5,000 Shillings per flat. Three months and several compound fractures later, the flats were empty. Dieter had a comfortable nest egg, and the world, or at least that part of it which owned property beset with similar problems, was beating a path to his door.

Then, having amassed a small fortune and purchased the lifestyle he had always dreamed of, complete with beach-side residence in Nyali, four cars and a boat, he suddenly decided to turn legit.

He had seen that his wealthy neighbours were prey to the same fears and aspirations as he was. They had a lot, and they wanted it protected. They built high walls, topped with shards of glass. They had iron grilles over their windows, and they kept vicious dogs.

But dogs could be poisoned. Walls climbed. Bars cut. And behind all these layers of protection, the fat businessmen, their bored wives and pampered children still felt vulnerable. They wanted someone to make them feel safe.

So Dieter set up his Security Services – which soon became abbreviated, without conscious irony, to Dieter Haas' SS.

He fetched experts in electronic security devices from Germany and, from the hard-core of the gangs which had so effectively cleared out the occupants of cheaper properties, Dieter built up a uniformed army of loyal and disciplined men now committed to protecting far more wealthy residents from all who would do them harm. For an initial set up fee and a monthly retainer, his clients' homes were equipped with the latest electronic gadgetry, supplemented with uniformed guards armed with truncheons and kiboko whips patrolling the grounds, keying in at strategic points every thirty minutes to ensure they stayed awake. These were backed up by patrolling radio alarm squads in vans whom

Dieter guaranteed could be at any premises that hit the yellow panic buttons strategically placed around the house within two and a half minutes.

It was a matter of some regret to Dieter that the government didn't let him equip his Askaris with a little of the more sophisticated weaponry he eyed longingly at the various arms fairs he attended in the Far East, but maybe one day . . . In the interim, he had decided to stockpile some significant firepower, just in case.

Leo had known Dieter Haas ever since he had been retained to defend one of Haas' property clearance operatives on a charge of sexually assaulting a fifteen-year-old in an attempt to persuade her parents of the wisdom of accepting a rent review.

Leo had won the case. Not with any great flights of oratory, or even, he suspected, through the triumph of right over wrong. Rather, it was as a result of the inadequate preparation of the prosecution. The Attorney General's men had consistently misplaced key documents and failed to call key witnesses on the right days until the presiding judge's patience had been exhausted and he had accepted Leo's petition to have the charges dismissed.

Two days after his release, the accused was found floating in Mombasa harbour – or at least, most of him was. The newspapers promptly ascribed the grisly murder to the girl's family, and her elder brother and father were arrested and heavily questioned for several days before being released, bruised and bloodied but with their alibis unshaken.

Leo however had put his money on Dieter Haas being behind the killing. Haas had paid for his henchman's defence, but it had been clear in all the briefings he had given Leo that his only concern was the reputation of his business.

Dieter Haas had taken to Leo, although Leo had done his utmost to remain distant. It wasn't that he disliked Haas, on the contrary, Dieter could be excellent company and a visit to his home for Sunday lunch was more akin to dining with the pastor of some small town in rural Germany than that of a man who ran a paramilitary organisation. If anything, Leo liked and quite admired Haas, but he thought him dangerous, and best kept at a distance. Not that Leo had any scruples about having his own property protected by Dieter Haas' SS, and at a discount price. Nor did it cause him to pause, even for a moment, before ringing Haas' number that morning.

"I wish you'd let me pay you," said Leo, frowning.

"Why?" asked Dieter Haas, pouring him a second of coffee. "Consider it a mark of our friendship."

They spoke Ki-Swahili, a language in which Haas was more comfortable than English. They sat beside his swimming pool in which the youngest three of his four children splashed, screamed and dived. It was still early. Leo had managed to slip out without either Tyson or Joseph noticing.

Unlike Leo's house, a mere couple of hundred yards away, Dieter's house was newly built. Ostentatious both in its design and in the size of its Nyali status symbols – its pool, satellite dish, and car port. There was also something unique about the house: it was the only house in Nyali, indeed, probably the only house in Kenya of a similar wealth, which had no protective grilles on its windows.

"If I'm not confident I can protect myself, then how can I expect my clients to trust in my boys and me?" he used to say. And when it was pointed out that even the Commissioner of Police resorted to dogs, bolts and padlocks to protect his own home, Dieter would simply smile smugly and his large belly would tremble as he laughed quietly to himself, satisfied that he had made his point.

"I just think it would be more ... professional," Leo ventured, declining the proffered bottle of schnapps to strengthen the coffee.

"What would money changing hands make you feel?" asked Dieter, smiling benevolently as the rubber ring was swung from the pool into his lap, soaking the pyjama trousers he wore.

"Better. Safer," admitted Leo. "More in control."

"Why? Suppose someone pays me more? What then?" Dieter asked, tossing the ring back into the pool. He stripped off his drenched pyjamas. "Better you trust in friendship."

"What if a better friend asked you to do the opposite to what I ask?"

"I have no better friends," said Dieter simply, before throwing his vast bulk, with a happy bellow, into the pool.

Tom Miles, a man of habit and a creature of routine, had rapidly established a pattern of behaviour in the Police Club. When not expected in court, he started the day with breakfast around seven, held informal consultations with any night staff who wanted his advice prior to their departure, read the morning papers the arriving day shift fetched in for him, then walked the grounds for an hour before settling down to his notebook and idling the remainder of the morning away. Lunch was served at twelve, then a nap, another stroll, perhaps a book, afternoon surgery, evening meal and bed. He recognised and rejoiced in the fact that he was progressively becoming institutionalised because being institutionalised felt safe. Reassuring. Structured. His life seemed every day a little less like that of a prisoner and a little more like that of a resident of a secure care home. Except perhaps that he was treated with more respect.

Sundays were different. Less guards on duty. More kitchen staff, barmen and waiters. The regulations that governed his custodial regime, already pretty relaxed, were even less energetically observed. Up country members of the club on a weekend break in the capital staying overnight. Nairobi-based senior police officers and their families dropping by to use the tennis courts or sit around the empty pool, sipping cold drinks. Even they, though they could afford private medicine, saw little inconsistency in consulting a foreigner held on serious charges about their concerns and, after an early, uncomfortable reserve, several invited Tom to sit with them, treated him to passion fruit juice and Fanta while listing their various ailments.

Tom, even whilst recognising the ridiculousness of his feelings, increasingly resented these weekend interlopers. Logically of course he fully accepted that they were the rightful users of the Club, but he couldn't shake off the feeling that this was now his territory, into which they intruded.

Lunch was a little better than other days on Sunday: usually a roast with over-cooked vegetables and thick, school-dinner-type lumpy gravy. Even the food, invariably anglicised, was institutionalised. They had asked him if he wanted to be escorted to church, or have a clergyman visit him. He'd thanked them but declined. On this Sunday however, he'd asked to see McKenzie, and had to excuse himself from a Chief Superintendent's description of his varicose veins, on seeing him, attired in a t-shirt and shorts, arrive.

"What? It's Sunday," said McKenzie on seeing Tom's raised eyebrow.

"I know. It's just that I haven't even seen you without a jacket and tie before."

"Aye, well. You wanted to talk to me?"

Tom steered his visitor away from the suddenly silent groups poolside and toward the clubhouse, "I want to ask your advice about oaths," he began.

"Whoa. Hold on! Stop right there. You know, I'm no lawyer. It's Leo Kane you should be consulting . . ."

"No, no. It's not legal advice I'm looking for," said Tom, shaking his head vigorously, "Or the insights of a priest. You're a Servant of the Crown. You've signed the same sorts of things I have. It's you I need to talk to."

"Well, OK . . ." said McKenzie uncertainly, "but remember what you and Kane discuss is privileged. That protection doesn't extend to anything you say to me."

"I understand that," said Tom, impatiently. "Look, it's simply this: I took an oath of secrecy back then. I swore not to reveal certain things and, well, I consider myself still bound by that oath. But if I give evidence in court, I'll take another oath. To tell the truth." Tom stopped speaking, frowned and simply shrugged.

"And?" prompted McKenzie.

"Well, how can I reconcile the two?"

"You can't. So don't give evidence. You have that right. Keep quiet. Problem solved."

"But I want to give evidence. I want to speak in my own defence."

"Well, that's a decision for you," said McKenzie, doubtfully, "in consultation with your council."

"But if I do . . . tell them what I know, what I've done, then what about the Official Secrets Act? Will I have breached it? Could I be prosecuted back home?"

"Dr Miles, you really need to be talking to a lawyer about this . . ."

"But what do you think?" insisted Tom, "I want to know what you feel?"

"I think there's a reason accused persons have the right to silence," McKenzie said quietly, looking round at the studiously disinterested police officers. "And I really think you need to be talking to Leo Kane about this, not me."

"Oh, I will," Tom assured him. "When the time is right."

All this time, I've thought of myself as the victim. The one it's all happening to. The prisoner in the dock. The corpse on the dissecting table. The butterfly in the killing jar. But now I realise I'm actually the one in control. The game's moved to a point where I suddenly hold all the vital cards. And I can choose how they are played. The balance of advantage has shifted. At the same time, all the things that mattered before no longer count. Whatever reputation I had is shot. My life, my family and my past have all become public property, open to all and sundry, like a rundown stately home. The fact that someone still lives there merely adds to the punter's voyeuristic pleasure.

My life is destroyed, and yet out of this comes a freedom. I guess that sounds crazy. How can a man in my position call himself free? Yet I am. Free at last to confront that which, for so long, has been locked away.

CHAPTER THIRTY-SEVEN

In the UK a select team of civil servants and Treasury Counsel had been working all weekend to draft the petition Leo Kane was due to present at 6 pm, Monday. A masterclass in task management. By 11.45 am Monday, Nairobi time, the product of their labour, a crisply argued six pages, was simultaneously e-mailed to the High Commission and Sena Chambers.

At Sena, Leo printed off the final page, perused it, and then passed it to Aliya.

"It looks good," he said. "Bloody good."

Kapadia's secretary checked the e-mail inbox. Comments from the High Commission had yet to arrive. She was to make the necessary amendments to the document so that it accorded to Kenyan Judicial conventions. She decided to give it another 30 minutes before starting. Leo and Aliya went out for lunch. The actual presentation of the petition was likely to be a photo call, and Leo intended to fit in a haircut before he presented it, in person, at the Chief Justice's Chambers at 10 minutes to 6.

In the bar of the Grand Regency, General Harris held forth on the virtues of National Service and the merits of short, sharp shocks to a polite circle of journalists.

At the Safari Club, Nick Easton heard a whisper that prompted him to off-load several billion shillings worth of stock.

In his room at the Police Club, Tom Miles inspected the bleeding gums of one of his custodians, and recommended a course of treatment.

Paul Muya, having already lodged his petition hours earlier, spent the remainder of the day reading the Bible.

Court re-convened at 10 am the next morning. The Chief Justice took his seat without a word, or a nod. He was clearly, massively, pre-occupied. At two minutes past the hour, a single gun sounded, and from the bell tower at the Cathedral down the street, a tolling could be heard. There was a silence. Then the Chief Justice rose, and everybody else stood too.

"His Excellency, the President, our beloved Mzee, departed this life at 8.45 this morning," he announced, solemnly. "There will be three days' official mourning during which this court will be adjourned. At midday today, I will administer the oath of Office of the President of the Republic of Kenya to Mr John Ole Kisii. In view of this development, the petitions presented to me are void. The President, once sworn, will not be called to give evidence in this matter. This Court stands adjourned."

"And the clock starts ticking," whispered Leo to Aliya. "Ninety days till elections. Well, well, well."

The Chief Justice turned to leave. Paul Muya's normally urbane face looked now like that of a child, suddenly lost and fearful among strange adults. He called after the Chief Justice, pleading with him to pause.

The Chief Justice turned, looking worn, and sad. "What is it, Mr Muya?" he asked, heavily.

"My Lord," said Paul Muya, desperately. "In view of the announcement you have just made, I want you to know that when we reconvene, the prosecution will close. We will not be calling any further witnesses."

The Chief Justice nodded absently, and left the court.

The reaction in the streets outside was muted. There was almost a sense of relief. Not because the President was particularly reviled, but rather because his passing seemed to many so long overdue. His people were, by hard experience, reconciled to death. Malaria, AIDS, and simply travelling in over-crowded mutatus accounted for too many of their fellow citizens, too young, and with too much left undone. In such a society, the idea of a man, even one as once great as the late President, kept alive, brain-dead, by a machine, was less than easy to contemplate. Many thought it an obscenity, when children were still dying for lack of pure water to drink. His time had come, several months earlier. It was a kind of blasphemy to keep his poor old heart beating and his juices flowing through a cocoon of wires and tubes.

For the last few months, it had been as though the natural development of the State had similarly been held in abeyance. As though the body politic too had been maintained in limbo on life support. In a vegetative state. Now life, of a sort, could begin again.

Outside the courtroom, Paul Muya's supporters, free now to declare their man as a potential president, conducted a muted demonstration-cum-prayer meeting.

The President's death presented the British Government with something of a conundrum. On the one hand, the dead President had been a staunch ally of the West in the Cold War days, an implacable enemy of Communism and an elder statesman of the Commonwealth. On the other hand, he had been undemocratic, corrupt, venal and, in his last years, paranoid.

Then there was this whole business about the Tom Miles trial. Whoever attended the funeral representing the United Kingdom would inevitably have to shake hands with the new President, and offer the Nation's sympathy. How would that look?

"There's nothing like a state funeral for getting things sorted out," the Head of Chancery cheerfully assured David Mowbray. "It's a summit, without the posturing. HMG will be able to talk to Ole Kisii, face to face. It's the best chance we've got. I think we should urge the PM himself to come."

Nick Easton gave a half laugh, and shook his head as though amazed that anyone so stupid managed to tie his own shoelaces in the morning. "I've already advised them to dispatch some lesser royal. Keep the formal representation as downbeat as they possibly can, and then let the rest of the UK delegation be personal acquaintances. If the Kenyans feel slighted, all well and good. A lesser royal and, if they must, the Minister for Africa. But no more."

After the funeral, John Ole Kisii spent several hours receiving formal expressions of condolence on behalf of his people.

The time allocated to each delegation, and the coverage given in the part of the media his party still controlled, was in direct proportion to the status of the visitor, and the cordiality of their current relationship with Kenya.

As a result, a delegation of ministers from Ethiopia received the same amount of time as the Vice President of the United States. The UK's Minister for Africa was allocated six minutes less.

The vapid royal who headed the delegation represented Her Majesty in her role as Sovereign of Great Britain. In her role as Head of the Commonwealth, she was represented by the Secretary General of the Commonwealth Secretariat. But it was the Minister for Africa, accompanied by Britain's High Commissioner, Mowbray, his Head of Chancery and McKenzie that Ole Kisii most looked forward to speaking with. Formal statements were out of the way in three minutes flat, and they settled down to some serious horse trading.

Ole Kisii was pleased to notice how uncomfortable Mowbray was in the presence of his boss, and took delight in taunting him about their earlier discussions.

"It's a . . . difficult business, Your Excellency," the Minister offered.

Ole Kisii shrugged, "I don't see the difficulty for men like you and me. It's a matter for lawyers, not for us."

"But our countries . . ."

"This is nothing to do with nations," Ole Kisii interjected, with a mischievous smile. "Isn't that right, Mr Mowbray? This is to do with Paul Muya and Dr Miles. They are the protagonists. We are mere spectators. We may roar and shout, and perhaps even cheer now and again, but we cannot join in the game."

"But you could end it. Right here and now."

Ole Kisii spread his hands, and widened his eyes. "Could I? How?"

"You could declare an amnesty. In memory of the late President, or in celebration of your advancement. You could pardon not just Tom Miles, but several other embarrassing legacies of an earlier age."

"I suppose I could," agreed Ole Kisii, as though the idea had never occurred to him, "but I'm not going to. You know, I have never understood the concept of such amnesties. If a crime is committed, the guilty must be punished. The appointment of a new President, or a significant anniversary or the birth of an heir seems to me to have nothing to do with the right and the wrong of it. Mr Mowbray, what do you say?"

Mowbray shifted, and mumbled a few platitudes.

"I should like to see him. Tom Miles," said the Minister, abruptly. He wasn't going to pussy-foot around any longer.

Ole Kisii smiled. "Of course. Visiting hours are a matter of public knowledge. If you want to see him at any other time, you will need to make an application to the Ministry of Home Affairs, but I'm sure they will look upon it favourably. Will you be talking to Paul Muya, too?"

The question took the Minister somewhat by surprise. He frowned.

Ole Kisii shrugged, "No? Oh well. I'm sure he's keen to talk to you."

An aide approached and cleared his throat, discreetly. Ole Kisii glanced up at the clock. "Now you must forgive me. Your Royal Highness, gentlemen: On behalf of the people of Kenya I thank you for your condolences at this painful time."

The delegation rose. In turn, according to their rank and status, they approached the President, and shook his hand, and nodded their heads, and a State photographer recorded each for posterity and subsequent publication.

As Ole Kisii shook the Minister's hand he held on to it, and whispered, "We are both riding on the crocodile's back, you know that? We dare not jump off, and if we don't hold on tight, the creature will devour us. How tight is your grip, my friend?"

"I like that man," admitted the Minister for Africa grudgingly, as the British delegation headed back to the High Commission. "But I want some action, and I want it now. I do not intend to return to London with nothing to show for my trip but a picture of me kow-towing to the bugger and a bag full of crap. Get me in to see Tom Miles. And I want to see Nick Easton again, too."

There were meetings. Lots of meetings. The Minister had allocated a further day to the matter, and he was determined to achieve some kind of breakthrough. He bullied, cajoled, pleaded and threatened. He had his photograph taken with Tom Miles, offered him assurances and gave him gifts. He even had Nick Easton call Paul Muya to see if some agreement could be brokered. But all to no avail. Disgruntled, he set about his officials and when that failed to assuage his frustration, had Aliya Zain called up at Nick Friedlander's funeral in Mombasa and treated her to a seven minute harangue on what he wanted to see happen and what he thought she needed to do.

On the eve of their return to London, while the Minister was ensconced with the day's batch of papers Her Majesty's Courier had brought out for him, and the royal was addressing a wildlife conservation society of which she was Patron, Nick Easton and McKenzie set out in opposite directions to fulfil missions of their own.

McKenzie had a few questions to ask Leo Kane, and a few thoughts to share.

Nick Easton had an envelope to deliver.

Every shop, hotel, bar, government office, school, hospital, in fact every public place in Kenya, other than places of worship, were required by law to display prominently an image of the

President. After three days of mourning, the old images of Mzee, some remarkably youthful in black and white dating back to the 70s, were taken down and replaced with new images of John Ole Kisii, bashed out by the Government printer who had been working, day and night, ever since the late President's demise.

Some, even in his own party, wondered whether this was a particularly valuable expenditure: after all, they argued, he might only be President for a further 87 days.

The opposition parties protested to the Electoral Commission about what they saw as blatant electioneering at public expense. Factions, parties and groupings which could not agree about very much other than their implacable hatred of John Ole Kisii came together briefly to see if they could develop a common platform. They couldn't, but two erstwhile rivals found to their and everyone else's surprise they could do business with one another and formed a coalition which promptly adopted Paul Muya as its flag bearer in the forthcoming Presidential campaign.

Paul, predictably, accepted the nomination with a bishop and two chiefs by his side and in the full glare of extensive publicity.

The ruling party adopted, unopposed, John Ole Kisii.

"Do you still think Paul Muya and Ole Kisii are hand in glove?" McKenzie couldn't resist asking Nick Easton.

"Wait and see," Nick Easton replied. "If a week is a long time in British politics, three months is an aeon out here."

CHAPTER THIRTY-EIGHT

The trial reopened, Paul formally closed the Prosecution's case and Leo lodged the almost inevitable plea of no case to answer.

The Chief Justice had nodded, finished his longhand record of the plea then quietly asked the Assessors to withdraw. Leo outlined his argument. Paul Muya rose to respond but the Chief Justice halted him with a raised hand.

"You have rested, Mr Muya. We will adjourn while I consider."

"Take a look at Paul Muya – watch him closely," Leo said to Aliya as he leafed through his notes with exaggerated nonchalance. "What's he doing?"

"Whispering furiously to his supporting attorneys – just like you are."

"I'll bet he is!" Leo chuckled. "Hopefully this will force him to show his hand. He's holding something back, I'm sure of it. He must have something more. Something he's saving to use in cross-examination. I want the CJ to ask him to respond to our submission. If he does, Paul will have to declare what he's got up his sleeve."

When the Chief Justice returned, it was clear that Leo's strategy had failed. In measured tones, the Judge concluded that natural justice and the rule of law both required that the trial should not be prematurely terminated at this stage. The defence should therefore proceed to call its first witness.

Leo swore under his breath. Aliya watched Paul Muya. Paul Muya smiled.

Opening the case for the Defence, Leo stood, his hands in

269

his pockets. He remained still for a while, shaking his head, bemused, then addressed the Bench as though it had only just occurred to him that they were there. After a brief reiteration of the weaknesses he perceived in the Prosecution's case, Leo called his first witness – General Sir Malcolm Harris.

Leo led the old soldier through the questions they had prepared and thoroughly practised. He moved forward with caution, as though leading a blind man through a minefield. He recalled the vigour with which he had torn into Paul's first expert witness, and had initially feared for the General's ability to stand up under a similar assault from Paul. However Leo and Aliya, indeed Kapadia himself, who was the most bruising interrogator Leo had ever seen, had each subjected the General to blistering cross-examinations, and been pleasantly surprised by how well he had held up. The old man clearly relished the verbal sparring and emerged from these bouts bright-eyed and unflustered.

Having taken the General through his career in outline, dwelling for a few minutes on how he had won his Military Cross (he had crawled across open ground under heavy enemy fire to recover a wounded, and conveniently black, soldier), Leo concentrated on the counter-insurgency operations in which the General had been involved, comparing and contrasting tactics adopted in Palestine, Malaya, and Kenya.

The General talked with enthusiasm about the validity of "getting out where the trouble was" and the value of initiatives such as the Combined Action Teams in Kenya.

"Sir Malcolm," Leo asked, "Were you ever actively engaged in the Aberdares or Mt Kenya forests?"

The General shook his head. "Not during the Emergency, no. But I co-ordinated a series of exercises there in '64."

"General, have you ever had any dealings with Mau Mau fighters?"

"Yes. When I returned to Kenya in '63 to help establish a training capability. Several of the chaps on complement then were ex-Mau Mau."

"Did you ever discuss the Emergency with them?"

"Of course! We were all old soldiers who'd shared a campaign. We talked a lot about those days."

"Sir Malcolm, how did you feel about those men?"

"Feel about them? I liked them! Admired them, too. Crack jungle fighters. Far and away the best we'd had to face, and I told them so, too! Wish I'd had fifty of those fellahs with me in Malaya. No question. And they told me how they felt about us: How'd they'd respected us. They'd hated the KPR and Kikuyu Home Guard, mind you . . ."

Leo was surprised Paul had let that bit of hearsay pass, and thought it best to hurry the General along to their *pièce de résistance* while their luck held.

"Sir Malcolm, have you ever witnessed an event which you would regard as a war crime?"

The corners of the old soldier's mouth turned down, and he nodded, briskly, "Once. In Palestine. Two British sergeants had been taken by terrorists and hanged. They'd booby-trapped the ground too so those trying to cut them down were blown up. Feelings were running pretty high. The next week, four of my chaps manning a checkpoint caught a couple of young Zionists with explosives and small arms on them. They could have apprehended them, but they let them make a break for it, so that they could gun them down."

"What did you do about it?"

"Had 'em charged with murder. No question. In a counter-insurgency situation," said the old soldier, with pride, "One cannot afford to let standards slip."

Leo thanked the General, and sat. Paul Muya rose, smiling pleasantly. He thanked Leo, greeted the General politely, complimented him on how well he had conducted himself during the examination-in-chief. Even asked if he would like a chair, or a glass of water. The General eyed him warily, as though suspecting he might have explosives strapped to his chest, and said firmly that he would not.

"Sir Malcolm, you took part in Operation Anvil, did you not?"
"I did."

271

"What was the purpose of the operation?"

Leo was on his feet. "My Lord, Sir Malcolm is not a military historian, nor was he part of the overall planning and command of the operation. Dr Miles is not charged with any matter relating to the operation. I fail to see the point of my friend's question."

"Mr Muya?"

"My Lord, the Defence has put up this witness as something between a character witness, although he admits he doesn't know Dr Miles from Adam, and an expert on counter-insurgency operations. He took part in Operation Anvil. So too did the accused. As a career soldier he presumably had some idea of what it was all about. I do not seek an authoritative historical account of the aims and objectives of Anvil, but I would like to hear this witness's understanding of the purpose of the operation in which both he and Dr Miles were actively involved in positions of command, albeit junior ones. I fully expect to be able to demonstrate to the satisfaction of the Court that there is a direct link between Dr Miles' actions during that operation and the charges he now faces."

"Very well, Mr Muya. You may proceed," The Chief Justice agreed. "The witness will answer the question."

The General tugged at the cuffs of his blazer. He knew this was what he was in the witness box for: Leo had explained to him his main objective was to draw Paul's fire over Anvil, a challenge the General relished. "Anvil was aimed at destroying Mau Mau support in Nairobi. Ordnance and supplies were being sent up to the terrorists in the forests from here. Anvil basically involved throwing a cordon round the city, then searching the entire place, sector by sector, weeding out every Kikuyu, Embu and Meru for screening."

"In your view, was this operation justified?"

"Yes. It was. Cutting off the enemy's source of supply is a prerequisite to ultimate victory."

"And was it a success?"

"Yes. The Mau Mau High Command was scattered. Many

272

of them were detained. The enemy lost the initiative. It was a great success."

"Some say the Operation was pursued ruthlessly and brutally. What do you say to that?"

The General paused, and frowned, pensively. "It was a very ambitious combined military and police operation. Overall, it was conducted vigorously but with discipline and restraint. There might have been one or two isolated incidents where individuals got carried away and exceeded their orders but I know of no such incidents involving British military personnel."

"So not in your view a crime against humanity?"

"Absolutely not!"

"I'm going to read you something, Sir Malcolm," said Paul, taking a thin book in a plain paper cover which the female attorney at his table offered to him, "to which I would like you to listen very carefully." He turned to the first of the marked pages and began: "*They came before dawn. One moment, the streets were empty and silent. The next, full of soldiers and policemen. They kept the engines of their vehicles running. The sergeants bellowed out orders, and the backs of the lorries crashed down. Soldiers with guns leapt out, their heavy boots and foreign oaths loud in the pre-dawn silence.*

"*Some of us were on the streets, even at that time. The soldiers went into action immediately. Men walking to work were thrust up against walls, their hands forced above their heads as they were briskly searched. The soldiers demanded to see their papers, and when they found out what we were, they hauled us off toward the lorries.*

"*Any who ran were brought down. The soldiers were thorough, efficient, and well disciplined. They were kept under firm control by their officers.*

"*It was the policemen who were worse. They kicked open doors, and dragged us, roughly from our sleep. There was nowhere to hide. Soon, there were hundreds of us gathered together, trembling with fear and dread, for we had heard stories about camps, where they were putting our people.*

273

"By the end of the day, they had taken every one of us from the city."

"Sir Malcolm," said Paul, as he gently closed the book and held it to his chest, "do you think what I have read is a fair account of Operation Anvil?"

As he listened, the memories flooded in on Tom with remarkable clarity: The soldier with thick gloves splaying out concertinas of barbed wire to establish ad-hoc holding bomas in the middle of closed-off streets. The tiny Welsh corporal screaming, "Kipande, Kipande! Show us yer fuckin' Kipande!" up into the dazed faces of Africans a good foot taller than him. The squatting lines of bruised and bleeding men – the ones who had tried to run, their heads daubed with yellow paint to mark them out for special interrogation at the screening camp.

And the hooded men, sitting in the back of a police truck who, with a silent nod, indicated which of the sullen huddle should be retained, and which released.

He remembered too the beauty of the sunrise that morning and the plaintive squeal of the dry bearing in the swivel of the Bren mounted on the back of a Land Rover. Most vividly of all, he remembered the two policemen standing over the crumpled figure in the narrow alley . . .

"Sir Malcolm?" Paul prompted, for the General too seemed lost in distant memories. "Is this a reasonable account of the operation you and Dr Miles took part in?"

With an effort, Tom dragged himself back to the present. The old soldier stood erect, glanced across for a moment at Tom, gave him a determined nod then turned to meet Paul Muya's stare. "From the point of view of one of your people on the receiving end of it, perhaps. Yes. I think I would have to say it is a reasonable account."

"Then you would be wrong, Sir Malcolm," said Paul, triumphantly, "what I read to you was an extract from the diary of a holocaust survivor describing an SS operation in Poland in 1943."

The courtroom exploded with voices. The Chief Justice

banged the bench with his gavel, but was unable to restore order.

"The Commanding Officer of that operation," Paul Muya continued, shouting above the confusion, "was sentenced to fifteen years for war crimes."

"Mr Muya!" the Chief Justice roared.

"Three junior officers involved were each sentenced to 10 years imprisonment!" Paul bellowed, "No further questions!" He flung the book onto his table and dropped back into his seat, his arms folded.

Leo was on his feet demanding to be heard. The Chief Justice threatened to have the Court cleared. When the hubbub subsided to a persistent mumble, Leo protested vehemently. Demanded that Paul's entire cross-examination be ruled inadmissible, that the entire case be dismissed, and that the Chief Justice recommend Paul be disciplined by the Bar Society.

The Chief Justice held up his hand against Leo's protestations, "Mr Muya," he intoned, his quiet voice trembling with anger, "I share Mr Kane's outrage. I have consistently warned counsel that I will not tolerate games to pander to the media or to score some cheap political advantage. I now intend to adjourn for the rest of the day to consider whether the fact that you misled me as to the relevance of these questions constitutes a grave contempt."

Paul tried to speak, but the Chief Justice continued, "I will not hear you now, Mr Muya. I strongly recommend that you spend the rest of the day considering your next words to this court very, very carefully. When we reconvene tomorrow you will have your opportunity to make a statement."

The reporters were out of the court before the Chief Justice was even halfway to his chambers. Leo glanced across at Paul who sat, with his hand on his female colleague's shoulder, whispering quickly into her ear. Paul turned as he realised Leo was looking at him. "So much for your expert, Coke," he said with a smile. "You should have accepted the deal I offered."

Leo realised that no matter what happened the next day, Paul

275

had won. He suspected that Paul would always win. It was something, like praying to God and being kind to children, he just couldn't help but do.

"Well, that didn't go very well, did it?" Aliya said, gently.

Leo sighed. "No, it didn't. Let's get out of here and start putting together a petition for a mistrial."

As they left the court, Leo turned, for a final look at Paul. The Total Man still sat very close, in discussion with the female attorney.

Aliya, who had walked on ahead, came back and stood beside Leo.

"Is she his woman?" Aliya asked, nodding at the woman with whom Paul was deep in conversation. There was something about the way they leaned in toward each other that, although they weren't touching, or even looking at one another, seemed, if not sexual, still profoundly intimate.

"No," said Leo, deadpan. "Mine. Once."

Outside the Court, Leo held up his hands to stem the barrage of questions, and the reporters, like a well trained pack, fell silent, thrusting hand-held microphones and digital recorders into his face.

Leo frowned, and bit his bottom lip, as though searching for exactly the right words. He half turned, to check that the ever present Tyson and Joseph were in shot, close by. He wanted them to be seen, not as they were, a comfort and surprisingly amiable company, but as an image of Government repression. Not his protectors, but representatives of the oppressive state against which he was battling. They were not there.

"Typical," he thought. "First time they can be useful, and they're nowhere in sight."

"This trial is a sham," he declared, "a show trial reminiscent of the worst excesses of Stalinism. The Prosecutor seems determined to exploit this matter for his own political advantage. This is wrong. My client deserves, and has a right to expect, a fair trial focused solely on the charges he faces."

The questions began: How much longer would the trial last? Was Leo going to apply for a mistrial? Leo began to answer but halted in mid-sentence and he and the reporters and cameramen paused and turned as around thirty people across the street exploded with chants and two large banners were unfurled: the first said 'Justice for Jembe' in English, and the second 'Death to the killer' in Ki-Swahili.

The chanting fell into a pattern, led by a young man in dark glasses and a fluorescent shell suit. While attention was focused on the demonstrators, a strong forearm suddenly appeared over Leo's left shoulder, jolting his head back, and held him firm. Before he could make a sound or react in any way, a voice hissed in his ear. "The spirit of Jembe," so close, he could feel the warmth of the breath. Then another hand appeared over his right shoulder. A vicious panga with an eight inch blade swung down, biting into his left hip.

Aliya screamed, reporters spun, and cameras fast-focused, automatic winders clicking and ticking like overwound toys. The panga blade was dragged fast up across Leo's stomach and chest, and over his shoulder. His assailant pushed him forward, turned and ran. Three of Dieter Haas' men, in the shadows just inside the High Court building, raced out, paused for a moment as their eyes adjusted to the glare after the gloom of the hallway in which they had sat all day, and opened fire with Heckler and Koch MP7s. Leo's assailant pirouetted clumsily as blood spurted from wounds in his upper chest, groin and thigh. The panga somersaulted from his hand. He fell heavily to the ground, thirty feet from the huddle of reporters and photographers crouching around Leo, trying to catch the last gasped word, or final image, as Aliya screamed over and over for someone to get help. The blood-stained blade clattered down beside Leo's dead assailant.

CHAPTER THIRTY-NINE

Aliya was left trembling, sick and profoundly scared. No matter what she did, she simply couldn't get warm. It was as though her internal organs had been chilled, and no amount of sun on her skin could get heat that far back into her. There were moments, and images, she recalled with a lurid intensity from amid the blur of those few seconds: Sunlight catching the panga blade just before it first bit through the material of Leo's clothes. The sick wail from the white female reporter on whose blouse his blood splashed. The clumsy, ludicrous heap into which Leo had collapsed. The butcher's block reek of his assailant's blood on the hot pavement.

She suspected that had she vomited or fainted she would now be feeling somewhat better. But she hadn't and the stark horror of the incident, its obscene and naked brutality lay cold and heavy within her. Undigested; undisgorged. She should have gone through some process, she thought, which would now allow her to deal with it. But she hadn't, and now she couldn't think what that process would be, short of a nervous breakdown.

Leo sat propped up in the hospital bed. He had needed twelve stitches in a wound on his hip, and a further eight over his shoulder. His stomach and chest had been protected by a toughened vest which, unbeknown to her, he had donned every morning since the start of the trial.

He asked the nurse to remove the operating gown that he still wore, and then asked her to hold up a small hand mirror so that he could see how he looked. He was slashed and stitched from mid-chest, just above his right nipple to the point of his shoulder and again across his lower belly and hip.

He was shaken, and he suspected that he too was in shock. He was convinced that the sudden summonsing away of the distraught and contrite Tyson and Joseph had been part of a well-orchestrated event, as had the demonstration. He was convinced too that the best way of dealing with the next few hours would be to concentrate on activity, and not give himself time to reflect on what so nearly happened, or indeed on what actually had.

The front of the operating gown he'd just had removed was stiff with dried blood. So were the sleeves and front of Aliya's blouse. An image of Jackie Kennedy, her pink suit spattered with her husband's gore, flashed through his mind. He asked for the gown back. The nurse promised to fetch him a clean one. Leo told her not to bother.

"It could have been a hell of a lot worse, but for that," said Leo to the shivering Aliya, in an attempt to cheer her. He nodded to the gashed black jerkin which had taken the brunt of his assailant's blade.

"A bullet-proof vest?" Aliya said, frowning.

"Well, I suspect that's a rather low-tech description of it: a friend of mine gave it to me as a precaution against the possibility of State reprisals. Apparently it's what the President of Malaysia's bodyguards wear. You know, the guys who are trained to get in the way of bullets."

"But not a precaution you thought it appropriate to advise Tom Miles – or me – to adopt?" said Aliya, her lips a thin, hard line.

"No," admitted Leo, frankly, "Tom Miles' physical protection is the responsibility of the State, not mine. I was pretty sure if anybody was going to get hit, it would be me. And I was right. So what's the big issue?"

"There is such a thing as being caught in the cross-fire."

The corners of Leo's mouth turned down as he pondered this possibility for the first time.

"And who were the guys with the machine guns?"

"Employees of that friend of mine."

"Paul Muya's outside: he's just talking to some reporters, then he's on his way up."

"Well, you can tell him he can piss off for starters. I'm not having him milking this for all its worth. Tell someone to send the reporters up here. I'd like to talk to them myself."

Twenty minutes later, Leo was sure he was in shock. A slick perspiration greased his horribly pallid face. His eyelids flickered up and down and the room seemed excessively bright. But he was determined that the press conference should proceed, staged exactly as he required.

On cue, the press entered. As Leo had insisted, Aliya, wearing the same black skirt and white blouse with Leo's blood in camera-shot over her left breast, sat silently beside the bed, her hands folded on her lap.

Leo declined to respond to individual questions, good wishes or greetings even from those court reporters he had known for years. He lay, pale and unsmiling, propped up, stitched upper chest exposed amid a lightning storm of camera flashes and a static of shutter clucks.

When the VOK cameraman confirmed with a raised thumb that the somewhat antiquated camera he was using, which rested on the shoulder of a crouching assistant, was ready, Leo reached out for Aliya's hand.

"A state which permits its advocates to be subjected to lynch law on the very steps of its highest court," he said, slowly and evidently racked in pain, "totters on the very brink of anarchy and moral collapse."

"Had you asked for police protection?" asked a reporter, thrusting a Phillips pocket memo cassette recorder toward Leo.

"Since Miss Zain's arrival, we have both – supposedly – been accorded such protection. This afternoon that protection was withdrawn, without notice."

"Are you saying this was a conspiracy?"

"I am telling you what happened. You must draw your own conclusions."

"Is it true you have refused to see Paul Muya?"

"I have no comment to make on that."

"People are saying you deliberately threw yourself between the assailant and Miss Zain?"

Leo allowed himself a tight, brave smile. He attempted a modest shrug, then winced in pain. "I'm a defender, remember?"

That didn't quite accord with Aliya's recollection, but she still marvelled at the performance.

There was a pause, as all present recognised the quality of this copy, and ensured they took it down, verbatim.

"Will you seek a retrial?"

"I've not yet had the opportunity to discuss this with my client," Leo said, adding with a self-deprecating smile, "I've been somewhat preoccupied in the last few hours, but my advice to him will be to seek a brief adjournment, and then we will proceed. He has a right to his day in court."

"Will you be fit enough to finish the trial?"

"If I am spared. And in the meantime," Leo added, turning a brave smile on Aliya, and patting her hand paternally, "my colleague and friend Miss Zain will lead Dr Miles' defence in my place."

"It's completely out of the question!" said Aliya, once the reporters had been ushered from the room.

Leo sighed, and stared up at the ceiling. "Stop pacing. It makes me feel ill. I don't know what you're so worked up about."

Aliya stopped pacing. She stood at the foot of his bed, her hands clenched around the metal frame of the bed so that her knuckles showed proud and pale. "Leaving aside the fact that you didn't have the courtesy to discuss this with me first, or even thought it appropriate to consult your client about it? Well, A, or one, I have precious little experience of advocacy. B, or two, no background in this legal system and, C, or three, as you never tire of telling me, the sight of an Asian woman defending a white man for killing a black hero is not going to help Tom Miles' case at all."

281

"Ah, but that was before," said Leo. "Before I learnt the error of my ways. All over Africa, millions watch Bollywood epics, did you know that? Many people know the songs by heart without understanding a word of Hindi. And in how many of those films is there a beautiful young female lawyer defending some noble cause? Have you seen *Veer-Zaara*? Oh, I forgot. You despise modern Indian films. Well, a shitload of others don't and Dilip assures me it's but the latest of a long list of Bollywood blockbusters featuring fetching young female lawyers appearing for the defence. And that's how they'll see you now! You're the heroine. They won't associate you with the paan-chewing factory owners and bloated Duka-wallahs who rip them off every day, but with their heroes of the Indian cinema. I don't know why I didn't think of it before."

"But I'm not qualified to undertake Tom's defence."

"On paper you are. And besides, you've spent the last few weeks watching a master at work, and you've argued all manner of cases and causes with me with far greater eloquence than most practising barristers. You'll do fine. Trust me. Look how you took that tosser Rosenberg. Fourteen ways this side of Friday, remember? Advocates with decades of experience couldn't have done that. Now please, leave me to my pain. I feel myself fading. Oh, and switch on the TV on your way out. Who knows? We may be headlining the six o'clock news."

The entire trial hung in limbo. As the clock ticked towards the presidential election the fate of Tom Miles was no longer the biggest story in Kenya as far as the world's media was concerned. There was an even bigger trial of strength scheduled three months hence.

The Electoral Commission set the date. Other parties and factions named their contenders for the highest office in the land, but they were a clutch of discredited mediocrities, threadbare and irrelevant. Former ministers, bitter men who felt they deserved better. It was set to be a straight contest between John Ole Kisii, and Paul Mumbu Muya.

The Old Man, and the Total Man.

CHAPTER FORTY

"What do you think this is all about?" Johnny Sandford asks me one night. "This whole business. What it's all for?"

He's been down in the mouth for a few days. Ever since he went down to Nairobi to attend some sitrep meeting or other. It's clear that he has something on his mind, but he doesn't seem willing to share it. Not with Foss, or me, and it isn't my place to ask.

So I stay quiet. Till now.

"It's about them, wanting us, out of their country," I venture. "Them wanting to drive whites off land they think of as theirs."

"Do you really think so?" says Johnny. "Then how do you account for the fact that Mau Mau have killed hundreds, thousands, of their fellow Kikuyu? While more whites have died in road accidents in Nairobi alone than have been killed by Mau Mau throughout the whole of Kenya? And don't tell me it's because of the fine job we're doing defending the white homesteaders. You've seen how many farms and shambas there are out there with a single white family, holding out. If they'd really wanted to they could have picked the whole lot off in a single night and we couldn't have got to more than a handful of them. No, you've got it wrong. So unfortunately, have all the rest of us. This is not the natives versus the settlers. It's not the end of anything. This is the beginning of something. What we are witnessing are the birth pains of an independent Kenya. The struggle of a nation to free itself from its past. Blacks aren't fighting whites. Commie insurgents aren't pitted against the forces

283

of western democracy. Young Africans are fighting old Africans. Kenyans are fighting Kenyans."

He looks at me, and he suddenly seems very old. "This isn't about them and us. It's just about us. We Kenyans. And Britain and all the Queen's horses and all the Queen's men, and her aeroplanes and her battleships, are as irrelevant as last month's horoscope. You can rain down bombs on the forest until there's not a living thing within it and pour in more and more regiments of troops until we're garrisoned like Germany but at the end of the day, we, us Kenyans, have to buckle down and sort out whether there's enough space and soul and God's good grace in this country to accommodate the men like Jembe, the men like me and, God help us all, the men like Foss, too.

"And I have a grim suspicion the answer is no. Something, someone, is going to have to give, and, as usual, it's going to have to be the men like Jembe."

He pauses, weighing up his next words. Uncertain how much he should reveal. Not quite sure, even then, how much he can trust me.

"I'm going to tell you something. Something I probably shouldn't," he begins, once he's decided, "We've got to kill Jembe if we catch him."

"I know," I tell him.

"Nonsense!" he cries, "It's Top Secret. I was only told at this month's sitrep. How could you possibly know?"

"I knew before I ever came here. I was shown the order during Anvil," I tell him.

"Why?" he asks, amazed.

"That's Top Secret too," says Foss, joining us suddenly. He seems to have an instinct for when to interrupt Johnny and me. "Isn't it, Miles?" he adds with malicious pleasure.

"I . . . Yes," I say, but I can't meet Johnny's eyes.

Things are never the same between Johnny and me after that. There is a distance. A barrier. It's as though in his mind I've changed sides. Gone over to Foss. He was willing to share secrets with me, but I'm not willing to let him in on what clearly

284

both Foss and I know. It's like I've betrayed him and he can never forgive me. He never shares his feelings and his fears with me again after that night. I feel every time he looks at me after that he no longer sees a fellow soldier, but a foreigner. I feel lonelier then than at any time other than the day of Anvil.

CHAPTER FORTY-ONE

With court scheduled to reconvene the following morning, Aliya called in on Leo in his room before retiring for the night. Half a dozen of Dieter Haas' men, in crisp dark suits and sunglasses, hover around the doorway. She had picked out several more in the hospital entrance and loitering in the car park.

Leo was sitting up in bed. On her arrival, he quickly reached for the remote control, and switched off the television he had been watching. But not quickly enough for her to have failed to catch a familiar strain of music.

She smiled broadly, "What are you watching?"

"Just a film," he said, sulkily, like a spoilt child caught out.

"Switch it back on."

"No," he said, abruptly, thrusting the remote control under the bed sheet.

She crossed to the DVD player, pressed eject and nodded as the disc emerged, its title spelt out in a rough scrawl.

"*Pyassa,*" she said, nodding, "I thought so."

"It's by Guru Dutt," he said grudgingly.

"I know," she said, rising. "What did you think of it?"

"Long," he confessed, "But it had subtitles, so I could follow it pretty well."

"So what was it about?" she said, sitting on the edge of his bed.

He shifted over, to make more space for her. "About this short, fat chap who's supposed to be starving to death because he writes poetry that everyone thinks is crap, until it appears he's topped himself. Then his poetry becomes famous and this

286

other guy, who's now married to the first guy's ex-girlfriend, makes a fortune out it. So the poet returns, denounces this other guy, sings a song renouncing the world and heads off for the Himalayas with a prostitute called, if my subtitles have it right, Rose."

She nodded, impressed.

"Of course that's only a very brief synopsis," he said. "There's a lot of walking through red light districts questioning the basic humanity of mankind, and suffering, and more singing. Still, all in all, I enjoyed it."

"Why did you get it?"

"Because I thought it would give us something to talk about. Something other than the trial."

She tilted her head to one side, and looked at him quizzically, "Why is it you always make me feel so much older than you?" She took a thin file from her shoulder bag and lay it on the bed. "The application for a mistrial. Kapadia says it's fine, but advises against presenting it. I'm going to see Tom. He's pretty upset about what happened to you. Feels, well, I won't use the word guilty. Responsible. Says he's determined now to tell all in court."

"Well, we'll have to talk him out of that breathtakingly stupid idea, won't we?" said Leo, reaching for his mobile phone, "I'll give him a call."

"Let me try first," said Aliya, "You have a look at the application. I'll call you once I've spoken to Tom. And tomorrow try *Shri 420*. Or better still *Chaudvi ka Chand*. Now there's a film . . ."

John Ole Kisii sat alone in a neglected corner of the otherwise immaculate grounds of Mombasa State House – a corner which he loved because, as its unkempt air proclaimed, it had found favour with neither of his predecessors. The hot, moist, coast aromas – salt, diesel oil and seaweed – were still, even after years of waiting on them at this their official coast residence, vaguely offensive to his sensitive, high grasslands, Masai nose.

It was late. There was little sound now of the traffic beyond the high walls which surrounded the grounds. The crickets were still and the frogs that had their home in the small, artificial lake had long since fallen silent. The old man could hear himself breathe, and feel his blood move sluggishly through his hardened arteries. He sniffed.

A discreet cough announced the arrival of his Chief of Internal Security. The old man closed his eyes, and felt a great wave of sadness move through him. Quietly, he began:

"There is a strange kind of safety in the centre of an army. Tranquillity in the heart of a turbulent crowd.

"All my life, I have been at the heart of the crowd. I told myself then, as I tell myself now, I have simply to do my duty. Then I was of the crowd. One with the people. I am not responsible for the crowd, I said to myself. I am not its leader. So I stood by, and watched the growing venality of our leaders. And I smiled, sad, to see the clay feet of the great men exposed. But I said, I am of the crowd, loyal to my people. I am not responsible. I am not a leader. Come and sit at my feet, Nikodemus."

The man who had stood in the darkness, listening, moved light-footed to kneel before his President.

"I watched," the old man continued, "older, and wiser, but still not disillusioned, as the boy I knew grew to be the man Mzee, wrapping himself in the cloak of the despot. I heard the accounts of the tortures, beatings and killings. Still I said, I am not responsible. I am one of the crowd.

"But now, I am responsible, and must choose whether I will or will not allow just such acts to be perpetrated in my name. I will not, Nikodemus. Not even when they are carried out by friends acting only out of a love for me and a determination to protect my interests. I can no longer claim that freedom. I am no longer of the crowd. It was you who organised the attack on the white lawyer."

It was not a question. It demanded no answer. The kneeling man sighed. "What do you want of me?" he asked, quietly.

The President reached out, and lightly touched the bent head before him, "I want you not to have done what you did. That's what I want. What I must now have, Nikodemus my brother, is your resignation. I will instigate an inquiry." He raised his hands, and shook his head sadly as he felt, rather than saw, the suddenly re-emerging hope. "An *independent* inquiry. You must look now to your interest. Look no more to mine. Prepare to defend yourself from this inquiry as I must now defend myself from the repercussions of your love of me."

"You throw me to the dogs," murmured Nikodemus bitterly, "like the muzungu threw Miles to us."

The old man nodded. "Yes," he agreed, "It's the same. Acts, once admired, embarrass us later. Heroes become perpetrators. Martyrs become traitors. Traitors, martyrs."

"Is there nothing I can do to . . ."

"Atone?" suggested the President, "maybe, yes, maybe. I want Tom Miles."

"Dead?" asked Nikodemus, hopefully.

The President laughed, a dry, stark laugh. "No, Nikodemus, not dead. Fetch him to me, then go. I'll give you 48 hours. Time, and money, too. But I can't give you the protection I could have acquired for you when I was still in the heart of the crowd. With the authority of this office, I now see, comes a crippling impotence. Bring Miles to me, then go, with God, my money and my love, but not with my blessing."

CHAPTER FORTY-TWO

Paul Muya pounced on Aliya as soon as she entered the Courtroom, with Kapadia wigged and gowned a pace behind her. He didn't even wait for her to reach the Defence table before racing up to her, wide-eyed. "Leo won't take my calls," he said, almost petulantly, "Neither do you."

"That's right," Aliya said. She knew he had rung her hotel room at least six times the previous evening, and four the day before. But she had all her calls screened now. Ostensibly as part of her new, enhanced security but in reality to save her the agonising calls from her family. She still Skyped them every day, but she wanted to be the one who chose the time, when she was sure she could keep up the rehearsed nonchalance.

Paul snatched at her arm, "Surely he can't think I had anything to do with . . ."

"I don't know what he thinks," said Aliya, shaking herself free, "But I'm not taking any chances."

"He must talk to me," cried Paul. "He must."

"Must he? Is it about Tom Miles?"

Paul nodded once.

"Then you can talk to me about it."

"Not about this, I can't."

Aliya frowned, "Why not?"

"Because you're not a Kenyan."

To Paul's surprise, Aliya laughed. "If they elect you President, will you sign me a certificate to that effect?"

First up, a piece of unfinished business: Paul's apology. Solemnly, he acknowledged his error, and expressed his regret. It was fulsome, but hardly abject. A ritual apology, all form and no substance. But he went through the necessary motions, and that was what the system required.

He remained standing when he came to the end. He clasped his hands in front of him, the brief notes to which he had referred only once folded neatly in his grip. He bowed his head, and awaited judgement.

The Chief Justice told him curtly that he had reported the matter to the Disciplinary Committee of the Bar Association and was content to leave further consideration of appropriate action in their hands.

"I note for the record that the Defence will today be led by Miss Aliya Zain, who will be assisted by Mr Deepak Kapadia. Mr Kapadia, you are welcome. It's many a year since you have appeared as a junior before me! Miss Zain, I want to assure you of this Court's determination that you be given every assistance. Please feel free to ask for an adjournment to consult your client or Mr Kapadia at any time."

The Chief Justice looked around the Courtroom, very much in control. Few would have recognised him as the man who had made a little publicised visit to Leo Kane's hospital room the previous afternoon to express his concern and sympathy and to discreetly check for himself the real extent of Leo's injuries.

"Today, a widely admired and well respected advocate who should be appearing before me lies in a hospital bed," he continued, "the victim of a brutal and callous attack on the very steps of this building. Today, I see advocates appearing before me who have been escorted to the door of my court by private armies. Mine is the constitutional duty to uphold the rule of law. I warn all those present and, mindful that my words may be widely reported, all those who may read this pronouncement that I will not tolerate further erosion of the basic freedoms and protections to which every citizen of the Republic is entitled by right. Now, Miss Zain, do you wish to recall your last witness?"

"No, My Lord," Aliya replied. The General had in fact already left the country, a hurt and bitter man, nursing the suspicion, not for the first time, that he'd been set up all along. "We propose now to call Dr Miles."

The inevitable rumble of noise was instantly stunned into silence by the Chief Justice's glower. "Miss Zain; Mr Muya. My Chambers. Mr Kapadia, you would of course be welcome, too."

The Chief Justice rose, sweeping his wig from his head as he left the Court. Paul was no more than four paces behind him. Kapadia rose heavily to accompany Aliya but she turned to him, and shook her head. "Stay here," she said, firmly. "Please," she added as an afterthought with a tight-lipped smile.

The Chief Justice didn't even wait to reach his Chambers. In the corridor, he turned, mopping his face with a large blue handkerchief. Paul Muya began to speak, but the Judge snapped, "You are here to listen, Mr Muya, not to speak. Miss Zain," he continued, more gently, "I don't want you to think that I am minimising your obvious ability. Nor do I want to appear in any way to question your judgement in open court but I want to be absolutely sure that you realise the implications of what you now propose. Mr Muya is here to satisfy himself that I do not give you any unfair advice or inappropriate instruction. He is free to interrupt our discussion, but only to challenge points of law, procedure or fact. I expressly forbid any expression of opinion on his part. You do realise that Dr Miles will have to speak under oath, and be subject to cross-examination by Mr Muya?"

Aliya confirmed that she did.

"And that by taking the stand your client will have forsaken his right to silence, and the Assessors will be free to interpret any refusal to answer a question as they see fit?"

Aliya nodded.

"And, unless I am persuaded that any part of the evidence threatens the life of an individual or security of the Republic, both your examination-in-chief and Mr Muya's cross will be conducted in open court and probably be reported extensively in the media?"

"I do understand all of this, My Lord," Aliya assured him.

"I would add that this is entirely Dr Miles' decision and that, whilst we do not for a moment think his appearance would do anything other than aid his defence, both Mr Kane and I have explained to him in detail the implications of his decision."

That was an understatement. They had pleaded, cajoled, threatened, warned and begged, but all to no avail. Tom Miles was determined to take the stand, no matter what. They had even asked McKenzie to get the High Commissioner to intercede, which he did but with a similar lack of success.

"Very well then," sighed the Chief Justice. "Let us return to our places, and let us remember the eyes of the world will be upon us, and conduct ourselves accordingly."

"Paul Muya's holding something back. I'm sure of it and so is Aliya," Leo had warned when he rang Tom late the previous night. "He's been playing this trial for the media right from the start. He's got something up his sleeve that he's going to pull out when he's on the stand, Tom. Must have. And by taking the stand you're playing into his hands."

"There is nothing he could possibly have that offers any threat to me."

"You've told us everything?" Leo asked.

"Everything you need to know. Everything that he could know. That's how you wanted it to be, isn't it?"

Leo shook his head. "No, it's too big a risk. You can't take the stand."

"Can't I?" Tom asked, surprised, "Surely that's my decision."

"Yes, it's your decision, in the same way that it's a patient's decision if they choose to drink themselves to death. But I presume it would be your duty as their medical advisor to persuade them against it, as strongly as you can. Well, that's the kind of obligation I have to you. And I'm advising you very, very firmly. There is nothing to be gained by you taking the stand. Nothing at all. Do not do it."

Tom Miles took the stand amid an atmosphere of high drama to face Aliya's examination-in-chief.

It was to be anything other than an interrogation: there was to be no space left for spontaneity, indiscretion or omission. Every question and every answer had been carefully scripted in Leo's hospital room and learnt by rote with Aliya and Kapadia in Tom's room in the Police Club.

The courtroom was packed, the atmosphere electric as Aliya began by walking Tom steadily through the preliminaries. There were no placemen keeping seats warm in the public gallery. Nick Easton, McKenzie and every other principal was there.

Paul Muya's normal style when the defence had the floor was to take copious notes, and scribble urgent instructions to his bevy of aides. During Tom's evidence however, he sat quite still, his hands thrust deep in his pockets, hunched forward slightly, staring at Tom like a cat contemplating, mystified, a suicidal canary.

"On 10 December 1954, were you transferred to a unit known as Combined Action Team 12?" Aliya asked.

Tom affirmed that he was.

"How would you describe your military duties in Kenya prior to that time?"

"Routine. Garrison duties. Occasional patrols. Escorting convoys."

"But you had taken part in Operation Anvil?"

"Yes, I had, although I think strictly speaking that was a police rather than a military action. Again fairly routine. Only the scale of the operation differentiated it from hundreds of other such police actions."

"Prior to your transfer to C.A.T.12 had you been involved in any direct military action?"

"No."

"Prior to your transfer had you heard of Wilson Mumbu Muya, alias General Jembe?"

Tom paused, as Kapadia had told him he should. "Yes, I had."

"Had you ever seen General Jembe?"

Again the pause, and then again. "Yes, I had. I spotted him at a political rally in August or September 1954."

"And what did you do?"

"I pointed him out to a senior police officer present."

"Can you name that police officer?"

"Superintendent Foss, although he was an Inspector then."

"And on the strength of that identification you were transferred to C.A.T.12?"

"Objection: leading," said Paul, quickly.

"Withdrawn," snapped Aliya, as fast. "Dr Miles, were you told why you were transferred to C.A.T.12?"

"I was told it was because I could identify Jembe."

"Who told you that?"

"Superintendent Foss. He was already a member of C.A.T.12 by that time."

Aliya led Tom through a description of his early days with the unit, keeping it dull, unexceptional, routine.

The atmosphere relaxed by degrees but the tension snapped back tight as she asked, "Did you ever see Jembe again?"

"Yes, I did. On the night of 30 April 1955. At a shamba in South Kinangop."

"Can you tell the court what you were doing there?"

"Superintendent Foss had received information that Jembe would be there. Major Sandford and the rest of the unit were out on patrol, so Superintendent Foss told me to go with him and we set off to apprehend Jembe."

"Go on, Dr Miles."

"When we got to the shamba, it was empty. We settled down to wait. It was a terrible night. Pouring with rain. After a time, two men appeared. One was Jembe."

"Then?"

"Then my recollection becomes very confused. At some point I received a trauma wound to the head which caused me to lose consciousness, and affected my subsequent recollection of events. When I regained consciousness, I was some distance from the shamba. I made my way back there on foot. By the time I got there, Major Sandford and the unit were already there. Jembe and Foss were both dead."

"Dr Miles," said Aliya slowly emphasising each word, "did you kill General Jembe?"

"No, I did not."

"My Lord," Aliya concluded, "I have no further questions for Dr Miles at this time."

Paul Muya rose, and stood, one hand in his pocket, frowning. "One thing I don't understand, Dr Miles: if Foss had you transferred to C.A.T.12 simply because of your ability to identify Jembe, why did he send you away at precisely the moment you would have been most useful?"

"I did identify Jembe," said Tom, simply.

"But neither the official report nor your previous evidence says that."

"Doesn't it? Foss turned to me and said "Is this Jembe?" – I said that I thought it was."

"In the dark? Your powers of observation are most impressive. Who was with him?"

"Another Mau Mau fighter."

"Really? One of his men perhaps?"

Aliya rose to object, but Tom shrugged and said, "I suppose so, yes." Aliya resumed her seat.

"Why do you suppose so?"

"I don't know. I just thought it would be. That's all."

"Who was he, Dr Miles?"

"I couldn't say."

"Couldn't you, Dr Miles?"

"No. I couldn't."

"Are you sure?"

"Yes. I'm sure."

There was a tense standoff, then Aliya asked for a recess.

During the 15 minute break, Aliya sipped a lukewarm Coke and stared, frowning slightly, at Tom.

"You didn't tell us about identifying Jembe," she said, gently.

Tom sniffed. "I forgot."

"Really?"

"Yes, really," Tom snapped. "It was a long time ago. Things come back. OK?"

"I suppose so, but it would be helpful if we hear about these flashes of recall before the Prosecution in future."

Tom treated her to a long, cool stare. "I know what I'm doing. What's the problem?"

"I'm not sure you do, but more to the point, I am very sure I don't. And *that's* the problem."

When they resumed, Paul Muya stood for a long moment, staring thoughtfully at Tom, as though considering quite how to move forward.

"Dr Miles," he began, "Remind me why you were posted to C.A.T.12."

"Because Superintendent Foss knew I could identify General Jembe."

"How?"

Tom frowned, "I'm sorry?"

"How did he know you were able to identify General Jembe?"

"Because I'd identified him successfully before."

"Oh yes," said Paul, nodding, "this was at the Kikuyu rally on the 23 September 1954. When you pointed Jembe out to Foss. In your estimation, how many people were at that rally, Dr Miles?"

Tom shrugged, "I really don't recall."

"Many?"

"Yes. Many."

"Contemporary reports say around 2000, would you accept that figure?"

"It may have been."

"Well, would you say it was significantly less?" asked Paul, speaking with a greater urgency. "No? Would you accept there were more than 100 people there?"

"Many more."

297

"More than a thousand?"

"Yes. I would say so."

Aliya half rose, but Paul threw out his hand toward her like a policeman stopping traffic. "Dr Miles, how did you manage to pick out General Jembe from among a thousand other Africans?"

Tom paused, and looked, Aliya thought, almost apologetically toward her and Kapadia.

"His description had been issued to all units in the Nairobi area."

Without turning, Paul held out his hand behind him, and snapped his fingers. Marianne Kane promptly offered up the appropriate document. "My Lord, I would refer you to the Republic's second exhibit. I quote: "*Wilson Mumbu Muya, AKA General Jembe. Around 30 years of age. Height around 5' 10", of slight build. Skin is of a dark coffee complexion. Eyes dark. Hair close cropped. Clean shaven. Nostrils wide. Full lips. Teeth evenly spaced. No tribal markings or ornamentation. Usually wears European clothes. May walk with a limp.*" Is that the description?"

"It may be."

"There's no maybe about it, Dr Miles. If you or your Counsel wish to contest the fact or to challenge the authenticity of this exhibit, you are of course at liberty to do so. I do have expert witnesses on hand who can confirm that this was the description issued in late May 1954 and still extant in September of that year. I will be happy to call them. Now, are you telling the Court that this is the basis on which you picked Jembe out of a crowd of over a thousand other black men? If so, you must be a remarkable man, Dr Miles."

Tom sat, in silence.

"Dr Miles?" Paul prompted.

"I put it to you, Dr Miles," said Paul, evenly, "that your identification of Jembe at the rally was not as a result of the description issued. I put it to you that you could recognise Jembe because you had seen him before. You had been shown a photograph of him on the afternoon of the 24 April 1954, had you not?"

"I had," Tom confirmed, so quietly he could barely be heard.

"Dr Miles?"

"I had," Tom repeated, louder.

"And several hours before that, you had not only seen General Jembe face to face, but you had actually spoken with him. Isn't that also true, Dr Miles?"

"Yes," said Tom, "That's also true."

CHAPTER FORTY-THREE

I approach my role in Anvil with no great enthusiasm, but no great concern either. I am still not familiar with the NCOs and the men I will be commanding, but my orders were clear, and I am enough of a soldier to be reassured by the fact that they leave me little scope for initiative, imagination or mistake.

We are to take up position at a designated road junction at 4 am and hold it till 7 am, or until relieved or instructed otherwise by a senior officer. I am to secure all main and side streets within a clearly specified zone, and await the police screening teams. Pending their arrival, I am to stop and search all blacks in the area and detain all men whose kipandes identify them as Kikuyu, Embo or Meru.

We have eight streets secured and flood-lit checkpoints established and working efficiently within thirty minutes. Engines are kept running to power lights. The morning reeks of exhaust fumes and echoes with roared orders. A rapidly growing crowd of men squat, resentful and scared, their hands on their heads in the middle of the road. A dozen squaddies, submachine guns at the ready, watch them. The muzzles of the Bren guns on the Land Rovers sweep the length and breadth of that mass of glowering humanity, as though sniffing out resistance.

I am walking past the end of the narrow alley – returning from making my final deployment of an NCO and six men. I don't even realise it is there. Dawn is breaking but the passage-way is still in total darkness; the wide overhang of the tin roofs on the buildings on either side reach out to each other across the alley, almost touching. Even in full daylight the alleyway would be dingy and full of shadows.

It is the reek of spilt petrol in the crisp morning air that first catches my attention: It is the sound, somewhere between a slap and blow, and the gasping choking that makes me stop, turn and haul my revolver from its holster.

I am pretty sure none of my lads are in this area, so I let off two sharp blasts on the whistle hung around my neck, and send a beam of torchlight dancing down the narrow gully.

Caught, frozen, in the beam of light, are two white men in civvies, and a half naked African on his hands and knees.

A mass of disjointed details leap out at me: one of the Europeans is wearing a tie, and a white shirt. His sleeves are rolled up almost to the shoulder. The other still has his jacket on. He wears a trilby hat, and has a cigarette, half smoked, clenched between his teeth.

The African's skin shines with sweat and blood as the beam of light plays over him. He is panting, like a thirsty dog. He wears only a pair of underpants.

The European with his sleeves rolled up is holding a jerry can. The other holds a pair of bolt cutters.

"You there! Step back from that man," I shout. I am surprised at the authority of my own voice. "Keep your hands where I can see them and step back. Now!"

The two Europeans stare into the torch beam. Neither moves. A glare of irritation and impatience pulls at the face of the man with the hat and cigarette.

"Fuck off out of it, Tommy," he shouts back. "This is police business."

"You heard the man," says the other. "On your way."

For a long moment, no one moves. The confrontation between us is vast, simple and absolute. Any movement, on either part, will be an act of aggression, or appeasement. There is no scope for compromise.

As they stand for what seems like ages, I am conscious that the man with the bolt cutters is panting too. The African's

301

back is arched, and a tendril of bloody saliva hangs from his mouth, to the ground. The beam of light quivers over them, exaggerating the trembling in the hand that held the torch. With profound relief I hear the clatter of boots as four of my men run up in response to my whistle, their weapons trained into the alleyway.

The African spits a bundle of bloody cloth from his mouth, falls forward, and lays still.

"Don't do this, son . . ." the man in the hat says, his tone more conciliatory now.

It is this change of tack which convinces me that what I am doing is right. "Remove their weapons," I tell my men, "and keep them in the back of one of the lorries until the police arrive. One of you go and get a field dressing kit and attend to this man."

The two Europeans let the jerry can and the bolt cutters fall, shake their heads, and seem to look with pity on me. Resigned, they step out of the alley and are escorted to the vehicles in the main street. I holster my revolver and cautiously approach the unconscious man.

He lays so still that at first I think he must be dead, but the breath rattling in his throat is even and regular.

He has been drenched in petrol. I turn him over gently. He groans and winces.

"They've made a mess of me," he wheezes, in good English.

I suspect that he has at least one, and possibly several, broken ribs.

Dawn is breaking, or my eyes are adjusting to the gloom. Detail in the alley begins to emerge. There is rubbish everywhere, and the walls on either side are stained and flaking. A door, kicked in, hangs off its hinges a few paces away.

"You live here?" I ask. The man's eyes narrow, and he grunts non-committally.

I sit back on my heels, and study the man.

I guess he would be in his early thirties. He clearly understands English, and speaks it pretty well.

302

"*I'm going to send you to hospital*," I tell him, speaking slowly. "*When the police arrive I will report this to them. Then they'll come and talk to you. My name is Lieutenant Miles, OK? M-I-L-E-S. First Battalion, Wiltshire Yeomanry. Tell the police I will give them a full statement of everything I saw.*"

"*I can't walk*," he says, glancing down at his left leg.

I follow his eyes, and see with sick horror, that the little toe has been crushed. Burst like an over-ripe grape. The pink flesh is bright and pale now that the bleeding has slowed. I can make out a shard of bone protruding from the pulp.

"*They did this?*" I ask, glancing at the discarded bolt cutters. The man grunts.

I am more shocked than outraged. "*I'll get a stretcher party*," I say. "*Remember what I told you. I'll be making a full report about this, and I'll make a statement to the police. You have my word. The men who did this to you will pay.*"

The man lays back, still and silent. When I get out of the alley I am surprised to see that it is now full daylight, and that the main road is crowded with detainees, several dozen of whose heads are daubed with bright yellow paint. I call off two soldiers, and send them for a stretcher.

Twenty minutes later, they tell me that the man in the alley has disappeared.

An hour later, a fat captain from Battalion HQ relieves me and tells me to report immediately to the Chief Superintendent in charge of the operation.

"*You just strolled off, and left him there?*" asks the uniformed police chief superintendent, unable to keep the disbelief out of his voice.

He assures me I have singlehandedly set back the resolution of this State of Emergency by at least six months. Dozens of whites, he says, and hundreds of blacks will die brutally and needlessly thanks to my interference that morning. One of the main aims of this operation was to find that man, he says. To find him, question him, and neutralise his influence.

303

"How do we handle the ... paperwork, Sir?" one of the Special Branch thugs asks.

The Chief Superintendent frowns. "That depends on whether Lt Miles understands the sensitivity of his current position. Whatever he thinks he saw this morning is covered by the Official Secrets Act. Any public disclosure will result in his immediate arrest and prosecution. He is of course at liberty to report his erroneous and unsubstantiated version of the incident to his superior officers, but if he did then I would naturally conclude such an action was politically motivated." The two Special Branch officers smirk, as the Chief Superintendent pauses. "OK, you two. Out. We've still got a lot to do today and I want to talk to Lt Miles alone."

He sighs, and pinches the bridge of his nose. "Sit down, Miles," he says, gently.

"How old are you? Twenty-two? Twenty-three? I've got a son about your age. I'd like to think that my lad would have done what you did today. That took grit, standing up to those two. But as you get older you'll learn that being brave and being right are two very different things."

He flicks through the papers on the file, finds what he was looking for, then turns it once more for my perusal: He is showing me Secret Circular No 10.

"That means, quite simply," he says once I've read it, "that my men were acting under orders, even if they might have got a bit carried away. Now, what happens next is up to you. Those two will be watched from now on: not just to ensure they don't go too far again, but for their own protection. Jembe won't forget what they did to him. Mau Mau will have them marked for retribution: they'll probably put a price on their heads. One way or the other, you have my word they'll be on a tight rein from now on.

"But what about you? There are at least a dozen known Commies we're watching in the British Regiments sent out here, and getting on for a hundred socialists – all of whom are feeding nonsense to left wing MPs back home at the bidding of their

Russian masters. If I thought you were one of them, I would have no option but to have you thoroughly investigated and in the meantime have you transferred to an appropriate set of duties where your suspected Communist affiliation can do no further harm.

"It could also become known among the white settlers that you're the one that let General Jembe go."

The Chief Superintendent smiles, infinitely sadly. "And if that happened, well, you'll be a much sought-after young man. The mood the white settlers are in, I have little doubt that some of the more embittered ones, like those who have had to identify the pieces of their wives and children, would put a price on your head. I advise you to think very, very carefully about your next steps."

"My Lord," said Aliya diffidently as she watched Tom stare blankly into space. "I wonder if we might recess for a few minutes."

"Is there some point you wish to take guidance on, Miss Zain?" asked the Chief Justice. "Some matter you need to clarify with your client?"

"Well, not really, My Lord, but . . ."

"Then I'm afraid I must decline your request. I remain determined to give you every assistance, but I will not interrupt Mr Muya's cross-examination again without reasonable ground. Carry on, Mr Muya."

Paul picked up a bulky envelope, and drew from within it a dozen copies of a black and white photograph. He nodded to the Clerk of the Court, who took the photographs from him, handed one to Aliya, another to Tom Miles, and gave the remainder to the Chief Justice, who glanced at them, and then passed copies to the Assessors.

Aliya's stomach did two swift somersaults. She handed the photograph to Kapadia, who took out a pair of spectacles, and studied the image, his face impassive. She glanced across at Tom Miles. He looked like he was about to throw up.

305

"Dr Miles," said Paul Muya, "Can you describe what is happening in this picture?"

"May it please the court," Aliya said, thinking hard and speaking fast, "I must object most strongly to the introduction of new evidence in this way. Cross-examination cannot be a licence to dispense with the rules of disclosure. The prosecution has rested its case. I urge that the court rule that this photograph is inadmissible."

Paul was contrite: the acme of a reasonable man. "My Lord, I do sincerely apologise that this document was not the subject of previous disclosure, but it has only just become available. With the Court's permission, we propose to enter it now among our exhibits."

"Proceed," said the Chief Justice, "Dr Miles?"

Tom stared at the photograph he held in trembling hands. He faltered, his voice cracked and started again. "The photograph . . . it shows the body of an African, the head is propped up . . ."

Tom glanced across, almost pleadingly, at Aliya. She rose once more, but Paul again pre-empted her, seeming to know what she was about to say. "My Lord, I should perhaps have said that this is an authenticated copy of a photograph which is among the Colonial Office papers held by the United Kingdom National Archives. Its authenticity has been certificated however we will be happy to call the Director of the Kenya National Archives and Documentation Service to attest to its provenance. Please continue with your description, Dr Miles."

Tom seemed almost resigned. "Beside the body kneels a British Officer. He has a Stirling sub-machine gun across his lap."

"As a doctor, can you describe the injuries of the dead man as they appear in the photograph?"

Tom wiped a hand across his face. "From the photograph, I can say that the deceased has suffered severe head and facial injuries. The wounding is consistent with a gunshot. The stomach is considerably distended. This is consistent with internal bleeding, again, possibly as a result of gunshot injuries."

"From the photograph, can you identify the corpse?"

Tom laid the photograph on the table in front of him and looked straight at Paul. "No".

"Why not?"

"Because the head injuries are too severe."

"But you know whose body it is, don't you Dr Miles?"

There was an absolute, massive silence.

"It is the body of Wilson Mumbu Muya. General Jembe."

"And the British officer kneeling beside the corpse. Who is he, Dr Miles?"

"He is me."

"Can you see the hands of the deceased in the picture before you, Dr Miles?"

Tom shook his head without even looking at the photograph.

"Where are my father's hands, Dr Miles? What happened to them?"

"They were removed. It was . . ."

"What do you mean, 'they were removed'? How were they removed?"

"They were cut off. It was standard . . ."

"Where are my father's hands at the time this photograph was taken, Dr Miles?" asked Paul, relentlessly.

Tom's eyes suddenly filled with tears and he looked down. "In the cardboard box on the ground beside me," he mumbled.

"Who cut my father's hands off, Dr Miles?"

"I did," said Tom, looking up. "It was . . ."

With a sickening thud, Aliya flopped forward onto the desk in front of her, slid sideways, and fell to the floor.

CHAPTER FORTY-FOUR

There was pandemonium in the Courtroom when Aliya collapsed. Her bodyguards raced forward, without their customary weapons, but determined to shelter her with their bodies if necessary. Kapadia held her in his arms, and sprinkled water on her face. The Chief Justice was about to ask if there was a doctor present, but stopped himself, just in time, and instructed the GSU men escorting Tom to allow him to see if he could do anything for Aliya.

Paul Muya watched, smiling.

"Oh well, you weren't the first advocate to have been overcome by the tension," Leo reassured her. "At least now we know what Paul had up his sleeve," he smiled, "Sorry ... I guess that's not a very appropriate expression in the circumstances."

Aliya stood, staring out of Leo's hospital room window, arms folded. "I didn't really faint," she snapped, tapping her foot irritably. "I prosecute war crimes, remember? That was nothing compared to some of the things I've had to look at and listen to. It was just that I couldn't think of any other way of stopping him. Paul Muya was brilliant; he handled it perfectly. He wouldn't let Tom off the hook, yet he managed to seem so crushed. He had everybody's sympathy, even mine. You couldn't help yourself. And Tom, he was so bloody distraught. Out of control. I couldn't think of any other way of stopping it."

"So you took a dive?" said Leo, admiringly, "Good one! I wish I'd seen it."

Aliya spun round. "Are you laughing at me? Oh yes, it would have been so easy for you, wouldn't it? I don't seem to recall you doing so terribly well when Paul pulled his little stunt with the General. So what would you have done?"

"Hopefully, stopped it before it got to that point. Did you challenge admissibility?"

"Yes."

"Contest authenticity?"

"Yes."

"Seek a recess in order to be able to examine the document properly?"

"Yes, yes, yes! Until the CJ's patience ran out. He said that the photograph was pretty simple and really didn't need detailed study. He also warned me against further interruptions."

"Well then, I don't see what else you could have done. To be honest, I doubt if I'd have had either the presence of mind or the sheer balls to do what you did."

Aliya frowned. "Really?"

"Yes, really."

Leo insisted on visiting Tom, with Aliya. Not for the first time, she noted the variable severity of his injury. The hospital staff fussed around him, tutting and clucking and telling him that he really shouldn't even be thinking about going out. He promised that he'd be back within the hour.

"What did happen to the poor bugger's hands, Tom?" Leo asked, studying the photograph.

"They were sent to Nairobi for formal identification. It was standard procedure in the early days, and still quite common later on, if a suspect was killed by a unit that didn't have a fingerprint kit. Ours was back at camp on the other side of the Aberdares. It was really no big deal."

"I suppose we can call an expert to confirm all that, but the damage is pretty well done, now. Why did it have to be you who had to remove the hands?"

Tom shrugged. "It was a weird night, and a lot of things

which made sense then don't stand up to critical appraisal now. They knew I was going to be a medical student. I handled all the first aid and minor surgery in the Unit. It seemed an act of respect for me to remove the hands rather than to have some Askari hack them off with a panga."

Leo shook his head. "You still think it was such a good idea to give evidence?"

"Absolutely."

"And you still intend to maintain, on oath, that you didn't kill Jembe?"

"Yes, I do."

"Yet you have admitted that this is you in the photograph? How do we explain that?"

Tom looked away, "Well, it seems ridiculous now . . ."

"Try me."

"These sort of trophy pictures were very, very common, in those days. Getting Jembe was the biggest thing by far that any of the Combined Action Teams had achieved. There was a series of photographs taken, of which this is one. The last. Other pictures would have shown Jembe with his hands still in place. But you see, when the group pictures were taken, I wasn't there, just like I said. But Johnny Sandford though we'd all get medals and commendations for what we'd done, and he said it was important that I had my share of the glory."

"Glory?" said Aliya, with distaste.

"That's right," said Tom, failing to pick up the irony. "The photograph was taken about four or five hours after Jembe's death."

"Is there any way that could be demonstrated from the picture?"

Tom shook his head again.

"Pity," said Leo, thoughtfully.

Aliya picked up the photograph, and turned it over. A Public Record Office reference was marked on the back, together with various stamps authenticating it. She made a note of the reference, picked up her mobile phone, checking her watch to ensure that it was still office hours in London. She spoke for a few minutes and ended the call. Five minutes later, her phone rang. She listened, thanked the person at the other end, and put the phone down, turning with a grim smile to Tom and Leo.

"I've just spoken to our Departmental Records Officer, who just spoke to a contact in the National Archives. This photograph is out of a file from the 537 series – Supplementary and Secret Correspondence. Almost all of them are open now but this one has extended closure. A hundred years to be precise."

Leo frowned.

"You do appreciate the implications of what I am saying, don't you?" said Aliya, exasperatedly.

"Of course," said Leo. "You're wondering how Paul Muya managed to get hold of it."

"Yes," Aliya said, "and I'm also wondering why a file on a relatively routine counter-insurgency operation is deemed so significant as to require its closure until the year 2056. I'm wondering what else is on that file. I'm wondering what else Paul Muya's got, and I'm wondering who's getting it for him."

Leo puffed out his cheeks, and exhaled slowly. "What do you think we should do?"

"Do?" snapped Aliya. "I'll tell you what we should do. A, or one: get ourselves access to the same documentation. B, or two: limit the damage. C, or three: go on the offensive. D, or four; stop trying to conduct a defence in the dark."

"Right. I'll ring McKenzie," said Leo. "He'll get us the info."

"You do that," said Aliya, "and Dr Miles, no more games. You have to tell us everything that happened."

"Now?" asked Tom, sadly.

"Yes" said Aliya.

"No," said Leo, "I want a shorthand writer present to record it."

"This can't wait, Leo," Aliya insisted. "We have to hear it now."

"There's no need for a stenographer," said Tom. He felt in

his jacket pocket, and pulled out eight closely written pages torn from a notebook, and carefully folded. Aliya took the pages and flattened them out in front of Leo. Looking over his shoulder, she read them with him.

CHAPTER FORTY-FIVE

Throughout those last days of April, the atmosphere in camp is hellish. The uneasy stand-off between the Kikuyu Home Guard and the pseudo terrorists finally breaks down on the last day of the month, resulting in one man losing an eye, and another with his belly ripped so that his pals have to hold his guts in while Johnny Sandford pumps morphine into him, and I desperately try to improvise something that will hold him together until we can get him down to a proper operating theatre.

It has been raining heavily, and several of our chaps are down with malaria. Almost everyone has a cold, and our kit seems to be alive with insects; some kind of thunder bugs that sting like crazy and bring you up in a rash and stink if you manage to slap one as it bites you. God, it's awful.

Added to which, there are hardly any Mau Mau out there in the forest any more. For weeks, any we do run into turn out to be pseudo terrorists working for one Special Branch officer or another. Sometimes, it seems as though they've all been taken, de-oathed and turned. It's clear that our time in the forest is coming to an end. If only we can get Jembe, then we can all stand down. That's what people say. Get Jembe, go home.

That night, to try and patch up morale, Johnny has this bright idea about taking the entire team out in three squads for a glorified exercise. Ostensibly, we were going to sweep an area of forest from the deciduous woods up through to the moorland. Actually, it is going to be a race. Johnny, Foss and I will each lead a squad.

About an hour before we are to set off, Foss says that he isn't going, and nor am I. Johnny is really cheesed off. More with me than with Foss. It is as though I am betraying him again. I try to explain that I have no idea why Foss wants me around, but it does no good. There's an almighty row, and some pretty strong words are exchanged. But Foss knows his law, I'll say that for him. He tells Johnny that he can bellyache as much as he likes, but as the senior police officer present, he has first call on any British military personnel, and he's right. But Johnny isn't the kind of man who is easily balked. "You two want to stay here? Fine. That's just hunky-dory with me. Stay. But you stay alone."

I suppose Foss could have hung on to the police reservists if he'd wanted to, but he doesn't seem much bothered. In fact, he's almost relieved when Johnny insists on taking the entire team off into the forest with two NCOs in charge of the squads Foss and I had been meant to lead.

At sunset Foss calls me over, and the two of us set off in one of the Land Rovers. Foss is behind the wheel. We drive for what seems like hours. Up over the moorlands, and down into a small hamlet, a miserable looking place, with only a few guttering oil lamps to provide any illumination. By then, it's pouring with rain again. The tarpaulin cover over the back of the Land Rover has begun to leak.

Foss is in high spirits. Laughing, he tells me to remove my side arm and stow it in the vehicle.

"Where are we going?" I ask.

It amuses him to keep me in the dark. He likes the sense of power. "To a date with destiny," he says.

I'm not sure what time we arrive at South Kinangop. I guess it must be around 9.30. Maybe 10. It seems to have been dark for a very long time. I feel light-headed on the journey. Nauseous, too. I have a temperature and I suspect I am going down with what seems to be plaguing half the team just at that time. Or maybe it was just a dodgy tin of processed meat or the fumes from the engine.

Foss halts the Land Rover a fair way from the shamba. We

continue on foot. I stumble, and want to use a torch but Foss vehemently rejects the idea. Nearly bites my head off, but as our night vision returns after the headlights of the Land Rover, it turns out that we don't need a torch anyway. Except for the twisted, knotted undergrowth, and I doubt if anything short of full daylight would have helped us much with that.

We enter the shamba. There is an oil lamp on a table. It's lit, but there's no one around.

There are also a couple of stools. The place smells of stale sweat in old clothes, human urine and animal excrement. Foss checks out the room carefully, and then, easing a small pistol from his pocket, searches out somewhere to secure it. In the end, he wedges it beneath the table top.

"What now?" *I ask. I am uncomfortably aware that I no longer have a gun, or even a blade.*

"We wait," *says Foss, cheerfully.*

"For who?" *I sigh. My patience is running thin.*

"For Jembe," *he says, simply.*

We sit there, in the light of that single, soot-stained lamp, for what seems like hours. We have to keep our hands visible at all times, Foss says. We shouldn't move suddenly, because they will be watching us.

To be perfectly honest, I suspect it's all nonsense.

Until I hear the tuneless whistle.

It's obviously a sign Foss has agreed with them. I see Foss stiffen. One hand slips from the table top. He rises, so that he is half crouching.

"Shield the lamp until our eyes become used to it," *a voice I thought I knew says in English.*

Foss looks across at me, seeking some confirmation. I shrug: it is too early to say.

"You are unarmed?"

"Come on in and see for yourselves," *Foss replies, holding his arms out in an expansive gesture.*

There are two of them. One wears the monkey skin jacket

315

and hat, and the patched hide trousers of a true jungle fighter. He is terribly thin. His hair is in the same kind of greasy dreadlocks as the pseudo terrorists in our camp. He smells even worse than them. When he moves near to the lamp, I swear I can see the lice moving in his hair.

The other is Jembe.

The two men enter. One minute they're outside, the next, with us. They say nothing. Just check us over for weapons, then stand back and stare.

Jembe looks at me. He seems much older than the last time I saw him. Old and worn-out. His hair is frosted with grey. He wears a threadbare jacket, a dusty pair of trousers and, incredibly, carpet slippers. He sort of shrugs in greeting, then his eyelids droop as though he's exhausted.

Suddenly, Foss snatches up the revolver from beneath the table and fires point blank into Jembe's stomach. Jembe doubles up, with a kind of a deflated whimper, and simply folds. I must have staggered backward, in horror or sheer surprise. I stumble over something and fall so that I am sitting on the floor, staring up at what is going on.

Foss turns the revolver on the other man who, throughout, has stood dead still. It's as though nothing can surprise him. Foss aims the revolver at his face, but the man doesn't flinch at all. Then, agonisingly slowly, Foss lowers his aim to around the man's groin, and then fires. The impact blows the guy off his feet and flings him up against the wall. There he lays, cursing in some language I don't recognise, pressing his hand against the wound to his side, just above his pelvis.

Foss frowns, and stares at the revolver as though seeing it for the first time. "Funny," he says, "I was aiming for his left bollock."

I begin to get up, but then Foss turns the revolver on me. "Stay where you are, Sonny Jim," he says, cheerfully. "That is Jembe, isn't it?" he asks, jerking his head toward the recumbent figure in the centre of the room although his eyes never leave mine.

316

I say it is.

A slow smile spreads across Foss's face. "Did you ever get to see my two mates after Mau Mau got them?" he asked. "You know, the two you interrupted when they were sorting that fucker out. Did you? They hacked off their bottom jaws, you know, while they were still alive. Did you know that? One of them was still alive when I got to them. Still had half his tongue lolling out of what had been his mouth. The poor bastard tried to tell me something. Something that was so important to him. His dying words. And I couldn't understand a fucking word of it. Just stupid spluttering noises. And it was all your fault, you little shit. That's why you're next. I'm killing these fuckers for Queen and country. But you, well, I'm going to do you a bigger favour than you deserve. I'm going to tell them you died a hero's death. Who knows? You may even get a fucking medal. Posthumous, of course." He raises the revolver once more, and I am staring into it. I don't know if I am saying anything but there is sound, somewhere. I suspect I am. I am probably begging and babbling. Pleading and sobbing and crying. I wet myself. In all that was happening I am most hugely aware of that. I feel the warmth, and I think, "Oh God, the last thing I'm ever going to do in life is piss myself."

Then Jembe groans, and Foss turns, and fires instead into his head, blowing half of the left side of his face away. I lash out with both feet, catching Foss in the shins, and knocking him off balance.

The other Mau Mau snatches his chance. Like a lizard with a broken leg, he slithers across the floor, leaving a trail of blood, and, fast as a snake's tongue, a leather thong flashes out and around Foss's throat. The sheer electric brutality of it leaves me breathless. Foss's eyes bulge, and he tries to beat at his assailant's head with his revolver. His feet kick and drum on the floor. Pretty soon, he throws the revolver away and tears with his fingernails at his own throat, trying to get a grip beneath the leather which has already bitten deep into him. There is this ghastly rattling sound, and then the terrorist hisses in English.

317

"Pick up the gun. Finish him. I can't hold him much longer. Finish him."

This should be some great moment of truth. Some huge dilemma during which I agonise over what to do and finally choose one path. I know just how important this moment is: Know that the whole of the rest of my life depends upon what I now decide, but I can't pretend it is hard. I barely pause for a moment before picking up the revolver, and finishing Foss. Not with a bullet, although I don't know why. Instead, I take the gun by its barrel – it is still warm – and hit him, as hard as I can, just above the left temple.

Then I hit him again, just to make sure. Just the way I recall the pseudo terrorists dispatched the Colobus monkeys that day in the forest. And that is it. The side of his head caves in. Within him, death rattles.

The Mau Mau, with a shuddering sigh, releases his grip, and slips the garrotte from Foss's throat. With the professional disdain of a barber stropping a razor, he slips the thong through his fingers, to clean it, then thrusts it back into the folds of his jacket.

"I . . . I didn't know this was going to happen," I blurt out.

The Mau Mau looks across at me, still for a moment, then shrugs. He stares at the revolver I still hold, like a mallet. "So what happens now, Muzungu? We have each killed the one we came with and we have each accounted for a dangerous enemy. We have a choice of standing heroes beside martyrs, or traitors beside crimes. Soldiers will come soon. Attracted by the shooting. Do you want them to find me, like this, and you, with that gun in your hand, his blood on your face and your piss in your pants?"

"What choice do I have?" I wonder, reaching up to touch the smear of blood on my cheek of which, until that moment, I have been unaware.

"We can both come out of this. Alive, and free. But only if you trust me. That is the choice. Will you trust me?"

I don't know why, but I nod.

He reaches out a bloody hand. "Swear!"

He grabs my hand in his. He sighs. "Now help me up and try to stop this bleeding. Then, get me away from here. That will give us both our freedom. Then, you return. Tell them he sent you away. Tell them, yes, tell them you were just obeying orders."

I patch up his wound as best I can, and then half drag him towards the door. "Good! They will find two dead heroes, in an empty building." He grunts. "Some people will wonder, but most won't. Most will be happy to accept the legend, whatever it might be." He is gasping in short, pained breaths. "Get me to where my people can find me. They know how to treat wounds like this. Then you return, and tell them you were caught in an ambush trying to fetch reinforcements."

There is something about him. Something that makes me trust him. Or rather, something that makes me obey him. He is a savage. Filthy and stinking. Only a few years older than me. He'd brought his comrade to that shamba deliberately to get him killed, yet there is something about him.

Something . . . great.

"Who was he?" said Leo, quietly, as he handed the pages back to Tom.

Tom smiled, mirthlessly. "Do you really need to ask?"

"Yes," Leo said, softly, "I really do. I need to hear it from your own lips."

Tom shrugged, "All I know for sure was that he was a Masai."

"Siafu. Ole Kisii: the President."

Tom tilted his head in acknowledgement. "I don't know. Not for sure."

Leo chewed his bottom lip, uncertain how to proceed.

"If only you'd told us all this earlier. Then we could have . . ."

"You could have done what?" asked Tom. "Even if I didn't kill Jembe, I still have a murder to cover up, don't forget."

"Foss? A brute who shot Jembe in cold blood when he was trying to surrender, and was going to kill Ole Kisii and you? Doesn't sound like murder to me."

319

"No? Others might not see it that way. I conspired with a wanted criminal facing capital punishment – an enemy of my country – in the killing of a well respected police officer who had been decorated for gallantry. When I actually had the power to kill his assailant and save his life. I'm probably guilty of treason too. What defence can I offer? And when I'd killed Foss, what did I do then? I helped, no, helped isn't the word. What is it? Aided and abetted? Facilitated? A leading terrorist's escape from justice. I should have arrested him. I had it in my power: he was weak with loss of blood and I had the gun. Had I been a stronger man, I would have killed him, too. And then I would have had that moment of glory Foss had intended to keep for himself. But I didn't. I've always told myself it was because I was a better man; too decent. But now I think it was simply because I was too bloody weak. Well, not any more. Tomorrow, Paul Muya will ask me again what happened that night and there'll be no more prevarication. I will tell him it all. Tomorrow I will finally have my postponed moment of morbid glory."

CHAPTER FORTY-SIX

Nikodemus Odendo was confused. Part angry, part relieved, mightily hard done by and sorely pissed off. He had been Head of Internal Security for a little more than three months. Prior to that, he had been in charge of security at Kenya's Embassies and High Commissions around the world, a post he had been rushed into after a security guard at the Kenyan Embassy in Sweden had seen fit to beat up the leader of an Amnesty International delegation in front of a dozen cameramen.

He thought he had understood what was expected of him in his new role, as clearly as he had in his last. Not to wait around to be told what to do, but to have the wit to target what or who presented a threat to the security of the State or the well-being of its President and discreetly take the appropriate action. So far, thank God, it seemed as though no one other than Ole Kisii had connected his people with the strike on the white lawyer, and Nikodemus Odendo was at a loss to account for the President's perspicacity. He, Nikodemus, was supposed to be the Old Man's eyes and ears, and he sure as hell hadn't told him. Still, at least Ole Kisii hadn't yet detected his hand in Johnny Sandford's timely demise, or in the unfortunate fuck-up at the Charge.

And now, after all he'd done for the Old Man, he was out on his ear. One last job, and then he was as good as on the run. It was all so bloody unfair, and undeserved.

Still, it made Nikodemus feel better about something that had been troubling him for some weeks.

His decision to target Paul Muya. Not for carefully orchestrated elimination, oh no, but for cultivation, and the exchange of a few unsought favours. After all, who had the most to gain from Johnny Sandford's timely demise?

"You devious bastard!"

"Worked it out at last, have we, Coke? I must say you took your time. So what's the good Doctor going to do?"

Leo shifted the phone to his other ear. "Spill his guts in court tomorrow. Maybe. It depends what you are offering."

"What I offered right from the start," said Paul. "I'm not interested in him, I never have been. It's Ole Kisii I want. The people need to know the sort of man he is. The moment Dr Miles names him, I'll withdraw all charges and personally guarantee his safe return to the UK, and although you may have the redoubtable Mr Haas and his gun-toting gangsters looking out for you, I can assure you my guarantee is worth even more."

"What do you mean, you've never been interested in Tom Miles? What about all the things you said in Court? What about the sermons you delivered and the speeches you've made?"

"I told you right from the start you weren't hearing me, Coke. I only ever spoke of a man from another tribe and another land: not Miles the Briton but Ole Kisii the Masai. I only ever referred to a young soldier: Ole Kisii, the Masai warrior. You listened, but you didn't hear."

"You're gonna make a hell of a President, Total Man," admitted Leo, grudgingly.

"With the help of the Lord, and the trust of my people," said Paul, piously. "What ever the future holds, I'll never forget my friends. What happens tomorrow?"

"You'll get what you want, as usual. But we want to handle it. Miles will describe the Masai who led Jembe to the shamba, and tell how he betrayed Jembe. But not to you. He wants it done on redirect."

"I think we can accept that," said Paul, "yes, I think that's his right. And yours. Very well, I'll close my cross first thing tomorrow."

"And Tom Miles will shoulder his," said Leo, grimly.

On his final mission for his erstwhile master, Nikodemus Odendo picked six of his best men, and headed off in a couple of Peugeot 504s for the Police Club at Muthaiga.

Like many of his predecessors, he was a pretty anonymous man. He couldn't expect the GSU men guarding Tom Miles to know him, so he dictated a sheath of instructions and authorities on Office of the President notepaper.

His mind wandered as they drove out from the city and climbed up through the expensive suburbs. Where had he gone wrong? At what point, precisely, had he lost that essential empathy with his master which was the hallmark of a successful Head of Secret Police? He thought he'd understood Ole Kisii. Knew what he wanted of him. Where had he gone wrong? he asked himself again. When had that vital link ruptured?

And what was he to do now? He'd never really travelled outside Kenya, Sure, he'd visited his nation's Embassies and High Commissions to check out security arrangements. Even there, in a dozen different countries in as many varied time zones, he'd still been on Kenyan territory. His own land. Where was he to go? What was he to do? He could have denied it, he supposed. But why should he? He'd acted for the best of motives, out of loyalty, and a genuine belief that that was where his duty lay. He'd expected Ole Kisii to be grateful. Silent and glad. Not to turn on him and cast him out like a leper, into the night.

The white lawyer was pushing Paul Muya. Ole Kisii, for reasons of his own, wanted to give Paul Muya his head. Rope enough to hang himself. And the best supplier of that rope would be the Wahindi girl.

So what had he done wrong? He'd neatly taken Kane out of the equation, without even killing him. Then he'd even got the bonus prize of their operative eliminated before he could be pressed to make any embarrassing statements.

This was a dirty business, everybody knew. Why the hell, if Ole Kisii was going to be so bloody prissy about things, did he retain a security service at all?

They arrived at the Police Club. Nikodemus was looking forward to throwing his weight about. The GK plates on the Peugeots ensured that they weren't simply waved away. A GSU sergeant tapped on the driver's window, which descended, electronically.

Without looking, Nikodemus thrust the memo with the President's signature on the bottom under his nose. The sergeant's eyes widened, and he rapidly waved them on.

When they come for me, I fear the worst, but am surprised at how resigned to it I am.

I assume they are here to kill me. When I find they are here to take me away, I go with them, unresisting. Without fear or trepidation, but rather out of curiosity. What does it matter where they decide to do it? I am in their power, totally. That brings with it a freedom, of sorts.

"Where are you taking me?" I ask the one in charge, idly, more to make conversation than out of any real interest.

He sighs. "What do you care, Muzungu?" Then he relents. "Do you smoke?" he asks, offering me a cigarette.

Without quite knowing why, I take it, although it's a good forty years since I last smoked, and even then, it had been a pipe.

He lights the cigarette for me, and takes a deep drag of his own.

"You say Sir or Your Excellency when you talk to him," he says. "Don't sit down unless he asks you to, and don't speak till he speaks to you. Do you understand?"

"I understand," I say.

He takes a final, deep drag on his cigarette and then flicks it out of the window. "Then you're lucky. I haven't understood from the very beginning," he says, sadly.

They swept through gates which were flung open for them on the double flash of the headlights: clearly expected. They drove to the front of State House, and round the side, to the back. In the grounds, there were small pools of light. Spotlights, set in the grass, threw light up into the trees, illuminating their lower leaves stabbing down like silver daggers. There were winged insects and small moths fluttering in the beam of every light. Although it was late, nothing was still. The slightest breeze moved the fronds of the bushes and caused the fanlike foliage of the Travellers Palm to tremble like a peacock's tail. Crickets and cicadas clicked and ticked like a score of metronomes. A bird cried – a scuttering tut like a scolding mother. From somewhere bullfrogs set up a cacophony of hollow croaks.

Nikodemus Odendo steered Tom toward a patch of darkness where he could just make out the faint light reflecting off white furniture. Odendo stopped, took Tom's hand, and reached out with it until Tom felt the back of a wicker chair.

There was a long silence. Tom was uncertain quite how to act. He began to shift uneasily and, although the evening was cool, to sweat. His eyes still couldn't penetrate the darkness. He felt he was inside some vast cavern. Or a glass bubble. He could see the sky, ablaze with stars, and even the lights of a plane. But ahead of him there was only the dark. And the silence. He strained to hear breathing, but he couldn't.

"Your Excellency?" Tom ventured.

There was a sound like sand on glass. "I don't expect on that night either of us ever imagined one day you'd call me that. Sit down, Dr Miles."

Tom felt his way around the chair and settled himself uncomfortably.

CHAPTER FORTY-SEVEN

"Can you recall '55?" asked Ole Kisii. "The old heroes were all in detention camps or internal exile. The young lions were all dead, shot down or strung up, save for Jembe, Kimathi and me. The forest was full of your soldiers and de-oathed traitors turned on their own brothers by the promise of their lives. Bad times. But I still believed in the future I glimpsed in dreams on the forest floor.

"Jembe wanted to make a deal with the colonialists: did you know that? His nerve had gone, and he cowered in storerooms and godowns in Nairobi, jumping at every shadow. He was a broken man. Desperate to save himself – and do you know why? Because he had a child he wanted to see grow to manhood! Think what a coup that would have been for the colonialists! He would happily have confessed to anything, betrayed any of us, in exchange for his life, but your people had issued his death warrant in that Secret Circular.

"I told Jembe I would help him. And I did. I helped him to preserve his destiny – to become a martyr. Paul Muya thinks he's assuring his father his rightful place in the history books, but by his own birth he's the one who turned him traitor! It was you and I that saved him from the curse of his too-loved son. We gave him to eternal fame. To his nation."

"You know what I remember most?" Tom murmured. "The blood. That night. His. Yours. Foss's. So much blood."

"Only things already dead are born without blood being shed," Ole Kisii said. "Paul Muya wants you to name me as his father's betrayer. That's what this is all about. That's what this has always been about. My enemies have nothing else to throw at me: There is only one skeleton in my closet. Jembe's.

"I will make you no threats, Dr Miles, I will not threaten you with stern retribution or offer you priceless rewards. Because I know I have nothing to fear from you."

"How can you know that? How do you know I won't reveal your identity in court tomorrow?"

The President shrugged. "Because I took the measure of you that night half a century ago. I have the measure of you still. You won't betray me. Because in doing so, you'd have to betray yourself. And then you would have nothing left. Go, Dr Miles," he snapped, impatiently. "Go back to your cell. You are under my protection, as you have been all along. No harm will come to you. The judgment will go in your favour. You will go home to your small, safe little life again with your secret, and mine, intact. You are no threat to me. You never have been. You never were."

"That's it?" cried Tom, bitterly. "At the end of it all, I'm just dismissed? I saved your life! I carried you out of that shamba . . ."

"No. I saved you that night. I offered you rehabilitation. That's what you really carried out of that shamba. My preservation was just the precondition I imposed which you happily grasped."

"I despise you," said Tom, bitterly.

The President laughed, a dry, wheezing, bitter sound that seemed to fill the air. "You have no vote in this country and no influence internationally. Why on earth should I care what you think of me?"

"What if you're wrong about me?" countered Tom. "What if I name you in court tomorrow?"

The President smiled. "What indeed? Do you want to?"

"What if I said yes? What would you do? Kill me?"

"Oh no! Not you. I told you, you are under my protection. But someone would have to die."

"What are you saying? Who would you kill? Leo Kane? Aliya Zain?"

The President shook his head, "You really don't understand, do you? Both are non-entities, just like you. Killing them, like killing you, would just cause me embarrassment and make no difference to the world. No, Paul Muya would have to die. You would leave me no choice. His life would be the cost of your small moment of glory."

The old man chuckled. "Then you would at last have achieved something quite unique: you would have been responsible for the deaths of Jembe, who should have been this country's president, Mzee who was, *and* Paul Muya, who otherwise probably will be."

"Mzee? I don't understand . . . ," muttered Tom, recoiling, appalled, from the implications of the Acting President's words.

"Of course you do," snapped Ole Kisii, mercilessly. "You're a doctor. How does a man on life support come to death, eh? I had his machines switched off! Because of you, I was left with no choice. They would have forced me into court otherwise."

"But that's not my responsibility! That was your decision. Just as it's you who was responsible for what happened to Jembe . . . and for whatever happens to Paul Muya."

"Don't look for easy excuses, Dr Miles. Together we killed Mzee. You and I. As surely as we killed Jembe. Big men just seem to die whenever our paths cross, don't they, Dr Miles? So shall Paul Muya be next?"

"Well?" said Ole Kisii to his aide, as the younger man came out to help him from his chair.

The aide paused. "If you'd said that to me, Your Excellency, then tomorrow, I'd name you in court."

The old man chuckled, "I know. But you're not him. If I'd been dealing with you, I'd have adopted a different strategy. I'll leave you to contemplate what it might have been. Make sure Nikodemus gets the money I promised him – all of it, mind you. I don't want to see him again. I've already said goodbye to too many loyal comrades for one lifetime."

CHAPTER FORTY-EIGHT

There was a strange kind of timelessness about that night for Aliya Zain and Leo Kane. Although in pain, and moving with exaggerated care, Leo refused to return to the hospital and instead followed Aliya to her hotel room.

Before the attack they had been staying in different locations, but Dieter Haas had insisted on establishing a secure cell – a strategy which demanded they occupy two abutting rooms at the end of a long corridor choked with a succession of glowering heavies.

It had been some time since Leo had slept. There was a DVD player in her room and he found himself thinking about the Hindi films he'd watched in hospital. He tried to remember the tunes, but couldn't. He couldn't really distinguish one plot from another just now.

All that he knew was that he wanted to be close to Aliya. Neither seemed at all tired. Had she asked him, which she hadn't, he would have said it was because there was a need to discuss the next day's business. But really it was because he was scared and there was no one else he felt a need to be near to. And, he reflected glumly, if everything went according to schedule, she and Tom Miles would be on the midnight flight to London the next day, leaving him alone to the mercies of a President he'd been instrumental in deposing.

She'd even, discreetly, made a provisional booking for the seats, thinking that he hadn't heard. But he had.

He felt a sick, sulky, childish loneliness. He had no doubt about what had to happen, no question that it should be any different. There was an inevitability about it now. The end game had begun. He recalled an old African saying: when you've already jumped into the river, it's too late to worry about the depth. Well, they'd jumped. The river bank was disappearing fast into the mists, and he had to brace himself against the flood waters.

Aliya came out of the shower, a hotel bathrobe wrapped around her and her hair turbaned in a towel.

She smiled at him. He looked down, and found himself studying her feet. For some reason, he felt that he wanted to cry. This he attributed to the painkillers he was still faithfully taking every four hours. He couldn't bring himself to look up at her, because he was suddenly overwhelmed with the thought that the next day she would be gone.

"Do you want to stay here tonight?" she said, softly.

Leo moved so suddenly he thought, for an agonised moment of stabbing pain, he'd torn at least one stitch. "I . . ." he mumbled.

"Don't embarrass both of us. I'm not propositioning you. I'm simply saying that if you want to stay here, that's OK by me. Because I don't want to be alone tonight. OK?"

He nodded, dumbly.

"Right," she said. "Then how about a Raj Kapoor film?"

They were barely through the opening credits when the mobile in Leo's jacket, Aliya's mobile, and the phone on the low table beside the bed all rang in unison.

CHAPTER FORTY-NINE

By the time Nick Easton arrived at the High Commissioner's residence it seemed as though all the important talking had been done. His case had been pleaded, his actions exposed, his character weighed and his future decided. It could all have been handled without the High Commissioner ever setting eyes on him again, but Mowbray felt a personal denouncement was required.

Accordingly, Nick Easton was invited into a room, where he had so often sat and shared thoughts with the High Commissioner, to be confronted by a stony-faced Mowbray, a Head of Chancery who could barely disguise his satisfaction and McKenzie, who simply wished that he could go home.

It had been McKenzie who had worked it all out after Leo's call. McKenzie who had detected Nick Easton's hand in the affair and convinced a reluctant David Mowbray of the truth.

"Why, Nick, why?" began the High Commissioner, unable to keep the bitterness from his voice. "How could you have betrayed my trust like this?"

Nick Easton raised an eloquent eyebrow. "I'm afraid you didn't come into it, David."

"So you admit you orchestrated this whole business from the start?" asked the Head of Chancery quickly.

Easton treated him to a long, thoughtful stare. "Orchestrated? No," Nick Easton replied, "And I've no idea what 'this whole business' is."

"You've betrayed your country . . ." said the High Commissioner.

Nick Easton shook his head emphatically. "Bollocks. If anyone's betrayed his country, you did, by caving in too early over the SEACOW loan. That bloody near ruined everything. If Paul Muya hadn't managed to get to Miles before he got to the airport, we'd have lost the best chance we've ever had of guaranteeing real change in this country."

"Change?" said McKenzie, doubtfully. "You want change, and you think Paul Muya will deliver it for you?"

"You really don't understand, do you?" Nick Easton said, shaking his head, sadly. "You think this is about me? You think I'm acting alone, out of purely selfish motives? How do you imagine I got to know about this Jembe business in the first place? Do you really think even I could get to sift through secret files solely to further my business interests? How do you imagine I found out about Ole Kisii's involvement in Jembe's death? The only reference is on the file containing the photograph of the good Doctor posing next to the body. Look at the record of who consulted what when. See if that file has ever been out of official hands. And you," he added, turning to McKenzie, "Did you check with your boss before you came running to the High Commissioner with this load of half-baked tittle-tattle? No, I thought not. This is not about diplomacy, this is about politics. This is about ensuring Ole Kisii loses the next election. We have got to free Africa from the curse of the Founding Father generation. For their sake, as much as ours. This is real life, and the best thing you can all do is hope I choose to forget this conversation ever took place, or you'll all be looking for new employment."

McKenzie held his stare. He was thinking. Fast and hard. Thinking of Leo Kane and Aliya Zain, out on a limb. Of Tom Miles, hung out to dry, and of Paul Muya, who was about to inherit the earth, on a proxy for the Nick Eastons of the world.

David Mowbray sighed, profoundly troubled. He had simply no idea what to do. Which way to jump. He knew he couldn't afford Nick Easton as an enemy unless Easton was crushed. And that didn't look quite so likely as it had an hour earlier. In fact it didn't look likely at all.

"Maybe we'd better all pause, take stock and talk to London in the morning . . ." offered the Head of Chancery.

"There isn't time for that," snapped Easton. "This gets sorted, one way or the other, out here, before London is up and functioning. You have to decide which way to jump, David. Right now."

"Then I guess . . . you win," said Mowbray, slowly.

"No," said Easton, "We all do. Tom Miles does. Britain does. You do. Let's chalk this one up to . . . a breakdown in communications, and let's forget it ever happened."

He stood and extended his hand. They each shook it in turn. Last was McKenzie.

"You've got balls," said Easton, ever inclined to be magnanimous in victory, "And a sharp brain too. If ever you think of leaving the FCO, give me a ring . . ."

CHAPTER FIFTY

"I have no further questions for the Accused."

Aliya Zain let out a long sigh. Leo had assured her that he'd never known Paul Muya break his word. Nonetheless, a small part of her expected that his resolution would fail and he'd find the prospect of Tom Miles at his mercy, slumped like a zebra harried to exhaustion by a remorseless lion, irresistible.

There was an audible groan of disappointment. The Chief Justice frowned, and tapped his ball-point pen on his pad, pensively. He shook his head slightly. "Very well, Mr Muya. Miss Zain?"

Aliya looked across at Paul, who gave her an encouraging smile. He was aglow; alive with triumph. Well, she told herself, not for the first time, what did it matter to her? A man from the High Commission had handed her a ticket for the midnight flight to Heathrow. They'd even arranged for a temporary passport to be prepared for Tom in case the police were unable to retrieve his belongings in time. This was the home run. They were all safe now. Tom Miles, herself and, if the promises of future Heads of State meant anything, Leo Kane too.

So why did she feel sick?

She was about to begin the re-direct, when a murmur behind her grew to a voluble dispute, executed in hissed whispers.

She turned, and saw a half dozen hard men in grey suits arguing with the occupants of the front public bench, some of whom had been in court every day of the trial and one of whom was Nick Easton. The Chief Justice snatched up his gavel and brought it crashing down, once. "What is this?" snapped the

Chief Justice, as the entire tableau froze, like statues in a party game.

The Attorney General, discreetly seated two rows further back, rose, "May it please the Court, these gentlemen are State House Officials. His Excellency, John Ole Kisii has announced his intention to attend this morning's session."

The protesters on the front bench hurriedly moved, Nick Easton frowned and the Chief Justice craned forward to consult with his clerk about the appropriate protocol.

"Mr Ole Kisii wishes to attend merely as an observer, and in his private capacity," offered the Attorney General, urbane as ever. "It is for that reason," he added, with a politician's smile, "that normal courtesies, including adequate notice to your Lordship's Clerk, are not on this occasion appropriate."

"I really must protest," cried Paul, with a glare of loathing over his shoulder at the Attorney General. "This is a blatant attempt to influence these proceedings . . ."

"You have always had a strange idea of what constitutes justice in this country, Muya," said John Ole Kisii, as he walked into Court trailing a phalanx of aides. "As long as I am President, Justice will be delivered in public, and the courts will be open to every citizen."

All heads were turned. All attention focused on the gaunt and shrunken figure in a suit that seemed one size too big for him yet who exuded an almost hypnotic power.

Only the Chief Justice seemed unaffected. "You are here, Sir, as a private citizen, I understand? Very well. Within that capacity, karibu. Welcome. Please find yourself a seat, and bear in mind that in this court, all statements are to be addressed to me, and then only when I invite them. Usher, find some extra chairs."

"And, Mr Muya," continued the Chief Justice. "I think you can leave it to me to ensure that members of the public do not influence these proceedings. The gentleman who has just arrived, to whom, given his wish to be here in a private capacity, I shall refer simply as Mr Ole Kisii, has every right to be here. Now, Miss Zain, please proceed."

335

Paul Muya sat hunched, gnawing at his bottom lip. Gone was the almost post-coital tranquillity of a few moments earlier. In its place there was fury, and a massive, untrammelled energy. He seemed about to explode.

Aliya was on her feet, when a clerk from Leo's chambers discreetly slipped a note to Kapadia, sitting, blank-faced at her side.

Kapadia read it, touched her sleeve gently and passed it to her.

It was from Leo. It said simply, "Change of plan. Kill time till I get there."

She glanced down at Kapadia, who raised his eyebrows a fraction: he understood no more about this than she did.

"Dr Miles, you have already told this court that you first met General Jembe on the morning of 24 April 1954. Could you describe the circumstances of that meeting?"

This was planned. This was what they had agreed at a hasty consultation before Court reconvened. Tom described the morning in detail. The two special branch officers. The hunched figure of Jembe, mutilated, beaten, and drenched in petrol. His intervention, and the brief conversation between the two. Through earlier testimony, the Court had developed an image of Anvil as a process of mass brutality. Not perhaps akin to the outrages perpetrated in Nazi-occupied Europe to which Paul had compared it; maybe more on a par with the images of dawn raids and township clearances in Apartheid South Africa. Aliya skilfully exploited this backdrop to portray the simple humanity of the young Tom Miles as all the more heroic.

With Aliya doing little more than prompting, Tom moved on to the night, a year later, when Jembe had died. He explained that he had been unarmed. Taken by surprise by Foss's action.

Aliya brought him up short, leaping suddenly to the removal of Jembe's hands. Just as he had explained it to Aliya and Leo, Tom recounted the reasons for their removal. The lack of fingerprint equipment. The application of a standard procedure. The ever-resourceful McKenzie had even managed to locate the relevant instruction, a photocopy of a faxed transcript of which she introduced in evidence.

She glanced nervously at her watch: where the hell was Leo? She had half-hoped for an objection from the Prosecution on the authenticity of the document, debating which she could have used up a good three quarters of an hour. Not a word from the glowering Paul Muya.

She asked Tom to describe how he had removed the hands, stressing throughout the care, precision and humanity with which the operation was carried out. She got him to say in open court what he had said to Leo and her: it was an act of necessity, carried out with the respect due to the dignity of a fallen foe.

She was about to ask Tom to go over the detail of his sighting of Jembe at the loyalist rally when, to her profound relief, Leo made his appearance, supporting himself with a hand on McKenzie's shoulder and walking with, for no good reason that she could see, a pronounced limp.

The Chief Justice asked her to pause, and formally welcomed Leo, congratulating him on sufficiently regaining his strength to attend.

Paul rose, and perfunctorily added his welcome, but there was no hint of friendship in his stare. No mischievous wink, no shared smiles now.

The Chief Justice asked if Leo intended to re-assume leadership of the Defence: Leo affirmed that this was the case. Then did they require a recess, the Chief Justice wondered? Leo thanked him but declined, assuring him that a few moments consultation with his junior would suffice. As he turned to sit he saw for the first time Ole Kisii watching him, with a bleak smile. McKenzie, squeezing himself uninvited beside Aliya and Leo as Kapadia withdrew, watched Nick Easton, whose basilisk stare gave nothing away. Leo glanced across at Paul, and began to understand. He bowed towards the President, but the Chief Justice cleared his throat, and Leo turned painfully. "I had almost missed your enthusiasm to play to the gallery, Mr Kane," he observed. "But you will bow your head only to the bench in

337

my court. The gentleman you were acknowledging is here as a private citizen. Am I clear, Mr Kane? Am I understood?"

"As always, My Lord," Leo assured him. "As always."

"What the hell is going on?" hissed Aliya desperately, as she and Leo went into a brief huddle.

"I'm not too sure myself," Leo confessed.

McKenzie leaned in towards them. "There isn't time to explain," he said, "I've told Leo what he needs to know. You're both going to have to trust me, and so is Tom Miles."

"OK," nodded Aliya, "What should I do?"

"Pray," said McKenzie.

Leo smiled. "I doubt that's worth the effort. If there is a God, Paul will have already lobbied him. Let's all just keep our fingers crossed."

"Mr Kane?" said the Chief Justice, as Leo indicated that they were ready to recommence.

"Thank you, My Lord. We have no further questions for Dr Miles. That concludes the case for the Defence. We respectfully invite the court to move to final submissions."

Tom stared, open mouthed. He shook his head, and said something, but whatever it might have been was lost in Paul Muya's roar of protest. Nick Easton was momentarily on his feet then, as quickly, he sat down. A clutter of journalists tumbled over one another to get out of the courtroom and start transmitting text. In the back rows, the mobiles were out.

John Ole Kisii sat deathly still, eyes closed, smiling.

"You have an objection, Mr Muya?" said the Chief Justice, over the hubbub.

Anger and confusion tugged at Paul Muya's face, twisting his lips as he spoke and setting his chin trembling. "My Lord, I . . . I . . ." he pulled himself up short, straightened his back, tried to calm himself, and began again. "My Lord, I crave the Court's indulgence. A short recess. A moment to consult my learned friend."

"Very well," sighed the Chief Justice. "Ten minutes."

CHAPTER FIFTY-ONE

"We had a deal!" cried Paul, his fist clenched and his shoulders hunched. "We made an agreement."

"I know. My instructions have changed. If I could have told you I would, but I couldn't. I think they made sure that was the case."

"But I closed! I closed on the promise that your man would name my father's betrayer!"

"Look, Paul, I understand. Really I do, and I'm sorry. But I don't see what we can do about it now."

"You could keep your word!"

"I don't have that freedom. You know that."

"But your client wants to tell his story," pleaded Paul. "I can see he does. You know he does."

"Yes, I think you're probably right. But he's not going to be given that freedom either. That's part of the new game plan. Shall we return?"

Paul made a desperate attempt to seek the leave of the court to adduce evidence in rebuttal of Tom's statements, but to no one's surprise, the Chief Justice concluded that all Tom said could, with the exercise of due diligence, have been foreseen. Final submissions were little more than a formality. A summary of what had gone before. The Chief Justice withdrew, with the Assessors, to prepare his judgment, leaving instructions that, until advised otherwise, everyone was to remain in court.

In the Chief Justice's absence, several of the more enterprising reporters attempted to get an impromptu press conference with the President, but Ole Kisii was having none of it. Sternly, he reminded them that he was there in a private capacity, and sat tight-lipped, grim and still.

The Attorney General felt no such compunction about inviting two of his most amenable colleagues in the press to join him for a sly cigarette in the hallway – where he took great pleasure in crystal-balling the next few hours.

Leo crossed to the dock, reached up, and took Tom's hand.

Tom smiled, wanly. He looked ghastly, absolutely worn out. "So I still don't get my moment in the limelight?"

Leo shook his head. "Afraid not. There's already been too much limelight. It stops here and now. The verdict's a foregone conclusion. You know that, don't you?"

Tom nodded. "But does Paul Muya?"

Leo followed Tom's gaze, and saw, with sadness, his friend, defeated. It was probably just a coincidence, but it seemed to Leo as though all those who had packed so closely around Paul throughout the trial now sat slightly further back, leaning away, as though made uncomfortable by his proximity. Even his own ex-wife.

"Oh, yes," said Leo, quietly, "I think he does. I think everyone does."

There was a flurry of activity, the usher called on everyone to rise, and the Chief Justice and the Assessors filed back into court. Tom remained standing as the Chief Justice sorted his notes, and the Assessors settled themselves into their place.

"It's 'not guilty'," whispered the GSU man a pace behind Tom. "You can always tell. The Assessors are looking at you. Meeting your eye. They never do that when it goes the other way."

Tom looked across at Ole Kisii, who smiled. In control, as always, and nodded slightly. Suddenly, an overwhelming desire to wipe the smile off his face devoured Tom from the inside. "I want to change my plea," he said urgently.

Aliya was the only one to react. She was on her feet in a moment. "No!" she cried.

340

"I want to plead guilty!" Tom insisted.

Ole Kisii barely moved. The smile froze, then faded. That was all.

"The case is concluded, Dr Miles," said the Chief Justice, sternly.

"The judgment is yet to be delivered," offered Paul, hope suddenly rekindled within him. "My Lord, Dr Miles clearly has something he wants to say, and I urge you to hear it."

The Chief Justice shook his head slowly, as Tom began to speak.

"I'm guilty. I killed. I . . ."

"Silence!" shouted the Chief Justice. "Usher, clear the court! I will not have this charade! Mr Kane, Miss Zain: calm your client. Go with him, and help him to collect himself. I will ascribe his remarkable behaviour to the tension of the morning. If, however, he repeats his assertion when we reconvene," he added, with a glance at the blank-faced Ole Kisii, "I will have no option but to hear submissions on the admissibility of his change of plea. Am I clear? Am I understood?"

CHAPTER FIFTY-TWO

Tom sat with his head in his hands, as Aliya paced to and fro in the small room to which they were shown. "What the hell do you think you're playing at?" she snapped. "The Governments of two nations are conspiring to get you out of here with the minimum of difficulty and you seem determined to screw it up: Why?"

"I want to tell the truth. To get it all out at last."

"This is a trial, not a group therapy session: save it until you get home, then go and see a counsellor."

"This isn't about me. This is about the truth. What about the truth?" said Tom, looking up, eyes reddened. "Doesn't that matter? Don't I owe something to Jembe, and those two special branch men they killed, and even Foss, and all the others who died? Don't we owe some honesty to their memory? To history? Isn't the truth what this is all about?"

Aliya let out a long sigh "No. It's about justice."

"Isn't that the same thing?"

"No. I thought so once, but I was wrong. If you go back in there, and insist on blurting out what you claim is the truth, then I can assure you that whatever happens next – to you, Paul Muya and even Leo, is not going to be just. A greater good, justice, will be served by keeping your mouth shut, and going along with things. Just as you have for the past 50-odd years without too many difficulties."

There was a knock on the door. Leo eased himself in. Tom and Aliya both looked up.

"I've got us another five minutes. What happens now?"

The mobile in Leo's pocket sounded. With a grunt of exasperation, he reached in to silence it, but Aliya stepped forward. "Take the call, Leo," she said.

Leo flipped the phone open. "Yes?" he snapped.

"This is Ole Kisii. Let me speak to Miles."

"I'm not sure that's appropriate . . ." Leo began.

"Remember who you are talking to," Ole Kisii said evenly. "Give Miles the telephone."

Without a word, Leo passed it over.

"Don't be a fool, Dr Miles," warned Ole Kisii. "What do you think this will achieve? The court will be cleared. No one will be there to see it. A futile gesture in an empty room. But it will have confirmed your guilt, and the penalty is mandatory. Death. Only one thing then will stand between you and the hangman's noose. A President's clemency. And even though you will have attempted to destroy me, I may be merciful. I may allow you to live out the rest of your life in one of our prisons which, I assure you, will not take too long. Better to let things be as they are. Let Paul Muya and the people of my country keep Jembe as a hero and a martyr. Don't force them to see a poor, broken, craven creature. Don't make Paul Muya have to accept that it was his own birth that turned his father traitor."

"But all this has nothing to do with you or Jembe . . ." Tom insisted. "I want to confess to killing Foss."

"Do that and it will all come out. Including your responsibility for Jembe's death. You still don't understand about that night, do you? Foss didn't need you to identify Jembe; he needed you because you were the only white man Jembe would trust. Jembe didn't come out of hiding that night to meet Foss: he came out to meet you! You weren't the spotter, you were the bait. He put his faith in you and me, and we both betrayed him. I led him to his Gethsemane and you delivered the Judas kiss. He would never have given himself up to anyone other than you. Do you know what he said to me as we approached the shamba that night? You gave him hope. What you did that day in Anvil. You restored his faith. Still maintain you are not responsible?"

"But I didn't know!" Tom almost wailed. "Foss used me. You used me. I didn't know!"

"You're a man, Miles. You were an officer in an occupying force. Don't pretend to the rights of a victim. Face up to what you did, and do the right thing now. Listen carefully to me, Miles," said the old man, more urgently and in little more than a whisper, "I'm going to tell you something only my doctor knows. My own death, my own devourer, grows within me. Sentence of death has already been passed on me. A tumour. Eating me from within. In under two years I will be no more. You know better than I what the final months will be like. I am a dying man, with a great deal to do and very little time to do it in. Too little time before I bequeath the future to the Paul Muyas of this world. But I will not allow them, or you, to snatch away my brief present day. I have waited too long. Now you know it all. Make up your mind."

The line went dead. The policeman outside knocked on the door and told them it was time.

"Have you decided?" asked Leo.

"Did I ever really have a choice?" sighed Tom. "He's won. Of course. He slips away scot-free and I help him to. Again."

"Perhaps, perhaps not," said Leo. "But let's just take this one step at a time. "

CHAPTER FIFTY-THREE

Tom apologised to the Court for his outburst and the public were readmitted to see him acquitted and discharged. Hoards of well-wishers slapped Leo's back and shook Kapadia's hand. Aliya eased herself away from the crowd and crossed to where Paul sat, alone. She held out her hand. He shrugged, and took it.

Leo looked over the heads of the crowd and nodded. As John Ole Kisii and the Attorney General made to leave the Court, two clerks from Sena Chambers advanced on his nod and served the President, in his private capacity, and the State's Chief Law Officer in his official role, with writs to respond to a civil action commenced by one Leo Kane on the grounds that they, with others, had infringed his civil and constitutional rights by orchestrating his illegal wounding.

Leo turned toward Tom and grinned. "One step at a time." he called out, holding up the forefinger of his right hand. "Remember the Mau Mau with a home-made musket? Designed for one shot? Well, I may be no more of a Forest Fighter than Jembe was, but I'm a Kenyan every bit as much as he was and this is my fight now. You've just seen me take my one shot."

The remainder of the day was lost in a welter of press conferences, due process, state protocol and court bureaucracy. Whether at the High Court, the High Commission, the Police Club or Sena Chambers, there always seemed to be a crowd of people around. Always something to be done. Something to be said. Somebody to be thanked.

In this swirling dust storm of noise, confusion and activity, like an ill-prepared wedding party, they set off for the airport – diplomats, reporters, police officers, including, to Aliya's delight, Joseph and Tyson, and Dieter Haas' guards all mixed up and bundled into the wrong vehicles, crushed thigh to thigh against people unknown to them.

As they travelled, Tom and Leo, the former in the High Commissioner's Range Rover, the latter uncomfortably, in a police Land Rover, thought of their previous attempt to reach JKI. Foiled, Leo still didn't want to accept how, by Paul Muya.

Well, Leo reflected with no particular sense of triumph, any attempt by the Total Man to frustrate Tom's departure tonight would be more akin to a devotee flinging himself before the wheels of the Juggernaut, for Ole Kisii had made it clear he would tolerate no further moves on the matter which he now regarded as closed for ever.

It was as a result of his iron-clad determination that, on arrival at the airport, they were quickly ushered to the Government of Kenya's tightly restricted VIP lounge. It was only there, with all formalities completed and a good 45 minutes left before departure, that things finally started to calm down.

Tom, once more the country GP, calm, self-possessed and easy company, introduced Leo to the High Commissioner. He stood, smiling a patient hospice smile, as Mowbray tendered guarded praise for Leo's courtroom performance and expressed exaggerated sympathy for his injuries.

It was clear that Mowbray regarded the odd-ball Mr Kane with a distant suspicion and a morbid fascination, convinced that he had embarked upon a course akin to suicide by issuing writs against Ole Kisii and the State that morning.

After saying all the right things, the High Commissioner eased himself away, to slip into a clinch with the Head of British Airways' Kenya Office – to be assured there would be no ticketing hitches, technical glitches or procedural cock-ups to delay the scheduled departure.

Leo and Tom found themselves side by side, silent.

346

Suddenly uncomfortable, Leo offered Tom his hand. Tom smiled, and took it.

"We've come a long way since that night in the police cell," said Tom.

Leo nodded in agreement.

"Yet after all of it, after 50 years and picking over the details in court, only we, you, Aliya and I, really know the truth about what happened that night."

"And Ole Kisii."

"Yes, and Ole Kisii."

"Leo," Tom began, falteringly, "it can be dangerous to share the secrets of powerful men."

Leo feigned indifference. "The thought had occurred to me. It will be good for you to be back with your wife," he countered, keen to change the subject. "This can't have been easy on her."

Tom nodded. "And what about you? Will you be spending this weekend with your boys?"

"Not this weekend. They're up-country with their mother's parents. I've kept them far away from all this since ..." he paused. Something fell exactly into place. "Yes. In fact as soon as I've seen you off I'm heading up there to collect them. And I intend to be spending every day I possibly can with them from now on."

"Good for you!" said Tom. He paused and looked down, and shifted uneasily. It was clear he had something uncomfortable he wanted to say, and Leo really didn't want to hear it. He looked around, almost desperately, for someone to draw into their conversation, but without success.

"Leo," Tom began again, "I know I've got you to thank for my freedom. I know that you've done everything anyone could have asked – more. Far more. You've put your career, and your life, on the line for me. I have no right to ask you anything more. But throughout this, you've never once told me what you think. What you really feel."

Leo sighed, resigned to the conversation he didn't want to have. "Tom, please," he pleaded, "None of this has been about right, or justice, or you, or Jembe. Can't you just accept that? It was about Paul Muya and Ole Kisii, and who gets to run this country."

"Sure, sure," said Tom, "I understand that. But it was also about a war crime. If killing Jembe was a war crime, then I'm guilty of it. He came out to meet me. Me."

"Forget it, Tom. Don't ever tell Aliya I said so, but every war crimes trial I've read about strikes me as an exercise in futility and hypocrisy. Hypocrisy, because only the winners get to try the losers, and futility, because the wrongs the accused are usually being tried for are so vast and awful they are too great to be redressed by the punishment one could heap on a single individual. You can only execute someone once. You can only lock anyone up for a single lifetime. It's impossible to make the punishment fit the crime. There's no fair retribution, and there's no effective deterrent. But the greatest hypocrisy of it all is that by calling a certain level of excess a war crime you legitimise every lesser act of slaughter and destruction. I think the South Africans have it right: there's no point looking for retribution – the very best you can hope for is an approximation to the truth, and some semblance of reconciliation. If not for today, then in the hope of stifling the potent myths of tomorrow. Ole Kisii made a political decision that Jembe was worth more to their cause dead than alive. Foss killed Jembe. You killed Foss. If you really want to know my view, I only think that's a crime when the courts conclude it is. Until then it's merely a series of events. OK?"

Tom nodded, but said nothing. Leo eased himself towards the bar, and was about to order himself a very large scotch when he felt the scrutiny of the uniformed police superintendent who had nominally been in charge of their escort. Leo, suspecting the man of contemplating how convenient a death resulting from a cocktail of alcohol and prescription painkillers might prove, smiled grimly and ostentatiously ordered a fruit juice. He then sought out McKenzie, also heading home on the midnight flight.

"I haven't had a chance to thank you."

"No need," said McKenzie, dour as ever. "Just doing what I'm paid for, same as you."

"Sure, sure," said Leo, who had a pretty good idea just how many risks McKenzie had taken in breaking up the relationship between the British government, Nick Easton and Paul Muya. "So how did British policy get to change so dramatically and so suddenly?"

McKenzie shrugged. "I'll play the patsy for my country, but not for the likes of Nick Easton. So I had a friend look into where precisely his links high up in the FCO were. Our Minister for Africa will be announcing his resignation tomorrow: he intends to spend more time with his family. It's not just here Easton's been buying politicians. Suddenly, UK PLC finds it likes the idea of doing business with John Ole Kisii a lot more than it did 48 hours ago. Never underestimate the havoc an unambitious man in possession of a secret can wreak. Anyway," he concluded, "I owed you, and Tom Miles, for the committal hearing. I'm sorry for that, but I was . . ."

". . . just obeying orders?"

"Aye," said McKenzie, with a wry smile, "just obeying orders. Did you tell Tom or Aliya about our little chat?"

Leo shook his head.

"Fine," said McKenzie, offering Leo his hand, "Let's keep it that way, shall we? You know," McKenzie added, thoughtfully, "I admire you, Leo, but I sure as hell don't envy you. Whether it's Ole Kisii or Paul Muya your country is shortly to get a President that's got every reason to hate you."

"And your Government's going to regard you as its favoured son, is it?" asked Leo. "A Civil Servant who shafted his Minister?"

McKenzie laughed. "I'd sooner take my chances than yours. I really do want to spend more time with my family. Good luck."

"You too," said Leo turning away, to find himself suddenly face to face with Aliya.

She had been chatting to Joseph. Her hand still rested lightly on his forearm. She looked tired, and a long strand of hair had somehow escaped the strict discipline she'd imposed on the rest. She smiled up at Leo, as she swept it back into place.

There was an awkward silence, then Leo asked, "Why did you tell me to take Ole Kisii's call? How did you know who it was?"

Aliya looked down. "McKenzie told me to expect his call. He told me not to tell you. Remember, he and I work for the same boss."

Leo laughed. "You are wonderful! Why don't you come out for a holiday?" he continued enthusiastically. "Once all the paperwork on this is sorted out. Come and see the real Kenya. Swahili Land. The land . . ."

". . . where everybody fits in. I remember. Leo," she said, "thanks, but no thanks. This may be your idea of God's little acre, but it still feels more like hell on earth to me. It's like you said that morning about the beauty and the decay. You see glorious colour, where I only see a gaudy daub. You see the exotic and the picturesque. I see the squalid and the tawdry. You want to stroll along the beach and feel the heat of the sand through the soles of your sandals. I want to walk across a London park and feel frosted grass crunch beneath my feet. You won't believe this, but I ache to feel the cold sting my cheeks, and see my breath steam. Anyway, my next holiday is already booked. A fortnight's skiing."

Leo looked suddenly crestfallen and Aliya felt bad. Why did he always manage to make her feel so much older than him?

"I'll e-mail you in a couple of days," she said. "Sort out any loose ends . . ."

Their flight was discreetly called, and with relief blatant on several faces, they emerged chatting easily, shaking hands and slapping backs, from the VIP lounge, to see Paul Muya, still and determined, with a bevy of his closest associates, six minders and a dozen cameramen gathered like a posse behind him. Leo noted with satisfaction Marianne Kane wasn't among them.

Paul smiled, when everyone came to a halt. Glances were

350

exchanged between Dieter Haas' men and the four or five armed police officers. Weapons were eased in holsters, and thumbs moved to safety catches. Tyson moved toward Leo. Joseph stepped in front of Aliya.

Paul spread his arms, in a gesture of resignation and acceptance, and then, alone, strode forward, a hand extended to Tom Miles.

"I just came to wish you well, Dr Miles," he said, with his easiest smile firmly in place. The first camera flashed as Paul stood two paces from Tom, his hand still offered. "I accept now you're not the man responsible for my father's death. I deeply regret the suffering these past few weeks must have caused you and your family."

Tom, warily, accepted Paul's hand, and there was an audible sigh of relief as cameras exploded all around. Then Paul Muya held firm to Tom's hand and said, quietly but with scalpel sharp precision, "Name the man who was, Dr Miles. You are safe, now. No harm can come to you, so do the decent thing. Do now what you wanted to do in court: tell my people who killed my father."

Leo knew any sudden movement could be disastrous. Gently, he eased himself between Tom and Paul, placed a hand on Tom's shoulder and turned him, effectively breaking the spell.

Paul slumped, and suddenly there was movement everywhere and in the confusion McKenzie thrust forward to bustle Tom and Aliya through to the departure gate.

Aliya turned, caught Leo's eye and half waved.

Then they were gone.

Feeling suddenly, massively alone, Leo turned, to face an equally dejected Paul Muya.

They both stood, hands in pockets, regarding one another.

"So what happens now?" asked Leo.

"I fight the election. Not with as strong a hand as I had hoped, thanks to you. You betrayed me," Paul said, bitterly. "You've betrayed our friendship."

"And you've been a loyal friend throughout, I suppose?" said

351

Leo, unmoved. "Why did you give me his defence brief on a plate? How did you know just where to be that night they let Tom Miles out? The only person I told was Marianne. Why did you think the boys would be in danger on the Charge? You've played me consistently throughout this whole thing. Hey, I'm not complaining about that. I'm not bitter. Well, not about that. I'm used to being used. But you used my ex-wife and turned my kids against me, and that does upset me a trifle more than somewhat. So don't give me a hard time about betraying friendships."

Paul shrugged, and reached out a hand. "I'm sorry, Coke."

"No you're not," said Leo. "You're only sorry that you lost. Do you know the thought that's occupied me most these last few days? The thing that really troubles me? If that had been my Land Rover that mysteriously exploded and not Nick Friedlander's, or if that guy with the panga had succeeded in taking me out, it would have been you who'd make the great oration over my coffin. You who'd say the final prayer beside my grave. You who'd comfort my children. Something about that thought makes me want to puke.

"You know, throughout this whole thing I've had this oppressive sense of a good thing dying. I thought you were someone special. Someone great. But it turns out you're not the Total Man after all. You're just another grubby chancer in the pocket of big business and foreign politicians.

"Whatever your destiny holds, my friend, it certainly doesn't give you the right to take my boys away from me. And if you ever try to do that again, then what's gonna happen to you, well, just take it from me, it'll happen fourteen ways this side of Friday, that's all. Now, get out of my way. I have a long journey to make, and it's one on which I really don't need you as a navigator."

352

Acknowledgements

A note on history and sources

The Final Charge is a novel. Characters other than publicly known historical realities are all imagined. None the less I have tried to be accurate on known events and true to the time and the facts. I have also tried to rely on first-hand accounts and primary sources. In addition to unpublished material in the UK National Archives and the Kenya National Archives and Documentation Service I have found the Library of the University of London's Institute of Commonwealth Studies a most valuable repository. I am indebted to the staff of all three organisations for their assistance and advice. I also acknowledge with gratitude the guidance on case law and judicial procedure a number of academics and legal practitioners in both the UK and Kenya have provided. I would also like to note my appreciation to all at Sandstone Press, and in particular to Moira Forsyth, for the unfailing encouragement, patience and enthusiasm shown to me. No expressions of appreciation would be complete without a heartfelt thank you to Kauser Alibhai for her consistent encouragement and wise advice from initial thought to final draft. All errors and omissions are my responsibility, as are the perceptions of the beauty, generosity and frequent grimness of Kenya past and present.

I have set the hearing of Tom Miles' case prior to the 2010 Constitutional changes in Kenya.

I have drawn heavily on the following:

HENDERSON, I and GOODHART, P (1958) *The Hunt for Kimathi*. London, Hamish Hamilton

SLATER, M (1955) *The Trial of Jomo Kenyatta*. London, Martin Secker and Warburg

PAGET, J (1967) *Counter-insurgency Campaigning*. London, Faber and Faber

CAROTHERS, DR JC. (1954) *The Psychology of Mau Mau*. Nairobi, Government Printer

MAINA, P (1977) *Six Mau Mau Generals*. Niarobi, Gazelle Books

ITOTE, W (General China) (1967) *Mau Mau General*. Nairobi, East African Publishing House

ITOTE, W (General China) (1979) *Mau Mau in Action*. Nairobi, Transafrica Publishers

CLAYTON, A (1976) *Counter-insurgency in Kenya 1952-60*. Nairobi, Transafrica Publishers

MBOYA, T (1963) *Freedom and After*. London, Andre Deutch

WACHANGA, H K (1975) *The Swords of Kirinyaga: the fight for land and freedom*. Nairobi, Kenya Literature Bureau

WA WANJAU, G (1983) *Mau Mau Author in Detention* Nairobi, Heinemann Kenya (English Edition translated by WA NJOROGE, N (1988))

Anyone wanting to know more about Mau Mau and the State of Emergency could do no better than read Caroline Elkins' Pulitzer Prize winning *Imperial Reckoning: The Untold Story of Britain's Gulag in Kenya* (2005) New York, Henry Holt and Co and David Anderson's *Histories of the Hanged: Britain's Dirty War in Kenya and the End of Empire* (2005) London, Weidenfeld & Nicolson.